wreck me

SPECIAL EDITION

JENN PLUMMER

Wild Lupine Books

Wreck Me

Aspen Ridge, Book 4

Published by Wild Lupine Books LLC

Editing by Katie Ducharme - Between the Covers Editorial

Cover Art by Qamber Designs

contents

join jenn plummer's readers' group

Stay up to date with Jenn Plummer by joining her Facebook readers' group, Jenn's Harlots. Ask questions, get first looks at new books/series, and have fun with other book lovers!

https://www.facebook.com/groups/jennsharlots/

Dear readers,

Wreck Me is book four in a five book, interconnected stand-alone series. You do not have to read them in order but for the best experience, I recommend that you do. Wreck Me contains minor spoilers of book one, Unravel Me, that pertain directly to the story progression of Wreck Me. While nothing is directly spoiled, please keep this in mind if you have not read Unravel Me.

Themes in Wreck Me include: panic attacks and anxiety, emotional/mental abuse from a parent, homophobia (not from a MC), manipulation and blackmail, explicit language, and sexual situations.

Please read responsibly. If you have any questions about this list, please don't hesitate to reach out to me directly.

Sending all of you love.

playlist

Siren Sounds - Tate McRae
Lovely - Billie Eilish
Home - Good Neighbours
Whatcha Say - Jason Derulo
Chemical - Post Malone
Stargazing - Myles Smith
Want You – Third Eye Blind
Enough is Enough – Post Malone
Good News – Shaboozey
Way Down We Go - KALEO

For everyone who's turned their back on love, never say never. Once it finds you, it will wreck you in the best of ways.

For Katie, because without you, these books wouldn't exist, especially this one. And if by some miracle they did, they sure as hell wouldn't be what they are.

carter

MY HAND CARESSES THE BUBBLY ASS OF THE SEXY brunette currently bent over, wiggling her pussy in my face. I lean forward, taking a deep inhale of her musky scent before relaxing back into the large chaise I'm occupying. She shakes again, swaying to the thumping base of the loud music playing throughout the club. She's a sexy little thing, her hips gyrating to the beat, the flesh of her meaty ass jiggling in waves. My hand connects with the side of her cheek in a loud smack, loving the way the flesh reverberates from the impact. Her bare pussy glistens, already primed and ready. I technically don't need to go down on her first, but I don't mind the taste of pussy, and knowing that she's come even before I've entered her takes a little pressure off the main event.

"Are you going to eat her or do you just like to play with your food?"

A deep, masculine voice pulls my attention from the pretty pussy in my face, as a stranger takes a seat next to me. My head lolls across the upholstered chaise in his direction, surprised by his close proximity. He's easily a few years older than me, closer to thirty than my twenty-five. He has rich brown hair that's combed back loosely at the top, sun-kissed skin, deep blue eyes, and a jaw covered in light scruff. Objectively, he's hot, like in the way a man can appreciate Chris Hemsworth.

"Why? You want a lick?" I quip as he shifts closer to me on the settee, his thick thigh resting against mine now. He smells of expensive cologne—woodsy and citrus—and I can't help the inhale I involuntarily take.

"Not of her," he marvels, his rich blue eyes drinking me in. I squint at him in confusion as the brunette turns around, her bright brown eyes lighting up when she sees we have an unexpected guest. She turns, straddling me and leaning in, shoving her breasts in my face as she reaches to palm his cock over his black slacks. Her skin is smooth under my touch as I roam up her body, stopping to grab her full breast, feeding a rosy-pink nipple into my mouth and sucking, swirling my tongue around her soft flesh until it's a stiff peak.

A hand that's too big and too firm to belong to the dainty thing currently in my arms moves to my crotch. My body stiffens, my spine uncomfortably straight for the position I'm lounging in, my movements rigid and uncertain, unsure how to handle this situation. I've had threesomes with two women before, but never thought I would entertain another man with a woman, especially if they swung both ways.

He leans closer, tilting his body completely flush against the side of my own as he rubs the palm of his strong hand over my rapidly hardening cock. There's something different about it that stirs something in the pit of my stomach. With a woman, they're delicate, their hands so much smaller, softer; they're timid and unsure of just how to touch you. I fucking love that about them.

On the contrary, he isn't afraid, he's rubbing me off through my slacks with the precision of someone who has a cock, who knows exactly how good it feels to be touched this way, and it's firing confused signals like strikes of lightning throughout my entire body, my cock responding greedily while my head grapples with what the hell to do.

"Is this okay?" the objectively handsome stranger asks.

I honestly don't know. Is it? I'm straight. I don't hook up with dudes. Hell, I've slept with every woman within the city limits. And the next town over. But his touch feels good, almost too good.

While he's waiting for my reply, there's a sudden pressure as he grips my cock firmer through my slacks. *Fuck*, that feels good.

The words are out of my mouth before I can stop them.

"Umm, okay. Yeah, it's okay."

The brunette pushes me onto my back, and I willingly situate myself so that she can straddle my face. I grab on to her hips, helping guide her pussy right down onto my waiting mouth just as I feel those big hands unbuckle my belt.

My heart stops beating.

Then my pants are unbuttoned.

Air leaves my lungs.

My zipper slides down.

My brain short-circuits.

Then it's those same, massive hands with thick fingers pulling my rock-hard cock free and stroking it from base to tip, squeezing and twisting at the head as I lick into the wet center of the woman on top of me.

He squeezes my dick just right and I can't help but moan into the drenched pussy in my face. I continue to eat her out languidly, her hips doing most of the work as she rocks back and forth on my mouth, but my mind is on what's happening to my dick.

Sex is my thing. I *love* to fuck. This is just sex.

Being a member of Temptations, an elite, members-only sex club an hour away from my small town, has its perks for someone like me. I love the variety I find here, the ease with which I can find a nightly hookup to fill a purely physical need to clear my head and give me the only hits of dopamine I get in my day.

Temptations has given me a place to unwind without worrying about commitment, expectations, or awkward conversations afterward about where this will lead. The answer is always the same—nowhere. Sex is a primal, purely physical release and nothing more. It's a stress reliever. There's no connection, no emotion, and most of all, there's no love.

He holds my cock tight at the base in his palm before a wet tongue licks at my slit, prodding it and lapping. No doubt cleaning up the precum leaking from me like I've never had a hand job before. I'm a fucking aficionado at sex. Sex is what I do best, and there isn't anything I haven't done—except be with a man.

He teases me, licking over the head of my engorged cock like it's a fucking lollipop, until I actually start to squirm, wanting more, chasing that feeling. Just when I'm about to say fuck it and move on, happy to sheath my dick with a condom and slide this pussy onto it, his mouth swallows me whole.

I nearly come on the spot.

The warm, wet heat of his mouth suctioning around me is almost too much. Pleasure scatters through my body, my hips stuttering, my ass clenching, my abs taut. It's so goddamn good. Squeezing her hips, trying to keep my focus on my task, I lick through her seam, spearing my tongue into her warm, slick center, fucking her with my tongue as her body shivers and shakes over me.

My hips jerk as his hands slide between my legs, cupping my sack just how I would do it to myself. The head of my cock slides into his warm throat as he swallows around it. I can't help but moan into her, pulling her body down further to drown out the noises flowing from me, not wanting to give him the satisfaction of hearing how good this feels.

Goddamn, he sucks me down like he's trying to suck my soul through my cock, like I'm the best fucking thing he's ever put in his mouth. He pulls back, lapping and sucking at my head before diving back down and repeating the process.

Fucking shiiit.

He pulls away just as I feel the first signs of my orgasm, my balls drawing up tight, the tingling at the base of my spine, my thighs twitching. Figuring he had enough playtime with my cock,

I put a little more effort into the pussy I'm feasting on, eager to slip her over my cock to finish myself off as soon as she comes, as long as she's okay with it.

I don't notice that the stranger hadn't walked away until my pants are roughly shoved down to my ankles, a pair of thick thighs straddling my own, the wiry hair of his bare legs rubbing against mine and catching me off guard, reminding me that it's definitely a man touching me right now.

He fists my cock in his big palm again, stroking it brutally, still slick with his saliva. But then there's a completely foreign sensation. What the hell is that? That's not a hand or mouth. Holy shit. That's a dick. On my dick. He has both of our cocks in one hand and is stroking them together.

Holy. Fucking. Shit.

What the fuck is happening and why the fuck am I so into this? I'd blame it on alcohol, but Temptations has a firm two-drink policy, and I don't drink more than one anyway. I never want to be anything less than clear-headed in sexual situations, consent being my number one priority—especially with my job. The last thing I need is someone falsely accusing me of misconduct.

The woman on me starts to shake, her pussy quivering as her orgasm moves through her, my mouth flooding with her cum. Her body slumps slightly forward as she slips off of me, having had her fill, and then I'm no longer blind to what's happening in front of me. There's no denying it. No ignoring it. I'm face-to-face with reality, unable to pretend something else is happening.

The man's striking blue eyes are set on my own, heavily lidded and aroused as he pumps our cocks together. My heart trips over itself, a foreign sensation moving through my body that I don't recognize.

I shift my eyes away, refusing to look into his while he jerks us both off, but not wanting it to stop. *What the fuck is happening?* Our partner saunters away and I'm left lying on the chaise as he fucks the life out of our dicks. His uncut cock is thicker than my own, but I'm slightly longer, my head red and angry as they glide against each other. He pumps his hand over our smooth flesh tightly, our balls lying together, nearly having me seeing stars.

"You gonna come for me?"

The fuck?

"Are *you* gonna come for *me*?" I hiss.

"I'll do whatever you want me to do, lover."

"I'm not your fucking lover," I snap through clenched teeth, desperately trying to hang on to a shred of control.

He looks down at our cocks, letting spit fall from his mouth as his hands work it in as lube. His shirt is unbuttoned, revealing washboard abs that clench as he straddles me, his hips undulating, legs spread wide over my thighs. My balls start to draw up against his and I know he's fucking got me. I'm going to come for this motherfucker.

His hands tighten around us as if he knows, squeezing our heads together brutally and twisting on every pass. It's one of the hottest things I've ever seen, and I can't explain why.

"Fuuuuck, I'm coming," I moan as my vision fades to black, my abs tightening as I slightly lift my back off the lounge, my fingernails digging into the soft fabric cushion.

And do I fucking come. Ropes of it spurt out of the tip of my cock like a goddamn volcano erupting after being dormant for a century. My cum covers our dicks, my legs shaking under him as my orgasm takes over. He doesn't stop his movements, jerking us easier now, using my cum as lube, but it doesn't last much longer. Within a few more strokes, he's following me over the edge of bliss, coming all over us, our milky white seed mingling together in a sticky mess over his hand and my abdomen. He groans as he unloads, a deep, masculine sound that is so rich and intriguing as it hits my ears.

The post-orgasm haze clears almost immediately and I realize what the fuck just happened as I scramble to get out from under him on the awkward surface of the chaise. The stranger's hands grip my bare hips, strong, warm fingertips pinning me down below him. Fuck that shit.

"Time to get off, or I'll move you," I grunt.

This motherfucker just fucking smirks at me, the corner of his lip tipping up in a partial smile, an eyebrow raising.

I move quickly, thanks to years of professional boxing and MMA training with my brothers. I flip us so that he's on his back and I'm out from under him. Releasing him and pulling up my pants quickly, I tuck my still-hard dick away and take a step back from the stranger without taking a second look at his reaction.

Just as I'm about to hit the front doors, ready to get the hell out of here before the panic gets to be too much, a large hand grips my bicep, pulling me into an alcove and shoving me against the wall. I could fight him off if I wanted to, but this is the only damn place that I have to decompress and clear my head, and if I lose my membership because of this dick, we're gonna have more problems than this one.

"The fuck do you think you're doing?" I hiss quietly enough for him to hear me but not loud enough that it would alert anyone to a possible altercation.

"I don't want to be done with you yet," he states almost pleadingly. I laugh under my breath as his hands fall on either side of my head, caging me in. He starts to descend in the direction of my mouth but he's reading this situation all damn wrong. Placing my hand on his chest, I give him a gentle shove back a step—not wanting to offend him per the rules of rejection at the club—but making damn sure my point is loud and clear.

"Yeah, well, we're done here. I'm calling it a night. That was a one-and-done, man."

"Doesn't have to be."

Fuck, he's not making this easy. He's definitely not supposed to be pushing so hard. How did this guy get a membership?

"Look, I got caught up in the moment. I'm not gay, in case you couldn't tell by the pussy I was eating when you joined us."

His eyes flick down to the outline of my rock-hard cock in my slacks, even though I just came.

"I don't care what you think you are or aren't, but your cock likes me, so maybe I can help you figure it out."

My mouth drops open slightly, not sure what the fuck to even say to that or what the hell is happening to me tonight. I've never had anyone read me so transparently, and his observations are spot on. With one touch from this stranger, he just confused the hell out of me, but he's right, my body is on board with everything he is offering. I've had great sexual experiences before, incredible even. But that? That was something entirely different. He affected me on a molecular level. Rewired my brain chemistry at its core, and that right there is why I have to get the fuck out of here. Now.

"It was sex, man. Nothing more, nothing less. Have a good night," I reply curtly before heading to the door and storming out of it. This time, he lets me go. I don't know if I could restrain myself a second time—from punching him or asking for a repeat—the fact that I don't know which messes with my head. What the fuck did I just do? And why the fuck did I just come harder than I ever have before?

After a late night at the club, morning comes sooner than I'm ready and my mind is swirling with the mystery man and how good his strong, powerful body felt straddling me, our hard cocks squeezed together. His uncut dick as he spurted cum all over us. The cum that mixed with mine that I had to wash off of me before bed last night. Everything about him was strong and masculine, and it really fucking did it for me. Which I'm struggling to understand today.

How the fuck did I enjoy that as much as I did? I've never been curious about men, but I've also never shared women with male partners before. My thoughts war with the events, everything playing over again like a fever dream. Did I seriously hook up with a man last night? The sheer power of my orgasm and how goddamn *right* it felt is enough to rattle me to my core, but damn, that was one hell of an experience.

Sitting at my desk at my family's distillery, earlier than normal, I boot up my computer to start my day on autopilot. I'm the marketing executive and brand ambassador for Aspen Ridge Distillery in a tiny town hidden away in Western Washington. My three brothers and I run the entire operation together with the help of a huge staff of qualified employees, whom we treat like family. The company has been in our family for decades, and while we weren't ready to inherit the business this young, we were all prepared for it, having grown up on the grounds, and each settling into a position of our own here—some of us easier than others.

My oldest two brothers, Sawyer and Dallas, are twins. Sawyer fills the CEO position, and Dallas is our COO; both of them are in roles they fit perfectly and have always wanted. Our brother Liam is doing what he loves most as one of our two master distillers, and then there's me, who kind of fell into this position and am just trying to do the best I can at it. We also have a little sister, Kinsey, who wants nothing to do with the family business and is about to start her second year of teaching kindergarten at our tiny town's elementary school. She's the smartest one out of the five of us for not making a career out of the family business. Working so closely with my brothers has its pits and peaks. And since I'm the youngest, some days, there are a lot more pits than peaks.

Like I summoned the fuckers—shithead, dickhead, and spunk rag barge into my office like they own the damn place. Which, I suppose we all do, but it's the one space that's mine here, and a little respect would go a long way. But I'm just the playboy younger brother that no one takes too seriously. So, why would they? I shake off the intrusive thoughts. They don't know I harbor some resentment for how much more at ease they each are in life, but isn't that normal when you're the youngest son of five kids?

Liam takes a seat in one of the chairs across from my desk, Sawyer standing off to the side with his arms crossed, as Dallas walks up to the front of my desk and drops a manila folder on top of it. The contents spill out slightly—a bunch of articles and a photograph.

My heart heaves, lodging itself in my throat as my palms start to sweat. I'd recognize that face anywhere—his rich brown hair perfectly coiffed, his chiseled jaw dusted with two-day scruff, blue eyes sitting behind a pair of round glasses that surprisingly suit him. The room starts to close in on me while simultaneously spinning as dread settles in the pit of my stomach. How the fuck did they get this?

I pick up the flimsy photo between my thumb and forefinger, looking at it with what I'm hoping passes as a puzzled expression, before flicking it back into the pile of paper.

"Who the fuck is this?" I ask my brothers, playing semi-ignorant, considering I don't actually know his name or anything about him. I'm taking a chance that they don't know what happened last night. Unless fucking Dallas and his girlfriend Blaire happened to show up and saw us. While Dallas and I are both members at Temptations, we have different interests, and Dallas has always headed to the back private rooms while I stick to the floor. We've never run into each other before organically. Plus, why the hell would he look into who I hooked up with? Nah. This is a bomb that I'm going to feel the effects of for a while, and I brace myself for the destruction.

"That," Dallas says as he points to the printed photo of the man who jerked both of us off last night, "is Griffin Nash. His family owns the entire fucking Northwest Explorer that has been dicking you around for months. Meet your pain in the fucking ass."

I cringe at his crass words that typically would roll right off me, but given last night's circumstances, and the fact that Griffin is clearly into cock, I bristle. I stare at the photo and try to comprehend what the fuck is happening. My entire body vibrates with anger. Panic starts to slither up my spine, infecting me with its poison. I grip my thighs under the desk, my fingers pressing firmly into the muscle.

A few months ago, I received an email from a personal assistant on behalf of a prestigious Pacific Northwest travel magazine, saying they were interested in doing a feature on the distillery. Their presence online and in print is well-known and has far more reach than just the Pacific Northwest. It could be incredible publicity for the business. I've spent months trying to get a meeting with the writer and being given the runaround.

Did he know who I was? Was this all some sick fucking game to him? Do my brothers know what happened last night? Fuck, what did I do? I have a near desperate urge to loosen my tie, and I don't want the move to look suspicious, but it's getting damn hard to breathe in here.

I lean back into my chair, doing my damndest to play it cool and hoping like hell none of them read my emotions. I've gotten extremely good at masking my anxiety, and I'm tapping into that shit hardcore right now, even if I feel like I'm failing to do so.

"Well, no fucking shit," I say smoothly after a whistle of surprise. "How'd you get this? I've been trying to find this asshole for months. He's the damn *owner*?"

Sawyer speaks up first, which is no surprise. "Yeah, a Nash. What are the damn chances of that? Wes Draven got the info. Man is talented. We should have gone to him a while ago, because he pulled all that shit in less than a day."

"That motherfucker shouldn't be hiding out in a small town like Aspen Ridge, he could be bringing in the big bucks in some place like DC as a PI if he wanted to."

"No shit, but our gain again since our family seems to be his biggest return client."

"No shit," Dallas adds. "Just be careful what you ask for, and don't repeat my mistakes."

Sawyer opens his mouth to say something we all expect to be snarky, but lucky for me, Liam speaks up, getting our idiot twin brothers back on topic.

"Will you two shut the hell up for two minutes? Don't even start your crap. Carter, what are you gonna do now? You know who he is, you gonna hunt him down and get him to do the feature or tell him to fuck off?"

Unfortunately for me, my shithead brother speaks up before I can make my own decision.

"Oh, he's gonna hunt him down. He's getting this story. They asked for it and we agreed. There may not be any contracts, but Carter can be persuasive. I'm sure you can work some magic and get us this feature."

"He's not wrong, Car. You're the one who got excited about this to begin with. You know what a game changer it could be for all the parts of our business—sales, expanded distribution, the events that Blaire has been hosting. We need this," Liam adds, and I know he's not wrong. When I got that email, I was ecstatic, but then it's just been bullshit ever since.

"Ehh. I'm fine if he tells him to fuck off. I think we're doin' just fine without all that press and attention."

"Fuck off, dumbass, no one asked you."

"Uh, pretty sure the four of us make up this goddamn distillery, so my opinion matters. Last I checked, I was the COO."

"Yeah, not CEO."

"Oh, fuck off on your high horse, shithead."

I drown out Sawyer and Dallas' bickering while my mind flashes to images of Griffin. A chill runs up my spine at the thought of seeing him again, and I inconspicuously wipe the sweat off my shaky palms on my thighs. I can't differentiate whether or not the feeling is foreboding or thrilling. Maybe a twisted mix of both.

Our distillery is the number one supplier of whiskey and bourbon to the entire Pacific Northwest, and we've only just started to expand to other states and territories. The Northwest

Explorer would damn near guarantee that expansion. It was an honor to have them reach out to us, but then they've done nothing but play games, and that level of unprofessionalism has been surprising. They've been setting up meetings and then cancelling, and all communication was through a personal assistant. The magazine can make or break companies just like ours, and I'm just greedy enough to gamble on it. It's not like my brothers are giving me much of a choice anyway, and I'll be damned if I let them down.

"I'm gonna find the fucker. And I'm going to get the feature *they* asked for."

Who cares if I already know what the asshole's dick feels like rubbed against mine. Or what he looks like when he comes.

Actually . . . an idea strikes me. I'm not against a little manipulation if it comes to it. I'm going to get that feature one way or another. I just hope that I can find him before he fucks everything up with the information he already has on me. He had better not have known who I was.

CHAPTER 2

Finn

MONDAY CAME HARD AND FAST, AND I WAS IN desperate need of more caffeine if I was going to get any work done today. I pull open my office door, tossing my bag onto my chair, and bolt straight for the break room to pour a mug of black coffee. I drop a pod into the machine and wait for the dark roast to brew, leaning casually against the counter, finding myself thankful for the rare moment of quiet in an otherwise busy room.

My family owns the Northwest Explorer, one of—if not *the*—most notorious travel magazines in the Pacific Northwest and beyond. I've been writing my entire life, majored in journalism at the University of Southern California, and couldn't get back to the PNW fast enough. There's something about this place that becomes part of your soul. Once you've been here, there's no place on earth that's quite like it.

My phone vibrates in the pocket of my slacks, making my jaw tick in annoyance, interrupting a brief quiet reprieve that I needed before taking on the day. Not ready to answer what I'm sure is my dad's bullshit, I ignore the call, knowing he'll make me regret it later. I head back to my office with my steamy mug of fuel, saying good morning to the small staff we have employed at this location as I prepare to catch up with my assistant on any new messages that came in over the weekend.

Relaxing into my office chair, I don't waste any time clicking open the file for my new story, the one I've been forbidden to write, last night on permanent replay in my mind. Did I expect to run into Carter Hayes at the club last night? Yes and no. But did I jump at the first opportunity to get close to him? Absolutely. I couldn't have fought it if I tried.

Truth be told, I thought he'd tell me to piss off the moment our legs touched, but he was so goddamn into me stroking him that I was convinced he was at least bisexual. To my surprise, I was his first, an assumption I made based purely on his little freakout, and damn if that doesn't make me feel good. Even if the events complicated my predicament even further.

The obnoxious vibration blares from where I dropped my phone on my custom walnut-built desk. An ostentatious gift from my father so that I "looked the part" while working at the Western offices. I know who's calling before looking at the screen, and he'll just keep calling if I don't answer.

To put it plainly, my father is an overbearing, pompous asshole who feels the need to check in with me to ensure I'm being a compliant, well-behaved son. After all, the Nash name is at stake here, and he's been convinced since the day I was born that I'm going to fuck everything up for him. A reminder I'm given multiple times a week.

Ever since I gave him the proposal for my next small town feature—Aspen Ridge, Washington—he's been checking in with me more frequently, making sure I'm heeding his latest order. *More like threat.* The conversation took me by surprise; regardless of my familiarity with his explosive reactions, this one was particularly intense, even for him.

I try to hide my embarrassment as I stand in front of my father's receptionist, Cynthia, knowing he's purposely making me wait so I know my place. As if he'd ever allow me to forget.

"Come in, Griffin. Take a seat. I'm pulling up your proposal now."

"Thank you, Dad," I reply, keeping my voice as stable as possible. I hate these meetings. Luckily, they only happen quarterly. We sit down in his stuffy-ass office in Seattle, and he goes through my proposal for locations and businesses I'll be highlighting as features in the magazine. He's a goddamn control freak and I've been doing this long enough now that he should trust me, but I have yet to prove to him that I've got everything under control.

I watch as his face transforms from annoyed focus to complete rage, as confusion grips me. What the hell did I send him? I quickly wrack my brain, ensuring that I checked ten times that the proposal was in the correct format and that it included all of the expected information. I always have my assistant, Trey, double-check it as well. There's no way we sent him a draft or something else entirely. Even so, my heart picks up speed behind my ribs, beating frantically as I try not to let it show outwardly. I can't be weak. Not in front of him.

"Where the fuck did you find this town? This family?" my dad bellows from his spot behind his desk. His face is a deep crimson red, his forehead pinched in anger. His rage toward me has been frequent over the last twenty-nine years, but never over a feature location for the magazine.

I cough into my fist to clear my throat before speaking. "They're hidden behind the Olympic Mountains, nestled up on the coast, literally engulfed in nature. It's exactly the kind of spot I look for." Plus, I recently stumbled across a whiskey from Aspen Ridge Distillery and went digging to find out more about them. "Trey has already reached out to one of the businesses for a meeting. The distillery that's listed there."

His rage explodes, and I dig my fingers into my thighs, bracing for whatever he's about to unleash on me.

"Stay the fuck away from Aspen Ridge! Stay the fuck away

from that family! Cancel the goddamn meeting! Do you understand me, Griffin? This magazine will NEVER feature that fucking family, or that disgusting town."

I blanch as confusion ripples through me. What the hell is going on? I've always had the ability to choose my locations, as long as I ran them by him first with these obtuse proposals and power-trip meetings. I'm good at what I do, and up until this moment, he's never had an issue with the locations of choice. Why now? But that confusion clouds my judgment, and I make a slip-up, questioning him.

"What? Why? That doesn't make any sense. Do you know that family? I've always been allowed to pick my locations. This town is enchanting; it's exactly the kind of place we like to feature."

He moves quicker than I'd expect him to, rounding his desk and lifting me to stand by the lapels of my jacket, shaking me roughly. I'm so stunned by his behavior that I react too slowly, my hands gripping his wrists for purchase, my eyes going wide. While my dad has always been verbally abusive, he's never outright put his hands on me. God forbid I suffered a mark or blemish on my skin and anyone found out where it came from.

"Who the fuck do you think you are, questioning me, Griffin? I'm the only reason you're even afforded the ability to write for such a prestigious magazine! Everything you have is because of me, Griffin! Everything! Don't you fucking forget it. When I say something, I expect you to comply, or I will destroy you. Do you understand?" His breath is hot on my face, reeking of stale coffee and cigars, churning the bile around in my stomach. I want to push. I want to argue. I want to dig deeper and find out more about Aspen Ridge, and the fact that my father is clearly keeping something from me only fuels that need. But I know I won't get anywhere by arguing. I've been playing this game my entire life, and I know when to shut my mouth. This is one of those times.

"I understand, Dad. I apologize."

He gives me one last shake before releasing his hold on me, causing me to stagger. He reads my compliance—something I've *perfected—and takes his seat behind his desk, straightening his jacket and returning to his work. I leave his office angry but more convinced than ever that I need to find out exactly what's hiding in Aspen Ridge.*

My father has been checking in with me more often since that conversation to make sure I'm abiding by his new rule. What he doesn't realize is that he's only fueling me, piquing my interest further.

I've spent the last few months looking into the town of Aspen Ridge and the distillery, and having Trey reschedule meeting after meeting to hold them off. My dad would find out if I met with them, and I can't jeopardize my position at his company. I love my job too much, and it's all I have. It's the only happiness in my life. But I need to find out more.

What started as innocent digging and research quickly spiraled into something so much more. From the moment I found Carter Hayes' picture on the distillery website, I felt drawn to him, and I couldn't have stayed away if I tried. While scrolling, my heart stopped as I settled on his photograph and spent too long staring. I've never seen such a beautiful man before, but there was something just behind his eyes that spoke to me, that called to me. There's a depth there that he's hiding, his smile not quite reaching his eyes. I felt a connection to him just from his photo. Touching him last night? Jesus Christ. There's something there that I can't explain or get my head around, but I'm far from being done with Carter Hayes.

My dad would see through on his threats to destroy me if he found out I was digging further into the town and family he seems to despise so strongly, and after the feelings Carter brought out in me thanks to last night's unexpected orgasms, I really want to avoid the fucker.

The Hayes family owns and operates the distillery, and it seems to be an institution in town. After my digging spiraled to focus more on just Carter, I was pleasantly surprised to discover his extracurricular activities included frequenting a sex club, something he doesn't seem to be trying to hide.

Discovering this little tidbit, I had to see it for myself. I know I should listen to my father and stay away. I should be working harder for him to finally be proud of me and see that I am competent and can handle running the conglomerate that he's built once he's ready to retire. Too bad for both of us, when I set my heart on something, I have to see it through. And right now? That's learning more about Carter Hayes.

It's tempting, though, to just drop this hunt I've suddenly become obsessed with, to finally be in his good graces. If he weren't such an evil prick. My dad is your typical egotistical asshole who doesn't realize what a loud-mouthed douche canoe he actually is. Everything that comes from his mouth drips with condescendence, misplaced arrogance, and garbled bullshit that I try hard to tune out. If he didn't hold my life in the palm of his hand, I'd walk away and never talk to him again. But as my life sits currently, he's right, I wouldn't have anything if I didn't have the job that I love so much. The career that I very much worked for, but is underneath him, regardless. He owns me, and he knows it.

Being able to travel through these gorgeous states and parts of Canada, discovering new places, tiny towns, must-eat diners, and the best hikes has been such a privilege. For as long as I can remember, I've wanted to travel and write about my experiences to share with the rest of the world. I've convinced my dad to expand from just the Pacific Northwest—but he's only on board if I continue to be his yes-man. Behaving. Complying. Being the perfect son, which couldn't be further from reality.

The only good thing my dad has done that I agree with is to make me genuinely work my way up, rather than just giving me a top position within the magazine because I'm his son. He did it to purposefully demean me, but I was grateful for it. I studied hard at one of the best journalism programs in the country, and have worked damn hard to perfect my craft. Investigative journalism isn't quite what I thought I would be doing, but man, if I'm not intrigued by this quaint town and the family that seems to be at its helm. Daddy dearest isn't exactly forthcoming with the information on why he wants me to drop it. Just expects his trained lap dog to comply, dangling a treat he knows I want in front of my snout. My career.

Swiping up on the green connect button, I answer his call to get it over with.

"Hi, Dad," I greet, keeping my voice monotone, neither overly friendly nor curt, remaining professional at all times so that I don't fuel the fire of his disappointment.

"Son."

His voice grates over me, a headache starting at the base of my skull. I imagine most fathers' voices bring memories of encouragement and comfort, but not mine.

"Remember, Griffin, I can take all of this away."

"Don't forget who made you, Griffin. And who can fucking end you."

"You're a goddamn embarrassment, Griffin. Fall in line or you're done."

"Are you even listening? Fuck, Griffin. Can you attempt to do the bare minimum?"

My dad's voice barks through the speaker, bringing me back to the present. Every time I hear the name Griffin, I can't control my visceral reaction. I was named after him, a gift my mother bestowed upon me, as if giving me his last name wasn't enough of a reminder of who I belonged to.

"Sorry, I was answering an email," I lie.

"When I call, you give me your full attention, do you understand? And you sure as shit don't ignore my phone calls."

I'm twenty-nine years old and still being spoken to like a

misbehaving child. If I weren't wound up so tightly in a spool that I don't know how to unravel myself from, I wouldn't take the abuse. But he's my dad, I love my job, and I have no idea how to walk away from this life when I have nothing else to go to. If I ever left, he'd make damn sure I was never published by anyone but him. A threat he's made before. He'd essentially ruin any chance I'd have of ever writing again, and writing is my life. It's all I have.

"Sorry, Dad. What can I help you with today?"

He huffs hard, not bothering to pull the phone away, and I crack my neck from side to side to ease some of the tension.

"Give me an update on the new locations you've found. It's been weeks. A monkey could have done faster work than you, Griffin. I should have let Dion handle this, but I thought my son could be more competent than he apparently is. You had better give me something good and fast. I'm getting tired of waiting. We need things to write about, Griffin, and we can't do that if you don't do your goddamn research and find them!"

Fuck.

"Sorry to be a constant source of disappointment for you, Dad. I'm working on it."

"And? What does that even mean? Jesus, Griffin. Can't you do anything right? I'm going to bring Dion in on this, it's clearly too much for you to fucking handle. You really are more incompetent than I thought. Are you staying the fuck away from Aspen Ridge?"

I take a deep breath, suddenly fearful about what could happen to Carter if my dad found out that I hooked up with him last night. Dion is as ruthless as my father is, and I don't need him poking around in my business, either. He's an eager little shit and loves to suck my dad's dick. Metaphorically. Although I wouldn't put it past him if my dad whipped it out and told him to get on his knees. A sudden image of Carter on his for me flashes behind my eyes. I feel an odd sense of protection over him. I've never met anyone like him, even if we didn't exchange many words. I can't let my dad or Dion sink their claws into him. There's no way he'll come out unscathed. I've been surviving his wrath for my entire life, and I can continue to take it.

"Dad, I'm sorry I'm a disappointment. I will get it to you soon."

Another audible huff, his breath whipping through the speaker of the phone, making my skin crawl. At least we're not face-to-face where the scent of scotch and cigars mingles on his breath, as drops of spittle fly from his mouth when he yells. My stomach rolls at the thought. My own father disgusts me, a deeply physical, emotional, and mental response.

"Last chance, Griffin. And do not forget about dinner tonight," he barks before disconnecting the call. My dad's an epic prick. Love our morning chats; sets the day up for success and a real positive attitude. My door opens after a quick rap of someone's knuckles, and even though I can already anticipate who it is, I'm still not happy about it.

"What?" I snap as Trey walks in. He raises his eyebrows at me, his only warning that he isn't going to take my shit. I take a deep breath, letting my rage simmer before giving him a fake, patronizing smile.

"Much better," he replies, walking into my office and taking a seat across from my desk. Trey has been my personal assistant, which he hates being called, since I was promoted to a travel writer. We've been best friends since high school, and when I got back from California, we picked right back up where we left off. At twenty-eight, he still has no idea what he wants to do with his life, so he's doing this until he figures it out. "Now, we still haven't replied to Carter Hayes' email on that meeting that he was promised. . ."

My heart stammers behind my ribs at hearing his name. I'm so thoroughly fucked when it comes to him. How is that even possible? Trey reads the change in my expression, which is the reason he brought Carter up to begin with.

"Why are you raising your eyebrows at me like that?" I ask, unamused, rage still simmering right at the surface.

"For real? You're gonna make me ask? You're such a little fucker. How did last night go? Did you find him?"

Damnit. Why do I tell this asshole everything? I let loose a breath and relax further into my chair, putting my hands behind my head, knowing full well he won't leave until he's been given a bone.

"Yeah. I found him."

"The sex club?"

My face must say it all.

"No, you didn't," he says through a deep chuckle. "Damn, that's some serious commitment, my guy."

"Not what you're thinking, buddy. At all," I lie, and he knows it. I'm openly gay, and Trey was the first one I came out to in high school. He said he figured, especially since I wasn't chasing girls the way he was, and that I looked like I was trying not to gag when I was making out with Bianca Lyman in the eleventh grade. I wrongly and unfairly assumed it would bother him, but nothing's ever changed between us. *I don't have to compete with you for chicks, man, this is awesome. They think you're way hotter than me.* And that was the end of it.

"I can read you like a book. You hooked up with someone last night, but it wasn't Carter Hayes?"

"It was my first night at a sex club, Trey, of course I hooked up with someone. Who the hell wouldn't?"

His phone buzzes in his hand, saving me from having to come clean to him about the specifics. He'll pull them from me eventually, but I need to hold out until I figure out a plan. Trey's shoulders drop, and he rolls his eyes at his phone.

"We're not done with this shit, 'cause I want details about what the club was like. What do you want me to say to Carter?"

I sigh. I want to meet with him, but I know my dad has ways of tracking every email that goes out and comes into this company.

"Let it sit."

"Real professional," he deadpans.

"We made contact last night, but I didn't tell him who I was. Let him sit and stew for a bit. He'll figure out who I am eventually, and then I'll deal with it." Trey raises his eyebrows at me as if he knows there's more to the story that I'm not telling him. I continue to keep my mouth quiet and grin at him in return.

"There's that cocky arrogance we all know. Alright, fine. I'll let him sit. I've got your trip planned to Emberleigh." He scans the tablet in his hands, looking for the information while I wait. "You leave in two weeks. Three nights, staying at the beach house. Is this a good idea while your dad breathes down your neck about literally everything right now?"

"I go that weekend every year, I'm not changing it. I have to get away."

"Okay, fine. I'll handle shit here."

"Oh! One more thing."

"Yeah? I'm not packing for you, dipshit, that is way above and beyond what you hired me for."

"I'm taking Carter with me."

I don't know how, but I'm getting him there. I need to. I have to.

***

Dinner with my parents is usually migraine-inducing. Since I relocated to the other side of the state to work at the Western office last year, they've chartered their private jet into Forks one other time besides tonight to force dinner down my throat. It's six p.m. when I pull up to the restaurant they've chosen for our family bonding time, and based on the valet-only parking, I'm sure I'm going to just love the overly ornate decorations, lavish furnishings, and one-bite, twenty-course meal we're going to share. I mentally clock how many burger joints I passed on the way here so that I can actually eat dinner tonight.

The hostess greets me with a bright smile as I walk up to the marble stand she's occupying, and after I share my name, she nods and leads me through the dining room to my inevitable slaughter. Adjusting my tie, I mentally prepare myself to survive the next two hours while my dad bounces between talking about himself and degrading me, and my mother drinks away her existence in a bottle of expensive wine.

My dad keeps my mom on a long leash, but there is no arguing who's in charge, and she knows not to bite the hand that feeds her. She likes to walk around with a stick shoved up her ass and behaves like a snooty, holier-than-thou queen bee. With her spending, lavish lifestyle, and trips abroad with her girlfriends, she plays the part of the dutiful wife to maintain the lifestyle that my father supports with his credit card. She was never an affectionate mother, and I look at her with the same regard I would a stranger on the street.

My steps falter as the hostess turns to present the table and its occupants to me, including a young, blonde, too-thin female turning in purposeful slow motion to give me her rehearsed million-dollar smile. I'd rather be staring at a slaughtered pig than the girl sitting with my parents. I do my best not to groan out loud, but my mind is flashing a bright neon sign that says Get Out Now, Finn!

"Griffin!" Her voice is fake and overly sweet, which grates on the current throb that is expanding in the center of my brain. "I'm so happy to see you."

The feeling is not mutual.

"Surprised to see you here, Lexi." I nod to her before picking up my cloth napkin and taking my seat next to her, across from my father.

"Son. I said six. It's six fifteen."

"Is it? I didn't notice. There was traffic, which may surprise you, but it was out of my control." My tongue is a little looser this evening upon seeing Lexi Fairchild here with my parents. My dad's jaw tics in frustration, and I know I'll pay for it later. But he won't berate me too badly in front of Lexi. One point for me, I suppose, even if this night just took a turn. Not sure which I would rather: an evening of my father's verbal abuse, or one where he pushes a relationship with his attorney's daughter onto me. Is an ice pick to the eye an option? Cause I'd take that first.

To make matters worse, my father knows I'm gay. He just refuses to believe it and thinks all I need is a little persuasion from a female of his choosing. Enter Lexi. Who, I'm assuming, doesn't know that I'm not into females, or knows and doesn't care either way because of my last name. Don't give a shit to find out.

My mom finishes off her first glass of wine for the evening and waves down the waiter, who places an ice-cold water in front of me.

"Lexi was gracious enough to join us for dinner to see you, Griffin. Isn't that lovely?"

Lovely? Does he know the definition of the word? I wouldn't use lovely and Lexi Fairchild in the same sentence. But I have to play the part or make my life that much more difficult later.

"Thanks for joining us," I say, keeping my voice monotone and uninterested, refusing eye contact with her.

"I'm just happy to see you. How are you settling in over here? I can't imagine living on this side of the state is enjoyable, it's very . . . what's the word without coming across as rude? Modest? I suppose?"

As if I haven't been living here for months. The Fairchilds live in the same multimillion-dollar neighborhood as my parents, fifteen minutes outside of Seattle. They flew here on my father's private jet for fuck's sake. I'm sure modest is exactly the word she's looking for. My eyes roll as I take a sip of my cold water. The main office building for the magazine is in Seattle, but we have a small office space on the west side and one further east. My dad will randomly pop into all of the buildings and wreak havoc, but he dislikes this one the most. Which is another check mark in the 'it's my favorite location' box.

"Definitely love it over here. Considering staying on a more permanent basis."

My dad's eyebrows shoot up his forehead, and I don't bother

restraining the smile that lifts my lips. Asshole. If he thinks I want to be back near Seattle and under his thumb, he's mistaken.

"Lexi, how is work?"

"Oh, you know, I work constantly. Lawyer life, right? Griffin, did I tell you that I'm a lawyer? Daddy is so proud, and I just love working with him. You know, your dad is our biggest client."

Of course I know this, Lexi; you've only told me during every interaction we've ever had.

The waitress returns and takes our orders. My mom hasn't said a word, tossing back her third glass of wine while we wait for the meal, Lexi filling any silence that could have let my headache settle. My father asks her questions while I stare out the window, my mind drifting to Carter, wondering what he's doing right now. Food comes and goes, and then my dad pushes Lexi at me. Again.

"We should get your mother home at a decent hour. Lexi should stay. Show her some sights tomorrow? We can charter the jet to come pick her up."

I nearly choke on my saliva at the suggestion.

"That won't work for me. I have back-to-back business meetings, and I'm scheduled to scope out a few potential locations for the upcoming fall season features that you're waiting on before I leave for Emberleigh." I would do just about anything to get out of spending more time with his choice of a wife for me.

Lexi lets out an annoyingly fake whine that she thinks is making her cute as a kitten, but it really grates like nails on a chalkboard. My father gives me a long, annoyed look that I brush off. We say our goodbyes, my zombie mother walking surprisingly well for polishing off a bottle of wine by herself, and I watch as they step aside to observe the forced interaction between me and stuck-up Barbie.

Lexi hugs me, plastering her boney-ass little body against mine while I keep my hands loose at my sides, refusing to touch her and give her any ammunition that I could possibly be interested in her. I should feel bad for being rude, but she's been brainwashed by her father, and she's a gold digger through and through. Just like my mother. Just like hers. I want a simple life, and even if I was straight, I would make Lexi miserable.

The women climb into the car while my dad gets too close for comfort, puffing out his chest, his face transforming to the one he reserves for me.

"Don't fucking embarrass me again. You will try with Lexi because it is a good match, and you need a wife. Stay the fuck away from Aspen Ridge, Griffin. Or you'll regret the day you were born," he snarls.

"Got it, Dad. Understood. Have a good night."

Prick.

He gives me the same disappointed look he's given me nearly every day of my life as he climbs into the back of the SUV. I watch as their driver pulls out before taking my keys from the valet and tipping and thanking him for his time. I'm in desperate need of a drink, and I make the drive home feeling drained. After ten minutes, the roads open up, and it's only me, the pavement, and the stars above. I roll all the windows down and just breathe, letting the tension release from my body the best I can right now.

My mind flicks back to Carter, the blissed-out look on his face as I made him blow his load all over us. Fuck, I want that again. I want his firm body under mine. He was perfect. The way he gave in to me, the innocent, confused, lust-filled expression written on his face as he stared up at me. I've never felt such a strong pull to anyone before, and it's only getting stronger.

I know it won't take long before Carter figures out who I am. Having Trey ignore his email will hopefully push Carter to dig deeper. If he's smart and I left any impression on him, he's already figured out that the person at the magazine screwing with him is the same person who stroked him until he came last night at Temptations.

So, instead of heading to the sex club after my nightmare dinner, I loosen the tie around my neck, stripping myself of my suit, to spend the rest of the evening at my rental house about thirty minutes from Aspen Ridge.

It's a three-bedroom, contemporary Northwest-style home, with two bedrooms on the bottom floor and a loft that covers half of the house on the second floor. Tall, vaulted ceilings over the living area make the space obnoxiously open. The moon illuminates the room through skylights that rest above thick, exposed beams. Floor-to-ceiling windows line an entire wall, with two French doors that lead to a massive deck overlooking a lake. It's extravagant and too much for one person, but my father likes to make sure I'm living to a certain standard.

God forbid I live in a modest house that is more than suitable for a single bachelor living on his own. According to him, the fact that I'm a gay man is bad enough; living in less than superior housing would somehow make people frown upon *him*. The place is sterile, stuffy, and clinical. I hate it. With white walls, plain art, and stiff furniture, it lacks vibrancy, depth, and warmth. It embodies the opposite of everything you'd want to come home to at the end of a long day to relax. As if living on my own wasn't hard enough, my living arrangements remind me that I'm a prisoner in my own life.

After a quick shower in one of the smaller downstairs bathrooms, I dress in a pair of sweats, pad barefoot over the hardwood floors to the bar, and grab the neck of my new favorite bottle—a twenty-year-old signature bourbon from Aspen Ridge Distillery. I chuckle as I pour two fingers over ice into my glass. If my dad only knew, he'd disown me . . . just for drinking the damn brand. I can't imagine his reaction if he knew his beloved only child fooled around with a Hayes. He already thinks I'm perverse for being a gay man, and now that he has forbidden me from contacting that family, it would solidify my place as the disappointment of a lifetime.

The fact that I can't do anything right in that man's eyes is a well-digested feeling that is an old friend of mine, one I've known the entirety of my life. It's turned me into a man who is constantly chasing the praise of someone who will never give it freely—or at all. And why I'm struggling so much with my new obsession with Carter. It was innocent at first, just wanting to see what could possibly have my father so strung out over them and their town, but after meeting Carter last night, after touching him so intimately, the way he gave me permission to get him off, I won't be able to drop it. Even if I find myself at the receiving end of his vitriol because of it.

If he doesn't want me to write a feature on an incredibly unique, enchanting town, then that's fine. But to forbid me from reaching out to a family altogether? It's just another control tactic and I don't know how much longer I can keep doing this, fighting myself every damn day to keep pushing forward, and for what? My dad will never see me as anything more than a disappointment. For as long as I can remember, I wanted to work for my family's business. Writing is an escape for me. Sharing people's stories, traveling, and discovering new places lights my soul on fire. Not everyone is as lucky as I am to find their passion so early. Every step I've taken has gotten me to this point, but there are plenty of days I have to ask myself: at what cost?

My father's expectations are unattainable and unrealistic. A game he's played since I was born. Time and time again, I'm set up for failure, and I want nothing more than to prove to him that he's wrong about me. That I can take over this company once he's gone and make it better than he had ever dreamed it could be. Because that's what I want, right?

It's hard not to wonder if we're both stuck in a similar cycle. My dad only cares about his precious empire and will use me however he sees fit to get what he wants when he wants it. I only care about proving to him that I'm worthy. When did my focus shift from telling stories to proving my dad wrong? Can I do both?

There's a huge part of me—a part I'm not ready to dissect— that would do anything to break free from it all, to stop feeling like I'm choking on his relentless demands, his vicious reminders of what a failure I am and always will be. I'm drowning in power, money, and privilege, and yet, none of it feels good. This can't be what life is about. I somehow want so much less than what I have, but so much more at the same time.

I pour another whiskey and head out onto the large deck. The Washington summer air is warm but not overly oppressive. It's something I love about this little part of the state. The seasons are favorably mild. A few overly hot, miserable days in the summer, and a few heavy snowstorms in the winter. I love everything in between.

The house sits on a large lake that stretches out in front of me; the mirror-like reflection of the stars above shines and sparkles on the surface. I take a deep breath of the pine-scented air, an attempt at calming my nervous system. I should have gone for a run today to clear my mind, but this will have to do. My bare feet pad across the cool wood surface of the deck, taking a seat in one of the many chairs that decorate the space.

I've always gravitated toward the outdoors. When the pressure gets to be too much, I would escape outside, regardless of the weather, and it would help calm the voices in my head telling me that I'll never amount to anything, that I'll never be good enough for anyone.

The solitude wraps around me in a comforting caress as I think about Carter. He's so different from everything I expected. In one night, one interaction, everything flipped upside down. I wish I could see the look on his face when he figures out that the writer who has been deliberately fucking with him the last few months is the same man who made him come so damn hard last night.

I didn't go there with the intention of hooking up with him. I went to watch. To see his routine, see what kind of things he was into. It sounds sick as fuck, but once I learned he was a member of a sex club, there was a dark part of me that needed to *see* it for myself. Getting vetted for a membership was easy enough, considering my last name.

He's the sexiest man I've ever seen, and I couldn't have stayed hidden in the shadows if I was chained to them. Everything about Carter Hayes called to me. His dark hair that fell into his face, his athletic body, chiseled abs, the blue of his eyes and how they reflected the dim, overhead lights of the club, making them almost iridescent. I wanted him. I want him again now.

I convinced myself I could go in there and just get a glimpse of him in person. But then I touched him, and the entire world shifted.

Every decision I make feels like a weight on my chest, but out here in the quiet, I can almost see my way through this mess. The mess that just got much more complicated. The weight of my problems isn't going to disappear, but for the first time in a long time, I feel hopeful. There was something between Carter and me, and I know without a shadow of a doubt, he felt it. My heart races at the thought. I just need to navigate this mess. There's a way for me to keep my job and to see Carter again, see if he felt the same way I did. I just have to find it.

carter

THE MUSIC SOFTLY VIBRATES THROUGH THE CLUB, BUT I only vaguely register it. For the sixth night in a row, I find myself sitting in the same spot, a whiskey on the rocks cradled in my hand, my fingers strumming against the cool surface of the smooth wood grain of the bar top, the same questions on repeat in my head. What the fuck happened that night that obliterated every other sexual experience I've ever had? Why the anonymity? The secrecy around taking a meeting with me that *he* initiated? Why ghost the damn meeting, follow me here, and fuck around with me? I hardly recognize myself anymore. I've never chased anyone, and now I've become obsessed with the one person who seems to have no interest in me.

Despite my best attempts, he's always in my headspace, filling it, consuming me. I've started to crave that feeling he brought out in me. None of it makes any sense. As if I've spent the last twenty-five years asleep, Griffin brought me to life. And now he's nowhere to be found. Where the hell is he? I've had his personal contact information for almost a week now, burning a hole in my pocket, and every time I unlock my phone to reach out, something stops me.

I'm barely surviving in this in-between dimension of what's

right and wrong. I'm not sleeping, this asshole on replay like a sick montage. Did he know who I was? He's been dodging my emails for months; could there have been some nefarious reason he wanted to catch me at Temptations? Oh god, what if he writes a story about *me*?

My sexual appetite is an ongoing joke in town, and it's actually a surprise no one has come along to try to exploit that yet. It's no secret that I'm a bit of a notorious playboy, and while knowledge that I'm a member of a sex club probably wouldn't be surprising, I can still imagine the look on my poor mom's sweet face, the questions about how I didn't even know the name of the person I let suck on my cock. Could I be any more of a fuckup right now?

I check my phone for the millionth time in the last twenty minutes, waiting for the shoe to drop. An article, a blog post— anything—that will taint my family because of my selfish actions. I'm spiraling, and there's no pulling me back. I have no anchor, no safe harbor. I'm a ship drifting at sea with no security to blanket it from the inevitable storm.

There's no other reason why he would have found me at Temptations and hooked up with me. This place is full on a slow night. Which means Griffin had to know who I was ahead of time. Things like this don't just happen. I don't believe in fate, coincidence, or that some other magical bullshit was at play. That asshole knew who I was, point blank. He got what he wanted and is going to hold it over my head—if he doesn't just release it. Something is seriously fucked up about the entire situation, and I need to get to the bottom of it. I just want his weasel ass to come out of hiding on his own and face me like a man.

I need him to come to me so that I can turn the tables back in my favor. If he's into me, I can use that to my advantage. If his plans are nefarious, I can get closer to him, maybe he'll hold off on whatever he's up to. At least, that's what I'm telling myself to justify why I can't control the pull to Temptations—to him.

So here I sit, night after night, waiting for Griffin Nash to show back up and seek me out. Anxiety swirls through me, and I have to take deliberate breaths to keep myself from spiraling further.

Small, feminine hands rake up my back, but instead of turning me on, I'm annoyed as fuck. I look up from the swirling amber whiskey in my glass for a moment to be polite and give my guest a soft smile. I'm immediately taken aback. She's gorgeous—long brown hair, soft skin, pouty pink lips.

"I'm Sarah."

"Carter."

"Are you watching or playing tonight?"

Fuck. Maybe this is what I need. Trying to let go of my piss-poor mood, I lean into her space, putting her breasts right in front of my face, and watch the moment her breathing hitches. I love this about sex. Watching my partner's reactions to everything I'm doing. Learning their bodies, their tells, what lights them up. This. This is what I'm good at. This is the space where my head clears of all the noise, where everything shuts off.

"Depends," I tell her honestly.

She steps further into my space, my legs opening and welcoming her between them. My hands move to her hips, the soft, bare skin of her waist warm under my palms. She's a tiny wisp of a thing, with small breasts that are less than a handful, hip bones protruding from her thin frame, her waist tucked in tight. My eyes track down her nearly naked body, her long legs close together, leaving a gap between them where her little pussy hides under a pink G-string. Her hands rub up my arms and over my shoulders, clasping at the back of my neck.

Fuck. Why isn't my dick waking up? Work, asshole.

With a last-ditch effort to get this going, I meet her eyes and suck her nipple through the thin lace of her bra, enjoying the way chills scatter across her skin. Sarah moans softly, a sound that normally goes right to my dick. Her hand reaches down, palming what should be my hard cock, and I release her breast, sitting back and putting some space between us.

"Did I do something wrong?" she asks sheepishly, probably not used to being turned down.

I sigh hard, disappointed with myself as shame washes over me. This has never happened to me before.

"Sarah, you are a gorgeous woman, and any other night, I would take my time to worship you like you deserve, but my head just isn't in it tonight. It's cliché and normally a bullshit excuse, but I promise you it's the truth, it's not you, it's me."

She releases a deep sigh, her shoulders sagging in what I hope is relief and not the disappointment currently weighing on me.

"I can't say I'm not disappointed. Everyone has eyes on you."

Not the one person I want to have eyes on me.

I shake off my intrusive thoughts and give her the best smile I can muster. "I'm sorry. Enjoy your evening, okay?"

She gives me a nod and reluctantly walks away, leaving me alone to my quiet brooding. A laugh rolls through me as I hold the glass of my drink to my lips.

"Something funny?" Mike, the bartender, asks me.

"Who the fuck comes to a sex club and sits at the bar all night like a lonely, sad asshole?" I say through another laugh, the absurdity of my situation finally hitting me.

"Apparently you. Not too late to get that sexy little thing back over here to make you feel better."

Mike's not wrong, but I wasn't either. My head's not in it. I'm too occupied with Griffin Nash. Torn between wanting to see him again to see if everything I thought I felt was real, and ripping his fucking head off to find out what his goddamn issue is and what his plans are.

I toss the remainder of my drink to the back of my throat, nod at Mike to charge the card he has on file, and head outside before my panic starts to eat away at me here on the floor of the club. The last thing people need to find out is that the 'always up for a good time' guy is actually a head case who's constantly worried about everything.

There weren't a lot of rules growing up in my family that my parents followed through with. Finish school through high school, then go to college or pick a trade, be considerate of everyone around you, and attend family dinners on Sundays. That last one hasn't gone away even though we've all grown up. If anything, it's a more solid line that we five kids don't want to cross. None of us want to upset our mom.

Showing up early, I walk into my parents' house unannounced, my mom cutting up vegetables and putting them into tinfoil for the grill.

"Hey, Mom, how are you?" I ask as I drop a kiss on her head. She's shorter than all of us by a long shot, with short brown hair that is highlighted with silver strands that have come in as she ages. She's the sweetest, most welcoming woman you'll ever meet and has the patience of a saint. But you'd have to be, raising five heathens. She had us boys all back-to-back, then a few years between me and Kinsey. I'm surprised that after having Liam so soon after the twins, she didn't end up in a psych ward, but then she had two more, so she clearly thrives in chaos.

"Hey, my boy. I'm wonderful. Ready for a full house. My favorite day of the week."

"You're a saint hosting all of us, especially since we've expanded so quickly."

"I love it, and you know it."

"I'm not complaining. Especially when Ivy brings dessert," I say jokingly, even though my sister-in-law, Ivy, who's a chef, does bring the most amazing desserts, and my mom knows it. "Anything you need help with?"

"No, no. Dallas will be here shortly, and he'll help me finish up. You go ahead and find your dad." I know she means well and that she certainly doesn't have favorites, but damn if it doesn't dredge up my insecure feelings. As the fourth-born and youngest boy, it's been hard to find my place in the family. My older brothers easily found theirs—Sawyer is the oldest and bosses us all around, trying to control everything going on. Dallas, his twin, is a heavy mix of the oldest and middle child. He has a wild side that comes with being a middle kid, but he's also our caretaker and the glue that keeps us all together. Liam is calm and collected, so close to my dad and easily following in his footsteps. Kinsey is the baby and only girl, who can do no wrong in anyone's eyes.

I've forced myself into a role of being the fun, energetic one who's always up for a good time, never backing down from a dare, and trying to make jokes about everything. But in reality? I'm fucking lost as shit and I always have been. I'm not naturally good at anything—my brothers are exceedingly talented at running our family business, boxing, hockey, and creating whiskey. My sister is an amazing teacher, friend, daughter, and is loved by everyone who meets her. Besides fucking my way through random partners, I don't have any idea what I'm good at or what I should be doing with my life.

It's nothing anyone has done or said, and the guilt for feeling the way I do weighs heavily on me, but it's bound to happen when you're one of five siblings. Someone is going to get left out, someone is going to feel out of place. I'm drowning in love and support from these fuckers, but I've always felt like some part of me was missing, like I'm not wholly myself, and I don't know what that part is or where to find it.

I chase that good feeling that comes with sex, with knowing that I've made another person feel good, at least in the moment. But other than an orgasm on my end, I've never felt anything other than a quick burst of satisfaction for giving them a release and doing it well; it is simply transactional. I've never felt anything other than empty with every partner I've had . . . *until Griffin.*

I find my dad at the bar at the back of the house, rearranging his bottles. He looks good, and even though he wasn't ready for it, retirement suits him well. He had several strokes before Sawyer and Dallas took over the company from him. I know my mom loves having him home with her full time rather than being at the distillery, even if the way we got here was less than ideal.

My dad had inherited the business from our grandfather, and then it was passed to Sawyer. None of us were expecting the strokes and the lingering health issues that followed them, but I suppose no one expects these things to happen when they do.

He's doing surprisingly well, all things considered. He gets exhausted quickly, has some facial paralysis on one side, and his speech is quite slurred. Any emotional or mental health issues he deals with privately with my mom and his therapist. We do our best to fill him in on what's happening at work, as he loves still being as involved as he can be. The distillery was his life; he grew up running around that land, watching his grandfather and then his father build what it is today. It runs deep in his blood, and not being able to work every day at the place that he loves so much has taken a toll that we're all aware of.

Another check for why I'm such a fuckup for hooking up with Griffin. Even if I didn't know who he was, had I not been at that damn club to begin with, he wouldn't have any information on me that could paint us all in a bad light. But I'm going to fix it. I have to.

"Hey, Dad. Rearranging or reminiscing?"

"He-hey, son, both."

"Yeah? Got a favorite?"

He pulls out a twenty-year-old signature bourbon from our distillery and shows it to me.

"This one. Small batch. Single barrel."

This is one I haven't seen before. The bottle is smaller than that of our other bottles, a distressed black label across the front. Aspen Ridge Distillery's logo is proudly on the small label around the neck. The amber liquid is darker, more of a caramel color than a diluted amber.

"It's beautiful, Dad. Hey, can I ask—" My words are interrupted as chaos unfolds. A loud bang is followed by my idiot twin brothers falling into the room from the doorway. Dallas is on top of Sawyer, his arm wrapped around his neck, Sawyer throwing punches into Dallas' ribs as they each grunt and groan.

"They'll never grow up."

"Nope. I got it, Dad," I say as I walk away from him and toward my idiot brothers, irritated that they couldn't give me ten frigging minutes with him without interrupting.

"Li! Gimme a hand in here with these animals!" I yell down the hallway, hoping Liam has already arrived before turning my attention back to Thing One and Thing Two.

"Shut your mouth, I know you took them all on purpose! Hannah said you did!"

"I fuckin' wanted them!"

"What are you gonna do with five dozen muffins, dumbass?"

"Eat them, shithead!"

"Not five dozen!"

For fuck's sake why are they the way they are? Fighting over goddamn apple cinnamon muffins that Ivy can't get enough of. Sawyer makes it his sole responsibility to make sure his woman is stocked with them from the coffee shop that our sister-in-law owns–Bean Haven. Dallas must have bought them out this morning. I chuckle under my breath, pretty quick way to get Sawyer riled up is to fuck with Ivy.

Liam meanders down the hall with Hannah right behind him, her lavender hair swishing around her face as she rolls her eyes at the two idiots plowing into each other on the floor.

"I told him it was a bad idea! I said that all I had was what I had already made since it was Sunday, and I've changed my hours to come here every week. He doesn't listen!" Hannah defends herself, as if we don't already know that Dallas is the guilty party here. She's been best friends with Liam since they were in preschool, and I've known the girl almost my entire life, so she knows the deal with our unhinged family. She throws her hands up in the air and bends down to the massive pile of males on the floor just as Dallas winces, Sawyer's elbow cracking into his lip hard.

Hannah braces her hands on her knees and yells into the fray, "Serves you right, Dal! I told you poking the bear wasn't a good idea, didn't I? You don't listen!" I can't help but laugh. For so long it's been just the five of us siblings, it's nice to have some other family around here to yell at these morons.

"Get them off each other! I don't want blood on my carpet again! Sawyer Hayes, don't you break any of his bones today!" our mom yells from the kitchen. I look at my dad, who is standing at the bar with a smile on his face.

Liam and I give each other a look and shrug, moving at the same time to grab a brother and yank them off of each other, putting some needed distance between them. I've got Dallas' arms pulled back hard, clinching them behind his back as he still tries to lunge for Sawyer.

"You don't own a monopoly on the fuckin' Bean Haven muffins! It's our sister-in-law's bakery, and I can eat as many as I want!"

"Will you give it a rest, dumbass?" I ask as I drag him out of the room and shove him down the hallway. "Why you gotta piss him off?"

Dallas shakes out his shirt, wiping the back of his hand across his mouth and smearing blood across his cheek. "'Cause it's funny. Why don't you try it?"

"Nah, don't need the beast busting my pretty face, now do I?"

"Right. What would the women think then?"

My imagination immediately conjures Griffin and the fact that I may be into men. Or am into men? Hell, I don't even know what way is up right now. And just like that, my mood deflates again.

"Oh, go figure, you're bleeding. Do you get some sick enjoyment from riling people up?" Blaire asks Dallas as she blots at the cut on his lip with a rag. He gives her a devious look I'd rather not have seen. "Don't you dare answer that, Dallas Maverick. Not at your parents' house."

"Gross," I say under my breath as I walk away from them.

Blaire works at the distillery as our event coordinator and has had quite the whirlwind romance with my brother. He's lost to that woman wholly, and after the life she's had up until this point, I understand why he's so protective of her.

The rest of dinner goes as smoothly as it can, considering the company we're in. All of my brothers are swooning over the loves of their lives. There's a tiny twinge of jealousy that flutters in my chest, but overall, I just don't understand how they can give themselves up so completely to another person. Especially after what Sawyer went through when Ivy left him at eighteen. The way he can just fall back into the fold, give someone else the power to completely wreck you—this is exactly why I stick to just sex. No feelings involved. No chance of anyone destroying me.

Griffin made you feel something.

Choosing to ignore the thoughts in my head, I help clean up from an early dinner and head home to change. There's only one place I want to be tonight, and it's only because I need to deal with Griffin Nash. It has nothing to do with him becoming a permanent fixture in my head.

Not at all. I'm in complete control.

CHAPTER 4

finn

"Hey fuckface, we're going out. Get off your ass and get dressed, no more brooding," Trey shouts as he walks into my house unannounced.

"Why'd I give you a key again?"

"'Cause you love me."

"I'm rescinding your permanent invitation. Give it back," I groan from my place on the couch where I'm currently writing on my laptop.

"Dude, what is wrong with you? If I didn't know you better, I'd say you were lovesick."

"I'm not lovesick, you idiot. Just trying to sleep my problems away, but my ex-best friend won't piss off and let me wallow."

"Well, if I'm your ex-best friend, then I guess you wouldn't mind if I take the Lexus out for a spin?"

That gets me standing up, the room spinning as I get used to the quick change in balance. Fuck, how long have I been sitting here working?

"Fuck you. Don't even think about it, Trey. No one touches her."

"Well, then I need daddy to drive me around."

"Daddy, huh? Are we sure you aren't gay?"

"Wouldn't that make your life so much easier? We could run off into the sunset together, and life would be grand."

"You couldn't handle me," I joke.

"Probably not, you freak. You think Carter Hayes can?"

I drop back down to the couch and groan like a baby. "Ugh. Did you have to bring him up?"

"Get dressed, or I'll do it for you, and trust me when I say neither one of us wants that. So get to it. We're getting you out of your writing cave. You've been locked away all weekend, and I know you're stressed. This will be good for you, and I don't have to roll up like a loner. Let's go."

Begrudgingly, and feeling kind of bad, I walk through the downstairs to the smaller bedroom I'm staying in, pulling off my sweatpants, taking a fast shower, and pulling myself together the best I can. I opt for a pair of jeans and a short-sleeved, button-up T-shirt.

Ten minutes later, I'm grabbing the keys to my SUV, and we're heading outside.

"You gonna tell me where we're goin'?"

"Want to take me to that sex club?"

"Are you insane? No. Plus, I'm still within the probationary period, and I can't vet guests yet."

I can feel his eyes on me as I drive, and I know he won't let this go. I can't say that I don't get it. Who doesn't want to check out a high-end sex club if they have the opportunity? If I hadn't been so lust-struck by Carter, I would be making that place my own personal playground.

"I expect that no to change to a yes once you can. We're meeting some friends at a new place that just opened, and thought you'd want to check it out."

Called it. Trey navigates, and after a ten-minute drive, I pull into the parking lot of a new speakeasy, *The Whispering Well*, written on an old-school sign on the side of a brick building. A hostess lights up when we walk in, the real reason for us being here making more sense.

"Hey, Ana, how is your night?"

"Hi, Trey. It's better now. Seat for two?"

"Actually, we're meeting some friends. I think they're already here. A group of them?"

"Yes, rowdy bunch? I'll take you to them."

I watch as they flirt for a moment, Trey on his game, before she weaves us through the open dining area. Plush, velvet, high-back booths are scattered around the walls of a floor that's raised higher. My eyes track a small set of stairs that lead to tables on the lower floor. A stage is in front of us with a band gearing up to play. I can't help but pick up every detail, and I'm impressed with the thought that went into the place. They should do well, and I hope the area can keep them in business.

Two men look our way and lift up their drinks as we approach, but it's the one who doesn't that makes me nearly trip over my own feet. I drop an elbow to hit Trey in the ribs, making him wince.

"Are you fucking serious? This isn't happening." I go to turn around, but he grabs my arm in protest.

"Dude, I didn't know he'd be here, but it's gonna look real fucking shitty if you walk out now that they've seen you."

Fuck. When I decided to make the move west of Seattle to work at this office permanently, I knew there would be a chance of running into him since he returned to this area after med school. I've been lucky the last few months until now. This is just what I need.

I stare at the photo on my screen as I bounce my leg in the back of the Uber, ready to get home. My trip to Coos Bay, Oregon, lasted two weeks, and it's the longest time I've had to be away before. I love traveling, but I like being home more when I have someone waiting for me. Nick smiles back at me on the screen, and I can't wait to get back to him. He's never too upset when I leave, but I can't stand the distance it puts between us.

Pulling up in front of the apartment that my dad rents for me —a place too large, and too fancy for my taste, but, Nick loves it and I "need to keep up appearances"—I quickly pay my driver on the app, grab my bags and jump out of the car. I'm eager to get to Nick. Even though he's never stayed the night with me, even though I persist, he stays at my penthouse when I'm away because he lives in a shared apartment with two roommates while he finishes med school. He says he needs full commitment before he can stay the night with someone, which I've always respected, no matter how often I've found myself not wanting to be alone anymore. We've been together for almost a year, and I'm finally ready to tell him how I feel. That's why I had to come home early. I couldn't wait another day without telling him that I love him and that I want to move forward in our relationship.

The elevator stops at damn near every floor to let people off. My heart is in my throat with anticipation while I wait until it finally reaches the top. I'm out the door with my duffel thrown over my shoulder before the doors can completely open.

I rush down the hallway and set my bag down outside the door, wanting to surprise him and wanting my hands to be free. I quietly unlock the door, and dread immediately washes over me. My spine straightens as bile rises in my throat. Moans fill the space of my apartment, one of which I faintly recognize, but he's never sounded so . . . vocal with me. Our sex life has always been very monotonous, but I just assumed it was because of our inexperience and how tired he always says he is.

I walk through the house, steeling myself for what I already know I'm going to find. Each breath I take feels like shards of glass going down my windpipe, a grasp so tight on my chest that taking each step takes an obscene amount of effort. I follow the noises to my bedroom, the door left wide open. My boyfriend is hammering into a guy I've met before, someone who he said was just a friend. Clearly not.

My mind blanks as everything kind of goes black.

"This is how you spend your time while I'm gone?"

"Shit! Finn! What are you doing back?"

"That's your response? That's the first thing you want to say?"

They scramble apart, everything moving in slow motion. I've seen these scenes in movies, where everyone moves quickly and frantically, apologies are thrown, people scream and yell. That's not how this plays out.

"What do you want me to say, Finn?"

"You're in my apartment, Nick, fucking someone who's not me, I'd say you should say a whole helluva lot more than what you have so far. Just get out. I want you to leave."

"Finn, we don't have to be over. I just need more than what you're giving me."

My dad's voice rings out in my head, reminding me that I'm a fuckup, that I'll always be a fuckup, that I'll never be good enough for anyone. Maybe he's right.

"If what I'm giving you isn't enough, Nick, then we should have been over a long time ago. You didn't need to fuck around behind my back. Didn't need to do it in my bed either. Just fucking get out! We're done."

Nick and his friend quickly get dressed, grabbing their things and heading to the door. He has the audacity to turn and face me one last time, but I can't bear to look at his eyes.

"Finn . . . you could—"

"GET OUT!"

"Dude, you've got this. Fuck them. I didn't know they'd be here. Just pull it together. We'll have a beer and then we'll bounce."

Trey's voice brings me back to the present, and I nod at him, but I'm still annoyed. Who wants to share a beer with a shitbag person that hurt you?

It's been five years, and I'm definitely over him, just don't like the reminder shoved right in my face. The worse part of our relationship wasn't the cheating, anyway, it was the gaslighting, manipulation, and guilt he constantly placed on me that fucked with me more. I just didn't realize how toxic the behavior was until I needed to get him out of my life. After I kicked him out, news traveled through our small group, and Trey found out that Nick had been cheating on me for the majority of our relationship. Explains the lack of sleepovers.

Trey fist-bumps everyone at the table: his friend Leo, Oliver, Nathan, and . . . Nick. I give them all a nod as I take my seat next to Leo. Trey and I have known him since high school, when we all played soccer together, and he's all around a good guy.

We order a round of beers, everyone chatting, the hostess coming back to check on things and flirt with Trey. I keep quiet, completely out of my comfort zone and feeling like I want to crawl out of my fucking skin.

"So, how ya been, Finn?"

"Don't call me that. Griffin is fine. And I'm great," I answer curtly as my phone goes off.

"That's how it's gonna be? Not allowed to call you the name you go by?" Nick has the audacity to question, and I just shrug my shoulders in reply. He's not worth it, and I don't want to hear my name from his toxic, lying mouth.

My phone dings with an incoming text.

> Dad: Just read your feature and it's subpar at best. If you can't produce quality work, I'll find someone who can. You're making the decision to replace you with Dion easier and easier every day. Get your head out of your ass and do your job. I'm ashamed you're a Nash. Ruining my good name with shit writing.

My shoulders slump as defeat sets in. Fuck. I just turned in my story on Pineview, Washington. I worked my ass off on that feature and I'm damn proud of it. The entire town deserves a spotlight feature, and I only focused on a few of the places there—a little Turkish restaurant run by the sweetest mother and daughter duo, an incredible rare finds book shop, and a burlesque theater with the best show I've ever seen, performed by extremely talented dancers that should be on a New York stage instead of hidden away in a small town in Washington. Bringing a spotlight to these places, bringing in tourism—knowing they can handle a boom—can make these towns prosper instead of crumble. We have the power to help, and it's a piece of my job that I take seriously. Of course he hated it.

Me: I apologize, Dad. I'll work harder.

Dad: You're damn right you will. We don't need stories on fantastical lands, we need grit. You're going to tank our reputation, Griffin, if you don't step it up. I expect more from a Nash.

Me: I'm trying

Dad: It's not good enough.

I'm not enough for my parents. I wasn't enough for Nick, and even if things could be different between me and Carter, I'd end up not being enough for him, either. I don't even know why I try anymore.

Sitting alone again on my couch with my laptop on my lap, I rest my head back against the cushion in frustration, defeat pressing in. Memories of Carter's crystal-blue eyes dance behind my eyelids as he looked up at me, shock and awe written all over his face as I worked our slick dicks together. He's easily the most beautiful man I've ever seen. His rich brown hair mussed and falling into his eyes, his flushed skin, his big, thick cock, and the ridges up the length.

His body aside, the feeling I got from the moment I laid eyes on him was unlike anything I've ever felt before. The way everything silenced in my head, all the pressure left, leaving just Carter. It was instant. As if everything in my life had brought me to that moment, I was rewarded with peace. God, I want that. I need that. Just for a minute.

Fuck it.

Not able to fight the pull any longer, I close my laptop, grab my keys, and I'm out the door heading to Temptations, driving a little faster than I should. I expected Carter to figure out who I was by now. Trey and I are both shocked he hasn't reached out again, except for the single email at the beginning of the week. Maybe he didn't feel the world shifting under his feet like I did. Maybe the entire thing was one-sided because I'm so goddamn desperate to have someone finally see me, to no longer be alone.

I shake my head of the thoughts while I drive on the empty streets before merging onto the highway. Temptations is roughly a thirty-minute drive, and I hope like hell Carter had nothing better to do on a Sunday night than go to a sex club. The thought freezes me for a moment. What if he's hooking up with people? *Cause what else would he do at a sex club, dumbass? Of course he's hooking up with someone.*

Nausea rolls around in my stomach at the thought. I don't have any claim to Carter Hayes, but he's mine. I don't know how else to explain it. *Mine.* And I don't want anyone else touching him but me.

The drive flies by, and before I know it, I'm pulling into Temptations, swiping my black membership card over the inside scanner and entering the club. I quickly check-in with the receptionist to reserve a room, and enter the main floor, loud music and naked bodies filling the dance floor and bar. The lights are dim, a red hue glowing off of everything tonight, my body vibrating with eager anticipation.

I do a quick scan, not seeing Carter right away, my heart throbbing in my throat, nerves completely shot. How am I going to feel if I see him with someone else? It was hot as hell to share him with that beautiful woman the first night, but the moment she walked away, a curtain had been lifted—both literally and metaphorically. I slowly prowl the outskirts of the main floor, my eyes scanning for Carter. I feel him here—a magnetism so strong, I couldn't fight it if I wanted to—and I want to get my eyes on him before he finds me.

After ordering a drink from the bar, I slip to the back and wait. I could go to the back rooms and see if he's there, but something tells me he's close; I can feel him. I do another perusal of the bar, and at the far end, enveloped in the darkest part of the club, is Carter Hayes, his dark hair falling over his forehead, his eyes focused down on the drink cupped in front of him. Relief washes over me upon seeing him alone.

I keep to the shadows, sipping on a whiskey that tastes all wrong, watching Carter sulk at the bar alone. Beautiful female suitor after suitor propositions him, and he turns down every single one. It's hard not to question whether he's just not in the mood or if I seeped under his skin like he did mine.

I can only wish.

Drink in hand, I weave through the crowd, their bodies a blur, nothing but a flash of movement in my peripheral, my eyes locked in on one person. The only one who matters. He's wearing a navy blue button-up shirt that is pulled taut over his muscles, his shoulders rounded as he nearly hunches over the bar. He still exudes confidence, controlling the room without giving it his attention at all. I'm just as affected as everyone else here. I want him. No one else will do.

The leather barstool creaks as I take a seat on it, my arm brushing against his. Carter bristles, sitting up straighter.

"The fuck do you want?"

My heart flips over in my chest as I realize he knows it's me without having to look. Looks like I did leave an impression on him after all. *Good.*

"Depends what you're offering."

His eyes finally look up to meet mine, the crystal blues sunken back and forlorn. He looks lost, almost panicked. I don't like it, and I don't know what put that look there, but I need to fix it.

"Let's go somewhere and just talk."

He arches a brow at me as if he believes my words about as much as I do. Picking up his whiskey, I shoot the remaining amber liquid into the back of my throat before setting it down next to my empty glass and walking away. I weave through the crowd again, paying no mind to the naked bodies and the few hands that dare to reach out and grasp at my arms to get my attention.

Stopping in front of the room I've reserved for the evening, I swipe my black membership card over the keypad, the door unlocking and giving me access. I nod to the bouncer, letting him know we're all good here, and hold open the door for Carter, feeling his presence behind me. My adrenaline spikes, anticipation a live wire thrumming through my veins as I ready myself to be alone with the man I haven't been able to get out of my head all week.

The room is simple. Lights are dimmed around the space except for one illuminating a queen-sized bed in the center of the room, made with simple white sheets, the headboard pushed against the far wall. A large wardrobe sits off to the side, filled with everything we could need for this kind of scene—toys, lube, simple restraints, a blindfold. Unfortunately, we won't be using any of that tonight. A large viewing window fills the entire length of one of the walls. My eyes flick up to the light placed at the top of the door, glowing red, telling me we have complete privacy for as long as we want it.

Carter hovers by the door while I walk further into the room, opening the wardrobe doors and glancing at the contents. I pull out a long, flesh-colored dildo, turning and smacking it against my palm purely to see if I can make him uncomfortable. Much to my dismay, Carter only looks annoyed.

"What do you want, *Griffin*?"

Ahh. So he's done his research. I'd hoped as much. The name slices over me like barbed wire, and I crack my neck to the side to ease some of the tension rolling through me.

"Finn."

"What?"

"Call me Finn."

I have no idea why I say it. Only the people closest to me call me Finn. But it feels more like me than Griffin ever did. I *hate* Griffin. My dad is Griffin. Griffin sounds all wrong coming from Carter's lips.

"I don't give a fuck what you want to be called. Imagine my surprise when I finally tracked down the dickhole writer who has been avoiding me, only to find out it was *you*. Was this all some sick game to you? You think fucking me around for the last few months only to, what? Follow me here to catch me in some illicit acts? Thought you'd take it a step further and get me to hook up with you? What's your endgame here, *Griffin*?" His tone is fierce, each word piercing and getting louder as he goes on. But I don't flinch. Even though his words shred what remains of my self-worth.

I replace the dildo, carefully closing the doors of the wardrobe and turning back to face Carter. He's wearing black slacks that were tailored to fit his athletic build. Strong legs make me guess that he's a runner like me, leading up to a trim waist and muscular chest. His biceps bulge at the fabric of the blue button-up shirt where they're crossed over his chest. His rich chocolate brown hair is quite long on the top, styled and tousled back out of his face now, the sides are shorter, but just enough so that it's off of his ears. My cock bucks as I take my fill of him.

Fuck. My hands itch to touch him again. It's almost painful not to reach for him.

I meet his eyes as I rub my palm over the thick outline of my dick, not making a single attempt to be inconspicuous about it. Carter's eyes track the movement—just like I wanted them to—his jaw ticking, his only tell that I've affected him.

"What's your endgame here, Nash?"

Can't say I love it, but it's better than Griffin, I suppose.

"How'd you figure out who I was?" I counter, walking aimlessly around the room, checking it out.

"Does it matter? Let me guess, since you don't seem to want to be forthcoming about shit," Carter says as he leans back against the door, crossing his ankles like he's catching up with an old friend instead of interrogating an enemy. But is that what I am? I certainly don't want to be. "Your family owns the Northwest Explorer, and while you've been playing me for months on actually doing the interview *you* requested, you've done a deep dive on my family—looking for a story. You started with me, 'cause you thought I was the weakest link, right? And tracked me to Temptations. What I need to know is what you plan to do with the information you have on me now. I'm assuming you'll be exploiting it since taking a meeting with me to feature the distillery seems to be out of the question."

I'll give it to him, he's got quite the pessimistic mentality. I wasn't expecting him to jump to such dark conclusions about me. When I take a step back, I can see it. But he doesn't know me from the next asshole, and I'm sure he has his reasons for being skeptical. He also doesn't know my reason for following him to Temptations. Too bad I can't tell him that without sounding like a fucking crazy person.

I saw your photo on the distillery website, and my knees almost buckled with how beautiful you are. Your striking blue eyes called to me like whispers, giving me hope that someone was out there, created just for me.

Instead, I take slow, measured steps in his direction and watch his reaction. Once I'm a pace away, his breathing starts to pick up, just ever so slowly, an increase in the rise and fall of his chest. He shifts so that he's standing upright, putting us at near eye level, his jaw ticking, eyes squinting at me like he can't figure out my play. I stop once we're toe-to-toe, his scent surrounding me—rich molasses and spice—sending my senses into overdrive.

Fucking delicious.

I don't say anything, waiting for him to be the one to break the silence stretching between us. I use the time to study his features. His blue eyes that swirl with so much depth, the beard that he keeps trimmed expertly close around a strong jaw. His lips are slightly puffy, pale pink and perfect to wrap around my cock.

"You're not gonna deny it then?"

"Why deny what you've already made your mind up to believe?"

As much as it pains me to let you believe I'm capable of hurting another person. But I can't have you, so this makes it easier.

"Because I want to hear your filthy mouth say it," he snaps. "You knew who I was when you hooked up with me, took advantage of the heat of a situation, just so you could get a story. Are you even into dick or just that pathetically committed to your job?"

That last part stings, and I know my eyes flash with agitation before my mask falls back into place. I grab my cock with my hand and give it a vulgar jerk through my slacks, the outline of how thick and hard I am obnoxiously obvious.

"What about this makes you think I'm not into men?"

"Maybe it has nothing to do with pussy or dick and everything to do with being a sadist?"

An image of Carter splayed out on my bed naked, wrists and ankles bound, begging me to let him come after hours of edging appears in my head and I contemplate the idea with a smirk, my head cocking to the side.

"Gotta say, my imagination is doing delicious things right now." I take a single step forward, my shoe stepping between his, our knees nearly touching. My leg can feel the warmth emanating from his body and my cock throbs at a relentless beat.

"The fuck do you want with me?"

A sardonic laugh bubbles free from my throat because how do I even answer that? I want to know everything about you. I want to know what you taste like, what you look like when you're sleeping and most relaxed and vulnerable. I want to know your favorite movie, song, and how you take your coffee. I want to tell you that you're the first person to quiet all the bullshit constantly filling my head and my evil asshole daddy dearest has threatened my life if I so much as look at you, little own touch you or make you mine, when every cell in my body is telling me to do just that.

You'll never amount to anything, Griffin.

You're such a fucking disappointment, Griffin.

It's bad enough that my only son is gay, the least you could do is not fuck up another thing.

You're an embarrassment, I'm ashamed you're my son.

"I fucking own you, Griffin. You're a Nash. Which means you are mine. Fall in line, or I will destroy you."

I roll my neck from side to side, the sick reminder that I can't do anything right in my father's eyes causing a familiar pain behind my eyes. I want to quiet the voices. I need to. So, I press.

"Isn't it obvious?" I finally answer, pressing my hips against his, my eyebrows raising at what I discover. "For someone who says he doesn't want me, you are *so* goddamn hard."

A sexy growl works its way up Carter's throat, a sound that makes my dick buck against the zipper of my slacks. The tension is a live wire between us, palpable, and making us both nearly pant at the close proximity.

He wants me just as much as I want him.

I roll my hips against his, watching his reaction. His breathing hitches, every rise of his chest rubbing against mine, his nipples hard peaks under the tight, thin fabric of his shirt. Fuck, I wish there wasn't any material between us. I want to feel his hard abs, his perfect chest. My fingers ache to drag my nails over the fine expanse of his sexy body.

"Lover, you can deny this all you want, but you feel it just as much as I do."

"I'm not your fucking lover."

He says the words, but they don't pack a punch. His eyes devour me, and he can't hide his arousal. He wants this, he's just too caught up in the other bullshit to make the move. The corner of my lips lifts on one side, challenging him.

"Fine. I'll make it easy on you, Carter."

"By walking out and never coming back?"

"I'll dare you."

His eyes flash at the challenge, and I wonder if he'll take me up on it. I don't even know what I'm pushing for him to do. Hell, we can stand here and grind our cocks together through the thin layer of our pants until we're both panting and filling our boxers with cum for all I care. Just as long as he gives me a piece of him. Just as long as my brain stays quiet. He's the first person to settle all the messed up shit in my head. Being with him is all I want right now, it doesn't matter that he falsely believes I could do anything to hurt him . . . or anyone, for that matter.

"You want it?" he asks, surprising me.

Jesus. Is he testing me? Yes, I want it. I want to devour him whole.

"Fuck yeah, I do."

"Then fucking *suck it*."

My eyes widen, my heart rate spiking, my mouth practically watering for him. He wants me to taste him again? I know he has to be testing me now. He's still unsure if I'm actually into dick, or hell, even him, but despite what he may be questioning, I've never wanted someone more. The dynamic is different; I'm always the one in control, never before trusting another person enough to let them lead, but I want to please Carter. I want to make this as easy as possible for him. My heart pulls as I realize all the shit that's probably muddling his head—me, the magazine, and from what I can only assume, the strong possibility that he's only been with women until now. Jesus, no wonder he's fighting it and panic dances behind his eyes.

I start to drop to my knees at his demand, going against every natural instinct I have to follow it, but I want him, and I'll let him lead this for as long as he needs to.

"I've been craving the taste of you since the first night," I confess truthfully. "But I need to hear you say it—explicitly—that this is what you want, Carter."

He hesitates for a moment, and I know I put him on the spot, but I need his consent. I need to know—games aside—he's here right now with me, and this is what he wants. His eyes search mine for a moment, and he must find whatever he's looking for because he nods his head.

"Words, lover. I need them. Then I'll make you feel so fucking good."

His eyes flutter closed for a moment as he releases a deep exhale, and I fear I've lost him. My feelings are quickly squashed as they open, burning with lust, and my heart picks up the pace in my chest, blood rushing to my cock, stiffening me hard as fucking stone.

"Yeah, I want this. On your knees, Nash."

My knees hit the hard floor as Carter makes quick work of his pants, his fingers shaking as he's slipping them down over his hips, frantically pulling his thick cock free. Goddamn it, thank fuck, he's eager for it, he wants this just as bad as I do.

I take over almost immediately. My hand wrapping around the cock I've been dreaming about all week. He's thick and smooth in my hand, and I give him a hard jerk, loving how his thighs tense up at the feeling I'm pulling from him. Using the flat of my tongue, I lick a slow trail from right above his sack, up the pulsing vein of the underside of his dick to the crown, flicking the bead of precum from it. Carter releases a rough exhale as he relaxes against the wall, giving in more, but not quite handing himself over to me.

I pump him twice, swirling my tongue around the thick mushroom head, lapping at the precum beading there. His salty taste explodes on my tongue and I moan around it, meeting his eyes as I do.

"Quit playing and suck it. You want my dick, Griffin? Show me how good you can suck it."

Fuck, I hate hearing that name from him. I flick my eyes up to meet his as I growl—deep and warning—before doing exactly what he says, sucking him all the way down. I relax my throat, letting his big dick slide into the cavity, my nose pressed against the pubic hair he keeps trimmed close to the skin. I fucking love that he's nearly bare. I throw everything I have into sucking him off, squeezing his hip with one hand and slipping my other between his legs.

He spreads willingly for me, giving me access to cup his balls. The urge to slip my finger behind them and stimulate his tight asshole is incredibly strong, but I have a feeling this would end quicker than it started if I do. Carter's hands stay firmly at his sides, closed into fists as if he's actively trying to hold himself back.

I use my hand on his hip to move him, urging him to rock, to fuck my face, giving him further control—which is difficult for me. It takes him a moment before he gives in, finally thrusting into my face, his thick mushroom head nudging the back of my throat. I shift, relaxing my throat, as I gag around his length for the first time, tears springing to my eyes. That seems to do the trick.

"Oh, fuck, yeah. Just like that. You like my cock down your throat? You like being on your knees for me?"

I want to answer him verbally, but I don't want him to stop, instead humming around him as I hollow out my cheeks on the next upstroke, sucking hard.

"Oooh, fuuuck. That's it, fuck that feels good." His hand twitches at his side for a moment, my eyes tracking the movement, waiting for that last thread of restraint to break. I take him all the way down and stay with my nose pressed against his pubic area, his euphoric, musky scent engulfing my lungs, his cock laying down my throat, and I swallow.

Once.

Twice.

Three times.

His hands thread through my hair as he forces me back, just long enough to break the suction and suck in a gulp of air, filling my lungs with oxygen, before he's pressing me back down to repeat the process. It's obscene, spit and his salty precum dripping from my lips, my gags and slurps mixed with his heavy panting, the only noise filling the room.

"Fuck. Fuck. You're gonna suck the cum right out of me. So fucking good. You want my cum?" He moans the words on jagged breaths, and it's music to my ears. "Shit. It's coming, fuuuck, pull back now if you don't want it."

I appreciate the warning, but I want it. Desperately.

I grip his hips with both hands, pulling him deep into my mouth as his cock swells, throbbing as he overflows me with his cum. He tastes fucking amazing—a musky, salty flavor that's my new favorite thing in the world. I gag around the heavy streams that shoot from his slit, swallowing back as much as I can in a greedy attempt to consume all of him.

"Fuuck, Finn, fuuuuuck."

Finn.

And just like that, I fall harder.

carter

My head flops back against the hard wall as I heave breaths into my lungs and work to steady my racing heart. Griffin—Finn—pops off my dick, taking languid licks over the sensitive head. Is he seriously cleaning me up? I look back down at him, my hands still holding the sides of his head, his silky strands threaded through my fingers. He grins up at me, a satisfied smirk pulling at his lips, making me want to smack the shit right off his face.

I let my hands fall to my sides as Finn slowly stands up, crowding my space, using the back of his hand to wipe the moisture from his mouth. He looks like a lion right before they pounce and devour their prey. Too bad I'm not some helpless gazelle alone in a field. I move my hands between us, stuffing my softening dick back into my boxer briefs. Finn grabs my wrists, lifting them above my head, and for whatever fucked-up reason, I allow it.

A moment passes between us before he dips his face into the crook of my neck, dragging his nose languidly across my pebbled flesh, inhaling deeply. The scruff of his facial hair is rough against my skin as he brushes his lips back and forth along the curve at the base of my neck and shoulder. My eyes flutter closed at the contact. Fuck. What is he doing to me? Why does it feel so good with him?

"Mmm. You smell as good as you taste."

The deep baritone of his voice sends the right signals to my dick, which, to my dismay, is rapidly hardening again. Finn lifts his head, practically nose to nose with me as he watches my eyes, my heart beating hard behind my ribcage, blood rushing to my ears. Just as his eyes flick down to my lips, I know I need to get out of here.

I easily flip our positions, pressing Finn hard against the wall and taking a step back. His eyes widen in surprise, but I don't miss the flash of disappointment that crosses his strong features.

"That's how it's gonna be then, huh?" he demands.

"That can't happen again and it sure as shit isn't going any further."

"So, you're just gonna come down my throat and call it a night?" He seems genuinely shocked by that, but I've given him no inclination that I'm a selfless man or that I'd even consider returning the favor. I still don't understand what the hell is happening between us or his true intentions.

"You weren't complaining while you swallowed it down and didn't spill a drop," I quip. "Such a good boy for me, *Griffin*."

I watch his facial expression as I taunt him, and I don't miss the slight flash of arousal that crosses his face at the praise, even if it was in jest. It's quickly replaced by the cocky asshole. We both seem to be powerhouses vying for control, the pendulum constantly changing who's on top. He purses his lips, nodding his head slowly as if digesting the situation and deciding how to proceed.

"So tell me, Carter, you seem to have quite the imagination. What exactly do you think I want from you? Why do you think I'm here? Seems like someone may not be so confident in his choice of extracurricular activities. Worried the public may think Aspen Ridge's iconic family has a sex addict running their empire?"

And there it is. I can't help it; my jaw goes slack, falling open. I didn't think he'd say it. With the taste of my cum still on his tongue, he just admitted his entire fucking plan and how he'll try to ruin my family. I'm an idiot. Panic rises quickly, the blood pulsing through my veins turning to ice as my face heats and my hands start to shake.

"You motherfucker! You signed a contract to come in here, an NDA! They'll drown you if this gets out!"

"Back the hell up, Carter. I was asking what *you* thought," he says in the most calm, slightly irritated voice he can muster. I study his face, so fucking confused, my rage and panic simmering to a barely contained boil right at the surface.

"Drop the games, Griffin. What do you want from me? My sex life is an open book because I'm a man who owns his shit. I don't do anything half-assed. I can speak to every single one of my actions. So what is it that you want?"

His eyes dart back and forth between mine as if he's searching for something to hold on to. His eyes are heavy, as if he's struggling with the weight of the world on his shoulders and he's hoping I'm his lifeline, his savior. He looks at me with so much depth that it nearly knocks the wind from my lungs. And then he speaks, the word barely a whisper above the sound of our heavy breaths and racing heartbeats.

"You."

My molars grind together, and before I realize I've done it, I have Finn's shirt balled in my fists, shoving him hard against the wall. My body wars with wanting to knock his teeth down the back of his throat and kissing him so hard he'll feel the bruises of it tomorrow. What the fuck is wrong with me? The tension thrums through us like a ticking time bomb.

Our breathing is labored, coming in hard pants as we share space. Anger courses through my body, my hold on his shirt so tight my knuckles are turning white. Fuck, I feel it in the marrow of my bones, Finn has the power to destroy everything. But all I can see are his perfectly plump lips, slightly parted as he braces for my next move. I know he feels it, the tension pulling tight, that I'm grappling for control and that this could spin either way.

He doesn't fight me, his arms lying slack at his sides. He's giving me the control again and time to decide, and I don't understand why. I meet his eyes, so fucking blue I could be looking into the clearest ocean. They swirl with mirth, dirty promises, and something else that he's keeping locked up tight. I want to know what that is. I want to know his secrets. I want to know what he needs saving from. I want . . . *him*.

For just a moment, suspended in this space with Finn, I feel *everything* rather than nothing. My heart pounds so loud I can hear my pulse between my ears, my hands shake where his shirt is balled in my fists, my stomach fluttering and in knots. It all feels so *good*. Everything in my head quiets. For a moment, it's just us, nothing else clouding my thoughts. The outside world disappears, and who we are no longer matters.

So, I kiss him.

His lips respond right away, as if he knew this was how it would end, as if any other scenario wasn't even an option. Finn's hands circle both of my wrists, holding me in place like he's scared this will end before he's ready.

His tongue melds with mine, the taste of my cum potent and an erotic reminder of what we just did. I suck it into my mouth, Finn moaning around the sensation. Our mouths move together easily, his facial hair rough on my skin. It doesn't occur to me until this moment that I'm kissing a man for the first time. Instead, it feels like I'm doing exactly what I'm supposed to. With exactly who I'm supposed to be doing it with. That thought right there is what should stop me.

I can't fucking do this. I don't do feelings. I also don't fuck around with selfish, rich pricks who could be fucking with my family. But maybe if I give myself to him, he'll give me what I need in return. Maybe if I give him more of me, he'll drop whatever nefarious plans he has up his sleeve and instead write the article I was first offered. The one my family wants and deserves. Even if it wrecks me in the process.

I kiss him like I mean it, like I can't control myself, and I lie to myself over and over again—it's just to get the article and protect my family. But, then, why can't I stop? Why is this kiss the best kiss of my entire life?

"Fuck, I can't decide what I like the taste of more, your tongue or your cock." Finn moans the words against my mouth as he kisses over my jaw, moving down to my neck, sending pleasure spikes up and down my spine. My head lolls to the side, lust-drunk and loving the way his beard scrapes against my skin. His hands release my wrists, moving to my waist and pulling me closer to him. Our bodies are flush, his cock pressing firmly against my hip as he grinds into me. I let him. He humps me like a cat in heat and I don't hate it. I want to be the reason he falls apart.

"So fucking desperate. Rubbing your cock all over me. Don't stop until you blow."

"Take me out so you can watch," Finn nearly begs, his voice deep and needy.

His words roll over me, and I find myself wanting to do just that. Wanting to see his thick, uncut cock jerk until it explodes. But I can't. I have to keep some fucking control here. Instead, I pull him closer to me, my hands rubbing down his back until I reach his ass, jerking him upward slightly so that my thigh rests between his legs.

Finn rocks, a steady movement rolling his hips, rubbing his cock back and forth over me, until his breathing hitches and I know he's on the edge.

I drag my tongue over his plush lips before whispering, "Come for me," against them. He ruptures, and I swallow down every one of his moans with my mouth as I kiss him. His big, strong body shakes in my arms, and it's such a new, surreal feeling that I want to make a core memory of it. If this is the only time I get to hold Griffin Nash while he comes undone, I don't want to forget it.

Finn comes down from his orgasm, and I release his mouth. His eyes are heavily lidded, lust clouding over those wild blue irises, and I like that I put this look on his face.

"Fuck. I don't know when the last time was that I finished in my pants."

"I'm sure it happens often. Didn't take you long either," I joke, my lips against the warmth of his neck.

"Fuck off, Hayes."

"You first, Nash," I reply with a small smile on my lips.

A beat of silence passes between us. And for a moment, we're just two confused people, suspended in this space that neither of us seems to want to leave. The outside world is pulling each of us in a different direction, but right here, between us, it's quiet.

"I don't know your plans, but whatever you do, leave me and my family alone, Finn. *Please.*"

He pulls back slightly so that we're eye to eye, one of his hands reaching up to cup my jaw. He looks pained, like he's holding onto something and trying to keep it locked up tight.

"You don't know me yet, Carter, something I plan on rectifying, but I would never ruin someone's reputation. Ever. I also would never out someone's sexual orientation or habits. I don't expect you to trust me with anything more than your body right now, but believe me when I say that will change. I'll make sure of it."

My heart flips over in my chest, a feeling so foreign I don't understand it. This man came into my life like a goddamn wrecking ball, and I need to get some sort of control back. But how can I when he's looking at me with those crystal-blue eyes like I'm the most important thing in the entire world. I've never been looked at like Finn is looking at me right now.

"Finn, I . . ." My mouth opens and closes several times before I close it for good.

Not wanting to finish my sentence, unsure what the hell would come out or whether or not I believe his words. *I want to believe him.* I step back, letting my eyes fall to the floor as I walk away, opening the door and leaving Finn standing alone. I don't stop until I've reached my car, the outside world instantly filling my head with noise, my body going numb.

My head has never been so clouded before. My entire life, I've lived in the moment, never taking anything too seriously—except my job at the distillery—and even if my actions tended to be a little seedy, I've never had a single regret, never felt bad about anything that I've done.

One thing's for sure; I damn well haven't ever had a hookup that fucked me up so bad after. It's like Griffin—*Finn*—crawled under my skin and rooted himself deep within the marrow of my bones. It's a mindfuck. The most shocking part of it all is that I'm not even that freaked out by the fact that he's a man. They've never crossed my mind before, and I've seen my fair share of naked male dicks and asses at the club, and they've never caught my attention, but then again, I wasn't really looking. It's something I need to dissect later because I'm officially confused as fuck.

The bigger issue that's taking up most of my focus is that being around Finn leaves me breathless and how I lost my head last night because of it. His touch ignites something in me that I'm convinced I was incapable of feeling. It's like being sucked into his orbit, making him the center of my attention while he lights me up from the inside out.

I don't know what these feelings are, but they need to stop. I'm still confused about whatever the hell it is I'm even feeling. Yet, he's the one person I can't have. The first person in my life to awaken some broken piece of me is the person who is hiding a world of shit. I can see it in his eyes. I should be thankful—Finn is systematically and ruthlessly tearing apart everything I thought I knew about myself. I need to put an end to it, and if Finn doesn't stay away, I'll have to. I just need to get him to write the article first.

What the hell could he even be hiding? I'm still not sure I believe him that he would never try to out someone, but that may just be my anxiety talking. I don't want to let my family down, I want to get them the feature that could change the trajectory of our distillery and our town, but at what cost? I thought I could whore myself out to him, but it's clear all self-control goes out the goddamn window when I'm with him. I can't explain it. Like I'm walking around asleep, and one look or touch from Finn awakens me. Everything looks, tastes, and feels different.

Fuck.

Why does everything have to be so complicated? Why can't I just have one thing in my life that is easy for me? That I can walk into and feel at ease, feel wholly myself, and not over-question fucking everything.

You feel at ease when you're with Finn.

He needs to be purely off-limits. I don't do emotional connection. I can't give up control. I can't. The thought alone scares the living shit out of me.

The pressure builds inside me, the panic getting louder and louder. My body feels warm while my blood turns cold. I need to move or I'll blow. Quickly lacing up my running shoes, I strip out of my T-shirt and haul out of my house. I live right on the edge of downtown Aspen Ridge in a modest house that my siblings have deemed my bachelor pad. Too bad I don't ever actually bring any dates home with me. Gives them the opportunity to be clingy. I don't do clingy.

Women easily confuse sex with emotions, and I'm positive I lack the latter. So, it's always been easier to fuck in a bar bathroom, the back of a car, an alley, or my favorite and first choice, Temptations.

Then why have you pictured Finn in your bed every night since you met him?

Confusion and anger nearly choke me as I pull my front door closed and hit the pavement, setting a brutal pace right off the bat.

My legs are quick to warm up, but I know I'll be paying for not easing into it later.

Clarity doesn't come after the first mile. I can still feel Finn's lips on my neck, the light stubble that scratched at my skin as he nuzzled into me, breathing in my scent, dragging his tongue up and down the throbbing vein there. Why is that so hot?

Finn is turning my world upside down and I don't fucking like it. Especially when it's not just me he holds power over. My sex life may be a running joke in Aspen Ridge, but no one but Dallas knows about my membership to Temptations. And he certainly isn't keeping tabs on me if we both happen to be there at the same time. I meant what I said that I own my choices, but that doesn't mean I want anyone to find out that I'm a member there. Our family? The businesses we supply to? Our customers? Our brand? Would any of them care if I were openly hooking up with a man? Fear latches onto me, propelling my legs harder and faster.

I need to be loyal. No, I *have* to be loyal. My family, this distillery, it's everything to me, and I have to protect it at all costs. Even if the pull to Finn is magnetic. Something tells me that fighting the tether that's wound tight between us is going to be one of the hardest things I've ever done. Choosing between my family and the man I'm suddenly addicted to is going to split me in two, one half loyalty and love, the other desire and destruction.

I just need to survive this nightmare. Get Finn to write the article, and then I'm out. No more physical contact. Purely professional. I can do this.

I look down at my watch. Mile three. The early morning sun beats down on my body from a near-cloudless sky that is rare for our area, warming me from the outside in. I relish the feel of it on my skin. I pump my legs harder, hoping the pain will push away the clawing desire to see Finn again. What the fuck is wrong with me?

I turn around, knowing the three miles back are going to be a grueling bitch. Maybe by then I'll have forced thoughts of that motherfucker from my head.

Once the front of my house is in sight, I sprint the rest of the way, pumping my arms and legs as hard as I can. Stupid fucking mistake after a six-mile run in the rare heat that my body isn't used to. But maybe I'll actually sleep later because of it. Without images of the sexy male who my dick seems to crave floating behind my eyelids.

I heave forward, holding myself up with my hands on my knees while I suck in gulps of air and dry heave. Sweat coats my body, my skin salty and raw. The run helped, but it's not enough. My mind is still swirling with a storm of shit I need to figure out. "Fuck!"

I need to hit something. Maybe one of my brothers will be down for a workout before we need to be at the distillery. I check my watch, and it's not even seven a.m.

> Me: Someone meet me at Dom's

I send off the text to my sibling group chat, my skin tight, my head pounding. I pace in my kitchen, chugging back a glass of water while I wait for one of them to respond. Goddamn, everyone is so busy now that they have lives and families of their own. I'm having a complete fucking meltdown and identity crisis, and no one is going to be up for meeting me for a reprieve.

> Me: For real? What the fuck? None of you are gonna answer me?

> Dallas: You didn't use the code phrase so I figured it wasn't important and I'm a little preoccupied

> Kinsey: Eww.

> Dallas: We're finished now.

> Sawyer: Poor Blaire

Liam: Ha. You walked into that one dumbass

Dallas: Shut the fuck up spunk rag

Me: For fuck's sake is anyone gonna meet me at Dom's or do I have to call Reid?

Liam: You don't want to do that

Dallas: I had a shiner for weeks. I still can't blink correctly

Dallas: Blaire says I'm crazy but I think that eye blinks slower than the other

Sawyer: You're an idiot

Kinsey: I can come hang out with you there if you want? I can't take a hit like they can but I can do my best for you.

Dallas: Do not hurt our little sister!

Sawyer: Use the code phrase if it's a need Casanova, otherwise, I gotta skip today. I was up with Ivy and Grace all night

Liam: Let us know when you're ready for a break, brother. Hannah and I are happy to help

Sawyer: We're good right now but I appreciate it. Not ready to leave them

Fuck. Is this code phrase worthy? We set it up as protection to bail each other out of shit if it was a situation we needed help with. But I can't even tell them my issues without it exploding completely. FUCK.

Me: I'm good. Don't worry about it. Just bored.

Kinsey: Want to meet for some coffee?

Do I want to do that? My sister is on summer break, and I really should be soaking up some time with her, but I just want to work this tension out of my system to clear my head. Guilt eats at me as I war with what to do. Shit.

Me: Yeah. Meet you at Bean Haven in twenty?

Kinsey: See you in a bit!

After taking a quick shower and doing my business, I pull on a pair of fitted khaki shorts, a navy blue short-sleeve button-up shirt, and my white Converse. Bean Haven is an Aspen Ridge staple. My brother Liam's wife, Hannah, owns the place and makes the best baked goods in the state. She closed for two days a few weeks ago because of some personal things she had going on, and the town nearly lost their shit. She keeps us all fueled with her coffee and pastries.

As I approach the storefront, I nearly groan out loud. Hannah's grandmother, Mrs. Nettie, sits outside at her little table that is placed there just for her during the summer months, with her little dog in her lap. You never know what you're going to get with Mrs. Nettie. You're either on her good side or this creepy ass other side she lets out sometimes.

"Hi, Mrs. Nettie. How are you and Winnie today?" I greet her, giving her what I'm hoping is a charming smile.

"Don't you hit on me, Carter Hayes, or I'll call your momma!"

My eyes bug out of my head. So, wild and crazy it is.

I gasp, pulling my hands over my heart to mock horror. "Mrs.

Nettie! You hurt my feelings! Now, why would you want to break my heart first thing on a Monday?"

"Oh, don't give me that garbage! You Hayes boys are all trouble. Except for Liam. Liam's the good one."

"Your secret is safe with me, Mrs. Nettie. I know you have to say that because he's married to your granddaughter," I say with a wink.

"Psh! The day you settle down, Carter Hayes, is the day I will let you give me that smooch you've been trying to get!" I laugh at her, reaching over to scratch Winnie's ears before pulling the door to the shop open.

Walking into Bean Haven, my sister, Kinsey, is already chatting with Hannah at the counter. Her light brown hair is worn up in a messy bun, her face bare of any makeup. She's such a perfect mix of both of our parents. Our mom's soft facial features and petite stature, our dad's hair color and blue eyes. She's wearing a pair of cutoff shorts that I think are way too short and a loose-fitting Aspen Ridge Distillery T-shirt.

"Hey, little sis. Hey, Han."

"There he is! Why do you look like someone kicked you while you were down?"

"Nah. I just got a lot of work stuff on my mind. What about you?"

"Well . . ."

"Oh, shit. So this wasn't a 'I just want to spend time with my brother' coffee date? You've got some shit you're gonna try to pull me into."

"Okay, I really need help. I can't live with Mom and Dad anymore, Carter. I love them so much. They're so amazing for letting me move back in after college. But I need out."

"Ugh. I get it. But, what do you need me for?"

The bell to Bean Haven chimes, and Kinsey and I both turn our heads to see our brother's best friend, Reid Knight, bend his head to walk through the door. Reid's been Sawyer's other half since Sawyer was in college at the University of Washington. He brought him back to Aspen Ridge with him one summer, and he never left. He owns a tattoo shop a few blocks down from Bean Haven. The man is covered from neck to . . . I've actually never seen the man in shorts, so I don't know how far down the damn things go, but on every inch of exposed skin, he's got ink. Ivy has nicknamed him Drogo because of his long hair and massive size, and I don't disagree with her.

Reid walks over to our table as he makes eye contact with us before placing his order with Hannah.

"Hey, man, how are ya?" I ask.

"Life's decent. How are you?"

Oh, I'm just dreaming about fucking the shit out of the man who's taken over all my headspace, but you know, life's a peach.

"Everything's good over here," I reply, my voice falling flatter than I mean for it to.

"Kinsey?" he asks her. My sister smiles coyly at him, and I have to squint my eyes at her. She had better not be flirting, I will shut that shit down so fast. She is not allowed to flirt. No boys. Even if there isn't anything about Reid that is boyish. He's definitely a man, just maybe like a superhuman one.

"Everything's okay. Happy that summer is here. You want to join us?"

"Yeah, that'd be great, shop doesn't open till four, so I've got plenty of time to kill."

Hannah places a mug of steaming coffee on the counter and a small ivory plate with an old-fashioned donut next to it. He must come in here a lot for her to know his order without him asking. I watch their exchange and am reminded how thankful my family is to Reid. One way or another, he's managed to help out all the women in our lives who mean something to us. He has a dark past that only Sawyer knows about, but none of us press. It's his story, but we're all grateful to know him and have him in our corner. Reid returns, pulling up a chair to sit in front of the booth. His large-ass body wouldn't fit next to me in the booth, and he knows how protective we all are of Kinsey. I appreciate him giving her space.

"So you two just catching up? I'm not intruding on any sibling bonding time?"

"Nah. Just hanging."

"Actually, I was just about to beg Carter to let me move in with him," Kinsey blurts, my eyes shooting up to her. I did not know that's where that conversation was headed. My mind flashes images of Finn in my bed, and that would never happen if Kinsey was there. Not that I have any intention of ever bringing Finn home with me.

"Whoa, Kins, that is not happening."

"Whaaat? Why? I'm a good roommate! I'm quiet, you won't even know I'm there. I can't live with Mom and Dad anymore!"

"Why don't you take the loft above Rogue? Blaire's moved out since moving in with Dallas," Reid interjects, taking a sip of his coffee. Kinsey's head snaps in his direction.

"Wait. Are you serious?"

"Yeah, why not? It's furnished. It's a studio. Don't think it's glamorous or anything. But Blaire enjoyed living there."

"I could pay you."

My eyes shoot back and forth between the two of them as they start to plan this out, and I don't like it at all.

"Whoa, okay, back up. No one is moving anywhere. Kinsey, Mom and Dad's is not that bad."

"It is. I need my own space. I'm twenty-two, Carter, I have a career, and I need to be on my own."

"What about above Bean Haven, then? We can talk to Hannah."

"And be woken up at the ass crack of dawn when she's there before the sun comes up to start baking? No, thank you. Love her. Love Bean Haven. That's a hard pass."

"Beggars can't be choosers, Kins."

"And I'm not begging. Reid offered, and it's a better option than the one you just gave me, without even talking to Hannah first, by the way."

"I'll ask her right now," I snap as I raise my hand to yell for Hannah. Kinsey quickly leans over the table, wrenching my arm back down.

"Don't you dare! I don't want to live above Bean Haven, Car, you know that would be rough."

The situation rapidly gets out of control as Reid and Kinsey start discussing options. Pulling out my phone, I open up the group chat.

> Me: We got an issue

> Me: @ Bean Haven with Kins and Reid and Reid offered to let her rent the studio

> Dallas: Fuck no. She's staying with Mom and Dad

> Sawyer: The fuck? No. Absolutely not. She's too young to live on her own.

> Liam: Tell her no right now.

> Dallas: Shut that shit down

Kinsey's phone chimes from her lap, and I smile brightly at her as she reads the messages.

"Really, Casanova? You're a dick."

"Look," Reid says, putting his palms up in peace, "I don't need you four Neanderthals comin' at me for bein' helpful. Kinsey, the place is yours if you want it and these dumbass brothers of yours let you breathe."

"She's our baby sister, man, you gotta understand."

"I do, more than you know, trust me," he says, a bit solemn and reflective. "But, I'm downstairs seven days a week and into the evening when I've got late clients. She'd be safe. And she's responsible. Just come get the keys if it works out. If not, don't worry about it." With that, Reid pops the last bite of his donut into his mouth and stands to leave.

"Why do you four have to be such overbearing dickholes?"

I shrug at her. Because I honestly don't know. She was a surprise, and we all just love her so much. Especially as we got older, and more so the last year since Ivy has returned. The real world out there is scary as fuck and we want to keep Kinsey safe from it all. Suffocating her probably isn't the best way to go about it, but that's just who we are. I try to think about it from Kinsey's perspective for a moment, and it really isn't fair to her. She's an angel and the best of all of us. She really doesn't deserve to be kept locked up and miss out on experiences because of our fear and need for control to keep her safe. We shouldn't overcomplicate her life, or she'll just end up resenting us all in the long run.

With a deep huff, I relent. "Alright. I'm for it. I've got your back. You deserve to live a little, and it's not like you want to backpack through Europe by yourself. Which is a hard no, by the way."

"You know I don't need your permission, right?" she snaps.

"Alright, spitfire, I know you're right. I'm just sayin' that you're gonna have a hard sell with our brothers and that I've got your back. They're gonna give you shit about it. But, I've got you."

"Eek! Thank you!" she squeals.

It feels good to support her doing something that makes her happy. Just wish I could figure out my own shit to make things in my life happy as well.

After getting home from Bean Haven and hanging out with Kinsey, I'm exhausted, and my mind has settled from unfiltered rage to calm curiosity. Maybe things really are just as simple as they seem, and I'm overcomplicating all of it. Maybe it isn't Finn who lit me up, maybe it's both men and women? That would make life so much easier if it turns out that Finn was just my first sexual experience with a man, and that's why I'm clinging to him.

That it has nothing to do with Finn per se and everything to do with the fact that he opened my eyes to being more open about who I'm attracted to.

Feeling like I need to explore this a little more, I grab my laptop and bring up my favorite porn website, quickly scrolling to the male-on-male section and flicking through the page until I find something that looks semi-interesting.

Pushing my gym shorts down, I slowly stroke my dick until it gets hard, cupping my balls with my other hand. I languidly stroke, watching one of the men drop to his knees and start sucking the cock of the other one. I mean, it's sex. It's nothing I haven't seen at the club, and my dick stays pretty neutral. Hmm. I click the back button and scroll through again, settling on a video titled Muscled Guy on Guy. The two men are big dudes, muscular, athletic builds, and strong hands. I skip over the story of it all and move the cursor to the main event. One of the men has the other one doggy-style in front of him, curled over his back and jerking his cock for him while he fucks his ass.

Electricity spreads lightly through my body as I start to really stroke my dick, timing it with the thrusts of the man in the video. It's much better, but still, not mind-blowing. I watch the facial expression of the man taking it, eyes blown, mouth agape, he's totally blissed the hell out. My mind takes over, putting Finn there instead, bent over and at my mercy while I fuck his tight asshole and stroke his cock. My body suddenly ignites, cock starting to leak precum from my tip.

Oh. Fuck.

I close my eyes and let go, imagining Finn's sounds while I drive into him over and over, making him beg for more. Fuck yes. His firm ass in my palms while I spread him apart, the wiry hair of his legs rubbing against mine. I raise my hand and connect with his ass cheek—hard—a loud moan echoing from Finn's mouth. Fuck, he's not breakable, I definitely like that.

I fuck into him, my thick cock stretching his asshole around it as our balls slap together. *Yeah, I fucking like that a lot.* My breath is coming in hard pants now, my abs clenching, my legs straining as I brutally stroke my dick.

"More, lover. Harder."

"Fuck, you want it rough?"

I jerk it hard, squeezing the head of my cock on every pass as I fuck my hand, lost to the image of filling Finn's ass, his strong body giving into me, his moans unabashed, flowing freely, chanting, clawing at the blankets under us.

My balls seize up suddenly, my orgasm taking over with force. "Finn!" I come hard, making a mess of my abdomen and chest. The video has long since turned off, so I just lay there to gather my bearings. What the fuck was that? Now I'm even more confused.

Alright, so maybe it is person-specific? Kind of? It went from definitely interested to mind-blowing real quick. Just my goddamn luck. What the fuck does that even mean? Am I bi? Something else? My cock likes women and *Finn*? I definitely liked the males on the screen, but it was Finn who pushed me over the edge. Can't anything be fucking simple for me?

"Fucking shit."

finn

AFTER SCANNING MY BLACK MEMBERSHIP CARD AT THE front, security opens the door for me that leads to the floor. The club is busier than I expected it to be for a weeknight. But this place always seems to be hopping. The floor is lively, music thumping through the speakers, bodies in a wide variety of undress, lingerie, and costumes, but I've got eyes for one person and one person only. I tried to fight the pull to come here tonight, but I couldn't.

Carter is already at the bar when I arrive, and my heart takes off like a rocket behind my ribs. Hunched over a glass of whiskey like last time, he looks dejected and lost. Does he not have anything else to do but visit a sex club? Or is he here for the same reason I am? Because he can't stay away from me. I try not to let my mind wander with the thought, even if it makes my heart thump wildly in my chest at the prospect.

Not wanting to waste any time, I take a seat on an empty stool next to him, our shoulders brushing against one another as I do. His spine stiffens, and I wonder if there will ever be a time that he relaxes when I approach him.

"Here to make my life more difficult, Griffin?"

Now, I'm the one to stiffen. Fuck, I hate that name, especially out of his mouth. As if he read my expression, he calls me out on it.

"Damn you really hate your own name, don't you?"

Instead of answering him, I nod my head to the bartender, pointing at Carter's whiskey. He quickly pours a whiskey on the rocks and sets it on a napkin in front of me.

"Thanks."

I take a sip, not enjoying the flavor as much as I enjoy Aspen Ridge's.

"Ever thought about getting them to stock yours?"

"You mean my family's whiskey?"

"Yeah, it's better than this shit they're pouring."

He scoffs and brings his drink to his lips. I track the movement. Watching as the cold liquid pours into his mouth, the slight bob of his throat as he swallows it down. Everything about the movement is an aphrodisiac for me, and I want to grab his face and suck his tongue into my mouth to taste the whiskey off of it. I'm positive it would taste better if I drank it mixed with him.

"Surprised you don't have some negative shit to say about it."

"None. It's my favorite."

"Fuck off with that shit."

"Believe what you want, but I'm serious."

We sit in silence, finishing our drinks while the music floats around us, the smell of sex strong in the air.

"Why are you here, Finn?"

God, I love the sound of that. So much better.

"You want the truth or a lie?"

He turns to face me, his knee rubbing across my thigh with the shift.

"Truth."

"I can't stay away." The silence stretches between us while his eyes bore into mine, reading my expression and looking for the lie he isn't going to find. Whether he wants to believe me or not. "And you can't either."

He releases an exhale, as if he's almost relieved. But maybe that's just me projecting what I'm hoping he's feeling.

"That so?" he questions just as we're interrupted by a visitor.

A female appears between us, her hands moving to each of our shoulders, making her interest in both of us known. I don't bother acknowledging her, my eyes focused only on Carter. The way his hair is styled out of his face, a piece falling forward into his eyes, my fingers itch to push it out of the way. His eyes are soaking up our suitor, and my heart squeezes painfully. He's clearly interested in her. How could he not be? She's gorgeous. Fuck. Even if Carter got on board with whatever is between us, would I be enough to sustain him? He's only been with women until me, I don't know if I have it in me to compete with that constantly. But, God, I want this man so much it hurts.

I remember what it was like to share him, but that was before I had him. I quickly weigh if I could do this, if I could really share him again. Part of me feels that if this is the only way I can have him, then I should take it, but when Carter turns around fully, his hand moving to her hip, bile rises up in my throat, and I know my answer.

There's no way I can share him.

The pretty female steps into his space, Carter sliding his thigh between her legs and pulling her close. Her hand leaves my shoulder to wrap around his neck, and Carter responds naturally, pulling her closer to him, and my fists clench, nails digging into my skin. Fuck, she's practically dry humping him. He keeps his eyes trained on me, like he's daring me to intervene, to stop this before it gets too far. Is he fucking serious right now?

"You're mine." The words are out of my mouth before I can stop them, my voice dark and menacing.

"The fuck I am."

As if to prove a point, his hands slide up the back of her thighs, under the short, sequined dress, letting it lift as he grabs her ass in his palms. His eyes meet mine as he kisses her neck, hands kneading into her bare ass, pulling her closer to him. My heart rate picks up—painfully so—as if it's being squeezed in a vise. I feel the moment my facial expression morphs from fury to unwarranted pain. I don't have any claim over Carter, he's not mine. We aren't anything more than two lost people who have an intense chemistry between us.

But it feels like so much goddamn more, and I want to explore that. Even if I'm jeopardizing every good thing I have in my life to do so.

I'm two seconds away from leaving when Carter's head cocks to the side, as if reading my discomfort, before pulling away from the woman. He gently pulls her dress back over her ass, giving it a little playful slap.

"You're very tempting, beautiful, but not tonight. I've got some business to take care of. Rain check?" He says the last two words while looking at me to further make his point, and I release a deep exhale of relief. Point taken. He can be with whoever he wants to, on his terms. He's in control. That's fine. As long as I don't have to watch him with anyone else. I'd leave before it got too far.

Fuck. Why do I feel so possessive over him? Doesn't he feel this between us? It's so strong for me. My pull to him is chemical, at a cellular level, deeper than anything I've ever felt before. I can't stop.

She leans down, pressing a chaste kiss to his cheek, and I can't help but wonder if they've hooked up before. My eyes close at the thought, and I suddenly feel like a fish out of water. I came in here so cocky, eyes only for Carter and so sure he was trapped in this bubble with me—no matter how toxic it may be—and I'm suddenly reminded that Carter is an active member of a sex club where he's most likely been with people who are currently here. It's a thought that didn't cross my mind until now. I've been so focused on just the two of us that I seem to have forgotten Carter had an entire life before I waltzed in and blew the lid off of it.

We're alone again, sitting in silence. I study the side profile of his strong face, and struggle with the urge to pull him into a hug. I hate admitting how badly I just want to hug him. I don't need anything more, but to hold Carter close would be a gift. For some reason, he has the power to silence all the demons in my head, and I love how whole I feel when I'm next to him.

The silence isn't uncomfortable, both of us lost in our own thoughts as time passes.

"You going to write the article, Nash?"

"Haven't decided yet, Hayes."

He nods a few times, letting my words sink in before he gives the bartender a wave and stands to leave. Fuck, that's it? I suddenly don't want to go back to my house alone, I want to stay and talk with him; I want to learn everything there is about him. I want more. I want everything. Doesn't he feel this?

It takes extreme effort to keep from smiling as the bell chimes over my head. I walk into the coffee shop and am met with a welcome, cool breeze. The interior is cozy while also being vibrant, a classy bohemian aesthetic that works for the space. A single table sits inside a semi-circle window, an elderly woman with a little white dog in her lap eyeing me suspiciously. Odd.

I take steps further into the inviting space, past the few small booths that line the wall opposite a large pastry display case. *Bean Haven* is painted in a loopy scroll on the wall above the counter, and live plants are placed throughout the room. It's hard for me not to notice every little detail. This is definitely a place worthy of writing about. But do the food and coffee meet my standards?

"Hey! New to town?" A beautiful young woman waltzes from the back room, her lavender-colored hair bouncing around her face. She's wearing a tank top and jeans, a sleeve of intricately and expertly done floral line work covering an entire arm in a delicate tattoo.

"Hey, just passing through, actually."

"Well, welcome to Bean Haven. I'm Hannah."

"Nice to meet you, Hannah. What do you recommend?"

"Well, my best sellers are apple cinnamon muffins, cinnamon rolls, and chocolate croissants. But my favorite is the plum and cream cheese Danish."

"How about one of each and an Americano?" I say, giving her a flirty wink.

She holds up her left hand and wiggles her fingers.

"Careful, I'm a married woman with a growly husband."

I laugh and put my hands up, palms facing her, feigning innocence. I was genuinely just trying to be friendly. She gives me a smile and works on my order while I continue to look around the space. I'd love to interview her, learn the story, and meet more people. The town is somehow cuter than anticipated, and I had already thought it was something special. It's a true hidden gem, both from its position hidden by the Olympic Mountains and the Pacific Ocean, and the quaint charm that the town exudes. I've never seen such an idyllic, charming town. It's as if it were hand-picked right from a storybook.

Patrons sit in various spots within the space, and I can feel the inconspicuous looks as they regard the newcomer. I've seen it all before; residents of small towns tend to be wary of outsiders, cautious, and protective. It's one of the reasons I gravitate toward them. What brings these strangers together to share in the common, collective goal of protecting the thing they all love?

"Here you go!"

"Thank you. Can't wait to try it all," I tell her honestly. After taking one last look around the coffee shop, clocking all of the little details that make it unique, I head to the door. The little old lady sitting off in the window squints her eyes at me as she watches me go. Like she wants to make sure that I've actually left before she dares to look away.

The warm, balmy air hits my body in a gust of heat as I step out onto the cobblestone sidewalk. A hand roughly grasps my bicep, jerking me into the small alley on the other side of the brick building, shoving me against the wall. I do everything I can not to slosh my hot drink on either of us as I figure out what the hell is going on and if I'm about to be mugged in a tiny-ass town.

"What the fuck are you doing here?" Carter hisses, his face pinched, clearly pissed the fuck off. Our bodies are near flush, his minty breath warm on my face. Any worry I had evaporates, replaced with a rush of endorphins, my heart settling, and a smile tugging at my lips.

"I was getting a coffee and breakfast," I reply innocently, holding up the white bag of pastries and the to-go cup in my other hand.

"In Aspen Ridge, asshole. Just openly stalking me now?"

I scoff, even if it's true. "Pretty full of yourself, Hayes. You know I'm a travel writer, right? I'm assuming you read more about me than just my name."

"So, what? Now you're going to blast my whole fuckin' town? Stay the fuck away from my family. Stay the fuck away from Bean Haven. Hannah has been through enough."

"Hannah, huh?"

"Yep. My sister-in-law. And we're protective of what's ours, Nash, so not so kindly, fuck off."

I don't know why, but his words strike a chord. I'm genuinely awed by Aspen Ridge and was interested in learning more about the place and its residents, even if I've been forbidden from ever stepping foot here. I wouldn't ruin an innocent woman's life and for him to accuse me of such pisses me off.

"Fuck you! You don't know shit about me," I snap, anger coursing through me now.

"Don't I?"

"Trust me, whatever preconceived notion you have, I guarantee you're way off base."

A deep chuckle escapes him and it only pisses me off more.

"Whatever. Are we done here?"

"No. We need to talk. And not fucking here. Up the road to the end of the street, take a right at the clock tower. Last house on the left."

"Inviting me back to your place so soon, Hayes?"

"Fuck you. Don't make a goddamn scene, and for fuck's sake, don't talk to anyone."

"Meet you at home, honey!" I say just to piss him off as I step out of the alley and take my time wandering through the quiet downtown. I wasn't expecting to run into Carter here, even if I was hoping to. Even if my dad has threatened my life to stay away from Aspen Ridge, the Haye's family and their distillery, I thought it was long past time that I take a trip to visit the tiny town hidden in the woods. I couldn't stay away, and no one knows I'm here but me.

Excitement courses through me at being alone with Carter again, at seeing the inside of the place he calls home. I take my time walking up the street, looking at every storefront I pass—a bar called The Night Owl, a bookstore called Book Bound, which I actually stop in front of to look through the window. The inside is whimsical, a large sign in the window display case with a Cheshire Cat perched on the top, arrows pointing left and right with different fictional lands written in loopy scroll—Narnia, Middle Earth, Neverland, and Westeros. I definitely want to go in here on my way back.

I continue up the road until I reach the large clock tower that sits at the very end of Main Street, signaling the end of their downtown area. I take my turn and walk to the end of the short, dead-end road. Rows of gorgeous Sitka spruce trees stand tall behind the few houses on the street. Lampposts wrapped in Christmas lights line the brick sidewalk. It's even more charming than I imagined it would be. I easily find a modest home at the end of the street. Sipping on my caffeine fix, I stand outside of it and look up. The house is ten times smaller than anything I've ever lived in, and I find myself extremely jealous that this is all his. I've always wanted to live in a place like this. Modest, comfortable, and cozy.

It's painted a faded-out blue, with white trim that's chipped and whitewashed. The grass is vibrant, and there's a small porch out front with no furniture. I wouldn't have guessed that Carter lived alone, but that makes me wonder. But, then again, he wouldn't have told me to meet him here if he had roommates.

Lost in my thoughts, I don't register Carter's footsteps approaching until he practically shoulder-checks me.

"Well, thank fuck my coffee is almost gone or you would have just spilled it all over me for the second time today."

"Get your ass inside the house, Nash."

"Yes, sir." And fuck if I don't love the way his face flames once the words hit his ears.

He opens the door, and I notice that it was left unlocked—interesting. The town must have zero crime, or Carter is just way too trusting. That or no one fucks with the Hayes family.

I follow him inside, Carter's warm, woodsy, sweet scent filling my nose. I take a deep breath, inhaling it and wishing I could bottle it up. Any tension I was carrying with me drains, even if the situation between us isn't ideal, something about being here and in his space is wholly comforting.

My eyes dart around for any clues to give me more insight into him. There are blown-up old-school comic book posters framed along the wall of the entryway that flow into the living area, and I'm instantly intrigued, my heart stopping as I study them. This is my thing. My favorite comics, and they're hanging in his house. I do my best to control my excitement at this find.

There's a small table in the modest entryway with a bowl cradling a set of keys and his wallet. Hardwood floors that are scuffed and knotted from old age extend as far as I can see, but I don't get much more time to take in his space as much as I want to.

Carter immediately spins on me, my back hitting the closed door behind me as he stays a foot away, his eyebrows pinched together, his cheeks still red. I meet his eyes through the lenses of my glasses, and I notice his darting all over my face, trying to get a read on me.

"Now, why the fuck are you in my town?"

I shrug nonchalantly. "It's not private property, I'm free to visit wherever I want."

I don't know why I continue to piss him off. I'm a glutton for punishment, apparently. I need him to hate me so that I can stay away, but I can't fucking stay away to begin with. I've created a cycle that I can't break free from. I want what I can't have, and I should walk away, but I can't let go.

"I'm not playing these fuckin' games with you. If you need me to beg, I'll fucking beg. But I need you to stay away from this town and the people in it. I don't trust you. If you aren't going to write a glowing article about us, just leave. Please."

His desperation about breaks me. I want to tell him the truth. I want to tell him that I tasted an Aspen Ridge Distillery whiskey and went looking for more information on it while searching for my next location, that I fell in love with the town before I ever stepped foot in it. I want to explain how my father is a controlling piece of shit, how he's forbidden me from writing a feature on Aspen Ridge or the distillery, how the only good thing in my life is my career and that he would ruin me if he knew I was here right now. That I know how fucked-up this is, but that I can't walk away now.

I'm dying to share how much I love my job. That I just want to tell stories and get a positive spotlight on businesses and places that could benefit from it. I want to learn about his family history, the town, the distillery. I want to tell him that my dad is a cruel sonofabitch and is twisting my arm because I don't know what else I'll do if I don't work for his magazine. I'd have nothing.

That from the moment I saw his photo, I've been madly obsessed with him. I want to tell him that from the moment I met him, I've been consumed by him, in every waking thought, in my dreams, that I'm lovesick and I've never felt anything like it before. I never believed in love at first sight, but fuck, what else could this be? Doesn't he feel it?

But I can't tell him any of this. He'd try to have me committed to a mental institution; hell, if the tables were turned,

I'd probably do the same. I just need time. I need to figure this out, and I need Carter to get to know me. So, I'll play the part of the asshole until I can figure out what to do and how to get everything we both want. Stepping into his space, walking him backward a few paces, I know what I have to do. Because I can't give him up, and I can't take a chance on my father finding out until I can make a plan to get Carter's family the feature they deserve, and he gives me an opportunity to explore whatever is between us.

"Here's what's going to happen," I say, speaking up. "I'm going to my family's beach house this weekend, and you're going to come with me."

He scoffs, his head jerking backward. "You're out of your fucking mind. I'm good."

"Yeah, see, lover, you don't have a choice. You're going to be a good boy and come with me to the house for a long weekend—I want three full days—and I'll write the article."

I'm going to fucking hell. The words burn on my tongue as I say them, my stomach churning acid as he pales. I hate myself in this moment. And I deserve to have Carter hate me, too. But I know how bad he wants this article, it's the Northwest Explorer for fuck's sake, we've had plenty of bribes over the years to get us to feature them. I feel like shit for blackmailing him. But I know he won't go willingly.

"You motherfucker," he seethes. "We don't need you. There are plenty of writers there. *You* need to get the fuck out of my life."

"But then who will be there to suck your cock, Carter?"

"Trust me, there have been dozens that came before you, and far, far better." I don't even flinch. Instead, I use my forearm to push him against the wall, holding them there, my free hand shooting out to grab his cock roughly, making him grunt. He's hard as steel, just as I'd hoped he'd be.

"Liar."

He bats my hand away, eyes squinting into slits as he glares at me.

"It's your choice, Hayes. Come spend the weekend with me, away from Aspen Ridge, and where everyone knows both of us, and I'll convince my dad to run the article."

Fuck.

Carter doesn't miss a beat, his eyes flashing up to mine at the bomb I just accidently dropped. The little nugget of information that gives him more detail into what's happening here. He doesn't question me or press for more information, and I watch helplessly as he files it away for later. I release my hold on him and take a step back, waiting for his answer.

"Get the fuck out of my house."

"I need your answer today."

"Get out!"

Leaving Carter's, I feel like a piece of shit. The exact person my father sees me as. I've accepted that I'll always disappoint him, but now I've thoroughly disappointed myself.

I wanted to pull him to me, stuff my head in his neck and breathe in his scent, hold him the rest of the day, learn about all of his likes and dislikes, tell him that the only reason I haven't interviewed them is because of my dad. Instead, I skip over the stores I wanted to check out, and respect Carter's wishes, getting in my SUV and driving out of town without talking to anyone else. If he doesn't agree to come with me to Emberleigh, I don't know what I'll do. There is no plan B.

carter

AFTER MY EARLY MORNING RUN-IN WITH FINN, I'M EVEN more lost. Seeing him walk inside Bean Haven like he belonged there was an out-of-body experience. My two worlds were suddenly crashing together, and I felt frantic panic claw its way up my chest. Once again, I found myself fighting with my desire to kiss him senseless or bury him in my backyard. Lucky for both of us, neither of the urges won out this time.

Deciding I wasn't in the right headspace to go into the office today, I got set up on my couch with my laptop, grateful that my job can be done remotely, and put on an Avengers movie to play for noise in the background. I get caught up on emails, reviewing contracts to send to Dallas and our CFO, Lorelei. I lose track of time and spend several hours working on a new marketing campaign and checking in with my project manager for our current accounts. The ease of the work is fairly mindless, not exceptionally challenging or fulfilling, but I'm proud of it. My family has worked hard to get where we are, and I enjoy being able to push the stakes higher to bring awareness to our brand and products.

Which then brings my head right back to Finn and the power he has to bring in more distributors, more businesses to supply to, and more events here at the distillery. Late last year, we started offering tours and tastings as well as events, and it has been a big hit. Our event coordinator, Blaire, is even thinking ahead to focus more on weddings and using the beautiful distillery grounds as their venue, and our spirits being served at the bar. It's been very successful, but it could always be better. The weight of that is on me.

My stomach rumbling reminds me that I'm human and should probably get some food in me. There's only one thing I want right now—a double bacon cheeseburger with garlic fries— but with Ivy on maternity leave from Barrel House and knowing they've cut down their menu, I settle on walking over to North Pass Market and Deli for a sandwich. I slip on my shoes, grab my wallet, and I'm out the door for the quick walk around the corner to the deli. The sun has retreated behind the clouds, and I miss the warmth of it on my skin. I love summer and haven't really enjoyed it yet, but it's something I need to make a priority. My brothers and I usually take a few trips to Grace Beach for surfing, even if wetsuits are still needed in the summer.

The walk is five minutes tops, and the only downside of living in Aspen Ridge is that there's no escaping anyone. Everywhere you go, you're going to see more than a few people that you know. This trip is no different. As I walk up to the deck portion of the deli to order at the window, Wes and Lily Draven are already standing off to the side, waiting for their food. I'm really not in the mood to chat with anyone, but luckily, Wes isn't much of a talker, unless it's to Lily.

"Hey, man. How are ya?"

"Couldn't be better," he replies as he tucks Lily under his arm possessively. "That info help you guys at all?"

Yeah, just wrecked my entire world, no big deal. Would have loved to live in ignorant bliss for longer than twelve hours, but that seems to be par for the course in my life.

"Like always. You really want to stay hidden out here in middle-of-nowhere Washington State?"

"Best way to live, in my opinion. Been a part of the rat race once, and I never want to do it again."

"I get that. Well, we're not gonna complain. You've more than helped out my family over the last year."

"It's not a problem. The work is simple."

I bark out a rough laugh. "For a dark web computer whiz like you, maybe. That guy was a ghost, as far as I'm concerned. They've got so many writers over there; I couldn't figure out who was who and which one was messin' with me."

And I definitely didn't know the identity of the man who jerked me off at the club.

After chatting for a few and ordering my food, Wes and Lily head out, and I'm left waiting for my order, so I scroll aimlessly on my phone, checking the distillery's social media accounts and pages.

Not wanting to run into anyone else today, I collect my sandwich and head home with my head tucked down. I'm usually uncomfortable with the silence of eating by myself, and that's why I tend to go out so much, wanting to fill the lonely space and time with strangers and the immediate, albeit quickly fading, gratification. But today, I just want silence.

The rest of the day goes by in a blur, my head focused on the ultimatum that Finn dropped at my feet. I know I don't have a choice, but for some reason, it feels monumental. Like, if I go with him, everything will change. By seven p.m., I'm pacing the length of my house, running my hands through my hair, trying to decide if I want to go for a run, head to Temptations where I'll just sit at the bar like a sad, lonely fucker, or punch something.

Deciding that I'll try the latter if my dumbfuck older brothers aren't too busy for me with their own new lives and families. Pulling out my phone, I don't have to scroll far to find the group chat that's always going off.

Me: Dom's? Really need somewhere to put my energy right now

Dallas: Yeah, I'm down. Who wants their face smashed first?

Sawyer: Meet you there.

Liam: Yep. Could get a workout in.

Thank fuck.

I get to Dom's gym, Knockout, before anyone else, which doesn't surprise me since I live the closest. Each of my brothers has purchased their own property on the outskirts of town, all wanting their privacy. Since I don't take any of my dates home, I prefer to live within walking distance of everything I need and don't mind the commute to the distillery every day.

My three brothers and I have been boxing at Knockout since I was a kid. Sawyer and Dallas have always been destructive and physical when it comes to handling shit, and after they gave each other a serious ass beating as teenagers, our dad threw all of us boys into boxing lessons. We each feel differently about it. Sawyer would have tried to be a professional fighter, even competing some and training with the owner, a former boxing champion and his son, Dom, who was headed to the Olympics before an injury kept him from it. But the distillery called to him louder, and the thought of leaving Aspen Ridge in case Ivy ever returned was unthinkable to him.

Dallas enjoys it, but you can tell it's just to handle his stress. He's a ruthless jackass, taunting you to the point of losing focus. He and Sawyer usually match up unless one of us needs something different.

I typically fight Liam. He has all of us in weight and height, but he's eerily calm and collected—until he's not. I pity the poor soul who gets on his bad side. Where Sawyer and Dallas wear that side of them front and center, projecting it for everyone to see, Liam keeps it on reserve. He can be a scary motherfucker when he wants to be. He's a kick-ass fighter but weightlifts to deal with his shit. I run and fuck. But hell, I love to get in the ring with these assholes.

Our little sister, Kinsey, is a spitfire. Chalk it up to having four older brothers, but she could probably take all of us in her sleep if she wanted to. While she never wanted to fight with all of us in the boxing ring, my dad forced her to take the self-defense classes that Dom offers here at Knockout. After she turned eighteen, she said she wasn't going to keep taking the refresher classes, and he threatened to pull her tuition at school. We all got a good laugh from it because Kinsey is also stubborn as shit, but ultimately, she takes the damn class once a year, and we hope she's learned enough to always protect herself if she ever needs it. I'm pretty confident in her, more so than our brothers, who don't know how to ease off of her and let her try things for herself.

I walk into Dom's, already in my shorts, a loose tank top hanging off my torso. Dom, his girlfriend, and her other two boyfriends are at reception with Emma in Aidan's lap. Their relationship still catches everyone off guard, except for me. I guess with how open I am about sex and what I see at Temptations a few times a week, it makes me kind of immune to different types of relationships. If they consensually share Emma, and she's happy, that's really all that matters. Which probably aids in why the whole reason hooking up with a man for the first time isn't making me lose my fucking mind.

"Sup? You all still sharing nicely?" The big motherfucker, Cruz, who's my older brother's age, straight up growls, standing up a little taller and taking a step in my direction. Dom puts his hand out on Cruz's chest, holding him back while I put my hands up to show I don't mean any harm, laughing under my breath at that rise I was able to pull from him.

"He doesn't mean anything by it, he's just making a joke, settle down," Dom says to talk the bulldog off the ledge.

"It was just a joke, and for the record, I was not inferring that you share her with anyone else. Emma, I meant nothing by it."

"I know that. Can't save your teeth, though, if Dom unleashes Cruz on you."

"Bit protective, yeah?"

"We are. If you ever settle down, you'll know what we mean," Aidan adds.

"Nah, not in the cards for me. Where's the fun in that?"

"Oh, we're having plenty of fun, my man," Dom says, giving me a wink.

"You four enjoy. I'm gonna go wait for my brothers back here," I announce as I head to the back. I get where they're coming from; that protective side runs deep in my brothers, and they all are fiercely overbearing when it comes to their women.

The smell of old leather and sweat assaults my nose as I head to one of the free rings. The dim lights of the floor illuminate the off-white mats, stained and looking like they're overdue to be replaced. For as long as I can remember, my brothers and I have been meeting here to go rounds in a ring, not because we want to hurt each other but because it feels better to fight than hold everything in. And right now, nothing else could be more true. I need this release. Running isn't enough. Sex has changed. Fighting has to work. I need it to.

My brothers trickle in, Sawyer leading the jolly band of asshats. He's focused, looking a little tired, no doubt from the newborn baby he's taking care of at home, but I won't let that fool me. Dallas is wearing a sly-ass grin, and I just know that he's going to be a huge pain in all of our asses. He's already making me want to punch the look right off his smug face. Liam is right behind them, standing just slightly taller and broader, his face unreadable as he drops his gym bag next to mine on the floor.

"Hey, fuckers. You ready to blow off some steam?" I greet them, stretching out my arms.

"Yep. And I see you looking at me, don't think for a second I'm slow because I'm going on two hours of sleep," Sawyer spits in my direction, pointing his finger at me like I'm a naughty child.

"Whoa, shithead, no one would underestimate you. Calm down, big boy," I taunt, poking the big, grumpy bear.

"You want first? Was ready to beat Dallas' face in, but yours is lookin' a little too pretty, Casanova."

"I'm down," I admit. He's who I came here to fight, anyway.

We take turns taping our hands and wrists, getting our gloves on, and making sure we're good to go to prevent any unnecessary injuries. Sawyer's a little taller than me, but we're close enough in size that it would be a decent match, if he weren't the obviously better fighter. He's calculated, a little slower and more deliberate, but I'm no weakling and can handle my own.

Plus, I'm not getting in here to win in a fight against a professionally trained fighter, I'm getting in here to blow off the incessant chatter in my brain telling me that I'm fucking up everything. That's what I'm telling myself anyway. Maybe I want the pain, maybe it'll make me feel better to take the hits. Maybe there's a part of me that thinks I deserve them.

Sawyer and I climb into the ring, stretching out our shoulders and legs before we meet in the middle and tap our gloved hands together. Being in the ring with Sawyer is like watching a perfectly choreographed dance that you're trying to learn in real time.

He's smooth, flawless, completely aware of his body and his opponent's at all times. His wife, Ivy, says it's magic, and I have to agree. Getting in here with him, you need to be in the right headspace or he'll throttle you. But he's also the first to pull his punches and take the hits if it means you working through some shit in your head. I'm hoping today I get the latter.

The moment we part, I take my first shot, trying to land one quick jab to his chin, but he's up on the balls of his feet, bouncing out of the way, his footwork that of someone who's done this a thousand times. I brace myself as we round each other, Sawyer taking his time, squinting his eyes at me as he sizes me up. I see the right hook coming, and the air whooshes past my face as I narrowly avoid the punch that would have my head spinning.

Music blasts from the speakers in each corner of the room, the bass thumping through the ground. I recognize the song from one I used to play when I was younger, its lyrics fitting for going rounds right now. I try to focus on the words, on my brother in front of me with his gloves in front of his face, bouncing around on the balls of his feet as he circles me. But my head is filled with the noise I can't shake. I know I should come clean to them about everything, but I'm not ready for whatever this is with Finn to end. That goddamn feeling I get when I'm with him. I can't fight it.

You're fooling around with someone who's fucking with our family's future. The one person hell bent on fucking you around, holding the article over your head, and you're too blind with lust to stop it. You're gonna fuck everything up and ruin everything we've built for sex. Always thinking with your dick, Casanova. Never can take anything too seriously.

Fuck this shit. Sawyer continues to circle me, a quick jab making contact with my ribs. The pain reverberates through my body upon impact, but I don't back down. We're in it now. I throw a few punches back, trying to get a better feel for him. He's much too cocky for someone who just admitted to only getting two hours of sleep last night. Sawyer weaves and ducks, making it damn near impossible to rattle his skull like I want, even though I know Ivy will hunt me down after. I don't know who I'm more afraid of. But right now, it doesn't matter.

Sawyer takes a step in and I see my opening. Shifting my weight, I go for it, throwing a hard punch straight on, the solid contact of my glove against his cheek making me grin. He stumbles back, blinking in surprise, his lips turning up in a smile as he rubs his jaw like he's trying to decide whether or not I just pissed him off or he's impressed. I got the upper hand on him for a change and damn if it doesn't feel good. Our brothers hoot and holler from the ropes, but I keep my focus.

"Alright, you're awake now, baby brother. Good punch. So, what's got you worked up, huh, Casanova?" he asks. But before I can respond, he's moving hard, forcing me into a defensive stance, my gloves up to protect my face as hits rain down on me. Based on the impact, I know he's pulling them. They're lighter, still just as calculated as ever, but I know his punches feel like the weight of Mjolnir, and this ain't it. Shoving him off of me, he goes willingly. Sweat beads everywhere, my body on fire, and *I love it*.

"Made contact with the writer for the Northwest Explorer."

"Fuckin' finally. He going to write a feature on us? They seemed so damn eager to get us front and center. Was not expecting all the fuckery you've had to deal with," he says as he takes another jab at me. I move quickly to return the blow, catching him with two rapid-fire uppercuts to the stomach. It does the trick, knocking the air out of him as he stumbles, bending over for a quick moment to force some air into his lungs.

"Ooo! You're gonna feel me later, aren't you, big brother?" I taunt. "Yeah, it's been a trip. But he's traveling to his summer house this weekend, and it's his only free time, I guess. Invited me to go with him. Was pretty persistent. Said it's go, or no story."

"What a dickhole," Dallas chimes in from the ropes.

"Need help packing?"

My head jerks back to Sawyer. "For real? You think I should go?"

"Oh, you're going. It's not even a question, especially after those hits. This could propel us forward even further, and you know it. We want to expand, right? Use that Casanova charm and woo the shit out of him." Sawyer pushes the end of his gloved hand into my chest, knocking me back slightly with every little hit. "Get. Us. That. Feature."

"I'm with Sawyer, brother. Sorry," Liam says, making me drop my guard. Sawyer takes full advantage, giving me his full strength and landing similar punches right to my stomach and ribs.

"Fuuuuck!" I hiss. My ribs are definitely going to be bruised after that one.

Sawyer steps quickly into my space, his arm wrapping around

my neck, bringing my forehead to meet his as I breathe through clenched teeth.

"You good?"

"As good as I'm gonna be considering I'm going to meet this dickhead for the weekend."

"Are we good then?"

"Always," I tell him honestly, hoping like hell it goes both ways, even if I fuck everything up. I know exactly what will happen if I go away with him. Fuck, why does life have to be like this for me? I just want peace and ease.

Collapsing on a bench inside the locker rooms, I pull out my phone and bring up Finn's number that I've saved and left unused. I know going away with Finn is what needs to happen for my family, but that flickering ember inside me roars to life when I think about the possibility of being locked away with him for three days in a place where no one knows either of us. That scares the shit out of me almost as much as losing the opportunity to work with him for this article.

Giving in to my brother's demands, and knowing it's what's best for the distillery and my family, even if everything in my body is telling me this trip is going to change everything for me, one way or another, I fire off a text to the one person I don't want to talk to, the one person I can't shake my head clear of.

Me: Send me the address

Pocketing my phone, I grab my bag and head home, ready for a hot shower and some food. By the time I park my car in the parking spot behind my house, my phone has gone off. I chastise myself for not having the self-control to make him wait for a reply, but I'm too damn eager to see what he has to say.

> Fuck face: No can do. We'll ride together. I'll pick you up early.

Goddamn, why does he have to make everything so difficult? Grabbing my workout bag, I head inside my house, kicking off my shoes at the door as another text comes in.

> Me: Not happening. I can meet you there. I want my car with me

> Fuck face: Who said we were driving?

> Me: Where the fuck is this place?

> Fuck face: It's a secret

> Me: You make it so easy to hate you

> Fuck face: You wish you hated me, lover.

> Me: I'm not your lover

> Fuck face: The way you come so beautifully for me says otherwise

> Fuck face: See you early then

I toss my phone into the tray on the table next to my front door, fuming. How the fuck am I going to survive a weekend alone with this bastard?

I know exactly what will happen this weekend. Finn is a force I can't fight. I'm weak in his presence, and I don't understand it. I've never had a one-night stand that I think about after. I've had good pussy that I went back for a few times at the club but walked away from them without another thought. Finn is different, and I can't explain it. His attraction to me isn't something he keeps locked up. I know he wants me, and my body gives in to the temptation every single time. There's the added question about what he meant about his dad, that he had to convince him to write the article. I make a mental note to get to the bottom of that this weekend.

My original thought that I could whore myself out for the sake of getting the article has gone completely out the window. I know I need to go into this trip with a clear head, but nothing that surrounds Griffin Nash is clear. He fills me with . . . everything. Things I never thought I would be capable of feeling. I lose myself completely. I can't let that happen. I need to go there, survive, get the article, and leave with some part of myself intact. But fuck if there isn't a loud part of me that desperately wants more of him. Wants to know what's different about him and chase the feelings he pulls from me. I've never felt as good as I do with Griffin Nash.

Can I actually go through with this? I know we'll hook up; it's inevitable. The tension between us is too strong, and we already know what each other sounds like when we come. It's not like the sex would be a hardship. Shit, can I fuck another man? I've had a ton of anal sex, I can't imagine it's any different. *Even if everything about it is different.*

Suddenly, I'm feeling like a fish out of water as my over-thinking brain fucks me over and I spiral. Does he even want that? Just because he's gay doesn't mean he'd want me to fuck him. Shit, why am I even thinking about sex with Finn? Why can't I just chill the fuck out? I can survive this. I have to.

CHAPTER 8

carter

FINN SHOWS UP AT THE ASS CRACK OF FUCKING DAWN,
walking into my house like he lives here. The front door slams, the
footfalls of his steps leading him through my house until he
pushes open my bedroom door to find me sprawled out in my bed
buck ass naked.

"You're still sleeping."

"Good observation, jackhole. Go away," I groan.

"You aren't packed either."

"No shit. Fuck off."

"Aren't you a delight first thing in the morning."

"The sun isn't even up."

"No shit. The sun doesn't seem to rise over here in your hole
in the mountains."

"Ugh. Fuck. Off."

"As much as I'm enjoying seeing your bare ass—what the fuck
is that?"

"What?"

Finn's hands are on me before I can react, one hand gripping
the back of my neck, pushing my head further into the pillow, the
other flat against the center of my back, holding me in place. I
squirm to get away from him but without turning over and

letting him have a front-row look at my hard dick, I only thrash slightly.

"Is that a fucking brand?"

I instantly still, forgetting that the damn thing was there since the pain went away.

"Fuck, it's still red around the edges. What the fuck did you do?" he hisses, hands lifting off my back, fingers trailing over the scar at the very top of my ass cheek.

"Don't worry about it," I snap at him, trying to jerk away.

"Tell. Me."

"My brothers did it while we were drunk on our annual boys' trip in February. It was a joke. Ended up doing something stupid while drunk; it's not a big deal."

"The fuck it isn't, Carter, this is permanent!"

"No shit. But you aren't my keeper, so get off of me."

His fingers continue to run over my skin in a soothing, almost affectionate way. My heart does that weird damn thing in my chest. It's a slow burn at first, just my heart skipping a beat, steadily beating faster and faster as his hand flattens over my skin. Then my breathing starts to come harder, my heart fluttering. The hand around the back of my neck is a firm pressure, holding me still, reminding me that he's in control right now, and for some reason that I can't understand, I allow it, knowing that at any point he would let me up if I really wanted him to.

My body hums with equal parts excitement and nervousness, the warmth of his touch as he slowly palms my ass, the desperate little moan that escapes his lips as his fingers dig into the meat of my flesh. My thoughts empty, but everything else in me is alive, rapidly losing control of my feelings and my body.

Then, his mouth is there, a small peck over my fresh scar. Once. Twice. And then his warm, wet tongue that my dick is more than acquainted with licks over the spot. My cock is throbbing, pinned between my body and the bed, already leaking precum. The urge to roll over and have his mouth on me is so damn strong, but I fight it, letting him have this moment. I let myself enjoy his hot mouth, dropping open-mouthed kisses on my skin. He stays in the area directly over my scar, and then he's gone, and I nearly whine.

I hear the whoosh of air only a split second before the hard sting of his hand against my ass. I jerk hard in response, but he holds me down by the neck.

"Did you just fucking spank me?"

"Don't. Fucking. Mark. Up. Your. Skin!" He punctuates every word, pushing my head into the pillow as he says them. And then he's letting me go, taking a few measured steps backward. I lay there for a moment stunned by the turn of events, even more stunned by the wave of emotions spreading through my body like a goddamn inferno.

"You've got ten minutes, Hayes. Get dressed, pack. Ten. Minutes."

I listen for Finn's steps to leave my bedroom, fading away the farther he gets before I roll over and do exactly what he said. With my heart in my goddamn throat, my head swimming with confusion, and my cock as hard as steel, I take the quickest shower of my life, pull myself together, and pack a weekend bag without having a shit idea of where we're even going.

I find Finn sitting on my couch, his forearms resting on his thighs, bent over and focusing hard on his phone. He's wearing a pair of khaki shorts and a black henley that strains over the muscles of his biceps. His glasses have slipped down the bridge of his nose, and I want so badly to push them back for him. I'm fucked. I'm failing at keeping myself in check, and the weekend hasn't even started yet.

"Hey."

"Hi," he says, his face lighting up in a smile like I'm the best damn thing he's ever seen. "Are you ready?"

"Ready as one can be when they're being kidnapped." All I get is a dirty little smirk in return, and somehow that's better than any reply he could have said.

. . .

After a tense three-hour drive to Seattle from Aspen Ridge, we drive right onto the airstrip to a waiting plane, and I realize why his ass picked me up at three in the morning.

"Of course you have a private jet. Because why wouldn't you?"

"It's not mine. It's . . . my dad's. It's just frowned upon if I fly commercial. Apparently it makes *him* look bad, even if I'd prefer not to travel this way."

I don't know why the sudden transparency, but I've got a feeling there's quite a story there based on his tone, and as much as I want to push, I don't think he'll give me any more, so I let it slide.

"C'mon, we're already late because you decided to sleep in."

"Maybe if you had told me what time to be ready, I would have been."

"Get your ass on the plane, Carter."

"You're not making this fuckin' easy. You know that, right?"

"Don't give a shit. Just as long as you get on the plane."

"Not until you tell me where we're going."

"Why? Scared I'm kidnapping you?"

"Are you kidding me with that shit? You are kidnapping me."

"Emberleigh."

"What?"

"That's where we're going."

I follow Finn to the stairs of the plane, climbing up and nodding to the flight attendant. I take a seat in the center of the plane in a large chair, Finn sitting directly across from me, when he could have gone anywhere since the entire flight is just us. The door is brought up and locked, and then it hits me that I'm really doing this.

"Where's Emberleigh?"

"Maine."

Finn's beach house isn't a fucking beach house. It's a goddamn mansion with private access to the beach. After a long-ass day of traveling and not moving my body, the energy in me is buzzing. I claim one of the guest rooms on the bottom floor and drop my bag on the ground, quickly changing into a pair of running shorts and shoes. I don't bother with a shirt, hoping that I can soak up some of the sun that this part of the country seems to get. We left Seattle early enough that even after losing a few hours to the time difference, it's only late afternoon.

The bottom floor of the house is a large, open floor plan, with tall, vaulted ceilings, too many rooms to count, a deck that spans the length of the back of the house, an in-ground pool, a hot tub, a sauna, and who the fuck knows what else. I find Finn sitting at the wraparound bar that splits the fucking enormous kitchen from the dining room.

"Here," he says as he throws me a bottle of water with a green label, and I uncap it, taking a few large chugs and wincing.

"Got an issue with Poland Springs water?"

"Damn good water, except it's cold."

"What the fuck is wrong with cold water?"

"It's bad for you, and I don't like it."

"Noted. Where are you going?"

"A run."

"How about ice cream and a walk downtown?" Finn asks, as if we're on a fucking family vacation and I haven't been blackmailed into coming here against my freewill. At least, that's what I'm trying to convince myself happened.

I grumble, and it reminds me of Sawyer. When the hell did I turn into the grumpy-ass older brother? I'm the goddamn fun one, always up for a good time, happy as shit. But here I am, stewing in a massive beach house, owned by the same asshole that is holding me hostage.

"How about no and we cut the shit, Nash. The hell do you want from me?"

A devilish smirk fills his face, his dark eyes squinting as he roams over my body, settling on my crotch. Heat sparks, traveling up my spine like an annoying itch I can't fucking scratch.

"Fuck no. Not gonna happen."

"You can fight it all you want, lover, but I know you want me."

"The fuck I do," I lie. "Whatever shit has happened before was a slip of judgment. I'm here for the story."

"You could say that for the first time, maybe even get a pass for the second. But anything after that?" He takes a step into my space, and like an idiot, I take a step back, like a cat playing with his fucking prey, I let him back me right up against the wall. Finn's hands press against the wall next to my head, caging me in. Somewhere in the recesses of my mind, I know I could push him away. I've been fighting my entire life with my three brothers, and they're each bigger than Griffin Nash. But I don't. "Nah, you want whatever this is between us. You just don't want to admit it."

He strikes a chord.

"You think this is because you're a man? I don't give a shit about that. I care that you hold something my family desperately wants in the palm of your hands and are using it to blackmail me to get what you want. You want me to fuck you? Fucking is easy. Sex is what I'm best at, and I've been doing it unattached for years. You're not getting anything else out of me."

His eyes search mine as I spew the venom from my mouth. The close proximity is fracturing the walls I'm trying to hold in place. Fuck, everything about him easily crumbles them. But then he goes and says something that confuses me further.

"Nah. As much as I like your cock, Carter, I want more than that."

Is he insane? What the hell is he even saying right now? Based on the look on his face, he's just as confused.

"That'll never happen." I blow out a breath as he leans in, holding the mask of indifference I've perfected over the years, bracing myself for him to kiss me.

My hands ball into fists at my sides, my fingers digging into my palms, fighting the urge to grab him and erase the remaining space between our bodies. The tension crackles between us like a live wire, and I desperately want to let him stoke this blazing inferno inside me.

But he doesn't kiss me. He pivots at the last second, running the smooth skin of his nose across the rough stubble of my facial hair until his lips reach my ear, his breath warm on my skin, goosebumps scattering and pebbling my flesh. I fight the chill that follows, but I'm just not quick enough. I know he feels how he affects me. Why the fuck does this guy get under my skin like this? Why do I suddenly feel alive when we're like this?

"Liar."

My hands come up quicker than I meant for them to, pushing harder than I would want. They make contact with his chest, and I shove hard. Finn stumbles back a few steps, his crystal-blue eyes wild with excitement and satisfaction.

"Fuck you."

"Anytime, lover."

For a moment, I'm tempted to hate-fuck him right here. Rip off his shorts, bend him over the pretty upholstered couch, and fuck his ass raw until I fill it with my cum, leaving him unfulfilled to take care of himself. But no. I'm not giving in to him.

"I'll be outside."

His hand shoots out, fingers clasping my arm. Sparks shoot off from the connection, causing me to stiffen as I stare down at where our skin meets.

"Wait."

"What, Nash?" I snap.

"Truce."

I finally look up to meet his eyes—a stormy mix of desire and desperation gazing back at me. My goddamn heart flips in my chest, bottoming out into the pit of my stomach. I don't like that look on his face. It does me in.

"What do you mean?" I ask with feigned irritation, giving him an opportunity to lay out his conditions.

"I know how I got you here was shitty, but can we just put everything aside for the weekend? No one knows us here, can we just . . . pretend?"

"Psh," I tsk, shocked that he would even suggest it, even if my mind is swirling with the possibility. "Pretend what, Nash? That you haven't been personally fucking with me for months, hunting me down at a sex club, fucking around with me, then black-mailing me to get me to skip town with you to hide away in your super mansion? I don't know what you want from me."

He exhales roughly, thick fingers carding through his hair. I track the movement . . . not able to hide his disappointment when he winces. His eyebrows crinkle inward, his lips turning down, and once again—I don't fucking like it. I want to fucking fix it, and I can't explain why. He deserves my wrath, not my kindness.

"Tell me what you want." My voice is calmer, my anger receding.

His eyes lift up, meeting mine, those goddamn crystal blues looking back at me, setting off a new sensation low in my belly. Fuck are those goddamn butterflies? What the fuck is happening?

"You. Okay? I want you. Can we just try to forget every shitty thing that I've done to get us here, and just enjoy the weekend together?"

I open my mouth to spew more lies. More bullshit. But the look of needy desperation on his face stops me. I've been lying to myself and putting all the blame on him. There were ways around this; I didn't have to come, and he knows it. I can't explain it, but I want him, too. I want to explore this, and that's the real reason I'm here. Even if I've been convincing myself that it was for the feature he'd write.

The fact is, as much as I don't want to let my family down when it comes to this life-changing opportunity, I'm terrified that once it's all over, I won't have a reason to see Finn again. That he'll walk out of my life for good and I'll have no fucking idea how this man successfully flipped what I knew about myself on its head.

"I'm sorry, Carter. There's a lot more to all of this, and I just . . ." He huffs out a long breath and pushes his hand through his hair, keeping his eyes downcast. I step into his space, gripping his chin between my thumb and pointer finger, angling his head up so that he has to meet my eyes.

"You just what, Finn? Tell me, I'm so fucking confused," I ask him, my voice coming out less tender than it should. His stormy blue eyes rake over my face, and then he pulls his plump bottom lip between his teeth, and I nearly groan. It's such a sexy move that I haven't seen him do before, and I immediately want to rub my thumb over it to pop it free.

"You're so beautiful, Carter."

"Flattery isn't going to win you any brownie points, Nash, fuck off with that shit."

He moves quickly, pressing me back against the wall, his hand moving to my groin, grabbing my semi-hard dick and holding it tight. I can't help the grunt that leaves me, and the asshole smirks.

"How about a blow job then?" he asks as he playfully nips at my bottom lip. Fuck, everything about him makes me lose myself, but makes everything inside me go crazy at the same time. It's a war of emotions, but sex is always what I want, and sex of any type with Finn is my newest obsession. I'm here, and I knew it would happen eventually. Plus, my dick is harder than it's ever been, and my heart is racing a mile a minute in my chest. I want him. So fucking bad. Even though in the far recesses of my head, I know he's using sex to get out of communicating with me, I still melt into him.

Grabbing a fistful of his hair, I wrench his head backward. "You want to suck my dick, pretty boy?"

"Fuck yes I do."

Pushing him down to his knees, he drops willingly, hands going to the band of my gym shorts and quickly yanking them down, my cock springing free and slapping my pelvis. Finn wastes no time grabbing it roughly with his fist, stroking from root to tip.

"Ughn," I moan at the contact.

It's so different from a woman. He knows exactly how rough to get, what could feel good and what wouldn't. I groan again as my head falls back against the wall, his hand jerking me hard, his other coming up to cup my sack, rolling my balls in his palm.

"What are you waiting for, Finn? You want to suck my cock so bad, then suck it."

He wastes no more time, his lips curl around the thick head of my dick, and my eyes roll back into my skull. His hands grip my hips, pulling me in further as he chokes on my cock. I move my hands to the sides of his face, my thumbs swiping back and forth across his cheeks, holding him still as his eyes flick up to meet mine, giving me a slight nod of his head in consent. I spread my legs further, his jaw relaxing in my hands as he passes the control over to me. The transfer of it is so fucking hot it makes my knees weak. This strong-ass man on his knees in front of me, about to let me fuck his throat with my dick. Fuck, it's bliss.

I pull back and drive in slowly, testing him out, seeing how much he can take. I press in until I feel his throat strain, running my thumbs affectionately across his cheeks as reassurance that I won't hurt him.

"Tap my leg if it's too much, and I'll stop, no questions asked. Relax your throat for me, breathe through your nose. I can't take it easy on you. I need you too much."

I feel the moment he gives completely in, my dick sliding into his throat further than I have before.

"Fuuuuck, Finn, such a good boy. Fuck."

I pull out to my tip, swiping it back and forth over his wet lips. I can't wait to see them bright red and puffy, spit and cum leaking from the crease. Pushing back in, I slide all the way home, much easier this time. Finn's hands stay on my hips, his fingertips biting into my skin but not pushing me away or tapping. I start to fuck his mouth without restraint, trusting him to tap out if I'm hurting him or he can't take anymore. I didn't go this rough on him at the club, and I want to test the waters now. It's pure euphoria. Finn's mouth is nirvana, and I never want it to end.

One of his hands slips between my legs, massaging my balls, slipping his fingers behind them and running along my taint. My heart is pounding as fast as my thrusts, his mouth open, spit dripping from the corners, tears starting to leak from his pretty blue eyes. My balls draw up from out of nowhere, my orgasm coming on fast.

"It's coming, Finn. You want me to fill this pretty mouth with cum?"

He jerks my hips forward at the same time my dick swells, pulsing ropes of cum down his throat. I moan unrestrained, Finn humming around me as he swallows down everything I'm giving him. After I'm empty, I start to pull out, Finn chasing my dick like he isn't done with it yet, lapping at my tip.

"Fuck, I love your taste," he rasps.

"Mmm. You okay?"

"Caring about my well-being, Hayes? That's unlike you."

I look down at him as a flare of pain shoots through me.

"I'm not a dick."

"No, but I'm definitely obsessed with the one you have."

"I'd never want to hurt you, Finn." The words are out of my mouth before I can stop them, letting him see a vulnerable part of me that I keep locked up tight. He cocks his head to the side while he studies my face, using his thumb to wipe his lips of the cum and spit coating them.

"I know, or I wouldn't have trusted you to do that," he replies simply as he stands, meeting me eye to eye.

"Oh. Okay. Good," is all I can come up with to say.

"I want you to trust me, Carter. I can't explain this pull to you without sounding like a lunatic. I really am sorry about how I got you here. Just . . . something was telling me to take you away. To escape with you."

"Damn, you really do sound like a lunatic. Should I be worried about never making it home?"

His eyes twinkle with mirth as he laughs under his breath.

"Don't give me any ideas, Hayes. Or I'll run away with you."

Silence stretches between us as we stand toe-to-toe, sharing air, both of us suspended in unsaid words. Words that are being held back by fear and the outside world. I don't believe in fate or coincidences, but there's something I can't explain about why my initial reaction to him running away with me is excitement and not terror.

"Okay," I tell him, his eyes going wide as they bounce back and forth between my own.

"Okay, what?"

"I'll put everything aside for the weekend. I'll try. You aren't alone in this. I feel it, too, I'm just . . ."

"Scared."

I release a rough breath.

"Yeah."

"Don't be. I've got you."

And fuck if I don't want to believe him.

Walking around the small town with Finn is as easy as breathing. We fall into step together like two friends who've known each other their entire lives. It takes me a beat to remember that I'm far from Aspen Ridge and no one here would know me from the next asshole walking around.

"What do you do for fun? You know, besides prowling a sex club for unsuspecting women?"

"Is this on or off the record?"

The growl that leaves his throat is deep and masculine, and even though I can't see those icy blue eyes behind his aviators, I know they'd be full of annoyance.

"If you're not going to try . . . you know what? Fuck it. Let's just go." Finn turns to retreat the way we came, my chest tightening with something that feels a whole helluva lot like panic. I reach out and grab his arm, pulling him into my space, just a breath apart. Not an hour ago, I agreed to try this weekend. I let him see a rare vulnerable part of me and I'm already fucking it up, falling back into my old habits, hiding myself from everyone around me.

"I'll behave." Finn's head cocks to the side as if he doesn't believe me. "I will, just . . . give me a break here." My throat cracks as I continue, "This is new for me."

"Walking around town with someone other than yourself?"

"Fuck, man, you're really gonna make me say it?"

"Sure as fuck am."

"Goddamnit, you can't make anything easy, can you? I'm not open with people. I've never been in a relationship. And this is not a relationship, but I don't go walk around town with someone I'm fucking around with."

"Never?"

"Never. I don't want one. I don't do relationships, full stop. And I definitely didn't know I was . . ." My voice trails off as I run my fingers over the coarse stubble of my face. I don't know why I'm opening up, but it's just so damn easy to talk to him. And for once, I have someone who seems like they genuinely want to hear what I have to say.

"Into men?" Finn finishes for me, even though I'm still confused as fuck on that one.

"Into men," I repeat, not hating how it sounds. "I think? I don't even know. Again, not saying this is a relationship either, it's not, just feels a bit relationship-y."

Finn's lips lift in a smile as he steps into my space, whispering in my ear in that way that he does that drives me crazy, his warm breath scattering goosebumps across my body.

"Lean into it, lover. It might surprise you."

He pulls back, his hand dragging down the length of my arm until he finds my hand, threading his fingers through mine. Electricity zips between us, causing my heart to beat rapidly in my chest. I use the fist of my free hand to rub the spot, hoping to relieve this budding feeling. Finn gives me his signature smirk and pulls me along to continue up the brick street and the rows of shops. His hand is warm in mine, and just like everything else with this man, he's given me something I've never experienced before. And I don't hate it.

"You ever had lobster?"

I think back for a moment to all the damn fish I've had over my life growing up in Washington, but lobster isn't something that's typically caught locally.

"Nah, I don't think I have, actually."

"Get ready for it, you're either gonna hate it or love it. There will be no in-between."

We weave through tourists and get in line at a shack by the water called When in Maine. It's jam-packed with people, at least twenty in front of us, so it must be good. Everyone seems to be getting the exact same order, though, and after five people walk away with what looks like an overflowing hot dog bun, I look at Finn.

"Lobster rolls. Lobster and mayo on a split-top bun. That's it."

"That's all they sell?"

"That's it."

When we finally get up to the counter, Finn orders our dinner and pays. We take our lobster rolls and head back to his mega-mansion, finding a spot at the edge of the water, taking seats next to each other in the grass. We eat in silence, the sun slowly setting behind the cove. It's so different here from Aspen Ridge, and I've only been here a few hours.

"What's it like growing up being one of five kids?" Finn asks, breaking the silence that stretches between us.

I crumple up the white paper, tossing it into the to-go bag while thinking over his question. He's so goddamn easy to talk to, but it's hard not to hold back not knowing his true motivations.

This could all be a ruse to get close to me and I'm the desperate asshole that would fuck it all up. Especially because I want to talk to Finn. I want to open up to him.

Lean into it.

"Chaos mostly. But it was good. I don't know anything different."

"Always wanted siblings, so that's why I ask . . . in case you think it was for other reasons." And once again, he's reading my mind.

"You're an only child?"

"Yeah. Parents wanted to throw everything into one kid and not have to divide their time. Or so they say."

"Sounds a little lonely, man. Even if it was batshit crazy in my house growing up, I couldn't imagine it any other way."

"Yeah, trust me, being an only child isn't all it's cracked up to be. At least it wasn't for me. There were so many times I wished I had somebody to have my back, be in my corner when I was up against my parents. It was always two on one, and it was a game I was set up to fail from the very beginning. Who knows, maybe they wanted it that way."

"Nah. It sounds like they love you and wanted to give you the best shot at life and not have to split resources. Shit was hard when we were little. Especially when shit went down with my older brother."

"What happened?" Finn asks, his voice full of sincerity and genuine curiosity. Truce. There's a ceasefire in place. I take a steadying breath, keeping my eyes focused on the colors reflecting off the ripples of the ocean.

"He, uh, he was in a relationship for a while, basically my entire childhood, I guess. I can't really remember back to before Ivy was around. They were together for years, and it was a relationship just like my parents had. So full of love and happiness. Then one day she was just gone."

"Shit, man, I'm so sorry."

"She didn't die; don't look at me like that. She just upped and disappeared shortly after she, Sawyer, and Dallas graduated from high school. No communication, no notice. Just here one day and gone the next. He fell into a deep depression. My brother Dallas had to step up. My dad was working crazy long hours at the distillery, Kinsey was still little, and Liam and I were little shit preteenagers. My mom had her hands full. But Sawyer wouldn't get out of bed. He was supposed to go to college, and he postponed a full year. He didn't eat. It lasted a long time and it gutted me. Seeing him find the love of his life, just to lose her. It destroyed him."

Fuck, I remember seeing my brother laying on his bed staring blankly at the wall. His eyes were devoid of any emotion, like he was completely broken.

Mom was crying again, even though she thought I couldn't hear in the pantry. I know it's because she's worried about Sawyer. I don't understand why he won't get up. I miss him taking me to Grace Beach and teaching me to surf. I miss him picking on all of us and driving me around. Dad really misses him being at the distillery. I thought I was going to miss him because he was going away to college, but he's still here, lying in his bed like he always is.

"Sawyer?" I call out as I open his door and walk in. He's lying in his bed on his side, hugging his pillow. He doesn't look the same as he did before Ivy left a few months ago. He's skinny now, his eyes sad and empty, like he's sick with the flu and it just won't stop eating him alive. "I need you to get up, Sawyer. We all miss you, and I want my brother back."

"I can't."

"Why? Tell me why?"

"'Cause my heart is gone, and I don't know how to function without it."

"Your heart is beating inside you, Sawyer. She didn't take it."

"It's not the same without her here, kid. You'll understand someday when someone steals yours."

"You need to get up, Sawyer."

"Car, I'm sorry. I can't do this without her. She took it when she left me, and I'll never be whole again." His eyes fill with tears as his body shakes with sobs. I crawl onto the bed with my big brother and hold him, letting him cry and mourn Ivy, all while promising myself that I will never let this happen to me. No one is taking my heart. I'll never give anyone this much power to wreck me.

He said that Ivy took his whole heart with him when he left, and I believed him. The happy, fun brother that I had grown up with was gone because he fell in love with a girl who didn't stay.

I can feel Finn's eyes on the side of my face, and when I can't take the silence and the power of his stare any longer, I turn my head. My eyes trace over his soft features, my breath catching. He's looking at me like he finally sees me . . . the real me. The person I keep locked up tight because no one wants to be around an anxious wreck. I'm the fun-time brother, not the anxious one who's emotionally closed off from everyone.

"It's getting late, you ready to head back?" I say, the back of my neck prickling with sweat—and not from the balmy heat of summer.

As if nothing had just passed between us, Finn stands, pulling his T-shirt off and dropping it at my feet. I look up from where I'm perched, resting my elbows on my knees.

"Nope. Now the fun begins. Ever skinny-dipped?"

"Who hasn't skinny-dipped?"

"Well? Have you?"

"I'm not skinny-dipping, Finn. We'll get caught, and that's the last thing I need. I can see the headlines now."

He raises his eyebrows in a challenge, and I know the words before he says them, the bastard.

"Dare you."

Reluctantly, I stand, raising my arm over my head and grabbing the back of my shirt, pulling it off and adding it to the pile accumulating in the grass.

"That's what I thought."

"You're a fucker, you know that?"

"If it gets you naked and in that water, I'm okay with it." He shrugs like it's no big deal. Finn is so calm and collected—my opposite. I may seem like I'm always up for a good time, and usually I am, but that's all a facade. The pressure I feel riding my ass constantly that I'm going to fuck up and ruin my family's reputation—make the wrong deal, say the wrong thing—is immense. I'm constantly anxious, and it's well hidden. Running and sex are the only things keeping me from losing my mind.

The sun having long set, there's not a soul in sight, and my shorts are discarded, leaving me in just my formfitting boxer briefs. Then I'm following Finn's bare ass as we wade into the fucking freezing water. We're hidden on the opposite side of a rock formation that juts out into the ocean, separating two sections of the water. The moon sits up high in the sky, illuminating the water just enough to see where I'm going.

Finn dips under the surface, and even though I know it's coming, I can't brace for the feeling of him grabbing my leg and pulling me hard underneath. I jerk up, choking on the salty liquid flooding my lungs.

"You're a bastard!" I say through coughs. "Haven't you seen Jaws? We're practically in Massachusetts."

"We're in Maine, but there are definitely great white sharks here."

"Why the fuck are we in the water at night then, idiot?"

"'Cause I wanted to get you out of your head."

I stare at him for a moment before he swims close to me and places his hands on my shoulders. We're both standing, the water up to our chests, and while I know we're out here completely alone, nothing but the moonlight casting down on us, the fireflies flitting around on the grass and under the trees, nerves still race down my spine.

As if he can tell, Finn's hands curl around my neck and shoulder, hauling me to him. I gasp at the contact, his legs wrapping around my waist, his taut stomach mere inches from mine.

We're face-to-face, sharing air, and nothing has felt easier. His long eyelashes are beaded with water, the blue of his irises so stormy in the light of the moon, but there's no missing the lust-filled haze that clouds them. Hell, I feel it, too. I always feel it.

"Finn . . ." I plead, my voice thick with warning.

"Shh, don't think. Just . . ." his eyes flick down to my lips before his breath hitches. With his eyes on mine, he pecks me once. Just a soft press of his lips. My breathing starts to pick up, my heart racing in my chest. "Just don't think."

"I can't help it . . ." I confess.

He just shakes his head and says softly under his breath, "Carter, let me help you . . . like you help me." The last four words are whispered so low that I almost miss them. I have half a mind to ask him what he means, but I don't.

Strong hands move from my shoulders to the back of my neck, one lightly rubbing up and down the base. Instinctively, I pull him closer, putting us nearly flush. I know he can feel my hard cock pressing against him. Based on the warmth radiating from him, I know I feel his. Nothing but the thin, wet fabric of my briefs separates our dicks.

Hell, I love the feeling of being this close to him. I move one of my hands languidly across his hip and thigh, over the globe of his ass and back again while we both struggle to steady our breathing. Even under the water, his skin is so rough under my palms, the thick muscles of his thighs tight and masculine as I grip him, massaging the pads of my fingers into him.

"Tell me what you want," I whisper.

He answers by licking his lips, a slow swipe across the plush, peach-colored bottom lip, before he descends on my own. The kiss is soft at first, like he's feeling me out, and I don't blame him. I know I've given him enough whiplash to leave him battered. But he still keeps coming back for me. Maybe I had it all wrong and he's a masochist.

But then a deep, desperate moan escapes from him, and he opens to meet my tongue. I respond by pulling back slightly and nipping at his bottom lip, getting him to moan a little louder. *Fuck.* These sounds are killing me, going straight to my cock. He keeps his hands on my neck, holding me where he wants me as he uses his thighs to lift himself a bit and finds a rhythm, grinding his hard cock up and down across my length.

I let Finn use me however he wants, releasing his mouth and peppering his neck with kisses, licks, and nips. I drag one hand up the smooth expanse of his ripped stomach, over every ab that he's worked hard to earn, until I reach his bare chest, my finger rubbing circles over his nipple until it pebbles under my touch and the cool water.

Finn continues his pace, grinding us together, my hard dick straining against the wet fabric of my briefs, aching to feel him touch me where I need it most.

He pulls my head closer to his body, and I let out a breathy moan.

"Finn . . . I need . . ." I whisper, my composure slipping.

"I know. Me too . . ."

I move one of my hands to his ass to lift him higher, and the other to push my briefs down just enough to free my cock. Never have I ever been so grateful for the night sky and the privacy it gives, shrouding us in darkness. I grip the globes of his ass, my fingers digging into the flesh and pulling him impossibly close. I take his mouth with mine again as he melts further in my arms. He feels *so* good.

"Fuck, Carter. You feel . . . Hell. I've been dreaming about touching you like this, holding you like this. I don't want to rush. Let me make us feel good."

God, when he talks like this. Finn muddles everything. I can't think clearly when we're close; everything else melts away, and all that's left is the two of us. I lose myself to him, and it's the best feeling I've ever felt. Nothing can top this right here with him.

A desperate moan works its way up my chest, Finn using it to fuel his movements. With one hand around my neck, he holds me close, his other grabbing my cock, holding it tightly against his own. We moan in unison, our foreheads resting together. Our breathing is ragged as he jerks us hard and rough, the water making the friction difficult. His hard cock pulses against mine, and I hold him by his ass, keeping him close to me as we chase this feeling.

"Fuck. It's not enough . . . I need to come."

"I know. Shit. Let's get to the house," I tell him, suddenly feeling a whole helluva lot more relaxed and irresponsible. Finn unhooks his legs so that he's standing on his own, and then we hurry out of the water, quickly grabbing our clothes and hustling to the stairs of his private deck.

We don't make it past the first step before his hands are on me, wrapping around my body and hauling me into him. I tumble back against the railing, Finn's hands all over me as we battle for dominance, our kissing frantic and bruising. Finn bites down on my bottom lip until my tongue tastes the familiar, metallic iron flooding my mouth. I wince, pulling back from him but he just grins, his lips turning up in a sly fucking grin that's all him.

"You think that's funny, asshole?"

"I think you taste fucking delicious, lover."

"Yeah? I got something else you can taste."

"Fucking happily."

Breath is stolen from my lungs as Finn drops to his knees for the second time today, forcibly dragging the wet briefs down my sticky thighs. My cock bobs free and Finn wastes no time grabbing it in his strong grip and licking up the underside of my length.

"Mmm," I moan as I thread my hands through his thick, wet hair, my eyes locked onto where his tongue is currently lapping at my slit, licking up the precum leaking from the tip for him. I prop my foot up a step, spreading myself so that he can take as much of me as possible. My hips chase the wet warmth of his mouth, bucking forward until he finally sucks me down, taking me all the way to the back of his throat and swallowing before pulling up, his tongue swirling around my engorged head, and then repeating the process.

It's fucking euphoric and hot as hell. Just like every other time. I've yet to return the favor, never actually having touched his dick before. Something about seeing this huge, strong, confident male on his knees for me, worshipping my dick like it's the best thing he's ever had, does it for me every time, but I do feel like shit for having not given him anything in return. I'm just not there yet, as much as I want him. I'm still so fucking confused.

"Fuck, man, I love it when you suck my cock. So fucking good, Finn. So goddamn good. That's it."

He hums under my praise, picking up his pace and sucking harder on every upstroke. He's blowing my damn mind. But that's not where I want to come. I want to fuck him. I can't explain it, but I want it more than anything else right now. I want inside that tight ass of his, I want to claim a part of him like he's done to me.

"Tell me you brought lube," I demand, my voice shaky as I do everything I can to hold off my orgasm. I want to fuck his tight ass; I want to bend him over the railing and drive in deep until we're both a mess.

"Fuck. It's inside. I can't wait any longer."

"Dammit. I want to come with you, Finn, touch yourself."

He pops off my cock, leaving it slick from his saliva, and stands quickly, claiming my mouth in another soul-searing kiss. Our tongues tangle, my hands gripping the back of his head hard, hauling his body against mine in a desperate attempt to get closer.

"Fuck, I want to fuck you, Finn. I need more."

"Trust me, this is gonna feel so fucking good."

Finn pulls back, lines up our dicks, tip to tip, and fists his cock, pulling back the foreskin before moving upward toward mine, enveloping the head of my cock and creating a sheath.

"Ohhh, fuuuuck," I moan, my knees nearly buckling, as I look down, my jaw goes slack in awe. He jerks us like that, using himself to create this breathtaking feeling for both of us. The suction it creates melts me, all coherent brain function long gone.

"Oh, hell yes. Look at us, Carter. Goddamn, you feel so good."

"Finn . . . oh my god," I pant as he wraps his free hand around my neck, continuing his ministrations that are driving us both to the edge. His chest rises and falls rapidly against my own, his breathing heavy and warm against my face as he brings us closer and closer to release. Neither of us can take our eyes off of what he's doing, our cocks suctioned tightly together. His jaw is slack, as if he's just as lost to this as I am. He pumps us, my orgasm right on the cusp, and like he fucking knows it, he squeezes just a bit harder, forcing me over the edge.

"Ohhh, fuuuuuuck, fuuuucck, just like that, yesss."

"Yeah? You like it? You like how I make you feel?"

"Fuck yeah, I do. Fuck. Fuck. Fuck. Don't stop," I chant.

"That's it, lover. So good. Let me have it. Come all over us, flood us with your cum."

I explode. My orgasm pummels through me with the power of a goddamn freight train.

My cum shoots out, filling the sheath he's created with his foreskin and overflowing between us, coating both of our cocks and Finn's hand as he continues to stroke us together, my hips gyrating greedily as he fucks us.

Just as it becomes too much, everything too sensitive, Finn comes with a long moan that makes my heart rate pick up. I can't look away. Watching our cocks tip to tip, Finn's jerking, his cum mixing with mine, is the hottest thing I've ever seen. He releases us before collapsing against me, the railing of the stairs supporting us, my hands rubbing up and down the strong muscles of his back.

His body is flush against mine and the way his bare skin feels against me is fucking mind-blowing. We stay like that for several long minutes, catching our breath and letting our heart rates find a non-life-threatening rhythm.

I wrap my arms tightly around his body, letting him sag against me.

"Holy. Shit," he breathes against my neck.

"Yeah . . . holy shit. You just blew my goddamn mind," I confess, because it's the truth. I've never come so hard before, never felt anything so intense.

I hold him like that for a few minutes with the stillness of the night surrounding us. It isn't until the chill of the night mixed with our wet bodies that I start to press against him so that he stands on his own.

"We should get going, we're gonna freeze or get caught."

"Wouldn't want that, now, would we?"

The moment shatters, and my walls slam down hard.

"No. We wouldn't," I snap a little harder than necessary.

"Yeah. Figured. Wouldn't want anyone to get the wrong idea about you. I get it. Been there time and time again."

His words sting. But I don't correct him. He thinks I'm so closed-minded that it would bother me that he's a man. But that's not it at all. Is it different? Yeah. But that's not why my heads fucked up over this. Sure, I don't want to let my family down, and I know he's hiding something, but that shit can be dealt with. It has everything to do with everything he makes me feel. I can't give in to that. I can't lose myself to someone else. The fact that, despite knowing that something is different when we're together, I still can't give him all of me. I don't do feelings, and Finn makes me feel fucking everything.

I promised myself a long time ago that I would never let someone have my heart, that I would never get close enough to someone else for them to have the power to destroy me, but here I am. Just stupid enough to fall into bed with the one man who holds all the power to do just that.

Walking back into the house is a silent blur. Both of us too prideful and cocky to break the thick tension. But that's the thing about whatever Finn and I have—even the angry silence between us is comfortable. There's still nowhere I'd rather be. How fucked up in the head do I have to be? I don't recognize the feelings stirring in my chest, my mind telling me to get the fuck out now, my heart feeling like it's finally found home. I don't do this shit. My head is lost to a million different things, I barely register Finn's words.

"Want a drink?"

"Nah. I'm gonna go shower," I reply curtly.

I walk through the house to the bedroom I claimed for myself, heading right to the massive walk-in shower and turning it on hot. My head is spinning, and it feels like I don't know myself anymore. The only thing that's certain is I'm never going to be the same after this.

finn

LAYING ON MY BACK IN MY BEDROOM, I FOCUS ON THE ceiling, feeling like a huge piece of shit. I shouldn't have said what I did to Carter after we both orgasmed. But he always pulls away after. The moment he finishes, his brain clears, and he takes ten steps back from me. I wanted to strike before he did this time, and I shouldn't have. He said he would try, and tonight he did. He gave me pieces of himself that I thought I would have to try harder to receive. There's no way he doesn't feel this between us. I recognized it from the first moment I laid eyes on him at Temptations. He's different. We're different. He's straight-up admitted to never doing anything like this before, so he may not even recognize this for what it is.

The shit he confessed about his brother, it's no wonder why he's so closed off. After seeing the aftermath of a love lost, being so young and not understanding the heartbreak? Carter has walls up that were directly because of that. I want to be the person to break them down, to show him how beautiful a relationship and being loved can be.

Feeling like a piece of shit, I get off my bed and walk through the house in search of Carter to apologize. His door is closed, but I don't let that stop me, letting myself into the room with confidence. The noise from the shower leads me to him, the door separating us barely cracked open. Steam fills the bathroom, and I hesitate for just a moment.

I've never wanted anything as much as I want him. If he would only give in to what this is between us. I'm going to find a way to save us both through this shit situation and then I'm going to open his eyes to how good we can be together.

I just can't come clean about everything yet. Do I feel guilty for manipulating him into spending the weekend with me? Slightly. But he needed it and he sure as shit wasn't going to face what he's feeling while being compressed by everything around him that has already decided for him who he is. Carter needs to figure that out on his own. If it isn't me? So be it. At least I gave him the opportunity to explore and find out. But I'm it for him. I feel it.

Slipping into the bathroom, my clothes already discarded, I'm careful not to make any noise. Carter's body is under the spray, his back to me, barely visible through the thick condensation that's collected on the glass shower door. His head is in his palms as the stream beats down on the back of his neck. I can feel the emotion pooling off of him in waves. For a moment, I see myself—alone, wanting comfort in another person, lost, and confused—and I want to be for him what I need for myself.

Without wasting another minute, I pull open the door, startling him ever so slightly, and step onto the tile floor. Instead of fighting me, instead of turning around and demanding I get out, he doesn't move at all, and I don't know which is worse. My feet slap against the wet tile floor, leading me directly behind him. Reaching for him, my hands rub over the strong, sinewed muscles of his back, trailing downward until I reach his hips, where I confidently fold myself over him, my arms curling around his body.

His firm ass is nestled perfectly against my crotch for the first time, and while I've dreamed of this scenario on more than one erotic occasion, there's nothing sexual about this moment. My hands rub up each hard muscle of his six-pack abs until I reach his chest, pulling him further into me. His head lifts, hands moving outward, palms lying flat against the wall to brace us, and I hold him.

He doesn't hug me back, but he doesn't push me away. My heart runs rampant behind the walls of my chest. I'm attuned to every fiber of him—every breath he takes, his body rising and falling at a natural, calm rhythm, the goosebumps that scatter across his smooth skin from my touch, the way his steady heartbeat is racing behind his ribs. I lean into his neck, pressing a firm kiss at the base, right above his broad shoulder.

We stand there for minutes, maybe hours, just me holding him as close as possible. But after I've decided that we should wash before the water runs cold, I take a step back, releasing him from my arms. No words are spoken as I pump soap into my palms, rubbing them together before returning my hands to his back. I start at his rounded shoulders, massaging my hands into his strong muscles, using my thumb to draw firm circles at the base of his neck. His body melts into me like warm butter. I can visibly see the tension leaving his body before moving down his sexy back. Ever so slowly, I work my way down his body. The water sluices over his toned silhouette, my fingers digging into his firm glutes, under his perky ass, and down the back of his thighs.

Carter stands there and lets me explore his body in a way that he never has before. It's always been fast and dirty between us, me allowing him to be in control so he can justify his actions in his head. He's never touched me more than he has to, never touched my dick, and I'm okay with that for now. I get that he hasn't been ready to take that plunge. I'll be what he needs right now. I just want to be enough.

My fingers touch his hips, applying a bit of force so that he turns around and faces away from me. I pump the shampoo into my palm, working it into a lather before massaging it into his scalp with the pads of my fingers. His head drops back to make it easier on me, more tension leaving his body as he sags against me. I work my fingers through his hair, scalp, and the base of his neck, running my fingers through his thick, silky hair, water rivulets cascading over his shoulders and down his back. He lets out a little breathy moan and it makes me feel so damn good to pleasure him in such an intimate way.

His eyes stay closed as I turn his body to face me, leaning his head back and allowing me to rinse his hair. Once it's running clear, Carter opens his eyes, reaching behind me to pump soap into his hands, and then he does the unthinkable—meets my eyes while his strong hands rub soap over my pecs, over my collarbone, and expand outward to my shoulders. His strong hands slide over my body, and I have to bite my bottom lip to stifle the groan that wants to release. I've never been touched like this before, and it's killing me. Carter's hands on me feel incredible. He washes the top half of my body slowly, his eyes tracking every inch his hands glide over, like he's just as mesmerized with me as I am him.

When his hands dip further down, smoothing over my hips and avoiding my groin, he pauses, and not wanting to make him uncomfortable, I speak up, too afraid the tension that has pulled taut between us will snap at any moment, breaking whatever spell he's under.

"It's okay. I'll do it," I reassure him, my voice soft and under-standing, even though my heart fractures slightly.

Running my hands across the soap on my abdomen, I work over the short, coarse hair of my pelvis, and just as I'm about to grab my dick, Carter's fingers circle my wrist, gently pulling it away. My head shoots up to look at him, my eyes flicking back and forth between his, trying to read his thoughts through his masked expression.

Without a word, his fingertips ever so slightly run up the length of my dick in the most delicate of touches, and the electric current that spreads through my body nearly brings me to my knees. The force of the pleasure just from his barely there touch is enough to make me come on the spot.

He hesitantly closes his fist around my hard length, his fingers wrapping around it, his head focused down, watching in rapt attention. His thumb slides over my engorged head, sending shivers down my spine, a whimper escaping my lips.

"You like that?"

A rough exhale leaves my lips, my heavy eyes trying to focus on his. "Yeah. Yeah, I like that."

"I'm making you feel . . . good?"

Fuck. My sweet man. He's so damn unsure and lost right now and needs reassurance. This I can do. *Easily.*

"Yeah, lover, you're making me feel so damn good. You're stroking me so perfectly. Please don't stop."

His fist tightens slightly, as if I gave him the courage to keep going, his own cock rock hard, jutting out in my direction. I reach for him, my palm facing upward and sliding under his sack, my fingers toying with the space between his balls and ass, rolling the heavy weight of them in my hand. We both seem to be insatiable, having just come and already easily working each other back up again. I've never experienced such hunger before. There's no rush this time, neither of us is in a hurry to climax, content to sensually explore each other this way.

"Finn," he hisses as I move up the thick length of his dick and take him in my hand, matching the steady cadence of his movements around me. Our chests are rising and crashing hard, our breaths panting as he meets my eyes again. His pupils are blown, the blue irises stormy with lust. And then the dam breaks. His free hand moves quickly, his fast reflexes always surprising, palm grabbing the back of my neck and jerking me forward, his lips crashing against mine.

I feel the power behind his kiss down to my toes, my body a live wire, completely giving in to him—I'm at his mercy, and for once, he's not exploiting it; he's giving in and giving as much as he's taking.

I reposition us so that our cocks rest together, both of our hands wrapped around them, pumping them in a steady cadence. I fucking love the feel of his cock against mine, so hard yet so damn smooth. My fingers overlap his, and together we work ourselves up to orgasm, the fact that we're doing it together only adds an additional layer of heady arousal to the mix. It's not one-sided. Carter is here with me. Touching me. Willingly giving and taking. He's so perfect, and this is more than I ever could have hoped for. My heart could quite possibly beat out of my chest, so worked up, but so content to feel this with him.

The water beats down on his back, the heat and arousal mixing in the air, making me lightheaded. I'm crushed against him, our mouths devouring, swallowing down every single gasp and moan we release. We don't break apart while our fists pump each other's cocks together between us. His strong hand squeezes us together, right on the verge of pain, and it feels so fucking good that I can't think straight.

My orgasm comes on quick, the feeling of his cock against me, his hand around us too much to stave off the rush of pleasure barreling through me. I break the kiss, just enough to speak with a rough exhale.

"Feels too good. So fucking good. You're making me lose my mind."

"You gonna come for me, *lover*?" His words an homage to the first time we were together, and that's all I need. I combust without warning. "Oh, that's it, Finn. Look at you falling apart for me," he says as he continues to stroke me through it. The pleasure spirals from the base of my back throughout my body. My legs shake, and if Carter's arm wasn't wrapped tight around me, my knees would give out. Just as my cum starts to erupt from the tip of my cock, covering our fists, I feel his dick swell in our palms and I know he's there, too.

"Give it to me," I pant out. "Come with me."

And he does. His body jerking against mine as white ropes spurt from him, mingling with mine on our abdomens, hands, and dicks. It's such an erotic display, and I fucking love the sight of it. I'll never get enough. Of him. Of this. It'll never be enough.

His forehead collapses against my shoulder as he sucks in

lungfuls of air. My clean hand comes up and curls around the back of his head to hold him to me, whispering words of praise to my man.

"You were so good. So damn good."

"Mmm," is all he can muster in reply.

I continue to stroke the back of his head, willing my heartbeat to slow down.

"I've never been touched like that before, it was . . . everything, Carter."

A heavy breath rushes from him, and for a moment, I hold mine, terrified that whatever this was is about to blow up. This time, I give him a moment, steady myself, bracing for him to run and lash out, but it doesn't come. Instead, he pulls back enough to look into my eyes for a quick moment before his wet eyelashes flutter closed, his lips pressing against mine in a chaste kiss. In silence, he rinses us both of the mess, rewashing us quickly and turning the faucet off while I tiptoe around the situation like a kicked puppy. It's not in my nature to be so docile and submissive, but fuck, I want this man more than anything, and I'll give him whatever he needs.

We dry off in comfortable silence, even though I can hear my heartbeat in my ears. Towels wrapped around our waists, we leave the bathroom to throw on our clothes. I watch Carter pull on a pair of loose gym shorts, sans boxer briefs. They hang low on his defined hips, his V on full display as the flat of his hand travels up his washboard abs to his chest. When my eyes meet his face, he's giving me a knowing look, an eyebrow arched, the left side of his mouth turned up in a smirk.

"Snack and a movie?" he asks after a moment, as if he didn't just change everything for me.

"Ye-yeah." I clear my throat so it comes out steadier.

Twenty minutes later, we're sitting in front of a large flat screen TV, a bowl of popcorn, sodas, and a bag of M&Ms sitting between us.

"So, how'd you end up running a world-renowned travel magazine?"

"My family," I say without thinking. The ease of our conversation makes me forget myself, and as much as I don't want to be, I'm terrified of telling him about my dad, his threats, the abuse, and my very real fear of losing my career. "What about you? Always want to do marketing for a distillery?"

"Well, you've obviously done your research and know it's been in my family for a few generations. But I didn't know what else I wanted to do. All my brothers eased into their positions within the family and business seamlessly. Sawyer is a natural-born leader, and Dallas is, too, but he's too reckless and brash. He makes the perfect COO, and Sawyer balances him. Liam has wanted to be a master distiller since he was little. My grandfather and another master distiller, Graham, taught him everything. My sister wanted nothing to do with the family business, and she became a teacher. I was the only one that has always been fuckin' clueless about where he was going and what he was doing."

Carter talks openly and without reservation, and I hang on every word. I'm taking him in, finally seeing inside the man who's otherwise completely closed off from emotional connection. The man I've fallen rapidly for.

The way he talks, nearly rambles, makes me wonder if he has anyone to talk intimately to at all. My heart pangs at the thought, and I scoot closer. I resituate myself on the couch so that I'm facing him, my leg pulled up, my elbow resting on the back, my head resting on my hand, and the movie long forgotten.

"So how'd you end up in marketing then?"

"My dad suggested it. Said since I was always so good with a crowd—I was a partier . . ."

"No!" I mock gasp, and he rolls his eyes.

"Some things haven't changed, I guess," he says, but there's no heart in it, like he's trying to convince himself that's who he is because he doesn't want anyone else to think otherwise. But I catch on to it. I notice everything when it comes to this man. "He thought I could easily fall into the field if I studied. I was so eager to do *something* that I just went for it. After I graduated, my dad . . . you know what? Never mind. Tell me about you."

I want to push. I do. And I have to grind my molars together to keep from doing just that.

"What do you want to know?"

"Everything," he surprises me by saying. So I give him what I can, completely forgetting everything else in the process.

"I'm an only child. Rich-ass parents. Sent me to private school most of my life, but at least I got to stay in Washington. I love this state, but I also love to travel. I've got a best friend, Trey, who's a pain in the ass but he's been the brother I never had. Played soccer my entire life, I run as a stress reliever, always knew I was gay but didn't come out until after high school, at least not to anyone besides Trey."

"How'd your parents take it?"

"Me telling them that they're only child was gay?"

Carter winces and I reach my hand out, rubbing small circles around his knee.

"Not great. My mom is . . . well, she's the wife of a rich asshole, likes to spend his money, take trips with her girlfriends, and is pretty numb when it comes to human emotion. She just kind of blinked her eyes and sipped her martini. My dad, on the other hand?"

"Are you out of your fucking mind? My son is not gay!" his voice bellows through the expanse of his home office, and I can't help but wince. I've spent years keeping this secret, and I can't live this way anymore. I need to be open about who I am and open to finding love with someone out there. I don't want to be alone forever. I want to be enough for someone else someday, and I can't do that if I'm pretending to be someone I'm not.

"I am, Dad. I'm gay."

"The fuck you are, Griffin! This is to punish me, isn't it? You're

acting out, and for what reason? This will not stand. No son of mine is going to fuck other men!"

"Jesus. It's more than that, Dad. Don't make it about only sex."

"I can make it whatever the fuck I want it to be, Griffin! No one will find out about this! You will keep it to yourself until your pathetic little rebellion is over with."

"Dad. Please listen to me, this isn't about you. It isn't about Mom or anyone but me. I am gay. It's not going to change. I'm not going to wake up and change my mind. There's no choice. This is who I am."

He moves into my space quickly, and I make the mistake of looking to my shell of a mother for help, but she continues to sip her alcohol as if she's completely unfazed by the situation.

"She won't save you, Griffin!" he screams in my face, spittle splattering across my skin, forcing me to wince. I brace for the hit I've been anticipating my entire life, but it doesn't come. His next words should cut deep, but I expected them. I knew it would end like this, but I needed to do it anyway.

"No son of mine is gay. You are a fucking Nash. You will drop this disgusting little outburst, or I will destroy you. Do you under-stand me? You will marry a pretty, obedient little wife someday, and you will not embarrass me. I'll kill you before I let you tarnish everything I've worked for, Griffin. Understand?

"Let's just say it didn't go well."

"I'm sorry. You deserve to have people in your life who love you for you and support you unconditionally, Finn."

A knot of emotion lodges in my throat, and I'm forced to swallow hard against it.

"How, uh, how do you think your parents would take it?"

Carter thinks for a second before laughing, confusing the shit out of me.

"My parents are awesome. They just want us to be happy. They've never put pressure on any of us to be anything other than who we are. Honestly, there's not much I could tell them that they wouldn't be supportive of. Hypothetically, I can't imagine a world where I told them I was hooking up with a man and they were anything but happy. They may be a little confused, though; I'm known as quite the playboy. My brothers and I all have nicknames for each other. Mine? Casanova. Before that, it was lover boy," he says through a laugh. "I can imagine the looks on their faces, and it's pretty priceless."

My heart pangs with a kind of jealousy I've never felt before. What would it be like to have a supportive family like the one Carter has? That just loves each other for who they are with no requirements or expectations.

"I'm glad you have that. I don't know what that's like."

"I don't take it for granted, Finn. It's one of the reasons I feel like shit for feeling the way I do."

"What do you mean?"

He huffs, combing his fingers through his damp hair before giving me more.

"I don't fit in. I'm not completely myself around anyone, and I've always just felt like I was floating around. All my siblings have roles, and I never knew what mine was, so I chose to just be the fun-time guy, the silly one, the one who's always down for a good time."

"But that's not really who you are, is it?"

He looks away briefly before meeting my eyes, his icy blues forlorn and completely wrecking me. I reach over to touch his face. To my surprise, he nuzzles into the touch, his eyes not leaving mine while he accepts the comfort I'm offering him.

"No, it's not. But I love them all so much. They have no idea I feel this way, and it's not their fault, so I keep it from them so that I'm not a burden. Everyone always has so much shit going on and I don't want to add to it. I wouldn't be able to live with myself if I hurt them, Finn."

"I get it, babe. I do."

"That's why I've got to protect it . . . no matter what."

I let his words wash over me, and I understand. From what little I know about Carter and his family, I want to protect them too. I've never had something to fight for like Carter does. I've spent my entire life putting everyone else first and not getting anything in return, and Carter seems to willingly give everything to his family, but has so much unwavering love and support from them. I'm always letting my dad bulldoze me, control most aspects of my life, because I'm too weak to fight back. Mostly because I've never had a reason to. Until now.

Our attention returns to the movie. We easily picked *The Incredible Hulk* and argued over who our favorite Hulk actor is. Carter starts to doze off before we get halfway through, and when I realize it's already the early hours of the morning, I know we've got to get our asses in bed.

Even though I'm not ready to be away from him, even for sleep, I set our junk food on the coffee table to deal with in the morning and gently nudge Carter to get him to go to his room.

"Hey, we're gonna pay for this if we don't get some good sleep. Time for bed."

He's groggy as his eyes barely open, but he nods his head, standing and wobbling on his feet. I wrap my arm around his waist and walk his sleepy ass to the bedroom he's claimed, pulling back the sheets as he drops his gym shorts and gets into bed naked. His dark hair is such a contrast to the white sheets, his long, thick eyelashes fanning over his beautiful face. My heart aches for him, and I don't know how I've rapidly fallen for someone I've only had a handful of interactions with. All I know is that I have, and I would do anything to keep this feeling. I've got to face my dad as soon as we return to Washington and figure out why it's so important to him that I stay away from the Hayes family and Aspen Ridge. I don't want to ruin my career, but I don't want to lose a chance with Carter, either.

I cover him with the blanket, and just as I'm about to leave, his voice shatters the last layer of protection I was holding over my heart.

"Stay with me?"

Without a word, I climb into bed with him. We don't touch, there's no cuddling, but just feeling the heat emanating from his body, hearing as his breathing evens out as he falls into sleep after our long-ass day, is enough peace for me. I haven't slept next to another person before, and I never want to sleep away from Carter again.

carter

I WAKE UP FOR THE FIRST TIME IN MY LIFE WITH A warm body splayed across mine. It's a bit disorientating as my body slowly wakes from the best sleep of my life. My eyes squint as I open them, looking up at the white ceiling. Finn's leg is thrown over my hip, my dick laying hard against his thigh, his arm banded over my chest, head resting on my pectoral. The top of his hair is in my face, and I can't help but take a deep inhale, his calming leather and woodsy scent filling my lungs.

Hell. When was the last time I felt so relaxed? Lifting my arm around him, I lean into the moment, rubbing my fingertips up and down his spine. It's a comforting caress, both for him and me. Everything changed yesterday, and I'm refusing to give it any thought right now. I don't want to dissect it. Finn said to lean into it, and that's what I'm going to do for now. Fuck everything else pressing down on me, I just want to be right here right now, enjoying the incredible feeling this man brings me.

Finn doesn't stir, even though my heart is pounding behind my rib cage, right under his ear. Instead, I slowly doze back off to sleep, nothing in the world rushing me to get up right now.

Sometime later, wet warmth surrounds my cock, pulling me from a deep, restful sleep. The suction is tight, filthy slurping noises reaching my ears. My eyes crack open, looking down my body to find Finn laying between my legs, his mouth sucking my dick down like a champ. My hands reach for him instinctively, threading through the dark strands of his mussed hair, my hips taking over, thrusting into his greedy mouth.

"Fuck, that's so good, Finn. Damn, I love your mouth."

I hold his head in my hands, enjoying the warm suction he makes when his cheeks hollow out around me. It feels so damn good to wake up like this—something I've never experienced before. My body slowly trying to wake from sleep while blood rushes to my dick, my head foggy, but chasing an orgasm I'm not ready for.

Finn pops off, pushing my thighs and repositioning me the way he wants them.

"Pull your legs up for me, feet flat on the bed, spread 'em, lover."

I do as he says, my breath hitching as he sticks two fingers into his mouth, soaking them with his spit. He must see the panic on my face because his expression softens, that sultry, lust-filled gaze of his pulling back and instead giving me the comfort I'm clearly in need of.

"Will you trust me? I want to make you feel good, that's it. But, if you don't like anything I'm doing, just say stop and I will, no questions asked. There are plenty of ways for me to worship you, Carter, and it's not a hardship to figure out what you like and what you don't like."

It was exactly the kind of thing I needed to hear to let go of any reservations I've been holding onto. Last night, touching his cock for the first time about did me in. I've felt so guilty for not giving back to him what he's given to me but to touch his dick was admitting what this was. What I am. As confused as I am about it. But, at the end of the day, I couldn't hold back. I wanted to. I want to make him feel as good as he makes me. I couldn't continue to deny either one of us that.

I give him a nod of agreement, my lips turning up in a slow smile. "Show me what you got, Nash. I trust you."

His fingers move back to his mouth, soaking them with spit before he grabs my cock with his other hand, feeding it between his lips and sucking me down. He plays with me languidly, taking his time to suck on me, pleasure rolling through me in waves. And then his fingers are sliding over my taint, rubbing circles around my asshole. It feels foreign but his mouth is doing amazing things on my dick and my head's focus is split. All I know is that I don't want it to stop.

"How are you doing?"

I pant out my reply. "Don't stop."

Finn chuckles and returns to my throbbing dick, his fingers pressing more firmly against my hole.

"You're being such a good boy for me, I love you like this. I'm going to press in, okay? If you don't like it, just tell me to stop, and I will, but try to relax and enjoy it if you can."

"I want it, Finn. Let me feel it."

His wet finger breaches my tight hole, and I clench around him instinctively, but the sensation isn't bad, and he slowly starts to press further inside.

"Relax and let me in, lover. I'm gonna take such good care of you."

I do as he says, allowing my body to relax, letting go to him. His mouth returns to my dick, lapping at the precum leaking from my tip before sucking on the head, his talented tongue making me go crazy. His finger starts to move inside me, and fuck it feels damn good. There's a tightness, a slight burn, and the sensation is odd at first, like it shouldn't be there, but I'm relaxed, and that's helping. But I'm so turned on, I want more of it.

"Need more, Finn . . ."

"Fuck, yes. Give me a second, babe. We gotta do this slow so I don't hurt you."

I move Finn's head back down, but instead of taking my cock

into his perfect mouth, he licks down my shaft, sucking on my balls and then going lower.

"Ohh, fuck, yesss," I moan as my hips gyrate against his face. He laps at my sack, sucking each side into his mouth, rolling them around with his tongue. I'm suddenly so damn glad that I keep everything trimmed damn near bare down there as I spread my legs wider for him, totally lost to everything he's doing for me right now. Spit trickles down my taint, his fingers there to gather it up, and then there's firm pressure again as Finn adds a second finger to my ass. The burn is hotter this time as he stretches me, and I have to actively remind myself to relax.

"You're taking me so damn well. Fuck, if you could see what you look like right now. Legs spread wide, cock leaking, my fingers disappearing in your tight ass. You're a dream, Carter. A fucking dream."

Finn's praise washes over me as I relax into it. His fingers start to move, and I know exactly what he's looking for. My dick disappears into his mouth, swallowing me all the way back at the same time his fingers rub over a spot inside me that has my eyes rolling to the back of my head. Stars dance behind my eyelids as pleasure builds like I've never felt before. My hips buck wildly and wanton.

"Oh fuck uhng-gah-aah fuuuuck."

"There it is."

I come. Instantly. Filling his mouth without warning but I don't have time to feel like an asshole for it. He sucks hard, forcing my balls to empty into his throat. My moans are loud and unrestrained as the best orgasm of my life wrecks my body in the best way possible. Finn sucks me through it, continuing to rub that sweet spot inside me. I can't believe I've never let anyone do that to me before, not that anyone has tried. Just as I'm about to squirm away from him, he pops off, using his thumb to swipe at the cum leaking from the corner of his bruised lips while he slips his fingers from me.

"Holy fuck. Pretty sure you just drained my life force through my dick."

Finn's laugh reverberates through me as he cleans up my cock, lapping at it like he can't get enough, even though I just nearly drowned him with my cum.

"C'mere," I say, wanting to take care of him.

"No need."

My eyebrows arch in confusion but as he sits up, his cum is splattered on his abdomen, dick, and the sheets between my knees.

"Not even embarrassed by it. That was the hottest fucking thing ever and I want a repeat as soon as you'll let me. You enjoyed it?"

Now that the post-orgasm clarity has arrived, I wait for the shame, embarrassment, or panic to wash over me, but they don't come. My heart is still going crazy behind my ribs as Finn looks down at me, but I won't lie to him. Not after what he just did. Not after I fucking loved every minute of what he did to me.

"Yeah, I enjoyed it."

His face lights up with a satisfied smile that makes my insides feel warm, emotion that I've never felt before and can't quite place, overwhelming me. When did this turn into something other than whoring each other out for our own selfish gain? It doesn't feel like just bargaining anymore, it feels like a whole helluva lot more. That scares the shit out of me.

***

"Going for a run. Wanna join me?" I ask, even though I don't feel any stress weighing me down today. It's like I can suddenly breathe after being held underwater. I came here with one goal, even if I was just clinging to it because I couldn't face the real reason. I knew coming here would change everything, and it has. I think I'm falling for Finn. I barely recognize the feelings because I've never felt this way before. This morning, I walked in on him pouring coffee and making omelets for both of us, and even though it was such a simple thing to do for someone else, the breath was nearly knocked from my lungs.

Nothing has come easy to me; I've never found my place in anything that I do—except for fucking my way through partners —but with Finn? It feels right. It feels *whole*.

Finn stands up from his place on the couch, typing away on his laptop. "Let me get my shoes, I'll go with you."

Ten minutes later, we're both shirtless and hitting the pavement. Emberleigh is a quaint, tiny town that reminds me of home, but with coastal vibes. Whereas Aspen Ridge has more mountains, Emberleigh is a coastal paradise.

We find a steady pace that matches each other, and I follow Finn up the sidewalk a few blocks until he takes us through a parking lot, and then a sharp right turn onto a gravel path marked with a sign that reads *Tide's Edge*.

The trail winds around the coast with gorgeous scenic views that take my breath away. I haven't done a ton of traveling and I've never been to Maine until now, but it makes me want to do more. It's gorgeous.

The cloudless sky gives the brutal sun no filter as it beats down on my bare skin. It isn't overly harsh and the ocean breeze offers just enough relief from the heat to keep me moving, but I'm going to feel the effects of it later. The gravel crunches under our feet as we keep a pace with each other, finding a rhythm that works for both of us, like we've been running together our entire lives.

The vast Atlantic Ocean stretches out in front of us as we weave along the narrow path. The waves roll gently, white caps breaking on the shore, seals basking on rocks and soaking in the warmth the sun provides. Finn's breath matches my own—steady, deep, and calm—as if he gets just as much freedom from running as I do.

With every stride, any lingering tension starts to unravel. The noise of the world fades into the background, leaving just the two of us. If life was only this easy. I try not to let myself imagine what it would be like to run my normal route with Finn by my side in Aspen Ridge. What it would be like to have a partner that shared a hobby that was just as therapeutic for you as it is for them.

Instead, I focus on the trail in front of me, Finn's steady breathing to my right, the endless ocean and rocky coastline to my left.

"So how'd you find this place?" I ask him.

"Tide's Edge?"

"This hidden gem in middle-of-nowhere, Maine."

"Ahh. My grandmother. She has a little cottage in the cove, and we used to vacation here when I was little. I'll show it to you if you want. We can grab some lunch down there if you're up for it."

My heart stutters in my chest, not realizing that someone here does know him despite what he told me. A hard smack hits my stomach and I involuntarily hunch forward.

"We don't have to go. She's the sweetest old biddy you'll ever meet though."

"Thought no one knew us here, Nash? That another lie?"

"Don't do that, Carter. Yeah, my elderly grandmother lives a few miles down the road. But she hardly leaves her cottage, and she doesn't have a relationship with my parents. It's not like it would get out. But you don't have to come when I go see her. It's fine."

I look over at Finn, his face pink from exertion, sweat beading along his forehead and over his shoulders. His eyes are focused, but I don't miss the flash of disappointment in them. I wonder if he's ever taken someone home before to meet her. I get the impression she's important to him and suddenly feel like an asshole.

"Have you ever been in a relationship before?" I ask out of nowhere.

"Twice. It didn't work out, obviously."

Unwarranted jealousy rises inside me. Finn isn't mine. Of course someone would have had him before me. It's not normal that I'm turning twenty-six soon and have never had a relationship before. Or that I'm just learning I'm into men.

"What happened?" I ask, wanting to know, even if it hurts me to hear it.

"First one didn't last long. Maybe six months. We were in college. He was on the soccer team with me, didn't want to come out to the team, or anyone, really. Got tired of being his dirty little secret. But it was fine."

I get the sense that it wasn't, especially at the time. To be with someone and care about them but feel like you aren't worth them fighting for has got to hurt and leave even a bit of a mark on you.

"And the other one?"

"We were together for a year, I went away for a trip, came home to him in my bed with another man. I ended it."

Damn. The jealousy evaporates and is replaced by anger on Finn's behalf.

"You loved him?"

"Thought I did. Now I'm not so sure."

He leaves it at that, and it doesn't go unnoticed that he doesn't ask me in return. I guess I'm that transparent. I've already made it clear that I don't do relationships. My heart just isn't capable. *You're falling for Finn, though.* I don't want to give anyone that kind of power over me. No matter how lonely most nights are. How I crave having what my brothers have found. Fuck that. I never want to give someone else the power to completely wreck me. I'm fine on my own.

But can I walk away from Finn now?

I push the nagging thoughts in my head away as we hit the end of the trail, spitting us out in a little cove where he slows to a walk. Tourists meander, lost in their own individual worlds, paying little to no attention to the two large men in nothing but workout shorts. The area is exactly what he said it was: a small cove with water on each side, a walking bridge, some shops, docks, boats, and up the road, a few scattered cottages. It's quaint and exactly the kind of place I picture when I think of coastal Maine. Not that I've ever given Maine a thought from my small town on the other side of the country.

"She lives right up here. You can either go grab a drink across the street at Barnacle Billy's, or you could come with me."

Shit. Do I want to meet his grandmother? That seems like a big, unnecessary thing to do, but at the same time, I'm kind of rabid to meet someone who's known Finn his entire life, giving me just a little bit more of him.

"Yeah, I'm good, lead the way." Finn's face lights up, and I know I made the right decision. I want to do more to make him smile like that.

We walk side by side up an old, narrow sidewalk, passing some shops and eateries, the ocean right on the other side of the street. The place is so charming, and I know my parents would love visiting here someday. I realize now the lack of traveling I've done in my life, and after seeing a different part of the country, I want more of it.

"This one's hers," Finn says as he nods to the right. At the end of a rocky driveway sits a modest cottage, and not at all what I was expecting after staying in the Nash mega-mansion and driving in Finn's Lexus SUV. They are obviously swimming in money, and it clearly doesn't extend to her grandmother.

A freshly painted white picket fence surrounds a patio area laid with brick. A red door sits front and center of the little building with the words *Apple Tree Cottage* burned into it. The shutters are painted to match the red door and the brick of the patio, and it's so quaint it reminds me of a fairytale.

"Finn! My boy! Oh, my boy! What a nice surprise! I was wondering when you'd make it up here this summer." A shorter, elderly woman greets us from the doorway with the brightest, most welcoming smile I've ever seen. She gives my mom a run for her money. This is exactly the type of woman she'll be when she reaches this age. The woman has naturally frosted hair, and her face reflects that of a beautiful woman who has lived a full life with laughter and peace. I can't help but smile at her as I stand next to Finn awkwardly.

"Hey, Grammy."

"And who's your friend? He sure is a looker!"

Well, that's unexpected. She and Ms. Nettie would make great friends.

"He is, isn't he?"

"Oh, is he more than a friend? Finn, have you been hiding a boyfriend from me?" I nearly choke on my saliva as I look from Finn to his grandmother, waiting for him to explain. What the fuck is happening right now?

"No, no boyfriend, Grammy. Just a friend who needed a little escape."

"More like someone he blackmailed to take a trip with him," I say with a playful smile. Even if it isn't as bad as I thought it would be. *It's been the best trip of your life.* "I'm Carter Hayes, ma'am. It's nice to meet you."

Her eyes widen as she looks to Finn for a split second before schooling her features and returning her attention to me. What the fuck? Does she know who I am?

"Well, everyone's story starts somewhere! It's nice to meet you, Carter. You boys thirsty? I've got lemonade."

"We'd love some water, Grammy, please."

"Did he make you run, Carter? This boy has been running his entire life. If it wasn't soccer, it was running. Tried to get him to join a cross-country team once, but he needed the immediate competitiveness that soccer gave him. At least he was moving his body, I suppose."

Finn laughs a bit and looks at me like he's enjoying me getting to know a bit more about him. Maybe he's just happy to be here with his grandmother.

"What about you, Carter? You played any sports?"

"Yes, ma'am. I've also been running for as long as I can remember."

"Running away from trouble, I'm sure," Finn interjects, and I give him an eye roll.

"I'm also trained in boxing and mixed martial arts."

I love the look of surprise on Finn's face, so I raise my eyebrows at him in a challenge. My face must say it all because he gives me a sultry look back that has my skin heating. I'd like to show him a thing or two later. Especially if it ends in orgasms.

"What was this oaf like as a teenager?"

"Finn? Oh, he was the best. I've got sixteen grandkids, and while Finn isn't actually my grandson, he's the only one who calls me regularly. Always checkin' in on me and making sure I have everything I need. More than I can say about any of the other ones."

My head snaps to Finn in confusion.

"She's my great-aunt, technically. My dad's mom's sister, believe it or not. But, she's been a surrogate grandmother to me for as long as I can remember."

I want to know more here. Finn led me to believe that he doesn't have any supportive family, but this woman right here seems to love and adore him.

"Are you close to your family, Carter?"

"Yes, ma'am, I am. I have four siblings—three older brothers and a younger sister—and we're all a little too close for comfort some days."

"Must be nice to grow up with a big family. Your mom is happy?"

I tilt my head at her briefly, slightly taken aback by her specific question, but I move on quickly, chalking it up to her relating to a mother of a family."

"She is. I've never seen that woman go a day without a smile my dad has put on her face. It's us kids who've given her all her challenges," I tell her with a laugh. "I couldn't imagine raising five kids, but she did it. I think my dad keeping her so happy made it easier."

Finn's "grandmother" smiles at me and nods her head.

"I'm glad to hear it. A healthy relationship makes all the difference!"

We spent the next hour talking, Finn's grandmother giving me little bits of the sweet child he was. Finn is relaxed in the patio chair next to me, his laugh genuine, a smile constant on his gorgeous face. It's easy to imagine life with him, and that scares the shit out of me.

We walk back to Finn's, side by side, eating lobster rolls that we grabbed from a food stand on the water. I scarf down my first one in two big bites, bunching up the white paper and stuffing it into the bag before pulling out my second. Finn chuckles next to me as he pops the last bite of his into his mouth.

"What?" I ask, unwrapping my roll.

"You really like 'em, huh?"

"They're fucking good. I can see how someone wouldn't, though. Kind of slimy, but also chewy? Weird fucking texture, actually, now that I'm dissecting it," I laugh, taking another huge bite.

"So, your grandmother knows you're gay, then?"

"I mean, yes and no. I never actually came out to her, but she's put it together over the years, I guess." He shrugs.

"You know, I was getting the impression you didn't really have anyone in your corner, but she seems pretty amazing."

"Yeah, she is. Our relationship is a secret, though. My dad would . . ." His words cut off and I give him a moment before I decide this time I am going to push him more. I want to know what haunts him; I want him to open up more to me.

"Your dad would what, Finn?"

His shoulders deflate as he looks up at the pink and purple painted sky.

"He'd cut me off."

I stop in my tracks because that surprises me based on what I know about him so far. He doesn't seem like the type of person who would kiss his dad's ass just to have money or live his lavish lifestyle with his fancy-ass car and mega-mansion on the beach.

"Hey, I can see where your head just went and that's not what I mean. Believe it or not, Carter, I hate his money. I'm grateful for the things I have and the life I lead, but it's not the life I want for myself. I always imagined I'd live in a small town, where everyone knows everyone. I'd have a modest house that fits my needs perfectly, and I'd be able to travel and write. Writing is all I have that's mine, Carter. And my dad owns the biggest travel magazine in the country."

The pieces start to come together. "It's not the money. He'd take your joy from you."

Finn sighs and I reach out and grab his hand, threading our fingers together and pulling him down the road. He doesn't need to confirm what I already know. His dad's a controlling piece of shit.

Once we're back at the mega-mansion, I head straight for the shower while Finn pulls out his laptop and settles in on the couch. I strip out of my shorts and step under the spray before it has time to heat up, welcoming the sting of the cold, refreshing water and enjoying a moment of privacy to get my head straight. Mere hours with Finn feel like months. Being around him is as easy as breathing, it's practically effortless, there's no awkwardness in the silence or in conversation, and we both seem to anticipate the other's unspoken needs. I don't even have that type of relationship with my siblings, who have known me my entire life, and all things considered, we're extremely close.

Everything is different with Finn. The pull to him is so fucking strong, it's nearly impossible to fight. What is it about him that does it for me? I'm oddly not freaked out at all by the fact that he's a man, for the first time in my life, I'm feeling things that I thought were impossible. The past two days have been some of the best of my life, and I'm trying not to stress over the situation that we're going to face once we leave this little bubble. But inside these four walls? It's easy to forget all of it and let go with him. It surprises me how easy, actually. When I'm with Finn, he has a spell over me, and I somehow simultaneously lose myself completely and feel utterly whole at the same time. All reasonable thinking goes right out the damn window. All there is left is Griffin fucking Nash.

This isn't me at all, and that fear is still holding me hostage. What the hell am I even doing? I don't play house, hell, I've never had a sleepover before. I'm meticulous about fucking and bouncing—no strings attached, no feelings, no sleeping next to each other, and talking about our pasts. I'm feeling good in the moment, and after my post-orgasm clarity returns, I'm emotionless. I've never felt a goddamn thing before.

With Finn, I feel alive, and because of that, I don't recognize myself anymore. I don't recognize these feelings that are brought out in me by him. I know I'm falling for him. But that can't happen.

An image of Sawyer lying lifelessly on his bed, brokenhearted and dead on the inside, flashes behind my eyes, and my walls get a little thicker. I just need to get through the weekend, get the story for my family, and then figure everything else out after. Right? I need to keep my head in the game, I'm here for one reason and one reason only. The story. I can't keep getting lost in Griffin Nash.

After my shower, my foul mood doesn't simmer, my thoughts spiraling, on the verge of snapping. I throw on a pair of shorts and a plain pocket T-shirt, grabbing my phone and laptop from my backpack, and head to the enormous living room. I take a seat across from Finn on the sectional, putting my feet up on the ottoman, dropping my head back, and getting comfortable.

I see the quizzical look Finn shoots in my direction, probably wondering why the hell I chose to sit across from him when he'd want me next to him. Maybe because I'm trying to get space from you, jackass? I clearly can't control my feelings when you're next to me.

My phone buzzes in my hand as I'm pulling it out to check my emails and get some work done. Unlocking my phone, I'm not surprised to see it's my sibling group chat, since I haven't checked in since being here.

> Sawyer: Checking in on you
>
> Dallas: Yeah, how's it goin' Casanova?
> Clearing out that small town like you did ours?
>
> Sawyer: Don't knock anybody up on the East Coast, that'd make for a real shit situation

I internally cringe. No worry about accidental pregnancy happening over here on the other side of the country.

> Me: I'm alive. He hasn't murdered me in my sleep yet
>
> Sawyer: There he is. Fuckin' finally.
>
> Dallas: But have you murdered him?
>
> Liam: There's the real question
>
> Sawyer: No murder. No pregnancy. Just get on his good side and get the story to him
>
> Me: I've got it under control fuckers
>
> Sawyer: Just remember you're working and not playing
>
> Dallas: Yeah no dicking anyone down while you're there

Liam: I think we drove it into his skull before
he left. But a reminder is always good.

Sawyer: No fuckin' around. You're working.
Work means no play Casanova

Liam: What he said.

Dallas: No play time means no putting your
dick into anything but your hand.

Jesus Christ. That's seriously how they see me? I know how to handle business. Fuck this. Fuck everything. I chuck my phone into the far end of the couch harder than I should, their words digging way deeper than they normally do. I know they're just joking, and I've given them a reason to behave this way, but fuck. I'm doing the best I can, and I'm drowning myself in worry constantly to not fuck things up.

"What'd that phone do to you?"

"Nothing!" I snap.

Finn's head bops back like I smacked him, a flash of hurt passing over his face, and I instantly regret my tone. Even if he is the reason I'm in this impossible fucking position to begin with. He's the fucking reason I'm in this mess, for some fucked-up reason, he's set his sights on me and everything is just fucked.

If he had just left us alone and never reached out, I wouldn't be feeling this way. I wouldn't be across the country with him clouding my thoughts, muddling my emotions, and controlling everything I'm fucking doing. It's his goddamn fault I'm in this mess. Not knowing who the hell I am, not understanding why I'm feeling the way I do. When I don't want any of it. I didn't ask for any of this!

I stand abruptly, looking around for my running shoes. I need to move. The pressure in my chest is closing in, my veins turning to ice. Fucking shit. I hate this. Hate that everyone views me as just this fun-time playboy who's down for whatever. I've never given them a reason to think I can't handle my shit, handle the business.

But you're also giving them a thousand to think you don't take anything too seriously.

Damnit, I hate feeling so weak. I'm frantically searching for my running shoes, needing to get this energy out of me before I explode.

"Where the fuck are they?" I practically yell. My body feels like it's overheating, but my insides are cold, my head hazy, my heart racing at an erratic beat. Fuck, am I having a panic attack?

Finn grabs my arm, spinning me to face him, his other hand moving to my cheek. I can't help but flinch at his touch, but he doesn't waver. He stands strong in front of me, looking directly at my face through the lenses of his glasses. His voice is strong when he speaks again, calm and confident.

"Hey, hey. Look at me, Carter. Look. At. Me."

I lift my eyes to meet his as he looks over my face, trying to read me, trying to figure out the unknown enemy making me spiral. It's clear he reads the panic on my face, and that makes me feel worse. I don't want him to see this side of me. I should punch him. He's the fucking reason for all of this shit right now. But that would just make me feel worse. I don't want to hurt Finn, as much as all of this is his fault.

His crystal-blue eyes pierce my soul with their depth. I've never been looked at like Finn is looking at me right now. Like he would burn the world down just to make me feel better. Like I'm the center of his universe, and he's ready to combust with me if that's how it goes down. The panic starts to recede like a tide moving out to sea, replaced by the fire that only Finn has the match to ignite.

"Talk to me. I'm right here, and I'm not going anywhere. Just talk to me." His words are so sincere, no sign of a hidden agenda or lies. "Tell me what you need, and I'll do it. No questions. Let me help you."

I slam my mouth against his in a bruising kiss. Just like every other time I've been with Finn, the stress evaporates into thin air. My mind goes blank as my heart thumps hard against my rib cage. I'm lit up with something completely new, a feeling so good I want to wrap myself up in it. An inferno that I'll gladly burn up in.

"This what you need, lover?"

Yeah, this is exactly what I need.

finn

I KNEW TAKING CARTER TO MY GRANDMOTHER'S WAS A gamble. It was clear she had some questions, but thankfully, she didn't call me out while we were there. I've never taken someone to meet her before, and while she doesn't know that I'm gay, she's not stupid, either. But I knew the moment Carter said his full name, it clicked with her, and it makes me wonder how deep this goes with my dad if my grandmother recognized Carter's name. I wish I knew the history there, but my dad isn't very forthcoming about anything and my grandmother has made it clear not to bring him up to her.

Carter seemed fine when we got back to the house until his phone went off. I know the signs, one text from my dad is all it takes and I've turned into a raging asshole ready to pick fights and start fires with anyone and anything in my way. But Carter's reaction surprises me. He's anxious, on the verge of a panic attack. I fucking hate it.

He kisses me hard, and I meet him in the middle, taking everything he's giving me without hesitation and giving it right back in return.

"I want to fuck you," he hums against my neck as he sucks and nips at my skin. Chills scatter across my skin at the thought of

Carter inside me. I've thought about being balls deep inside his virgin ass more times than I can count. I know he's using me right now, but I'll give him whatever he needs to feel better.

"It's been a while . . ." I confess honestly.

"I'll take it easy on you. I *need* you, Finn."

Fuck. If I hadn't made up my mind before, I definitely have now. I've never been needed by anyone. I want Carter to need me. I want to be enough for him.

Carter pushes me against the wall, sinks down to his knees, and my brain nearly short-circuits. His fingers dip into the fabric of my shorts, pulling them down my thighs in one swift motion. My hard cock bobs free, slapping against my stomach. Fuck, is he really going to—

"Ohhh, fuuuuck. Caaarter."

His lips suction around the head of my cock and I nearly black out. His mouth is warm and wet, and just the fact that it's Carter is enough to blow my mind. I know I'm his first, and that makes everything a million times better.

"Yeah?" he asks hesitantly, uncertainty flickering in his eyes. I reach my hand down, pushing the dark strands of his hair out of his face.

"Yeah. So fucking good. Don't stop, I want to feel your mouth on me. Suck me hard."

"I don't know what I'm doing, if this sucks, at least I warned you."

"Carter, get out of your head for me. It's already the best BJ I've ever had. So fucking suck it. Make me feel good."

And boy does he suck it. Carter eagerly laps at my cock like it's his new favorite snack. He's uncoordinated, messy, and it's obvious he's never done this before, but everything he's doing feels amazing. What he lacks in finesse and skill, he more than makes up for in enthusiasm. It's clear he's trying to make me lose my mind. My balls are covered in saliva and Carter fondles them with his free hand while stroking me hard with the other, his cheeks hollowing out as he sucks on my head.

"Jesus Christ. Fuuuck. Just like that," I praise him as my hips start to drive into his mouth. I don't go easy on him, trusting that if it's too much, he'll tap out. My thrusts become frantic as I chase the feeling he's giving me.

"Don't you dare come, Finn. Not until I'm in your ass."

"Get me ready then, 'cause this feels too fucking good."

Carter doesn't waste any more time, sliding his wet fingers behind my balls as I spread my legs further to give him more access. And then his fingers are there, swirling and teasing around my asshole. I'm assuming he knows what he's doing and doesn't need me to guide him. He presses one finger in slowly, just to the first knuckle, and I can't help but wince. It's been a long damn time since anything was up there.

Knowing I need to relax, I focus on his wet tongue currently licking my dick like it's a popsicle. Before I know it, one finger becomes two, scissoring inside me and working me open. He doesn't search for my prostate, just focuses on stretching me out.

"I need you to take one more for me, relax. I fill my lungs with air, slowly releasing through my nose as Carter presses three fingers into my tight hole, twisting and fucking me with them.

"Mmm. I love you like this. At my mercy. Fuck, I can't wait to get inside you."

His words hit their mark, and I can't wait another moment longer.

"Fuck me, Hayes. I need it."

"Condom? Lube?"

"Fuck. Yeah, in my wallet."

Carter grabs the wallet from my discarded shorts and pulls out the condom and a lube packet. His mouth returns to mine, a mess of tongues, our hands gripping each other everywhere as we stumble to the closest bedroom, knocking into walls, the door bouncing open.

"Get your shorts off," I demand as Carter pushes me hard onto the bed. My hand moves to my cock, stroking it slowly as I watch Carter drop his shorts, his knees hitting the bed as he prowls closer to me. It's one of the hottest things I've ever seen. This gorgeous man, who's never had a sexual experience with another guy before, is crawling up the bed to fuck me.

Carter's blue eyes are trained on mine as my free hand reaches up to remove my glasses.

"Don't you dare." His voice is stern, but so damn sultry smooth, making my dick leak precum, chills scattering across my skin. "The glasses stay."

A smile lifts at my lips but quickly evaporates as he kisses the tip of my dick, taking his time to kiss up my body. My heart bangs hard against my rib cage, and I almost can't believe this is happening. Carter sits on his knees between my legs and quickly sheaths himself with the condom, adding more lube on top of it. His sinewed muscles are taut, straining as he readies himself. Coating two of his fingers with some of the lube, he makes eye contact with me, and then his hands are on me again. The gel is cold as he presses two fingers into my ass, lubing me up and stretching me just a bit more, making me moan, gyrating my ass against him.

"You ready?"

"Yeah, fill me, lover."

Carter lines up his cock with my ass, my legs spread wide, his hand on my hip as I suck in a deep breath. I bear down just as he starts to press himself inside me, slipping the head through my tight rim. The burn is real, and I know I could have benefited from a bit more prep. But I want him so much it hurts, and the sting is worth it. It makes it real.

Carter starts to press in slowly, and I take a deep breath, relaxing my body and adjusting to the sensation.

"Fuck, you're so tight, Finn. So. Fucking. Tight. I'm gonna come in this ass so hard."

Just to fuck with him, I squeeze hard around his big girth, making him groan. He slaps the side of my ass, and I can't help but laugh.

"Damnit, I don't want this to end too soon. Let me all the way in; relax for me."

After a minute, Carter finally bottoms out, filling me completely. He's so fucking deep, the bite of pain still there, but I want this so bad.

"You good?" he asks me, concern lacing his tone.

"Mmm. Yeah, fuck me. Fuck me hard."

Carter pulls out, dragging the head of his dick over my prostate and making me see stars. My legs shake as he pushes on my thighs, pressing them back toward my chest. Fuck, I forgot how intense this is. He drives back in hard, nearly knocking the wind from my lungs.

"Oh, fuck yes. Jesus Christ, your ass, Finn. So goddamn good."

He's not wrong, it feels phenomenal. My body is like putty in his hands as he drills his dick inside me over and over, holding me in place as I accept each and every one of his powerful thrusts.

Carter falls over me, his chest collapsing on mine, and it feels so good to have him flush with me, skin on skin. I grip him hard, my hands pulling him impossibly close, as I seek out his mouth. He meets me in the middle, tongue slipping behind my lips in a kiss so fucking good it seers.

"I need to come," I practically beg.

"Stroke it. Get yourself there. You're gonna come with me as I fill you up."

"Oh, fuck."

Carter lifts slightly, giving me just enough room to grab my dick, stroking it hard with each of his thrusts.

"Just like that. Look at you, Finn, so hard for me. You like me filling your ass?"

"Yes! Don't stop."

His hands are all over me, and it's such a contrast to the man I arrived here with. Who'd take every bit I offered him but wouldn't give anything in return. Now, he's inside my body, edging me closer and closer to a life-changing orgasm. How can so much change in forty-eight hours?

"I'm never gonna get enough. You feel so damn good, baby."

Baby.

It's all too much. His dirty mouth, the press of his sweaty, naked body against mine, his hands roaming over every inch of my skin. My orgasm comes on fast and hard, my balls drawing up close to my body, my dick thickening, my spine tingling.

"Fuck, Carter, fuck! I'm coming!" I moan.

"That's it, baby. Fuck, look at you, making a mess like such a good boy."

My entire body shakes as cum spills from my cock in thick ropes. Carter's hand moves to my abdomen, dragging his fingers through my mess before lifting it to his mouth. He comes a moment later on a long, drawn-out groan while he sucks my cum off his fingers.

"Fuuuuuck."

His cock throbs in my ass as he spills inside me, filling the condom with his cum. By some miracle, Carter manages to hold himself back when he collapses on top of me, his weight pressing me into the mattress. With him still deep inside me, his hands grab my face, cradling it, my arms wrapping around his body in return. My heart is pounding, a humming sound buzzing between my ears as worry starts to claw at my chest. It's the most vulnerable I've been in years, and it scares the shit out of me.

"Please don't freak out. I can't—I can't handle it if you freak out right now," I whisper, my words barely audible.

"I won't," he whispers back, his lips brushing against mine. "Thank you."

"I've never been thanked after sex before."

"You know what I mean. I needed an outlet and you didn't hesitate to give it to me. This . . . ugh. This is different, Finn. I don't want you to think I just used you. I wanted this. Wanted you. Thank you for giving yourself to me like this."

His words find their home deep within my heart, and I didn't realize how badly I needed to hear them. I let myself relax in his arms, hoping like hell he means it.

"What do you wanna watch? I'm in the mood for Marvel."

"Hell yes. I'm good with that. You good with *Spiderman*?"

Carter looks at me like I have ten heads, and I don't understand. It's not too much of a stretch that two men in their mid-twenties like *Spiderman*, especially since we both seem to enjoy Marvel. But . . .

"*Spiderman's* my favorite."

Okay, maybe that's a coincidence.

"Mine too. Which one? I swear I'll punch you in the nuts if you say the wrong one."

Carter cups his package with both hands and braces himself for an attack.

"Are you serious? Tom Holland is the best. Go fuck yourself if you think differently."

"What?" I yell in shock. "Tobey Maguire put *Spiderman* on the map for cinema. You say *Spiderman*, people picture Tobey Maguire. And if they don't, they're either not true fans or too young to know any better."

"I don't know if I can stay here with you for a minute longer. Tom Holland is a king."

"I'd like to see you try to leave, dumbass. I'll chain you to the bed."

His brows wiggle at me in a challenge.

"Can we agree that Andrew Garfield comes last, then?"

"Agree."

"Rock, paper, scissors for which one we watch?"

"Deal."

Carter and I throw our fists out, chanting as we go. Carter won with scissors to my paper.

"Suck it! Tom Holland it is!"

"No fuckin' way! Best outta three, are you nuts?"

"Fine. You're such a whine-ass."

We throw our fists for another round. I win with paper covering his rock.

"Alright, may the best man win, Hayes."

"Eat shit, Nash."

"Rock. Paper. Scissors. Shoot."

Carter slams his closed fist over my two outstretched fingers, winning the match. I groan loudly, dropping my head back to look at the ceiling.

"Hope you're ready to enjoy a night with my boy. Better get comfortable!"

I grab Carter by the arms, pulling him into my space, situating us so that his back is leaning against my chest, his ass between my legs as we stretch out on the immense sofa. His deep sigh is all the reassurance I need that it was the right move.

He puts on *Spiderman 2002* with Tobey Maguire without saying a word, putting a huge smile on my face that I don't need to hide. I want to talk to him about his texts, about what upset him and why, but I don't want to ruin what we've created right now. So I just leave it open-ended without pressing too hard.

Nuzzling into his neck, I keep my voice low, just letting him know he has someone if he needs, trying so hard for it not to come out as a plea. I desperately want to be there for him, want to take care of him the way I wish someone would take care of me. "If you want to talk about it, I'm here, judgment-free."

Time seems to freeze, suspending us, and with every passing moment, I wonder if he'll talk to me at all. Just when I've accepted that he isn't ready to open up on a deeper level to me, his voice cuts through the thoughts in my head.

"I feel like an asshole for feeling the way I do, but I'm just lost and sometimes the pressure gets to be too much. Everyone sees me as one way, but like I said before, it's not really me, and sometimes I just want to be the mess and have it be okay. I've manufactured this version of myself, and it's not one I'm proud of. My brothers all have their shit together, and most days, they don't think I do."

"I know you love your family, but who cares what they think?"

Kettle, meet pot.

"I do. I love them so much, and they're good people, Finn. I just want them to look at me like I'm not this fuck-off playboy guy. I've never slacked on anything when it comes to my job, and yet they still berate me that I'm out here fucking around instead of working."

"Why do they think you're here?" I can't believe I haven't thought to ask him what he told his family. I've been so consumed with only Carter, with getting him alone, that I didn't take anything else into account.

"Told them the truth, that it was the only way you'd write the article. That it was the only time you had free."

Okay, so not too far off base.

"It's never too late to reinvent yourself. You're never too old to start over, never too old to try something new, or to say this no longer brings me joy, I'm moving on. Life is short. Do you want to live it giving your family a fake version of yourself because you're scared of burdening them with being human?"

Carter looks up at me from where he rests on my chest like I've grown two heads, but I know my words ring true. He doesn't say anything else, but I can tell they affected him. I hope he takes the advice that's so easily and freely given. I wish it wasn't so hard for me to take my own.

At some point during the movie, Carter's shirt has ridden up, my fingers toying with the bare skin, rubbing soft circles and loving the pressure of his body against mine.

"I can feel your hard dick in my back, Nash."

"If you weren't such a tease, Hayes, I'd be able to stay flaccid for more than five minutes."

"I can't help you with that. Pretty sure my dick is raw and my balls are empty from how much we've fucked around this weekend."

"I can fix that for you."

"Watch the movie, Finn."

"Yes, sir."

Tonight, it's not even a question of where we'll sleep. Carter climbs into bed with only his boxer briefs on, and I slip in behind him, his back to my chest, our limbs twined together, my arm wrapped around his waist.

"I've never slept next to anyone before you," Carter whispers the admission, barely audible over the white noise from his phone, but I hear him clear as day.

"Me neither."

The next day, Carter and I wake up slowly, something I don't do often, but am really enjoying the pace of. I make us a breakfast of scrambled eggs and toast, and Carter pours us both coffees, leaving mine black and pouring way too much milk and sugar into his own.

"You up for the beach today?" I ask him, wanting to get his ass out in the sun and into the ocean.

"Hell yeah. You have surfing here in Maine?"

I give him a little laugh. "Yeah. Yeah, we got surfing here in Maine."

Our entire morning is very domestic, but neither of us makes comments, just move around each other like two people who've lived with each other for years rather than days. We clean up from breakfast and then head to our bedrooms. We each change into our swim shorts, pull the surfboards and some beach supplies from the mud room, and Carter helps me strap everything down before we hit the road.

We drive the Jeep with the windows down, Carter's arm resting on the windowsill, my hand itching to hold his, but not wanting to make the move. I take him to a three-mile stretch of beach on the coast of Emberleigh that has prime surfing. As we take our spot on the beach, I look out at a group of people who are already out in the ocean, and the waves look perfect. It's a hot one today, and I spray myself down with sunscreen and toss Carter the bottle once I'm done with it.

"What? Not gonna lotion me up, Nash? What gives?"

"C'mere, my baby, daddy'll take care of his boy," I coo, my arms outstretched reaching for him.

He barks out a loud laugh, batting my hands away. "Fuck off with that shit!"

I laugh with him as I pick up my board.

"Race you, Hayes?"

"Get ready to eat shit, Nash. Winner gets a blow job."

"Deal." Knowing this is not a bet I'm losing today, I shove him in the chest and take off.

"You dirty fucking cheat!"

My feet slap the water's edge as Carter's palm connects with my back, giving me a hard shove and knocking me off balance. I catch him tossing the surfboard down and fall on top of it, pushing under a wave as I follow him into the ocean, laughing. We paddle out next to each other until we take a seat and wait for the perfect ride.

"I won, so don't even try to get out of it," I tell him with a smile.

"Yeah, 'cause you're a cheat. I should have known better by now." He says the words, but there's no grit behind them; he's being playful back, and my heart swells.

"Damn right. Anything to get you."

"That so?"

I splash water in his direction, spraying his face with mist. "Yeah, it is."

We spend the next few hours surfing, and to my surprise, Carter is actually really good. As I watch him ride his last wave, swim to shore, and walk up the beach to our spot, I realize I haven't had this much fun in years—maybe longer—and I don't want this to ever end. I'm prepared to give up everything for a chance with Carter. I need to tell him how I feel, come clean about everything, and make a plan for returning to Washington to take on my dad. I can do this. Carter's worth it all.

After riding my last wave of the day, I join Carter on the beach, collapsing on the towel he's laid out next to him as he pushes a sports drink into my hand.

"Thanks."

"You weren't too bad out there."

"Is that a compliment? What have you done with Carter Hayes?" I mock gasp.

"Oh, shut up. Take it or leave it, you may not get another one."

"Oh, I know I will. You dish out praise and compliments like your life depends on it when your cock is down my throat." Carter chokes on his drink, which makes me laugh. He leans into my space to smack me, but I grab his wrist before he can make contact, pulling him hard into me. I'm lying on my back, Carter lying next to me, resting on his elbow and hovering slightly above me. I look up at him as his smile fades away, his expression morphing as his eyes become heavily lidded, lust taking over.

"You're so beautiful," I whisper as I brush the dark, wet strands of his hair out of his face. "I'm so obsessed with you."

The corner of his lip lifts on the left side, just enough to tell me he liked my words. I don't expect any more, but he surprises me as he leans in and drops a chaste kiss against the corner of my lips.

"What was that thing you did the night after the beach?"

"What thing?" I play innocent, even though I know exactly what he's referring to. It was hot as fuck and something I've always wanted to try.

"By the stairs, when you put our dicks together and jerked us off like a twisted mix of a Chinese finger trap and a water wiggler."

I can't help it, I burst out laughing. A deep belly roll laugh that I haven't felt in years.

"Goddamn, what a visual you just gave me."

"It's true! What the hell was that man?"

"Docking. You liked it?"

"I want to do it again."

"That good, huh?"

"You blew my mind."

I roll closer to him so that we're blocked from anyone seeing anything inappropriate, grabbing his dick quickly through his pants and finding him already hard.

"You want it, lover? Want me to sheath your dick while I jerk us until we both blow?"

Carter's breathing picks up, and I love how responsive he is to me. He leans in, nipping at my bottom lip, making me hiss.

"Let's get you home then, and I'll take care of us."

I'm on cloud nine as Carter and I put the beach stuff away. I haven't had this much fun in so long, and I've never been able to be so openly affectionate with another person. Carter is still figuring out who he is and understanding his sexuality, but he's surprisingly open to everything we've done.

"I'm going to go make a phone call and check on things before I jump in the shower. Movie night and burgers?" he asks.

"Sounds good to me. I'll go take a quick shower and order us some food."

Carter heads to the other bedroom for some privacy, and I head to mine with a smile on my face.

Walking into my bedroom, I have to do a quick double-take to understand the sight in front of me. Bleach blonde hair flows across one of the pillows, her face buried in her arm, naked body on full display from the back, a plump ass completely bare right in front of me.

"What the fuck?" I practically snarl. The woman sits up, grabbing the sheet and holding it to her full breasts, confirming what I already suspected.

"Lexi," I gasp. My heart stops and for a split moment, I'm frozen to my spot, unable to comprehend what the hell is happening. "Get dressed! What are you doing here?"

"I'm here for you. You're on vacation, I wanted to surprise you."

This reeks of my father. That fucking bastard will stop at nothing to get me to do exactly what he wants. Does he really think trying to force a woman on me is going to make me any less gay? Make me the dutiful son that he wants so badly?

"You can't be here, Lexi. Get dressed, now, and you need to leave! Quickly!"

"Griffin, you can't be serious. I flew five hours to be here with you, let's enjoy our time. Your dad said we could even extend the trip."

"There is no 'we,' Lexi. Now get out!" I'm in full panic mode now, knowing Carter could be done at any moment, grabbing the baby blue dress that's lying on the armchair and throwing it at her. She pulls it over her head, finally covering up her naked body, and then slips from the bed.

"We could be great together, Griffin. Why won't you give us a chance?"

"Because I'm gay, Lexi! I'm fucking gay. I'm into men and only men. A life with me would be miserable for both of us and not something that was ever in the cards."

"Surely that's not true," she says as she walks up to me, dragging her nails down my bare chest. I'm on the verge of yelling, of pushing her back a step, but Carter's voice breaks through like an icepick to my heart.

"What the fuck is going on here? Who is this?"

"Hi! I'm Lexi, Griffin's girlfriend." My head spins, a hot flash washing over me, and I sway slightly on my feet. Carter's head whips in my direction so fast that it probably hurts, his eyebrows shooting up, a quick flash of pain crossing his face before his stony walls are slammed back down in place, fracturing my heart in the process.

"Girlfriend?" he repeats, eerily calm, more inquisitive than alarmed. The transition of his emotion is subtle, but I caught it—because I know him. I anticipate a panic attack rising, but it's the complete opposite. Like he's broken, empty.

"She is not my girlfriend. I can explain. Give me a minute, and I'll explain everything."

"Well, hopefully fiancé, but we're taking things slow." Holy fuck, my dad had to find the one bat shit crazy broad in Washington State to sic on me. Carter just nods his head in slow motion, retreating and taking my heart with him. I have to get to him, I have to explain.

"Lexi, we aren't anything. I just told you I was gay, you need to leave, now!" My fingers grip around her dainty wrists just tight enough that I have her attention but not enough to come close to causing her pain. I grab her purse off the dresser and push it into her chest. "You're leaving. Go back to the airport, call your dad, and go the hell home."

"You're actually serious."

"Deadly. I'm sorry, I don't know what you've been told, but we were never going to be a thing. I've been polite, I've tolerated family dinners, but this was never going to be anything more than two people being friendly."

"Wow." It seems as dense as she is that it's finally sinking in. She rips her wrist from my hand, and I release her immediately as she storms outside. By the time the slam of the front door echoes through the house, Carter has retreated to his bedroom. I jog down the hallway to get to him, finding him packing.

"Carter . . . can we talk?"

"No."

"Wh—" I clear my throat of the emotion currently clogging it, making my speech come out strangled. "Where are you going?" I try to hold back the tears that are threatening to spill over, stinging my eyes. He's really not going to let me explain? I would never do something like this. I know how it feels to find someone you care about screwing around behind your back, and I can imagine what's going through his head right now. But none of it is correct.

"Home."

"Please stay."

"Can't."

He continues to shove his clothes into his bag, wrapping up his computer and phone chargers, throwing an Aspen Ridge Distillery sweatshirt over his head, and covering the torso that I'm well acquainted with.

"For fuck's sake, Carter, will you give me more than these one-word answers?"

"No."

"Can I explain? *Please.*"

"No."

Fuck this. Reaching for his bag, I rip it off the bed and throw it into the closet, forcing him to give me a reaction other than borderline empty. He's withdrawing into himself, and I wait for the signs of an oncoming panic attack, but they don't seem to be there. Instead, he's dejected, almost vacant. I don't know what's worse.

"Look at me." My shoulders slump as his jaw ticks back and forth, his fists clenching at his sides, but he doesn't make eye contact. "*Please,*" I beg, my voice thick with emotion I'm not bothering with hiding.

He finally lifts his eyes from the spot across the room he's been focused on, his beautiful blues connecting with mine. His face is drained of color, eyes that have been so full of life and happiness the last few days are now hollow and lost. He seriously jumped to the worst-case scenario and isn't going to let me explain. How can I even push to explain when he's already made up his mind about me?

Carter remains unresponsive, having disconnected himself

from everything we shared over the weekend, everything that's between us. He's going to bury down everything he feels at the first sign of turmoil. Once we return to Washington, we've got a whole helluva lot more than this to face, and I stupidly thought that I was enough that we would face it together.

The silence that stretches between us is oppressive, almost suffocating, and I find myself at a loss for words.

"Okay," I say solemnly, accepting defeat. Carter's eyes flash with surprise, and then he nods his head a few times as I step out of the room. I've been fighting for love and acceptance my entire life. I can't do it anymore.

CHAPTER 12

finn

THE TEXT COMES WELL INTO THE EVENING, AND BASED on how I left things with Lexi, I knew it wouldn't be long before he found out what happened in Maine. I know he's the reason that she showed up there.

Dad: My Western office. 7am sharp.

On autopilot, I shower, shave, and put on a pair of khaki slacks with a navy button-up shirt. After styling my hair and putting on my glasses, I grab my things, leaving behind my laptop since I know I'll be returning after this meeting, and make the thirty-minute drive into work.

My dad is already in his office when I arrive, the tension in the air thick with disappointment, his anger palpable even through the door. His secretary gives me a look that says I'm deserving of everything coming. Pretty sure she's been fucking him the last few months, but I wouldn't call her out on it. If she wants to bed Satan, that's her prerogative. I knock twice on his door before opening it, not waiting for him to invite me inside, as is the normal etiquette he expects.

To no one's surprise, he's sitting at his desk, a cigar in his mouth, even though it's barely seven in the morning. His hairline is receding, the once-chocolate-brown, lush hair now thinner and dusted with grey. His beard is full, his cheekbones and jaw strong like mine. He's still handsome, even in his fifties. I'm the spitting image of him, having only gotten my mom's blue eyes. I can see my future in front of me, sitting at a desk, angry at the goddamn world because I'm chasing something that I'll never get. His eyes rake over me like claws, making my skin crawl. He truly is disgusted by me, I'm that much of a disappointment in his eyes. Suddenly, nothing in the world is worth having to deal with him anymore. Not after he ruined the single best thing I've ever had. Even if Carter and I didn't have the greatest start, I know it was real. It is real. The past few days changed everything for both of us.

"You want to explain to me why you're such a fucking idiot? I spent all evening trying to come up with a reason why MY son was shacked up with Carter Hayes and why Lexi had to fly back to Washington in tears because you kicked her out on the streets! The fucking streets, Griffin! Thomas and I have been in business together for two decades! Her father is livid, and I have to make amends."

"I don't have anything to say."

"No, that's not good enough. I want to know why the fuck that scum was in my goddamn house with my son!"

"Dad, I'm almost thirty years old, it's none of your business what I was doing." I don't know where the sudden courage comes from to talk back to him, but I feel so depleted that fear has taken the back burner for a change.

"Are you fucking him? Jesus Christ, Griffin, I knew you were pathetic, but to stoop this low? You're a fucking disgrace! You disgust me!"

"I'm in love with him." My father's face pales. The red of the anger slowly fades away and is replaced with an ashy grey. I didn't mean to say the words, but they came tumbling out of my mouth. They aren't wrong, though. I think I knew I loved him from the moment I saw him, and then I gradually fell in love with him more and more through every interaction.

"I don't know what is worse, Griffin. The fact that it's a man or that it's a Hayes."

"Why do you hate them so much?"

"Because he took everything from me!" he screams, his voice echoing off the walls of the office and piercing my ears.

"Who?"

My dad moves around his desk, and I brace for whatever is coming. He grabs a fistful of my shirt and jerks my body twice, my hands reaching up to clasp around his wrists.

"You're going to get your fucking shit together or I'm done with you. So help me, I will cut you off and leave you with nothing but the clothes on your pathetic back. You're going to apologize—no, grovel—to Lexi, and you're never going to see that piece of shit ever again. Do you understand me, Griffin?"

His breath smells of stale cigar, and I try not to dry heave as he shouts the words in my face. When I don't say anything, he shoves me harder than he ever has before. I'm so caught off guard that I stumble backward, grabbing at the wall to brace myself from falling right on my ass. My dad may be an emotionally abusive asshole, but he's never hit me. This has been the closest. I'm not scared of him, but I am pissed. Anger courses through me at an alarming rate. I hate this man. My own father.

"Do you understand?" he screams again, his voice so loud I know the rest of the office can hear him.

"What aren't you telling me? Help me understand!"

"It's none of your fucking business, Griffin. I'm your father, and you should have loyalty to your family above all else. I have expected respect and obedience from you, and you seem to fail at every turn. Fucking fix this or I'll make you regret it."

Knowing that his threat will ring true if I don't figure something out, and fast, I nod my head in agreement before following it up with words. "Yeah, Dad. I'll fix it."

"Get the fuck out of my office. I can't stand to look at you any longer, you pathetic mess."

With that, I leave my father's office to find his receptionist pursing her lips in a smirk. I roll my eyes and walk out of his office with my head held high and shoulders back. I'm not going to let him embarrass me. He's the one who should be embarrassed about how he treats his own son. I've always worked hard to make him proud. I've always done everything he's asked for. He will never be happy, nothing will ever be good enough. But I put up with it time and time again because I don't have anything other than this. My career is everything. *Until Carter.*

Not wanting to spend a moment longer than I have to here, I take a deep breath as I push open the large glass doors, inhaling the fresh air. Once I'm in my car, feeling more alone than I ever have before, I know I need to talk to Carter. It's all I want right now. Taking a chance, I pull out my phone and send off a text, not giving a shit how desperate I sound.

> Me: Please give me a chance to explain.

"C'mon, Carter, please answer me." I bounce my leg anxiously, wishing like hell he would just let me explain everything. Something I should have done the moment I realized he was giving in to what we have. Miscommunication is the death of everything, but fear held me back from doing what was right by telling him when I had the opportunity. When he doesn't respond, I send another one.

Me: I miss you

I don't know how long I stare at the screen, willing him to reply, even if he tells me to fuck off, I just want to see those three little dots appear. But they never come.

I spend the next three days sleeping on and off, drinking too much whiskey, sick to my stomach, and not finding clarity. My phone goes off, and I'm desperate enough to hear from Carter that I snatch it off the coffee table with shaky fingers. My body deflates when I see that it's from Trey.

Trey: Dude this is not okay. Don't ice me out

Trey: I'll come by and you don't want that

Me: I don't want company

Trey: Well look who it is. Glad to know you're alive

Me: You're a shit friend if you thought I was dead and you're texting me instead of coming by

Trey: Fuck off. I'm coming by

Me: No. I changed the locks

Trey: The fuck you did asshole

Me: I'm fine man. I just want some quiet. I'll check back in later

I toss my phone back onto the table, take more than a few long pulls from the whiskey bottle, and throw my arm over my eyes. I doze off at some point and wake to the telltale click of the lock of my front door. Hard footfalls bring the intruder closer and closer, but I don't bother moving, too drunk to give a shit, and hoping maybe he'll just leave. Or better yet, put me out of my misery.

"God damn, it reeks like old cheese and tuna that's been left to bake in the sun."

"Fuuuck you, no it doesn't," I mumble, my words slurred.

"This is worse than I thought it would be. Shit, haven't seen you like this before, not even after Nick."

"Why are you here, Trey?"

"Cause I'm in too deep, asshole. You're my best friend, and I'm not gonna let you drown yourself in alcohol and sorrows. You're better than that. Plus, you know too much, and training a new best friend would take too long, so I've gotta keep you alive."

"Fuck off!"

"Damn, how much have you been drinking? Your liver is not going to be happy with you. C'mon, time to get up."

I groan as Trey grabs my shoulders to forcibly sit me up on the couch, the room swaying and spinning like a motherfucker.

"If you puke on me, we're gonna have issues. I'm making you some coffee, then your ass is getting in the shower, 'cause I wasn't lying, your ass reeks dude."

"Just leave. You've got better things to do than deal with my shit."

"The fuck I do. I don't know what your dad said this time, but it's not true, Finn. You're deserving of love, you're deserving of friendship, you're the best kind of man there is out there, you were just born to shit parents, and you don't know how to break the cycle. Do you hear me?"

His words open up the dam that I've been holding back, the tears flowing freely from my eyes. I've spent so long trying to be good enough for everyone around me, and the emotional and mental damage inflicted by my dad is to blame.

"Shit, man, it's gonna be okay." Trey sits next to me, wrapping his arm around my shoulder and pulling me into him while I cry it out. "Let's get you sobered up and then we're gonna get shit figured out. This isn't how your story ends, bro." My best friend holds me while I lean onto his shoulder, sobbing and wishing like hell I could get through this. I'm lucky to have him in my life—at least I've got this.

After Trey forces some coffee down my throat, he helps my still half-drunk ass to the shower and pushes me in with the cold water streaming down on me. I collapse on the stone bench and let the water beat down on me for a while before Trey comes back to check on me.

"You still breathing?"

"Yep."

"Good. Making sure you didn't drown while I was cleaning up the pigsty out there. Wash, or I'll do it for you."

"Fuck off," I grumble with a half-smile even though he can't see me through the frosted door. But I don't dare test his patience more than I already have, so I stand and reach for my soap.

"Thatta boy. I'll be back, and I expect you to smell more human and less wet dog."

I flip him off, but I get to work on scrubbing the last three days off of me. Pretty sure the alcohol is leaching from my pores at this point, and I know he's right, this isn't a good look, nor is it me. This isn't how I handle stress.

After I've finished up business in the shower, I've sobered up enough to walk on my own and think a little more clearly, but I'm exhausted. I dry off quickly, pulling on a pair of joggers and a T-shirt, and pad through the house to find Trey in my living room with my laptop open.

"Thanks."

"Never have to thank me. You'd do the same for me, brother."

In a heartbeat.

I sit down next to him and pull the fleece throw blanket over my lap.

"Aww, look at the little baby!" Trey coos, giving me shit for feeling like ass and being vulnerable.

"You can leave now."

"Nope. You're stuck with me until we figure this shit out."

"What are you looking at?"

"The article you started on the distillery. It's damn good."

"I've been researching them for a few months, and from what little I managed to pull from Carter—they're a damn good family. I don't get my dad's problem. Have you heard anything?"

"Well, I did a little digging because I thought this entire thing was fucked from the beginning. Turns out your dad and Carter's parents went to college together at UDub."

My eyes must bug out of my head because Trey laughs nervously. "Yeah, that was my reaction, too."

"So we knew there was history, and it probably started there. Find anything else?"

"Not yet, but I'm still digging. Carter give you any details about his parents?"

"Not really, no. They seem like a fairytale couple, though, super in love and great parents."

"Well, I'm not giving up."

"I think I need to pay my dad another visit. Did he return to the underworld?"

"I wish. But he is back at the Seattle office. You gonna take a trip?"

"Yeah, maybe if I press again, he'll give me a little more. I need to understand what the hell is going on here."

"You ready to tell me what happened in Emberleigh?"

"I'm in love with him."

"Well, no shit. But does he feel the same?"

I think about every interaction I've had with Carter over the last month, how neither of us could fight the pull to each other, his smile when he laid next to me and we shared air, the comfort we found in each other's presence, how easily our bodies came together.

"Yeah, he does; he just hasn't accepted it yet."

"Has he been with men before or you his first?"

"Definitely his first," I reply with a smirk.

"You worried about that?"

"I'm more worried about him never admitting to being in love with me than being enough for him."

"Want me to smack him? Sometimes a good throat punch is all someone needs to remove their head from their ass."

"Nah, I'll do it if he needs. He's a stubborn asshole, but I'm not ready to give up on him. I thought I loved Nick and I was so fucking wrong. What I feel for Carter was instant, life-changing."

"Love at first sight shit?"

"A hundred percent."

"It's gonna work out, brother. I got your back, and we'll get through it."

We have to. There's no other option.

***

The next day, I make the three-hour drive into Seattle to the Northwest Explorer's main offices, ready to talk to my dad again and see if we could have a civilized conversation. I didn't give him a heads-up that I was coming, and hopefully, if I act like I'm going to be compliant, he'll be open to being a little more transparent with me.

After parking my car in the parking garage, I pull out my phone to send Carter a text. I've been messaging him once a day for the last few days. I don't want to be pushy, but I want him to know that what we had was real, and hopefully he'll be open to talking to me and giving me a chance to explain. As much as I was heartbroken that he wouldn't give me a chance to do that at the moment, I have to put myself in his shoes as well and attempt to be understanding of how he reacted.

The situation we found ourselves in wasn't exactly conducive to transparency from either of us. Based on our brief history, he's been programmed not to trust anything I say. But I have to fix that. We've been speaking with our bodies for long enough, and I hope that with time, he'll let me use my words.

> Me: I hope you're ok. I can't stop thinking about you.

Pocketing my phone, I take a deep breath and head into the office, nodding to security and taking the elevator to the top floor, where my father's office takes up the entirety of it. All the worker bees are on the floors below. Cynthia, the evil minion receptionist, gives me a look that would strike lesser men down, but I just return it with a cheeky smile.

"Good morning, Cynthia. Here to see Satan, I'm sorry, my dad. Same thing though, am I right?" I joke just to piss her off even though my mood is sour.

"He has appointments all day, Griffin. You'll have to schedule something at a later date."

"Yeah, see, that's not gonna work for me, Cynthia. Because I just drove over three hours to see him. He is my father, and I'm not going to schedule a time to sit and talk with him."

She huffs as my father's office door opens and the man of the hour appears.

"I've got this, Cynthia. Thank you."

"I know it's unannounced, but I needed to speak with you."

"Hopefully to share something I can finally be proud of," he mutters, as if I can't hear him a foot apart as we walk into his office.

I grind my molars and swallow my pride, saying the words that need to be said to smooth things over between us and buy me the precious time I need.

"I came here to apologize."

His facial expression doesn't change, the bastard.

"I'm sorry for how I treated Lexi, she caught me off guard and I had to put out a fire because of it. I apologize for the embarrassment it caused you, and I'm going to work on making amends."

"It doesn't change what you did or what you said, Griffin."

"I realize now that—" The words practically die on my tongue, but I know I need to get them out. "I realize now that my feelings were not reciprocated and that I was being a fool. I'm going to fix it."

"You came all this way to tell me that? That's what you have for me?"

Fuck.

"I wanted to be a man and apologize to your face."

"Your apologies are worthless until your actions prove otherwise. Are you cutting ties with that pig?"

I dig my nails into the flesh of my thighs through my slacks at his insult.

"I already have. We aren't speaking. Can you explain to me why you hate them so much? If I could just understand."

His jaw tics, anger rising, but I need to understand.

"I told you, Griffin. It's none of your goddamn business. Now stay away from them, focus on Lexi, and maybe I'll reconsider having your ass replaced with Dion."

I exhale a defeated breath, but I agree.

"I understand, Dad."

"If you're lying to me, Griffin, just to save face, I will find out. Don't fuck with me. Last chance, or you're on your own."

I nod my agreement. "I understand. Thank you."

With bile rising up my throat, I leave my dad's office feeling like a slimy piece of shit for playing his sick fucking game, but the last thing I need is for him to ruin my name by blasting me publicly and bringing Carter into that. I need to protect him at all costs, and I don't trust my dad not to put me in front of his firing squad and let Carter go down in the crossfire. Once I'm in my car, I pull out my phone and text Trey an update.

. . .

Me: Omw back. He seemed to accept my apology and I still have my job right now. If we're gonna find something on my dad, we gotta do it now.

Trey: We're going to figure it out. He'll slip up somewhere and we'll find it

Trey: You doin okay?

Am I? I don't really know. I'm going through the motions to get shit done, but I don't think I'm okay. Not really.

Me: I'll get there, just not today

Trey: You've got me

Me: I appreciate you

Trey: Up for company tonight?

Me: Sure

Trey: I'll bring the pizza

Me: Hitting the road, I'll see you later

With that, I start the long-ass drive out of the city and back into the mountains with Carter on my mind the entire way. I kissed my dad's ass to buy me more time, to get something together to get us out of this damn position. Whether or not Carter and I end up together, I'm still always going to do the right thing. I didn't think I'd ever be in a position where I needed to choose between the love of my career and the love of my life, but here I am, and it's no competition. I just need to make sure that when I go down and lose the job I've dedicated my life to, it doesn't negatively impact Carter, and I've got myself set up ahead of time. I need a game plan. Which means I need time.

carter

SLEEP ELUDES ME. FOOD IS TASTELESS. MY DRIVE IS gone. This is exactly what I didn't fucking want. I never wanted to be so wrapped up in another person that they had the power to destroy me. I'm a shell of the person I was before Griffin Nash walked into my life uninvited and flipped the entire fucking thing off its axis.

This is why I stick to transactional, emotionless sex. Finn's words ring in my head, *"lean in,"* churning the bile around in my stomach. How could I have let myself lean into those moments with him? My walls were taken down for the first time in my life, and I'm stunned stupid I thought even for a moment I was falling for him. Was I that caught up in everything?

I should be panicking, I should be angry. But all I feel is the bitter sting of regret. Regret over letting myself fall into Finn's clutches so easily. Regret over being so goddamn weak when it comes to him, regret for falling for him. Because that's what happened, isn't it? I don't do feelings, and this is why. I can't believe I didn't fight it harder. I was stupid to think for even a moment that I could give him parts of me without falling for him. Fucking stupid.

My heart feels like it's in goddamn pieces, my emotions so raw and unrelenting. I would rather go back to feeling numb all the time than feel the pain of losing someone I can never have. He should never have gotten this much control over me, so much so that when I saw her in his room, quickly getting dressed, Finn's face panicked like he was desperately scared of me finding his dirty little secret, it shattered me completely. I'm furious at myself for allowing this to happen.

There's a nagging voice in the recesses of my mind telling me that everything was a lie, that he was fucking with me and could share the information with whoever he wanted. *Aspen Ridge's sex-crazed youngest child, looking for attention because he's sad and didn't get enough of it at home.*

Would he really do that? The pain in my heart stabs violently, a relentless reminder of how far I've fallen and all the control I lost to him. Sawyer was right when he explained how he felt when Ivy left. Finn took my fucking heart and now I have to learn to survive without it.

I go through my morning routine when my phone buzzes with an incoming text. He's been texting me once a day, and I'm just pathetic and heartbroken enough that I find myself waiting for it to come.

Finn: Please give me a chance to explain.

Finn: I miss you

Finn: I promise it wasn't what it looked like, but I want to explain in person.

Finn: I'm watching Spiderman. The Tom Holland one.

Finn: What we have is real, lover, it's not just going to go away

Finn: Plese tkl to me. I need u

Finn: I hope you're doing ok. I can't stop thinking about you.

Finn: I dreamed of you last night, of your beautiful face resting on my pillow, looking back at me. Your hair was in your face and when I reached out to push it away, you disappeared. I miss you.

Finn: I'm thinking about you, lover. I hope you have a good day.

I skim through the texts again, reading his latest one, my heart banging against my rib cage. Fuck this shit. I need to get over this. I need to come clean to my family that we won't be getting that feature in the Northwest Explorer, that Finn very well could spread information that paints me in a negative light. Then, I need to be a man and face Finn.

Driving over to my parents' house, I feel the weight of the world on my shoulders, the tension a heavy pressure, but I breathe through the panic clawing its way up my chest, threatening to take over and consume me. I need to hold my shit together and get through this.

The rain pelts down on my windshield, the clouds dark and stormy, the weather reflective of my mood. I find myself missing the sun that was always out in Emberleigh, or maybe I just miss the little bubble that Finn tucked us into. It was so easy to fall into a rhythm with him in a place where no one knew us. Where there was no magazine, no distillery, no family ties pulling us in the direction that loyalty demands. It was just simple. Until it all came crashing down around us.

I pull down the long lane that leads to my parents' drive, the wild lupines' lush colors leading the way, even in the grey haze that covers everything from the dark clouds above. Needing to get this conversation over with, I jump out of my car, jog up the porch stairs of my house, and knock on the door twice before opening it and slipping off my shoes.

"Hello?"

Sharp nails on wood scatter across the floor with a little bark, and my nerves instantly settle.

"Garbage!" I coo as I drop to my haunches and pick up the little ball of fur. My mom rounds the corner with a genuine smile at the sight of me, and my heart aches at how badly I'm about to disappoint them.

"This is a nice surprise," she tells me. Amy Hayes is the most welcoming, patient, loving person, and has always been so supportive of us kids. I hope my dad is willing to keep my indiscretions between us, because she has to have a line somewhere. And finding out her youngest boy is a member of a sex club is probably it.

"What's this angel doing here?" I ask as I pet the sweet puppy.

"*Billy* is staying with us while Liam and Hannah take Charlotte camping. They leave in the morning, but I wanted to get him settled today."

"Why didn't they ask me? He's half mine!" I protest like a child. Liam and his daughter, Charlie, found the little thing whining in a dumpster a few months ago. I instantly fell in love with him, and looking back, it's probably because I'm lonely as fuck.

"Because you've been a little preoccupied, son."

She's not wrong.

After giving Billy a bunch of love, I stand and brush off the dog hair clinging to my pants and shirt.

"Dad home?"

"You know where to find him, I'm going to get a few things done around here."

"Thanks, Mom," I say, giving her a big hug and pressing a kiss to the top of her head.

I walk through their house, knowing that my dad will be in

his office or the formal dining room where the bar is. Whiskey runs through his blood, having grown up on the grounds while his grandfather and father continued to grow the distillery to what it is now. Their shoes are hard to fill, and while it seems like my brothers aren't feeling the pressure of that, I sure as shit am. Especially because my position is new, as in, I'm the first person to ever hold it.

"Hey, Dad, you busy?"

"C'mon in."

"I wish I was coming here with good news, wanted it to be a surprise once it was done, but now it's not going to happen, and if it does, it just may not be great, and I want to let you know face-to-face."

He takes a seat on one of the barstools that surround his in-home bar and gives me his full attention. His words come out slightly slurred, with a bit of a stutter, but he holds strong and doesn't let it stop his communication. He's such a strong role model for all of us and always has been.

"You can tell me anything, and we'll figure out how to get through it as a family."

Here we go.

"A few months ago, I was contacted by a big magazine about doing a feature on our family and the distillery. Which was a huge deal. But then they started rescheduling our meetings, taking longer than necessary to email me back, just dicking me around. And . . ." I swallow the lump in my throat before continuing. "I could be being overly skeptical and worrying for nothing because this may be a stretch, but I don't get the feeling that they want to do a feature on us, but more of a smear campaign. Their writer tailed me and, without giving you too much info on your son's sex life, got some info on me that may not be great for the family or the distillery to have exposed." Even if it's not going to surprise anyone.

"What kind of info?"

Fucking kill me now.

"Can you keep it from Mom for as long as possible?"

"Jesus, how bad can it be, son?"

"I'm a member of a sex club."

His facial expression doesn't change, which surprises me.

"Oh, that's not that bad. Not ideal, but you aren't exactly quiet about your sex life, son. Is it seedy or clean?"

"Dad, Jesus. Of course it's safe. That's the appeal: safe, clean, and it was supposed to be discreet. But there are red flags everywhere I look. I haven't gotten to the bottom of it, but I don't want to be the reason the distillery gets dragged through the mud. If this gets out, they could make it look way worse than it is. I don't know what way this is going to go, and I regret getting myself tangled up in it, but I need to protect you all from everything you've worked hard to create and how far you've come. I think that we should be prepared for me to step down from my position at the distillery to avoid any negative press it could bring."

"Carter." My mom's voice comes harsh, a tone I'd grown up hearing when she scolded her five heathen children. "That will never be an option."

"How much of that did you hear, Mom? Or do I need to jump out that window?"

"Stop it. You think I don't know about sex? You're almost twenty-six, and I knew you were going to be a wild one the moment I saw you sneaking Savannah Erikson out of the house at fifteen. Plus, how do you think I got five children and two granddaughters?"

God, if you're real, strike me down right now.

"You're being rash in your decision, and it sounds like there's more to it than just your worry over the distillery."

She could always read every single one of her kids like a book.

"What magazine?" my dad asks, saving me from having to discuss my sex life with my mother.

"The Northwest Explorer."

Both of their eyes get big, and that constant friend of mine rears its ugly-ass head and sends ice through my veins, my heart rate picking up its pace.

"What am I missing here?"

My dad opens his mouth to speak, but my mom's hand covers his, resting on the bar. My mom speaks up instead. "It's just a large magazine, very . . . well-known. But whatever happens, we will face it as a family. Is there anything else?"

It's on the tip of my tongue to tell them that I've been hooking up with the man I'm worried could cause all this damage, but I feel like one bomb in an afternoon is probably good. Plus, have I even accepted the fact that I'm bisexual?

"No, I'm on my way to the distillery to talk with the boys. I just wanted to let Dad know face-to-face because everything is so unsure."

"This is why we have lawyers, Carter, if you're really concerned about it. But I highly doubt that such a well-known travel magazine would publish something that would be better suited for a gossip magazine. Talk with Sawyer, get the lawyers into a meeting, and then we will navigate it. This isn't the first time we've had a scandal."

That surprises me, and my eyes lift to my mom for her to explain.

"Nope, a story for another time, my boy. Now get out of here, go face your brothers."

"So quick to send me to my demise?"

"Never. We trust that you can handle yourself in all things. We love you, and we're proud of you. The only reason you will ever leave your position at the distillery is because it no longer fulfills you or brings you joy. Not because you are scared. We don't react out of fear; we face it and move forward. Do you understand?"

Not realizing how badly I needed to hear that, I wrap my

mom in a huge hug, her arms wrapping around my midsection, her head resting on my chest.

"Yes, Mom. I love you."

"Love you, too, my boy."

"Alright, give me my wife," my dad says, his voice shaky but strong.

"She's all yours. Love you, Dad."

Having a massive weight lifted off my shoulders, I leave my parents' house and take the drive to the distillery.

Sawyer's office is my first stop. I find him relaxed back in his expensive office chair, hands behind his head as if he were waiting for me. "Was wondering when you were going to show up to work. How was Maine? Can't say it's on my list of places to visit."

My heart picks up as I try to push back the memory of my weekend with Finn. The nights we spent wrapped around each other, how it felt to have all of his attention directed at me, the way we floated comfortably around each other, how we shared the best sex of my life. How, for the first time in my life, I realized that I was capable of loving another person, even if I didn't want to.

"Maine is actually beautiful, it's similar to AR but sunnier. But we gotta talk, and it's not great. Gonna affect us all. You want the news first or call the boys in?"

"Shit," he huffs, leaning back in his chair, pulling out his phone to text our brothers. Sawyer sits in his chair, studying me while we wait for them to come up to his office. Dallas walks in first, barreling in like he owns the place.

"What up? Family get-together? Did you bring snacks?"

"No one brought snacks, dumbass, take a seat, we're waiting on Liam."

"Shit, he always takes forever. Maybe I should go get Gloria so I'm more comfortable. Why can't he have an office in here with the rest of us?"

"He does, but he also has one closer to the vats and houses

because he works over there more. Do you live under a rock? How do you not know this?" Sawyer snaps, bemused.

Dallas just shrugs as he lounges in a chair next to me, shifting around and groaning, complaining about how bad Sawyer's guest chairs are. Liam walks in a few minutes later and takes a seat with us, ending our misery of dealing with Dallas.

"Sorry, had to finish helping Graham with whiskey fungus inspections."

Sawyer rubs his hand across his jaw in irritation. "Shit, is it spreading?"

"Not any more than expected. Angel's Share is part of the process, and we're not a small-scale distillery; it's to be expected. I think our great-grandparents did a service to the town by building this place out in the middle of nowhere, but we want to make sure it doesn't start to spread onto everything."

"Let me know what you need. We don't need black soot covering all of Aspen Ridge if we can help it. Floor's yours, Casanova. What do you got for us?" Sawyer says, nerves starting to take over.

I go through the whole story again from the beginning. Leaving out the parts of hooking up with Finn and how we spent the entire weekend wrapped around each other. I come clean about Temptations and avoid Dallas' eyes so that Sawyer and Liam don't find out that he is also a member if he doesn't want them to know that. Unlike what I told my dad, I go into further detail about how I was hesitant from the beginning, that talking to a journalist in any aspect who knew my sexual habits, and was digging into my family without coming to us first, has left me with the impression that he was looking for dirt rather than gold.

It feels awful to talk about Finn this way because, deep down, I don't think he would do that to me, and the thought nearly makes me hyperventilate. I wanted to believe him so badly when he reassured me it wasn't in him to ruin someone's life, but then how the hell did he get me to fall for him only to find out he's got a goddamn girlfriend on the side? What was the point of all of this if it wasn't to do something nefarious? The pieces don't fit, and my anger at myself and Finn overrides my rational thought.

After I verbally vomit it all for the second time today, I feel fucking exhausted.

"Well, that explains your shitty-ass attitude the last few weeks," Sawyer says after I'm finished.

Dallas chimes in, and it's not very helpful, but he's also not wrong. "We should bury these assholes; show them they can't fuck with us."

"That is not how we do things, dumbass. I'll call our attorney and prepare to respond on the off chance they print something negative. But I wouldn't even stress it, Car. If they know we know, they're going to anticipate a reaction. I'm sure it's going to make them think twice about running an article. But it doesn't sound like something the Northwest Explorer would even run. It sounds like he's a fucking tool and was bored and fucking with you."

Now it's my turn to deflate into my chair. I run my hand through my hair, trying to breathe.

"You really think so?" I ask, looking for clarification. Needing it.

"Yeah, I'm sure. And if they're dumb enough to run it, we're going to fight them on it. They've got no basis. Plus, what kind of assholes are running that place?"

I just shrug, because other than the little I know about his dad, there's a part of Finn that only I saw that isn't capable of doing something like this to anyone. He genuinely seemed so passionate about writing stories and using his voice and platform for good. Maybe Sawyer is right and I have it all wrong—there has to be something else deeper going on here.

After a long-ass day, and pondering my family's reactions, there's one more person I need to talk to. I need the full story, I need to understand. Sawyer didn't get closure when Ivy left, and I want to make sure that I have that. Even if the situations are completely different, I feel like I'm not going to find myself again until I reclaim some of that power. He wants to explain so bad, then I'm going to give him the opportunity and make it damn clear that we're done.

No matter how much the thought nearly brings me to my knees in pain.

finn

I SIT WITH A COOL WHISKEY GLASS IN MY HAND, shirtless, my grey sweatpants riding low on my hips. It's the same as every night over the last two weeks. I'm completely empty. Broken.

My phone buzzes, and if I wasn't so desperate to hear from Carter, I wouldn't bother looking. I pick it up, Carter's name flashing on the screen with a text message. I nearly slosh the remaining whiskey over the rim as I jerk upright in my seat. Unlocking my phone with trembling fingers, my heart in my throat, I read his text, the words stunning me.

Carter: I'm outside.

It takes me a moment before my body catches up to my brain, and I'm moving quickly through my house. Wrenching open my front door, Carter is standing there in the flesh. The urge to grab him and pull him into my arms is strong. I just want to hug him, hold him close to me. I can barely contain the relief that courses through my veins, the tears that want to fall. Fuck, I've missed him.

"We need to talk."

"That's never a good thing, but considering we haven't spoken in over two weeks, I'm not going to complain," I reply, my voice coming out as strangled and broken as I feel.

I open the door further and Carter walks into the house, and as he walks past me, I inhale his woodsy, sweet scent into my lungs. My fingers twitch at my sides, and I have to ball them into fists to keep from reaching out and touching him. He looks like he's lost a little weight, the tan that he worked for in Emberleigh already faded. He spins on me, and the empty look in his eyes tells me that he's not here to work things out. But I'm not going to let him go this easily. I can't.

"I just need to know the truth. All of it. Nothing is making sense to me anymore. So, please, after everything, give me that. You said you wanted to explain. I need to hear it, but if you lie to me . . ."

I let out a long breath, running my hands through my hair. This conversation is long overdue.

"In case you missed it, my dad's a top-notch asshole. Always has been. He's ruthless when he wants to be, which is almost always, and I am his one and only failure, the golden child that he desperately wanted. He gave me the best education money could buy, tutors, coaches, but I have always fallen short in his eyes. The fact that I'm gay just makes it all the worse. I've been trying to be enough for him my entire life and always come up short, Carter. I'm never good enough."

Carter's eyes are filled with a stormy mix of empathy, rage, and confusion, and I'm uncertain which emotion he's feeling the most.

"I feel for you, Finn, I do. He's a piece of shit and I wish like hell it was different for you. But that doesn't explain the shit that's going on. I want to know why. Why offer the distillery a feature? Why tail me? Why force me to go away with you? Why ask me to lean in? Fuck, Finn. Was I just some sick game to you? Try to turn the straight guy? Do you really have a goddamn girlfriend?!" He huffs loudly while every piece of my heart crumbles. "So explain it, or I clearly made a mistake by coming here." He snaps out the words, each one shattering my heart a little bit more.

"I don't, Carter. She's nothing to me, I swear. Lexi isn't anyone but a lost girl whose dad is pressuring her to marry rich. Our dads are business partners. Mine refuses to acknowledge that I'm gay, and apparently Lexi is his key to showing everyone that his son isn't an abomination. They have been trying to arrange our marriage for a long time. Lexi is on board because I'm a Nash. She wants the life that she has grown up knowing, and I'm her ticket to keeping it. I've never touched her. Never even been alone with her until I saw her standing in my bedroom in Maine. That's the truth."

Carter looks at me—really looks at me—and I hold my breath and wait for him to give me some semblance of a clue that he believes me.

"Fuck, Finn. Your dad's a piece of fucking work. Now what about the part where my family is involved in this shit? How do we fit in this fucked-up situation?"

"I'm still figuring that out. Every piece I have given to you, Carter, that was all real. When I said I love my job more than anything, at the time, I meant it. My dad owns one of the most popular and well-known travel magazines there is. He knows how much working there means to me, and he uses that to get me to comply."

"Why don't you just leave and go somewhere else if he's so fucking bad? Finn, he can't control you. You're so much damn better than this."

"Because he would ruin me! The magazine may be big, but the communities are small. He would make sure no one hired me anywhere else. He would sully my name, and no one would publish me. Up until recently, I haven't had anything in my life that I cared for more than travel writing." *Up until I met Carter*

Hayes. "I stumbled on Aspen Ridge by accident. I was given a twenty-year-old signature bourbon from your distillery as a gift from my best friend. I wanted to know more because that's what I do, and I found Aspen Ridge. Carter, when I tell you I fell in love through just photos, I did. I had Trey immediately reach out, and then I gave the proposal to my dad for Aspen Ridge to be the focus of my next feature."

"Okay . . ." he says, urging me to go on, leaning his shoulder against the wall next to him, his muscular arms crossed tight across his chest.

"He flipped. He's always been prone to violent rage, but Carter, he freaked. Forbade me from ever stepping foot in Aspen Ridge and especially from speaking to your family."

"What? Why the hell would he care?"

"Our parents know each other, or did at one time."

"What?" he asks me, his eyebrows pinching together with the same confusion I'm feeling.

"I don't know the details because he doesn't talk to me, just expects me to listen, but my dad despises your family. He went ballistic, Carter."

"So why the hell didn't you stay away, Finn? Why fuck with me?"

"Because I couldn't! I fucking couldn't!" I yell, my voice cracking with emotion. Doesn't he feel this between us? Why is he fighting this so hard? "I saw your photo online and I couldn't stay away! I tried! I needed to know you, Carter. I needed to see you in the flesh. It was a pull I couldn't fight."

Carter stands tall, rigid and in a defensive stance, his fists balled at his sides, eyes narrowed at me in frustration. My knees nearly buckle from the piercing, fierce stare alone.

"What was your plan then, huh? Fuck around with me, get me to open up to you, then what? I was just something you couldn't stay away from and then you were going to what? Keep me your dirty little secret? Drop me altogether? When were you going to fucking tell me I meant nothing and that we were never going to get that feature?"

"You mean everything! I didn't know at the time, Carter. I was being impulsive because you consume me. But you don't know what it's like to work for him, to be his son. I didn't have a plan for handling it, but I was going to figure it out. I didn't want to hurt you, but I didn't want to lose you. You opened up to me in Maine, and I was going to tell you everything. I wanted to figure it out together!"

Carter's face pinches as if he's in pain, and I see the panic before it starts to hit. My hands instinctively reach out to him, but he pulls away and my heart stops in my chest, the air snatched from my lungs.

"I don't believe you."

My head jerks back as if he had slapped me. I would have preferred it.

"This is over. Whatever you think happened in Maine stays there. It's over. I agreed to your stupid demands, I went on your little fucking trip, gave you what you wanted, and I should force you to write the article you promised me, but we don't want it. I want nothing from you. Tell your dad to eat shit and that he got his way, something I'm sure he's plenty used to by now."

I feel like I just took a sucker punch to the gut. My heart falls into the pit of my stomach, bile rising up my throat and burning. My head scrambles with what to do.

"What do you mean this is over? We're not over." *We can't be.*

"Yes we fucking are."

"So you can fuck me but you won't admit what's between us? Happy to have me on my knees for you and share my bed, but that's as far as it goes?"

"I never wanted this! I have never wanted commitment! You're not special, Griffin. Just because I've fucked you doesn't mean I want more from you."

Griffin.

A sardonic laugh that I don't recognize erupts from my chest. His words are knives slashing across my flesh, ripping through muscle and puncturing vital organs. His eyes flash with surprise, either at his own words or my reaction, but I don't give him time to react further, and he doesn't get to see how deep those words wound. I'm never going to be fucking good enough for anyone. Never be enough for someone to choose me. I thought he felt everything between us. I thought he would trust me to tell him the truth, but I'm not enough. Without a word, I turn on my heels and head for the door.

"Finn, wait . . ."

Carter trails behind me, his footfalls hard on the wood floors of my house.

I snatch my keys from the bowl at the entryway table, my body on autopilot, a quiet, calm, stillness settling over me—numbing me. A defense mechanism I've perfected. I've felt so much pain and heartbreak over the last two weeks of silence between us, and now I'm just empty.

"I didn't mean it like that. Fuck. That came out real bad, let's talk this through," he backpedals.

I'll never be done with Carter Hayes, but I'm not going to be used and abused so he can live out some sick fantasy and never fully give himself to me. He keeps fighting this magnetism between us instead of leaning into it, and I'm not going to stand by to wait for the next time he wants me. If he can't have my back, if he can't trust me, if he can't choose me, then I can't stay. Even if he's wrong. So very, very wrong. I said my piece, was truthful, and he still doesn't believe me.

"You knew exactly what this was. We were fucking. That's what I do, Nash. I fuck. I don't do feelings. I can't," he says, his voice softer but firm. Little goddamn liar. He's only trying to convince himself. That's what this is really about. He's been doing feelings this entire time, he's just choosing to ignore them.

I whip around to face him, my face pinched with anger and frustration. His steps halt, even taking a hesitant one back like he can feel how he's finally pushed me too far. This is it. All in or nothing at all. I can't do the in-between for a moment longer. Not after I'm choosing him over my family, over the goddamn job that I love so much, over everything that I have. I choose him knowing I am walking away from everything. If he can't be all in for me, then I'm done with him. I'll forever feel love and gratitude for Carter because he gave me the strength to walk away from a life I should have left a long time ago. With or without him, I'm going to survive this and start over. I just hope like hell it's with him by my side.

carter

FOR THE SECOND TIME IN FIVE MINUTES, FINN IS wearing an expression that damn near guts me. I can't read him, but my heart felt like it was breaking as I watched him walk away from me. I shouldn't have said what I said, and it's killing me. I lashed out to hurt him the way he's hurt me, but it wasn't worth it. Seeing the pain flash across his beautiful face, how he stumbled back with the force of my words as if I had physically hit him, feels worse than any pain I've ever felt. I've fucked everything up because of my fear, and seeing the pain on his face that I caused is enough to break me completely.

He takes another step in my direction and I cross my arms over my chest protectively. As if that has ever saved me from the tsunami that is Griffin Nash.

"Oh, wicked lover, you can lie through your teeth all you want, but I know the truth, whether you ever admit it or not." His voice is a deep, sexy baritone that caresses over my entire body. *Just like it always does.*

"Yeah? What's that?" I whisper as one of his hands makes contact with my hip, the other grabbing my throat, gently nudging me closer into his space. I go willingly because when have I ever denied him? He's a master at diffusing the heated situations that I rain down on us. I should be freaking out, but there's no panic, no fear, no anxiety—just a plethora of emotions that I'm trying to swallow down and ignore.

His voice is as strong and resolute as he is when he speaks. "That you want this. Want me. Want *us*. This is the real deal and you know it. Neither one of us expected it, the only difference is I'm the only one chasing it. You're scared because everyone you've been with before me hasn't made you feel half of what I have."

"You're wrong." I whisper the words against his lips as he descends on me, our faces so close, his breath warm on my lips. That ember deep inside me is being stoked and he's the only one with the power to make it rage.

"Am I?" He pulls back and arches a brow behind his glasses, his gorgeous blue eyes a mix of that cocky arrogance I can't get enough of and apprehension that fills me with guilt. Sex has always been a way to empty my mind, a stress reliever because it felt good, but he's wrong. I didn't feel anything at all with everyone before him. Sex with Finn? I feel *everything*. And that scares the shit out of me.

But what's worse? Having him and chance losing him or walking away and ending it before it's even had the opportunity to be something more? The last few weeks have been a reminder of what life was like without him, and it's miserable. He brings light into my life when I didn't realize it was so dim to begin with.

It dawns on me why it was so easy for Sawyer to accept Ivy back into his life after she crushed him by leaving. Because it was never an option to begin with. He was always hers, just as I'm Finn's. He claimed my heart as his, and whether I fight it or not, he's keeping it.

But the fear is still strong and holds part of me hostage. Fear of losing him and not recovering, fear of giving up the power to another person, fear of coming out in a relationship with a man— especially after the reputation I've made for myself with the female population—fear of how to protect Finn from his father, fear of him resenting me if he loses everything to be with me.

I open my mouth to argue, to cut him deep again, because giving in is so hard. But it's his eyes that are flooded with uncertainty and pain that do me in. My heart feels like it's in a vise grip. It physically aches to see that I'm the reason he's hurting. So, I tell him my truth.

"They never made me feel *anything*."

His eyes flash with surprise, but I don't give him the chance to respond. My lips crash against his, taking his mouth in a heated kiss that ignites my entire body. It's as if a dam has broken, and all the emotions I've kept locked up tight since the night I met Finn finally flood forward in a rush. I swipe my tongue against his seam, wordlessly asking him to open for me as our hands grip each other, lining our bodies up flush in an effort to get as close as possible.

"You're everything I didn't know I needed," I confess after pulling his plush bottom lip between my teeth and releasing. "What are you doing to me, Finn?" His hands slide up to the sides of my face, forcing me to look at him straight on.

"Making you feel, baby."

Our mouths connect, teeth clashing, tongues tangling as we race to rid each other of our clothes. My fingers connect with his bare skin, grateful he was already shirtless, tracing over each defined ab, the hard plane of his chest, loving the feel of him under my palms.

Finn's fingers finally remove my belt and unbutton my pants, my zipper forced apart as he shoves my pants down my legs, and I shuck them off.

"I'm sorry," I say between kisses. "I'm so fucking sorry."

"God, Carter, me too. I'm so sorry."

I swallow his words, kissing him and throwing every ounce of feeling I possess into it. It's more than a kiss, it's a promise, a claiming. I worship his mouth the way he deserves, giving him all of me and taking all of him in return.

Once I'm completely naked, I drop to my knees, quickly dragging his sweatpants over his hips, boxer briefs in tow. His hard dick snaps free of its confines and bobs against his abdomen, all thick and veiny.

Finn steps out of the jeans and I toss them haphazardly off to the side. Running the flat of my palms up his thighs, the thick, tight muscles, the coarse hair that feels so good on my skin. I look up at him from where I'm perched on my knees at his feet. Grabbing his hard dick with my fist, I slowly stroke it, once, twice, loving the way his eyelashes flutter over his beautiful blue eyes, the moans that escape from his full, bruised lips. I'll never tire of the reactions I can pull from this man. His hips gyrate and chase my mouth as I flick my tongue over the tip repeatedly.

"Suck it, lover. You know how I like it."

I moan as I lean up, bringing my lips to his uncut tip, pulling the skin back and licking the pearly bead of precum leaking from his slit before wrapping my mouth around his engorged head and sucking hard. His head drops back against the wall as a long, deep moan reverberates up his chest.

"Mmm. Just like that. Your mouth feels so good."

Wanting to be as close to him as possible, I suck him all the way down my throat, my hands caressing over his pelvis, hips, and onward until I'm gripping his strong ass, pulling him deeper into my mouth, tears springing to my eyes.

"Jesus Christ, Carter. Fuck, yeah, such a good boy for me."

I let his words urge me on, but I don't need them, I just need *him*. I need him closer. I need all of him. I'm frantic, needing *more*. I suck him like I'd die without him, but it's just not enough. I feel desperate, out of control.

It hits me suddenly and with zero apprehension. Something settles deep within my psyche, into the marrow of my bones, and finds its home. Popping off his dick, I stand abruptly, my hands gripping the back of his neck and pulling his mouth to mine in a deep kiss. He doesn't miss a beat, not wasting any time to open for me, meeting me halfway, equals in everything.

"I need you," I tell him.

"Lover, you've got me. I'm yours. I've been yours since the moment I saw you."

"Make me *yours*."

He pulls back, his hand moving to the side of my face, angling my head so that he can meet my eyes and read my face.

"You are mine, Carter," he practically growls.

"Then fuck me, Finn. Make me yours in every way."

A rough exhale leaves his lips, his warm, minty breath brushing against my face. He runs his thick fingers through my hair, pushing it out of my face as his eyes study me.

"You sure?"

"Yeah, I'm sure. Fuck me, baby."

A playful smile plays at the lips I love so much.

Finn grabs my hand and pulls me to his bedroom, where I kick the door closed behind us. He wastes no time getting his hands on me. His mouth trails open-mouthed kisses everywhere he can. My hands thread through his hair, pulling him closer to me as he works his way down my neck and over my chest. He stops to swipe his wet tongue over my nipple, teasing and nipping.

"Ugh, fuck."

Finn just moans against my skin, moving to the other side and lapping at my sensitive flesh. He slowly works his way down, sucking and biting at my skin, leaving a heated trail everywhere he's touched. It feels so damn good.

Dropping to his knees, his fist grabs my hard length, pumping a few lazy strokes that feel so good my knees nearly buckle before his mouth opens. There's no teasing—the finesse that he typically has when he blows me is nonexistent. He sucks me like it's the last time he'll ever get to do it, as though he wants to bury a piece of himself deep within me. *Too bad he already has.*

"Fuck, I love my cock in your mouth, but I want you to fuck me, baby. I *need* you to fuck me."

His eyes look up at me full of warmth and happiness as he hears the pet name that he loves so much. I hope it feels as good as it sounds. His hand slips between us, cupping my balls and rolling them gently before sliding over my taint and rubbing that sensitive spot behind my sack. Goosebumps break out across my skin, his chuckle reverberating through my dick.

"Mmm," he moans as he pops off. "Need lube. I'm gonna love prepping you." Finn spins me around with his hands on my hips, forcing me to bend over the bed. "Don't move, I want you spread open for me."

Even though my legs are shaking with anticipation, I stay put, my body bent over the edge of the bed, my forearms holding up my chest while Finn grabs the bottle of lube from his end table drawer.

He returns quickly, his large hands gripping each ass cheek, massaging deep into the muscle and making me groan. Spreading my ass wide open, nerves rustle their way to the surface. As if he can feel it, his hands release me, caressing over my skin in such a loving touch that it settles me.

"I'm gonna make this so good for you. And we can stop at any point. If you don't like anything I'm doing, just tell me. No safe words needed, no means no to me, and I'll stop."

I release a rough exhale. "I'm good, I want this."

And then he's spreading me open again. I expect the cold trickle of lube, but what I get instead is his warm, wet tongue.

"Oh shit!" I exclaim as I nearly jump out of my skin.

"Shh, let me take my time with you."

His tongue laps at my hole, making it sloppy with his saliva. He swirls around and around, my head getting fuzzy with the new sensation. He presses firmly with his tongue, barely breaching the tight barrier before lapping at it more. Fuck, the pleasure is indescribable.

"I need to touch myself, Finn, it's so good." I reach my hand between my legs to stroke my aching cock, but before I can get to it, he smacks my hand out of the way.

"No. Wait for me. It'll be worth it if you hold off."

I groan unintelligible words as he feasts on me. Just when I think I can't take it anymore, I hear the pop of the lube bottle and then feel a cold trickle of liquid directly down my crack. Finn spreads my ass cheeks open wide, his thumbs catching the lube, alternating rubbing over my tight rim. Over. And over. And over again.

My legs shake under his onslaught, and we haven't even gotten to the penetrative sex part. My breaths come in hard pants, my back arching into him.

"I'm going to press in now, breathe for me." And then he's breaching past that tight rim, sliding a finger into my ass. I know to relax since we've done this much before but goddamn this is gonna burn.

"I love your ass, Carter. Fuck, if you could see what you look like right now. Your big, strong body bent over, taking my fingers. Fuck, I can't wait to feel you squeeze around me."

Fuck, yes. I grip the sheets with my fists as Finn's lips trail kisses up my spine, one finger moving to two, then he's searching, and as soon as he finds that spot, my cock jerks hard under me. I'm leaking streams of precum, stars dancing behind my eyes as he ignites this inferno. I moan loudly, feral and wanton. I've never felt so needy, a type of desperation that makes you feel out of control. I feel . . . alive.

After a few minutes of pure pleasurable torture, Finn finally pulls his fingers out and pushes my hip to get me to move onto my back.

"I need to see you while I fuck you for the first time, Carter. I want to look into your eyes as I claim you."

His words go straight to my heart, pounding mercilessly against my ribcage. Flipping onto my back, I spread my legs wide to make room for him to fit between them.

"Condom?" he asks.

"I've only been with you since we first hooked up. And I'm tested monthly to remain a member at Temptations," I confess sheepishly.

He settles between my legs, our cocks pressed against each

other, trapped between our abdomens as his mouth descends on mine. Our kiss is slow and methodical, a sensual, languid caress of our tongues, capturing each other's moans and swallowing them down.

"I did the same thing. I'm clean, and I haven't been with anyone but you in a long time. The idea of nothing between us makes me fucking feral."

"So, no condom?"

"No condom. Are you ready? Be sure. We don't have to do this. I want you to be comfortable, I know what a big deal it is to let someone else inside your body. I want you to trust me, Carter."

His words nearly break me and I fucking hate that I lashed out the way I did. I don't want him to question anything, I want us to both be in this.

"I'm sorry, Finn. I didn't mean anything I said; I was scared and confused. I trust you. I choose you. I want this. Want you, baby, so fucking much."

His face goes molten, and he doesn't ask any more questions, just lines up his thick cock with my open hole, pushing my legs back and looking down at where we're about to be joined.

"Bear down for me."

I do as he says, Finn's thick head pressing against me without too much resistance. I can't help but wince as he gives me a moment to adjust to his girth.

"You're way bigger than three fucking fingers, man."

"Shh, you can take it. Be my good boy, Carter?"

"Fuck you," I grit out through clenched teeth, even though there's a smile lifting on my lips.

"Happily." His cock slips all the way in, his chest collapsing onto mine as his hands find my face. I let out a loud groan as I'm filled for the first time.

"Fuck, I love you." Time freezes, my eyes wild as I stare into his. Those three words wash over me, stunning me. Finn loves me? "I know this isn't the best timing, with my dick buried in your ass for the first time, but I couldn't hold it back another moment. I love you, Carter. So fucking much it hurts."

I seize his face with my hands, the burn, the ache, our families, the magazine article, the distillery, everything outside of this little room disappears. Pulling his mouth to mine and giving him a bruising kiss, I know I feel the same way. I didn't want it. I fought it hard. But just like a storm on a path of destruction, Finn wrecked all my plans, knocking down every single wall of protection I built, ripping me bare until the real me was left raw and open.

"I love you, Finn. Fuck, baby. I love you too."

Finn's eyes fill with tears, and my heart nearly bursts from the abundance of emotion filling me.

"You love me?"

"Yeah, baby. I love you. You came into my life and wrecked everything I thought I knew and wanted." Finn pulls back slightly as my hands clasp his face, my thumbs brushing the tears away from under his eyes. "But you showed me everything I've been missing; you've shown me who I really am and what I want. I'm leaning in, baby. I'm all in."

"Fuck. I needed to hear you say that," he whispers on a rough exhale, his forehead resting against mine. My hands glide down the strong muscles of his back, grasping his ass and squeezing.

"Finn?"

"Yeah?"

"I need you to move now."

"You want it, lover?"

"Fuck yeah I do. Show me what you got."

Finn pulls out and then slams back in, and a moan spills from my lips as his dick rubs against my prostate, the burn from the stretch just a small simmer now. He doesn't hold back or restrain himself, he fucks me like he needs this just as much as I do.

"Ohhmygodohfuuuck," I mutter, my words unintelligible and garbled as I hold him close to me.

"Fuck that's so hot, who knew you'd like bottoming?"

"Don't care . . . just . . . don't stop. Fuuuuck."

Finn chuckles as he sets a steady pace, his dick hitting that spot inside me that has only ever been touched with his fingers until now, my cock throbbing and leaking precum like a motherfucker between our bodies.

"God, you know how long I've wanted to do this? It's better than I imagined."

My eyes snap open, my hands moving to his hips to steady him so I can let the fog clear for a moment.

"You have?"

"Fuck, yeah. Wanted to fuck you the first night I met you. Went home and jerked it twice to thoughts of slipping into this ass."

"I didn't know . . ."

"I don't bottom. Ever."

"What?" I ask, blinking rapidly at him.

"You heard me," he whispers as his lips brush back and forth over mine, his cock rocking slowly inside me.

"But you did with me."

"Because you didn't know you were into men and I wasn't about to force my cock on you. I wanted you, any way I could get you. You've always been different. Something snapped into place that night, and I haven't been the same since."

My mouth hangs open slightly and Finn takes full advantage of it, licking into me while I'm shocked silent. I came here tonight to break things off and instead got so much more than I started with. He starts to move again inside me, short thrusts, staying deep and driving me crazy. I pull my thighs up higher on either side of his hips, angling my pelvis upward, deepening his penetration, and I see stars.

"Ohfuckingfuck, I'm gonna blow, I can't. Ohmygod, fuck."

Finn lifts up just enough to make room for his hand, grabbing my aching cock with his fist and stroking just the way he knows I like it. The combination of him filling me, rubbing against my sensitive prostate, and his rough hand stroking me hard, I combust.

My ass clenches around his cock as my dick throbs in his hand, pearly white cum shooting out against both of our chests. My eyes nearly roll to the back of my head as one of the best orgasms I've ever had rolls through me. He rubs me through it until I'm spent, but he doesn't stop fucking me, doubling down on his thrusts, chasing his orgasm.

Dragging my fingers through the mess on my abdomen, I gather up some of my cum on two fingers. "Open for me, baby, taste my cum while you fill me with yours." I press them into his mouth, his tongue swirling over my digits and sucking the jizz off of them.

"Fuuuuuuck, Carter!" he chants my name like a prayer as he falls apart, his dick twitching inside me, warm jets of his cum coating my insides. Fuck, I never thought I would ever like, no scratch that, fucking love, having a cock in my ass, but here we are. We'll be fucking doing this again. And soon.

After our breathing has evened to a less concerning rate, Finn lifts off of me just enough to look at my face. His beautiful blue eyes look tired but so damn happy and satisfied. I love that I'm the reason for it.

His fingers brush the hair out of my face, his fingertips so light on my skin. "How are you feeling?"

I wiggle a little, making him groan, his forehead dropping down to rest against mine. "Like I'm ready for you to exit my body now," I say with a little laugh.

"Fair enough. But you're okay? I didn't hurt you?" he asks as he pulls out of me. The rush of cum dripping from me is instantaneous and my cheeks heat.

"Fuck no. We'll be doing that again."

"Thank fuck. I'm okay with bottoming if that's what works for us but now that I've had your ass . . .?"

"You want more, huh?"

"Oh, definitely."

"So, what now?"

"Now," Finn says as he stands, his naked body on full display for me. "We go take a shower, then we talk and figure this out."

I nod my head in agreement, following him to the massive stone shower in the bathroom. We take turns washing each other's bodies in the comfortable silence. I'm full of emotions that I don't know what to do with right now, but for the first time in my life, I feel content and at peace. I'm willing to fight for this. Fight for Finn. Fight for me.

finn

CARTER LOVES ME. IT SURE AS HELL FELT LIKE HE DID, but thinking it and hearing the confirmation from his own lips are two completely different things. Loving him is the easiest thing I've ever done; it's everything else that is complicated and messy. I just hope that I can be enough for him to stand by me while I figure this out. I don't know how I'll survive it if he walks away from me. I've accepted that I'll never be man enough for my dad, that I'll always be an inconvenience to my mom, but to not be enough for Carter? That'll destroy me. It already came too close to it.

I work silently in the kitchen, making us sandwiches and putting them on a plate with some chips. I juggle the plates, with two water bottles under my arms, and join Carter on the couch, handing him his food.

"It's not cold."

"Yeah . . . you hate cold water, remember? Your 'it's actually not good for you' spiel stuck with me."

Carter gives me a knowing smile and my heart pounds behind my ribs. It's such a little thing, but I love it so much. I want to make him smile like that every day, and if he wants room temperature water like a freak, then so be it.

We dig into our dinner quietly, both of us refueling and lost in our thoughts of the turn of events. My heart feels full but my mind is whirling, waiting for the other shoe to drop. Now that I have him and he's in this with me, I have to do everything I can to keep him, and that means putting myself first for the first time in my life. I need to untangle myself from my father and hope like hell he doesn't try to ruin me in the process.

Carter finishes his food first, setting the plate on the coffee table in front of us. He shifts his body so that he's facing me, his elbow resting on the back, holding up his head. His hair has dried from our shower, the longer strands of the top falling into his face. He hasn't shaved in a few days, and the scruff has come in thicker. I like it. Finally ready to talk through this together now that we've shared orgasms and our stomachs are full, I start the conversation.

"Okay, so how are we going to get through this shit storm?" I ask as I pop my last chip into my mouth.

"Well, I should probably start by telling my family I'm into dick."

I inhale hard, a piece of chip lodging in my throat as I sputter, coughing roughly into my fist, my eyes wide as I struggle to get in oxygen.

"Damn, you okay, baby?"

"Yep," I say through bouts of coughing while I try not to let a chip kill me. It'd be his fault if it did.

"Okay, so I probably wouldn't say it like that, but if that's how you want to come out, then that's on you."

"I don't know, I've given it some thought and think that may be the best way," he says, laughing, looking like he's picturing his siblings' reactions.

"How, uh," I start nervously, "how do you think they'll take it?"

"I'm not gonna lie and say that their opinion of me doesn't matter. My family and I are close. But I can't imagine them being pissed or disgusted. They're pretty open. I've just made quite a name for myself with the ladies, and they're gonna be shocked stupid. I definitely got around."

"Those days over?"

"Yeah."

"Yeah? A taken man?"

"You're damn right I am."

As if he knew I needed to hear those words, tears fill my eyes again.

"Hey, it's okay. I meant what I said. I love you, Finn. I'm not going anywhere. I fought it as long as I could, but I can't anymore." His strong hands touch either side of my face, his thumbs swiping away the few rogue tears that escaped. His lips press firmly against mine in a chaste kiss that steals the breath from my lungs, then his firm lips are kissing under each eye, finally resting on my forehead. I've never felt so perfectly connected with another person before. Like my soul has finally found its missing half.

"I don't want to hide you, but I think we need to get a plan together before we blow the lid off of everything."

His words don't hurt because I understand them. I know it's not about coming out or keeping me a dirty little secret; it's giving us both time to do this the right way.

"I'm not going to argue that. My dad lost his shit when he found out you were in Emberleigh. He's really got some grudge decades in the making, and I don't know what the deal is yet, but I want to find out. He's a hateful asshole, but I want to under-stand why it's directed at your family."

"I don't get it either."

"Got any family demons hiding in the closet, Hayes?"

"Hell if I know. I don't think so. My dad is from Aspen Ridge. He returned here after college with my mom and got preg-nant with Sawyer and Dallas. Everyone loves them."

"We'll figure it out. He made one comment, though, that I keep coming back to. He said he 'took everything from me.' I asked who, and he just continued to flip out and threaten me."

"Well, shit. Who? My dad?"

"Hell if I know. But I'm going to figure it out while easing out of working under his thumb. I don't want to ruin my writing career, but I refuse to work for him any longer."

"You think he'd really make it so no one else would hire you? Your own father?"

"Without a shred of doubt. He would," I reply honestly. My dad doesn't make idle threats. A deep growl rumbles from Carter's chest, his hands tightening into fists.

"We'll figure this out. You aren't going to lose your career because of him. You aren't his fucking pawn. I'm right beside you now." My heart swells at his words.

"Thank you."

"So right now, let's keep this quiet. We can sneak around, right? Until we figure everything out?"

"Yeah, I mean, if you're up for it, there's always Temptations," I suggest.

"You want to play out in the open, baby?"

"I'm not against it. Especially if that's the only way I can have you."

He gives me a heated look before looking away quickly, his face morphing into concern.

"I do need to come clean as well, and I owe you an apology."

My spine tightens, but he continues to hold my face, stroking his thumbs delicately back and forth across my cheekbones.

"Okay?"

"I'm sorry for leaving you in Maine and not hearing you out. It was shitty after everything we shared that weekend. I panicked, and I let that fear control me against all reason. It wasn't fair to you."

"I understand it, as much as it hurt."

"I trust you."

His words blow me away, and my head bops backward, his hands dropping to my thighs. They mean just as much to me as hearing that he loves me, and my eyes well with tears.

"Baby, don't cry. We're going to get through this together. But I'm sorry for not staying, and I'm so sorry for the things I said when I got here. You didn't deserve to hear those words from me. Thank you for sticking with me, for not giving up on us."

I wipe the tears from my eyes and nod, swallowing down my emotions.

"You weren't the only one who went to Maine with less than innocent intentions," he continues, and dread festers in my stomach briefly.

"What did you do, Hayes?"

"I convinced myself that everything I was doing—regardless of what I was feeling—was all to get close to you to butter you up to get the story I wanted."

I can't help it; I laugh. "You're a dick. I'm not even offended because there's no way you could whore yourself out to me and keep your emotions off. I felt every single goddamn one. In every look. In every touch. Every kiss. Every time we made each other come. It's real. Raw. We're the real deal, Carter Hayes, and the real you can't ever hide from me."

"Fuck, I love you," he says right before he pounces, pushing me back into the couch. We make out like teenagers, slow and methodical, until I pull him down the hall and into my bed.

"The first thing I want to do once we're out is move closer, sleeping away from you after knowing sleep next to you isn't something I'm willing to do for long," I tell him. Carter snuggles into me, throwing his leg over my hip and nuzzling his face into my neck.

"I second that."

CHAPTER 17

carter

IT's been three days since Finn and I decided to be together. Three days of allowing myself to love another person and be loved in return. Since we decided to keep this from everyone right now, I've been taking the drive out to his place every night, but I want him in my bed, I want him in Aspen Ridge. The more I'm here without him, the stronger the pull is to blow the lid off this shit so I can move his ass into my house and be with my person.

I know it's fast, I know I've never been in a relationship with anyone before, but for the first time in my life, I've found someone I can be vulnerable with, that I feel like myself with, and I'm willing to fight for that and put in the work.

I've been working from home, something I'm thankful my position allows, but today I'm in the office, walking into a meeting with our event coordinator, who also happens to be Dallas' girlfriend, Blaire, for a meeting, texting Finn as I go.

> **Me:** I can still feel you when I walk or sit down fucker

Finn: Same, did you have to go so hard on me? I think I'm going to be sitting the rest of the day and not moving, maybe icing my ass.

I laugh as I stare down at my phone. Last night we decided to take turns fucking each other. Neither of us went easy, but the best part was watching him stave off his orgasm while I fucked him raw until I filled his sweet ass. He was only allowed to come once he was in me and by the time he was, he did not fucking hold back. Eager little shit.

Me: Must be nice to have the ability to work from home today

Finn: You could if you wanted. Round two?

Me: You're insatiable

Finn: Only for you

Finn: Come to me tonight?

Me: Yeah. How about a little playtime at Temptations tomorrow?

Finn: We need to talk about limits first

Me: Now that's a conversation I want to have while you're naked in bed

Just as I hit send, a hand slaps down hard and my phone gets smacked out of my hands, crashing down to the ground, and I scramble like a newborn giraffe to pick it up and close out of the message app.

"What's got you smiling like an idiot?"

Dallas, the dick.

"Why do you have to be a dickhead, Dal?"

He just shrugs while I check to make sure he didn't just break my damn phone.

"You heading to meet my woman?"

"Yup. Gotta let her look at the good-looking Hayes once in a while; sure she's fed up with seeing your mean mug all the time."

"Well, now I'm coming with you, Casanova, can't have you stealing my girl."

If he only knew I wasn't Casanova anymore and that I'm taken by a man. I laugh out loud, and Dallas looks at me like I've lost my mind.

"Your goddamn mood swings are all over the place lately, you're giving me whiplash."

"Fuck off, dickhead," I say as I push past him.

"Whoa, where'd that pair of balls come from?" he taunts as he pushes me back to get in front of me, speeding up his pace to get to Blaire's office first. I grab his arm and pull him behind me, giving him a little shove and walking faster.

"You're not coming to this damn meeting, Dal, fuck off with that shit."

"Like hell I'm not, she's mine and I'll damn well be wherever I want when it comes to her!"

We end up shoving each other back and forth until we're practically brawling, stumbling into Blaire's office and crashing to the ground.

"Oh, for fuck's sake. Not you, too! Carter, you're better than this!" Blaire yells as I struggle to shove my dickhead brother off of me.

"Should I even ask why you two are fighting?"

"He wanted to take the meeting alone with you, baby girl. That's not happening."

"Oh my god, Dallas, don't be ridiculous! It's your brother!"

"The good-looking one!"

"You all were bred in a lab! There is no one good-looking brother! It's all of you!"

Dallas shoves off me and stands quickly. I follow suit, straightening out my shirt and pushing my hair out of my face. Blaire's eyes are blown huge as she slowly backs up as my brother prowls her with his head cocked to the side.

"Did you just say all my brothers are good-looking, princess?"

"I did."

"Oh, baby girl, mistakes were just made." Dallas' head turns to face me, sending his next words in my direction, but I'm already moving. "You'll need to reschedule your meeting, Casanova, my future wife needs to be punished."

"Oh for fuck's sake, Dal! I don't need the dirty details!" I yell as I slam her office door and walk quickly down the hall. Just as I'm home free, Sawyer's voice yells for me as I pass his open door. I turn on my heels and pop my head in.

"Thought you had a meeting with Blaire to open up wedding dates for next summer?"

"Yeah, well, fuckin' dickhead came with me and kicked me out. Apparently Blaire needed a punishment," I say with a shiver.

"Fuck. How many times do I have to tell him not in the goddamn office? Ugh. I'll deal with him. How are you? Just wanted to check in on you."

"I'm hanging in there."

"Try not to let it ruin your life, brother. There are more important things out there to live for. Whatever happens, we'll take care of it, and it'll pass."

God, I hope he's right, even if we're talking about two different things here.

"Thanks. How are you? When do I get to snuggle my niece?"

"Ivy's ready for a date night, I am not."

"No! You? Protective of your baby daughter? Impossible!"

"Yeah, yeah. You'll be the first I call, though, I know you're good with Charlie when you babysit her."

"Wait, you mean I was supposed to be babysitting Charlie? Not the other way around? Shit, I'm messing everything up."

"Fuck off, Casanova. Let me know if you need anything. I may have a life of my own, but I'll always be there for you."

I hope he means it.

Later that night, I'm lying in bed with Finn as he brushes the hair from my face, something he does often, the move making my heart swell each time.

"Talk to me about limits, about your likes and desires," he says.

"Hard limit is sharing. I can't do it with you. It's never bothered me in the past, but I also didn't feel anything but sexual gratification until you."

"Thank fuck. Same. What about voyeurism or exhibitionism?"

"I'm indifferent to voyeurism; it doesn't do it for me, but it's not a hard limit either."

"Same. I'm not really into it. What about others watching you? Us?"

"Not a kink for me. Like, it doesn't get me off knowing others are watching, but as you saw yourself, I tend to stick to the main room. Part of me likes to put on a show, knowing others could be wanting to be me or be my partner for the night is hot, but it's not a deal breaker if you aren't into it."

"That first night at the club with you was my first time at a sex club, period. My first time fooling around with anyone in public openly. I was definitely into it," Finn expresses.

I perk up.

"Yeah? You want me to show you off?"

"Yeah, I think I'd like that. Being claimed publicly by you."

"Fuck, just the thought of that is making me hard, baby. Tell me your hard limits for playing."

"I'm not into impact play unless I'm the one giving it. Not really into role play or asphyxiation, definitely no degradation."

"Praise?" I interrupt to ask because I think I already know the answer.

"Yeah, I think so, for you too, huh?"

"Yeah, which is new since you. I like knowing I'm making you feel good."

"Before you, I needed to be in control. I've only bottomed twice, and I hated it both times. With you, it's easy and I thoroughly fucking enjoy it."

"Thank fuck, because I love fucking you."

"Don't get any ideas, Hayes. Save it all for tomorrow."

I huff out a protest, but Finn just pulls me further into him. Our bodies wrap around each other like they do every night, his strong heart beating against mine.

"I love you, Carter."

"I love you, too, baby."

My drive to Temptations is a blur, I can't get to Finn fast enough. The day dragged on. It was meeting after meeting and email after email, and I'm drained as fuck. All I want to do is collapse into Finn's arms, but tonight, we're playing at the club, and the thought gives me a jolt of energy that I needed. Plus, I have a surprise for him, and I know he's going to lose his mind.

I park my car and practically jump out of it, tripping as I jog up the stairs to the main entrance, wincing as the plug sitting snugly in my ass shifts from my quick movements. I ordered it online a few days ago as a surprise for Finn and have had it in for the last hour. The amount of prep I need for him to fuck me is ridiculous, and I wanted to make things easier on him.

Swiping my matte black membership card with gold writing on the first scanner outside the heavy door. Once I'm inside, I greet the receptionist, check my keys and wallet, and then scan my card again. The doors open as the music reaches my ears, a sensual beat that has my dick perking up, knowing I'm about to see my man. It's the first time Finn and I have been here since we sat at the bar and bickered, fighting the pull we both have always felt. I'm ready to show him off as mine.

I find him sitting at the end of the bar by himself, a whiskey on the rocks cradled in his palm. I don't take my eyes off of him as I cross through the floor, homed in on my man, everything else blurring together.

"Fuck, you're here. Jesus, took you long enough."

"I'm here, baby," I say against his plush lips right before I take them in a kiss that makes both of us breathless.

"You want a drink?" he asks, and I shake my head no. I just want him. "You're sure about this? I know you've probably hooked up with other members frequently, if you're not read—" I silence him immediately with another kiss, shoving my tongue in his mouth and swallowing down his moans. He tastes of the whiskey he's been sipping on and I eagerly suck on his tongue. He turns to face me fully, his legs spreading on the stool so I can step between them, his strong hands grabbing the back of my thighs. My hands hold his face, angling him just how I want him, my face bumping into the thick rim of the glasses I love so much.

"You're so fucking perfect for me, baby."

"God, don't stop. Give me more."

I pull away from him, grabbing his hand and leading him to the chaise lounge we first fooled around on, sending my thanks to the powers at play that no one is currently occupying it. I push Finn down onto it, taking a moment to look at him. His legs are spread, his black pants stretching tight over the hard muscle of his thighs, a baby blue henley fitting him in all the right places. My mouth waters looking at him, and he's all mine.

Our first night together flashes through my mind, and I know exactly what I want. I continue to look over him, the hard lines of his athletic body, the thick outline of his cock. I get to his face, his heavily-lidded, lust-filled blue eyes, his strong jaw, and the stubble that covers it. Fuck, I love him so much it hurts.

I keep my eyes on his as I unbuckle my pants and slide down

my zipper, pulling them down over my hips and removing them completely, the plug bumping against my prostate and making me groan.

Finn gives me a questioning look, but gets the hint and shimmies his pants down his thighs. My hands connect with his knees and rub upward over the wiry hair covering his thighs until I reach his hips. Using him for balance, I straddle him, leaning down and claiming his mouth. It's there that I completely lose myself to him. If anyone's watching right now, I wouldn't even notice. All that matters is that I'm here with Finn. It's hard to believe it wasn't long ago I lay underneath him for the first time while he claimed me as his own. Because that's exactly what he did that night. I didn't know it then, but he took my fucking heart that night for himself and I'll never give it back.

I break away from his lips and meet his eyes to check in with him, but he beats me to the punch.

"Are you okay?"

"Never been better," I say as I nip at his bottom lip, making him growl.

Sitting up on his thighs, I press two of my fingers into his mouth. He sucks around them, getting them nice and wet for me. Removing them, I take his dick in my hand, smearing his spit around his hard shaft. I work him for a moment, stroking slowly from root to tip, making his hips buck under me.

"Shh, baby. Be patient."

Finn growls, arching his lower back and pressing his dick further into my hand. He starts to weep for me, so I swipe the bead from the tip, licking it off my fingers and moaning.

"Fuck, you taste so good."

Never did I ever think I would enjoy the taste of another man's cum, but here we are. I'll take anything he'll give me and ask for more.

Having enough of torturing him, I scoot up further so that our cocks rub together. I moan the moment his slick flesh comes in contact with mine. His skin is so soft and warm, rock fucking hard, and feels so good rubbing against mine. I fist us together, holding our cocks tight in my hand while my other reaches up his chest, toying with each of his nipples.

His hands grab at my ass, pulling me into him, and I watch his eyes the moment his fingertips brush against the gem of the plug. Finn stills under me, his fingers pressing against the flat end of the toy.

"Carter?"

"Yeah, baby?"

"You didn't . . ."

"Hell yeah I did. Now let me work us up so you can take me home and remove it."

"Ohh fuuuuuck, yessss," he moans as he bucks wildly, fucking my hand from beneath me. Pleasure zips up and down my spine as my orgasm barrels closer. The firm pressure of the plug rubbing all the right places in my ass, Finn's hard cock against my own as I stroke us toward oblivion. It's all too much.

"You gonna come for me, *lover*?" I ask him as he watches in rapt attention as I work us over, my fists wrapped around our cocks, jerking us hard. I feel the moment he falls over the edge, and I'm right behind him. His stomach muscles tighten, balls drawing up, my name on his lips as he blows. I'm right with him, our cocks jerking as we cover us with cum. It's so fucking hot watching our releases mingle together as they spurt at the same time from our dicks. The sight immediately turns me on again, and I know one time won't be enough tonight.

"Fuck, that was good," he says on a rough exhale, his head falling back hard against the chaise. "You're so fucking good."

I lean over him, kissing his lips, his cheeks, and down his jaw, not able to get enough of him. His hands wrap around my waist, and we breathe for a moment.

What I want next is gonna require a whole helluva lot of lube and the safety of his apartment.

We clean ourselves up, and to my surprise, I don't feel an ounce of worry about being seen or judged. Temptations is a safe environment for all members to explore their sexuality and kinks, and it's a relief that I've now seen and felt it firsthand.

Finn and I are forced to drive separately, but I follow him the entire way back to his place. The driving is getting old, but I'll do it for as long as possible until we can figure everything else out. He's worth it.

finn

I PULL INTO MY DRIVEWAY WITH CARTER SECONDS behind me. We barely make it inside before I've got his clothes torn from his body. I lock the door and then shove him against the wall, his body bouncing slightly and pulling me into him. We're a mess of mouths, tongues, and hands as we work our way to my bedroom. I want inside him so goddamn bad, and knowing that his ass is nice and stretched open for me excites and pleases me to no end.

"Hands and knees on the bed, let me see that ass."

Carter obeys, crawling on all fours onto the center of my bed, resting his cheek on the sheets and propping his sexy ass into the air. I strip out of my clothes, grab a bottle of lube, and kneel behind him, my weight shifting the mattress under us. His skin is so smooth as I run my hands over his ass, squeezing into the muscles and working my way up over his hips, and lower back.

"Fuck, do you have any idea how goddamn sexy you are?" I practically growl. Carter fists the sheets under him, staying so still and perfect for me. Spreading his ass, I get my first glimpse of the pretty jewel sitting against his asshole. "Fuuuck." I can't believe he did this for me.

"I'm gonna remove the plug, take a deep breath and push out

for me," I tell him, wanting him to know exactly what's happening to him at all times. Unless we agree otherwise.

My fingers grip the base of the plug and I pull slowly as Carter pushes out, successfully removing it from his ass. I toss it off to the side for us to clean later and stare down at his hole.

A deep, primal growl works through my chest at the sight. He's so fucking ready for me. Leaning in, I lick up his taint to the top of his ass, swirling my tongue around his open hole, dipping my tongue inside. Carter mewls, and groans, pressing his ass against my mouth in search of more.

"You taste so damn good. You like it when I eat your ass, lover? You like my tongue all over your hole?"

"Uhng-gah-aah!"

I chuckle against his skin. "I'll take that as a yes."

Reaching around, I grab his thick shaft and tug on it while continuing to feast on his ass, making him a moaning, whining mess under me. I fucking love seeing him melt like this. My big strong man, a fucking puddle because of how good I'm making him feel. Talk about a fucking turn-on.

"Finn . . . I'm gonna blow, baby. Fuck me."

"Mmm." I take one last long, languid lick up his ass before straightening my spine between his legs, sitting up tall. I pop open the bottle of lube and coat my weeping dick with it, rubbing my fist up and down and making sure I'm thoroughly coated.

"You ready for me, lover? How do you want it?"

"Fuck yes, baby. Hard. Fuck me into the mattress."

I nearly blow right there.

Lining up my cock with his hole, I press inside, sinking easily into him in one smooth motion. The world turns on its goddamn axis at the feel of his tight ass around my dick.

"Oh fuuuuck, yessss. Goddamn, I love your ass. You okay?"

"Yes, shit, yes, fuck me. Fuck me." He chants it, begs for it, and do I fucking comply.

I ride him hard, holding his hips steady as I withdraw and thrust back in.

"Look at you taking all of me. This." Thrust. "Ass." Thrust. "Is." Thrust. "Mine."

"Yessss!" Carter screams, his moans echoing off the walls and burning me up from the inside out. I collapse on top of him, flattening his body to the bed as I grab both of his hands, weaving my fingers through his and holding them tight.

"Shit, baby, it feels so good. You're hitting everything just right."

"Love making you feel so good, Carter. Fucking live for it."

I thrust into him, Carter meeting me stroke for stroke as he pushes his ass back out into me.

"Need to come, baby. Please. Fuck, I need to come."

I back up onto my knees, dragging Carter with me so that his ass is in my lap and back is to my chest. His head lolls onto my shoulder as I slow my pace. Gripping his hair, I tilt his head so that my mouth has access to his neck. I lick and lap, bite and nibble at the skin as Carter shakes and writhes in my arms.

"You're gonna come from just my cock buried in your ass tonight. Don't touch yourself," I whisper to him, daring him. I know he can do it. He's close already.

"Ohh, fuuuck."

"You're doing so damn well taking all of me, making me feel so goddamn good. I want you to come. Let me have it."

I reach around us, finding his nipples and pinching, alternating between bringing him a bite of pain and soothing it with gentle caresses. I lick up the length of his long neck and back down again before sucking on the spot where his neck meets his shoulders.

"Come, Carter. Milk me and take me with you."

That seems to do the trick. I fuck into him from below as he shakes in my arms, his ass squeezing tightly around my cock and pulling me with him. My orgasm hits hard, Carter's ass sucking the cum right out of me. We both gasp for air as we work to come down from this mind-blowing feeling. The chemistry between us is like nothing I've ever come close to experiencing before.

I run my hands over his body, stopping to flatten my palm against his heart, feeling the rapid beating beneath it.

"You did so fucking good. I love sex with you," I praise him.

"You fuck like an animal, Nash. I'm obsessed with it." I laugh against his neck.

"Knew you could come like that. So fucking hot."

"Jesus, at first I thought you were crazy, but you got me there. Fuck, baby."

"I love you."

"I love you too."

I'm done waiting. Trey and I aren't making any progress. Everything is a dead end. Other than yearbook photos and class lists, there's no other connection we can find that would explain my dad's hate for the Hayes family and why he's so damn adamant about me staying away.

He's texted damn near every day, asking when I'll be in Seattle and when I'll be making things right with Lexi. I did send her a simple text apologizing for how rude I was, but after everything I told her in Maine, I'm pretty sure she took the hint that I wasn't interested.

My phone chimes again, another bullshit text message reminding me how my life will be over if I don't deliver, and what a failure I am, just propels me to do one last drop-in to try to talk him off the ledge.

I wake up at four-thirty, having spent the night alone, and I'm not happy about it. Driving back and forth is starting to get to Carter, and he hasn't spent the night here since our evening at Temptations. It's been days and I fucking miss having him in my bed.

After getting ready, I get into my SUV around six to start the three-hour drive into Seattle, knowing that I'm just going to have to drive back once I'm done. It's bullshit, but I've got to see him in person and he hasn't been working at the western office lately. Talking on the phone and giving him the opportunity to hang up on me isn't an option.

After getting stuck in traffic for an hour, I'm arriving at the office building a full hour later than I had hoped I would. After I've parked, I shoot Trey a text to let him know where I am and that I won't be in the office today, and then send Carter a text telling him I'm thinking about him.

Taking a deep breath, I lock up my vehicle and make the trek to the top floor to no doubt fight with my asshole father. His ass-face receptionist, who I would expect to be here, isn't in her normal place, so I let myself in through the glass doors and walk to the back where my father's private office is.

My footsteps pause, the moans and thumping audible through the second set of closed doors catching me completely off guard. Knowing that my mom is in Paris this week, I steady myself for what I'm about to see. Like picking up a shoe after you've killed a spider, I have to check to make sure what I'm hearing is in fact, my piece of shit father cheating on my mother. Blood rushes between my ears and I almost can't believe this is fucking happening.

With a shaky hand, I twist the silver doorknob and push it open. I expected his secretary, whom I've suspected of sleeping with him in the past, but what I find is so much better. I quickly pull out my phone and snap a photo, making sure my dad's face is front and center in the frame.

Lucky for me, they are both facing my direction, and I don't have to see my indisposed father's shriveled dick. Instead, I get a front-row view of him barreling into none other than Lexi Fairchild. Her blonde hair is splayed over his desk, where she lies bent over, dress flipped up, my dad right behind her. Neither hears me until I start slowly clapping. My dad's head shoots up, his face red and angry.

"Get the fuck out, Griffin!" he roars, his voice thundering through the room as he pushes off of Lexi and bends to pull up his pants. Lexi pushes the hair out of her face as she looks at me, her eyes going wild with panic.

"No, I don't think I'm going to go anywhere."

"This isn't what it looks like, Griffin," Lexi tries to argue.

"It's exactly what it looks like, Lexi. I'm not blind. We were never going to be together, and I couldn't care less about what you do, but I highly suggest you run for the hills and figure yourself out before you are tangled any further with men like him. No amount of money is worth this." It's more kindness than she deserves after her role in shattering my weekend with Carter in Maine, but I don't fully blame her. She's the product of her father's demands, just like I am, only I'm choosing to break the cycle, and she's continuing it. I hope she gets her life together before she winds up spending it numb and empty like both of our mothers.

Lexi scrambles past me to leave the office, and I'm left staring at my father.

"I never want to hear you say that I'm a disappointment again after what I just walked in on," I seethe.

He doesn't say a word, and I turn on my heels to leave. It's better he stews for a bit, wondering what I'm going to do with the information I just gained on him, rather than fighting it out now. For the first time in my life, I have the upper hand and he knows it.

Once I'm in my car, I start it up to crank up the AC, the heat of the day already sweltering, especially in my office clothes. I always suspected my dad wasn't faithful to my mother, but to suspect it and see it firsthand are two completely different things. I gave up the fantastical dreams of a kid that my father was going to suddenly wake up and be the role model and protector that all the other kids I went to school with had. But this cements my feelings for the man who created me. All he's ever cared about is power and how to gain more of it by weaponizing his money.

I'm struggling with the best course of action. I immediately want to use every vile piece of hate he's ever thrown at me, every time he's used me, bullied me, left me to fend for myself, embarrassed me, made me this human who is constantly seeking praise and never feeling like he's good enough for anything, to crumble him. But I don't want to be anything like him, and that's exactly what he would do if the tables were turned.

I gave him almost thirty years of my life, breaking myself to become someone he could be proud of, but it was never enough, and it was never going to be enough. I was set up for failure from the moment he had me. He's always looked at me as a piece of his business, an asset that he can mold and control. I've lost too much of myself and too much time because of him. This ends here. Adrenaline is coursing through me as I unlock my phone and quickly bring up Trey's chat.

Me: Done already

Trey: Fuck bro. That was like ten minutes. I knew driving up there was gonna be for nothing

Me: You won't feel that way when I show you the photo I just took

Trey: Give me more than that

Me: Sure you don't want the surprise later? Kinda want to see your face when you see what I found

Trey: Fuckin' tell me or I'll cut off your dick and feed it to you

Me: Just walked in on my dad with Lexi Fairchild bent over his desk

Trey: No fucking way

Trey: You were just given the fucking keys to the city brother

Me: No shit.

Me: Now, what do we do with it?

Trey: We either burn it all to the ground

Trey: Blackmail the mother fucker and
take over

Trey: Or

Me: Or???

Trey: We take the high road and use it as
leverage for him to let you silently walk away
and start your life over.

Everything that was already running through my mind. I know I won't ruin the business because that's not who I am. I love my damn job, but I also am fully aware that unless I force a takeover, I'm not going to have one. But even if I do that, will he ever really and truly go away? I know what I'm doing without thinking too hard about it.

Me: We'll talk about it and get a plan together.

Trey: I got you no matter what. Where you go,
I go

Even though I still don't have the answers I want, with the evidence of a lifetime that could end all of this bullshit, I take the long-ass drive all the way back across the state, feeling a whole helluva lot better than I did this morning and one step closer to starting the life I've always wanted.

CHAPTER 19

carter

I CAN HEAR HIS FOOTSTEPS AS HE JOGS DOWN THE hallway and whips open the door. Finn looks at me, bleary-eyed and tired, but with so much emotion it makes my heart swell.

"What are you doing here?"

I shrug. "I couldn't sleep," I tell him matter-of-factly.

"So you drove thirty minutes in the middle of the night?"

"You can't come to me, where you should be, so I came to you. A few hours of sleep with you is better than none at all away from you."

Finn's face softens, his breathing shallow, a look of awe on his face. Without another word, he reaches for my hand, leading me to his bedroom, where I strip down to my boxer briefs and crawl into bed next to him. We reach for each other on autopilot, both wanting nothing more than to just be close, to feel the comfort and warmth that we bring each other. I'm so at home right here. I want to protect this little bubble we've built, but it's not good for us. We need to get out and live—together. I know that we need to stick it out, wait until we have better control of everything with his dad, but I don't want to wait any longer. Even if I am scared shitless about coming out to everyone.

"I can't keep this up much longer," I confess, hating the position we're in, hating that my speaking the words out loud just makes the pressure of everything that much harder.

"My sweet man," he breathes as his hand strokes across my forehead, brushing the strands out of the way. "Me either. Even if we didn't have all this other shit going on, coming out is a big deal, are you sure you're ready for that?"

"I'm going to tell my siblings first, then my parents. But everyone else can fuck off. They'll figure it out when they see us together. I don't care about anything else anymore. I just want you, Finn."

"Fuck, I love hearing you say that."

"Yeah? What else do you love?" I tease.

"The way you hate to drink cold water, the way your eyes squint in pain before a panic attack, giving me just a moment to help ease it back before you spiral, your love of Marvel, the way that you are so unapologetically yourself with me, the way you put your family first, how hard you love, the way you fight and challenge me, your heart, the way you fuck."

My heart nearly explodes with emotion, tears springing to my eyes. I've never been spoken to like that before.

"Fuck, I love you, baby."

"I love you more than anything."

Our lips connect in a long, passionate kiss, just a firm press of our lips together, our hands held tightly between us before we break apart.

"Are you sure you're ready for this?"

"More than ever. Why?"

"I walked in on my dad with Lexi bent over his desk, skirt around her waist."

I jump up onto my knees, pushing Finn hard in the chest.

"Ow!"

"I've been here for twenty minutes! Why didn't you start with this shit?"

"Needed to make sure you were fully in it."

I can feel the rage building in my bloodstream, my fists clenching hard. Are we seriously taking ten steps back again? Before I register what's happening, which doesn't happen often, Finn has grabbed me, flipping me hard onto my back, bouncing slightly on the bed as he pins my wrists above my head, his legs straddling me.

"Get those thoughts out of your head or I'll fuck it out of you, and trust me, I won't be sweet about it. I was joking. I was going to tell you, but I was so surprised to see you and enjoyed you being so needy."

My breathing starts to settle a bit; I believe him, I just want to know how this is going to affect us.

"Tell me what happened."

"Are you going to be a good boy?"

I practically growl at him, my dick throbbing under where he's sitting on my lap, his warmth seeping into me. I know he can feel how hard he makes me without even trying.

"Finn . . ." I say in a warning tone.

"I'm going to blackmail him into letting me go silently. I want a clean break from him in every aspect of my life. I want the ability to work wherever I want without the fear of him leering over me like a puppeteer."

His words stun me. I know his relationship with his dad is emotionally volatile, but the effort and courage it takes to fight back is immense. I couldn't imagine the weight of having a toxic parent, of loving them purely because they're your parents, constantly trying to make excuses and justify their behavior, convincing yourself that you're the reason for it—that somehow you're deserving of it. I'm going to spend my life healing every single wound and scar left by his piece of shit dad.

"Are you sure, Finn?"

"I've only ever been this positive about one other thing in my life. So, yeah, I am."

I know the answer before I ask it, but I want to hear it anyway. "Which is?"

"You, lover."

I smile up at him as he releases my wrists, and my hands move to either side of his waist, gliding up and down the smooth expanse of his torso.

"So, what's our plan?"

"Well, I'm going to go in there tomorrow morning to lay it all out. I don't anticipate him going down silently right away, but I'm confident he doesn't want anyone to know he was fucking his attorney's daughter."

"Damn, I'm so proud of you. Do you know what you want to do? Where do you want to go after?"

"I've been thinking about my options. I may have worked at the Northwest Explorer, but my name is on every piece I've done. People know who I am. I'm a damn good writer, but I wonder if people will always wonder if there's a story there, and I don't want it lingering over my head."

"You can't leave writing altogether, Finn. You love it too much."

"You're right, and I won't. I think I'm going to create my own travel blog for now. It'll be a slow roll at first, but all I've ever wanted was to tell stories, Carter. Real stories about real people. My dad has this massive platform, and I was only happy to accept his abuse for as long as I did because, for the most part, I've been allowed to do exactly what I want to. But I've been living behind the fear of the unknown. It was easier to take his abuse than it was to rock the boat. I'm ready for the next chapter. I'm ready to rock the boat."

"God, I love you. Your integrity, your courage, your resilience. You are my home, Finn. We're going to get through this together. I think this is perfect for you, and while you grow, you've got me. You're never going to be alone again." His eyes shutter closed for a moment, opening with tears beaded on his thick eyelashes. "Do you want me to come with you to talk to your dad?"

"Would you?"

"In a heartbeat."

He laughs, and I tilt my head, looking up at him while I try to read his humorous expression.

"I can't wait to see the look on his face."

"After we're done there, I'm going to come out to my siblings."

"Carter, you don't have to . . ."

"No, I do. I want to. I need to. I love them and if we're burning shit to the ground, we might as well do it together."

"Do you think they'll react okay? I know I've asked before, but I don't want you to get hurt, and that fear is just a reality for others who've come before us. This entire concept that we have to come out like it's some fucking announcement that needs to be made, as if we need permission to love who we love. But the fear is real, Carter. You think you know someone until you tell them you're gay, or bisexual, or anything else that's not in their realm of what they consider normal. I don't want you to get hurt."

"I'm not afraid. If they aren't supportive, or hell, even if they couldn't care less, I need to know. Because those aren't people I want in my life to begin with. So, better to figure that out now at twenty-five than later."

"I just need to say it again. You don't have to do this right now. Don't do it for me."

"I'm doing it for us, Finn. You're worth it. You're enough, you're all that matters to me."

The emotion that consumes his face is enough to bring me to tears. I fucking love this man.

"Okay. I'm with you. No matter what."

"No matter what."

The next morning, Finn and I get ready together in his bathroom, both of us vibrating with nervous energy for what we're about to do. The drive is fucking exhausting, and I can't believe he just did this back and forth yesterday. I haven't had to drive into the city in a long-ass time and I don't plan on repeating it any time soon. I love the seclusion Aspen Ridge gives us, our tiny town where everything is practically within walking distance. There are no big box stores, no skyscrapers to block the natural views of the mountains. Our air is crisp and clean, and I wouldn't want to live anywhere else.

Once we've been on the road and the sun has come up, I send a text to the sibling group chat letting them know I won't be at work.

Me: Got something to take care of and won't be in today. I set up my out of office reply, and left some things for Marcus to take care of.

Sawyer: Should we be concerned?

Liam: Did something drop we haven't seen yet?

Me: No, just got some stuff that needs my attention

Kinsey: Lay off of him, he's a big boy

Dallas: Big boy who needs his lil sis to come to his rescue

Kinsey: Dallas I will throat punch you so hard you'll need to eat through a straw

Sawyer: Thatta girl

Me: I'll check in later

I pocket my phone and take a deep breath. They can't make anything easy.

"Go better than you thought?"

"Eh. None of us gets a whole helluva lot of privacy. Comes with the territory of being close, but goddamn, sometimes I just want to be able to say something and not get the third degree."

"I have no idea what that's like, but I can imagine it could be a little suffocating sometimes. At least they love you."

I look up at Finn as he drives and smile. I really want them to love him, too.

We arrive at a large office building in Seattle, and I swear to Christ, it's goddamn hotter in the city than in Aspen Ridge. I use two fingers to loosen the shirt around my neck, but I'm not about to complain.

"You okay? You don't have to come with me."

"I'm good, I promise."

"If you feel any bit of panic, Carter, just give me a look and we're out of there."

"Baby, I'm good. I'm going to have your back. Let's go put an end to this shit so I can take you home with me."

Finn gives me a chaste kiss and we walk into the building. I'm acutely aware of his every move, every tick of his jaw, the way his eyes dart around, and I know that I made the right decision by being here with him. Sliding my hand down the sinewed muscles of his forearm, I thread our fingers together and hold his hand. His shoulders relax, and he exhales a breath that he was clearly holding.

There's only one word that comes to mind when walking through the building—opulent. Especially for a magazine like this. I know they're popular, but it's clear the Nashes didn't get their money from it. At least, not all of it. Everything is marble and glass, and compared to the rough grounds of the distillery in the country, with our raw materials, gravel roads, and rocky land-scape, I can't imagine living in a concrete jungle like this. I hope Finn falls in love with Aspen Ridge because there's no way I'm living anywhere else. I'd be miserable. Everything he's told me so far leads me to believe that he hates this shit just as much as I do, and that he's craving the comfort and peace that a small town brings.

We ride the elevator in silence, my thumb rubbing small circles across the back of his hand, a silent reminder that he has someone in his corner, that I'm not going anywhere. It seems to keep him grounded, and I'm surprised to find that I love the feeling of being someone else's comfort. The bell rings, and we step off on the top floor. My nerves ratchet up a few levels, but I breathe through it, I'm here to support Finn and I'm not going to let anyone fuck with him. His dad seems like a top-notch fuck-face, and I'll be damned if Finn has to live under his thumb for a moment longer.

To our surprise, Finn's dad is standing in the doorway of his office with his arms crossed, looking like he's waiting for our arrival. Finn's dad exudes the exact false bravado that one would expect from someone of his stature. You can practically taste the thick arrogance wafting in the stuffy room. His physical traits make it clear that he's Finn's father, yet he looks so different at the same time. His face is rounder, deep lines crease his forehead like his brow is always furrowed with anger. He shares the same jawline as his son, but his facial hair is salt and pepper. At first glance, he looks polished—based off the suit that has been tailored to fit his physique— but men like him can't hide that they're actually desperate, weak fucks.

"Griffin. What the fuck is he doing here?"

"Let's go have a chat, Dad. You're gonna want to hear this."

"I'm not speaking with you in front of this bastard." His dad's voice rises a notch, and my blood starts to boil over. Who the fuck does he think he is?

"Fine, we can do this right here, then," Finn says, keeping his composure, unlike me, who is slipping and about to lose it on this dick. "I am done being your puppet. I am done letting you control my life. You've controlled me long enough, Dad. I'm done."

A maniacal laugh bubbles up from his dad's mouth, and I take a step closer to him, wanting nothing more than to knock his fucking teeth out.

"The fuck you are. You're my son, Griffin! You can't just be fucking done!"

"Oh, I can. And you're going to be done, too. You're going to let me walk away from you and the magazine peacefully and without issues, and I'm going to start a new life on my own that you won't be part of. You and I both know what I caught you doing, you sick fuck, and if you as so much think about sullying my name to anyone, I will make sure everyone knows what a low-life cheater you are. You're all about appearances, Dad, what would everyone say if they found out you were fucking your lawyer's daughter?"

I stiffen next to Finn as his dad throws his head back and laughs. I can't believe this is the man who raised such a loving, compassionate, loyal man. I reach down to thread my fingers through Finn's, giving his hand a little squeeze, letting him know that he's got this. Even if I want to handle this my way, I know he needs to get through this on his own.

"You're such a stupid boy, Griffin. You have no proof. It's the word of a disgruntled, spoiled little boy who didn't get his way, trying to get his dad's attention. No one will believe you."

"Maybe. If I hadn't taken a photo of you in the act. Don't worry, there's no nudity shown, but it's very clear what's happening. Poor girl," Finn replies with a shudder.

"You fucking bastard! So, you're here to ruin me? Take everything that I've worked hard for? I fucking made you, Griffin!"

"I don't want anything from you! All I want is to walk away from your toxic, abusive bullshit and never hear from you again. You've controlled me long enough. You can continue to live your life, and I'll be free of you. That's it. I'm leaving the Northwest Explorer, effective immediately, and walking out of your life. You're going to let me go."

My mouth nearly drops open in awe of him standing up to his dad. I can't begin to fathom the strength it takes to confront your abuser, especially when the abuser is your own father. This man should have been Finn's safe place, his guardian in everything, his mentor, and instead, all he's done is use fear and control to wield him how and when he sees fit. I release Finn's hand and take several confident strides into his dad's space. I'll give it to him, he's a cocky bastard, but I've got a strong feeling it's only there because of the piles of money and power he stands on and inside he's really just a sad, weak, little man.

"Just gonna interrupt here for a second. Hey, I'm Carter, Finn's boyfriend. Pretty sure you know who I am already though, amIright?" I taunt. "You didn't create shit. You may share DNA, but it ends there. Finn's the best man I've ever fucking met and it sure as shit isn't thanks to you. Finn is way too fucking humble to threaten your slimy ass further but I'm not. Going to just make this real fuckin' clear so you understand the world of shit you're in. You won't so much as utter his fucking name after we leave here. If you think about reaching out to your competitors or making his life harder, we'll release the photo. You've done more than enough damage to him, and I'm going to guarantee he gets a fresh start with the ability to write anywhere he damn well wants and feels all the love that he deserves. And I'm gonna be the one who gives it to him. Every damn day. You understand me?"

I can feel Finn's stare burning into the back of my head. I know I was only supposed to come here for support, but I also needed to make sure he was protected and that this asshole knows we're a team. He matters, and I choose him.

"Answer him!" Finn yells after a silent, tense moment.

"Get the fuck out of my office before I call security!"

"Answer me. Do you understand?" I grit through clenched teeth.

"I understand. You're dead to me, Griffin. You were a mistake that I regretted from the moment your mom tricked me into getting her pregnant. You're fucking dead to me! Get out!"

"Likewise."

With that, Finn squeezes my hand and pulls me out of the office and toward the elevator. Once safely inside, he collapses against the wall, running both hands over his face. I pull him into a hug, one of my hands cradling the back of his head, the other wrapped around his upper back.

"It's over, baby. You did it. You're free. I'm so damn proud of you."

"Please don't you ever leave me, Carter. I'm so scared of not being enough for you."

"Are you kidding me with that right now? You're mine, Finn, and I'm yours. We're in it now, and there's no leaving for either of us. Look, I know it's gonna be hard, baby. I know there's gonna be days where you want to kick my teeth in, but I promise you I will try, I will put you first, I will fight for you and love you. I'll take care of you. You're enough for me, all I need. You're it for me. End game. You've wrecked me in the best way, and I can't spend another moment apart. Move in with me. Marry me. Spend the rest of your life with me; just don't ever think that you aren't good enough for me. If a day comes that you feel that way, then tell me so I have the opportunity to fix what I'm doing."

"You'd marry me?"

"Fuck yes, I'd marry you. I'm in love with you!"

Finn is finally smiling, his hands wrapped around my waist in return.

"Let's start with moving in together. I fucking hate my house."

"Thank fuck, baby. I hate it, too. I want you in Aspen Ridge with me, you're gonna love it there."

The elevator door slides open and I grab his hand again, walking out of this dumbass building.

"I understand why you hate the name Griffin now."

"Ya think?"

I've never seen such disdain and disgust on anyone's face before. The man doesn't even know me, but it was clear he hated me. What kind of father talks to his own son that way? My heart breaks for Finn, that he had to deal with that shit. If his dad had no reservations about talking to him like that in front of a stranger, I can't imagine what he's like behind closed doors.

I take the wheel this time, Finn letting me know that I'm the first person he's ever let drive his vehicle. It's the only thing he's bought with his trust fund that is lavish, and I'll give him this one. The damn thing is a dream and I'm glad he doesn't have to give it up.

I merge onto the highway and pull farther and farther away from the city, away from the cage that was locked around Finn, and head toward our new life together.

One hurdle down, two to go.

carter

From the beginning, I haven't had any difficulty in coming to terms with my sexuality, but now that I'm faced with speaking to it—with coming out—I'm suddenly nervous. My biggest hurdle was accepting love and giving it to someone else, regardless of their gender. Am I completely ready to share this part of me with my family? Can't say I'm eager to have this conversation, especially when they've only ever known me as a playboy. I'm confident nothing bad will come from me sharing my sexuality with my family, but I know I'm going to get some shit for it.

But I don't want to keep Finn in the dark. We deserve to live out in the open and not have our lives and actions ruled by fear over what people will think. I want to start living with him, and this is just one more step in that direction. Finn's dad's reaction replays in my head and I wince. The pure disgust was loud and clear. My heart pangs for Finn to have that kind of man as his father, and I really want my family to accept him as one of us, just like they have with Ivy, Blaire, Hannah, and Charlie.

While I know Finn is anticipating my family reacting badly, because that's the only experience he has had, I'm confident that it's just going to be an uncomfortable conversation rather than a negative one. They're going to be surprised, but nothing will change, except for maybe some jokes here and there—especially from Dallas. My poor Finn. He deserves all the love and support in the world, and I really hope that my family can be that for him. We've just gotta get through some hurdles first. And this is the first one.

Ready to get this shit over with, I relax on the couch that sits inside our tasting room at the distillery and pull out my phone, bringing up my texts. My only unread message is from Finn, and I open it up with a smile on my face.

> Finn: You've got this. I can be there in 10 if you want me

> Me: Nah, I've got it. They're a crazy bunch of assholes. Better to pull the Band-Aid myself.

> Finn: K. I'll be at your place waiting. I love you

> Me: Love you too

Closing out of his chat, I open up my sibling group chat, ready to get them here and do this. My mind and body are now oddly at one with each other—calm. Which is such a contrast to who I've been for as long as I can remember. The tension that normally sits tight at the base of my neck is gone, the panic and anxiety that rises so quickly has receded. I'm at a place for the first time in my life where I feel completely and truly at peace. And I'm ready to live that openly rather than hiding.

I type out the only words that I know the five of us can't ever ignore. The seven little words that will make all of us drop everything and anything and come running.

> Me: Grandpa caught me drinking his whiskey again

We created our code phrase after Sawyer and Dallas literally got caught drinking our grandpa's whiskey. Liam and I came to the rescue, coming up with an elaborate lie that they were just interested in the family business and were taste testing and some other bullshit we came up with on the fly. We've each used it a handful of times over the years, but have a pact to never abuse it. Dallas is the only exception because, well, he's Dallas. I think, given the circumstances, it's appropriate for me to use it for the first time.

A reply comes immediately.

Dallas: Where?

Me: Distillery. Got some news. Need you all to come

Sawyer: Be there in 15

Liam: Same

Dallas: Already omw

Kinsey: Be there shortly

I release the pent-up air I was holding in my lungs, relaxing further into my seat, letting my head drop down on the back of the velvet-upholstered couch. Now I just need to wait for them to get here. I don't think any of them are going to care, my family loves hard and unconditionally. But I know it's going to shock the shit out of all of them. I'm a notorious playboy. Reformed playboy now. I laugh as the realization hits me while I stare up at the large wood beams in the ceiling. Jesus Christ. People are going to get a good laugh at this.

I've fucked my way through this town, not something I'm crazy proud of, but we were all willing partners. I've had more than a few conquests that tried to settle me down, who fell for me and thought they could change my ways, but I never felt anything with any of them.

Turns out, I was just waiting for Finn Nash to barrel into my life, knocking the whole goddamn thing off course, making me feel something other than immediate gratification in the moment. I feel everything with him. And I sure as shit don't want to keep him hidden.

The rumble of a motorcycle and several cars hits my ears from outside as my siblings arrive. I take a deep, steadying breath, letting myself picture Finn waiting in my bed for me, glasses on his face, book in his hand. Yeah, I've got this. It's worth it. *He's worth it.*

"Dude you're pale as fuck, are you dying?" Dallas says as my siblings walk in, Dallas leading the pack.

"I wish," I grumble under my breath as my stomach rolls slightly, but I take a deep breath, imagining Finn's warm hand covering mine and squeezing, and I focus on staying in control.

"Really? How shitty are you going to feel if he is dying, dickhead?"

"So, we're back to dickhead? Thought I was dumbass? Get it straight, shithead."

"They're interchangeable depending on the day because god forbid you do anything consistently." Sawyer and Dallas bicker back and forth, and I shake my head.

"Hey, Casanova, what's got you so blue?" Kinsey says as she plops down next to me on the couch. Meeting at the distillery made the most sense. Needed a private place, but didn't want to have to kick them all outta my house, and I want to be able to leave when I'm ready for space. Liam starts to pace, running his hands through his hair, wracking up my nervous energy as Sawyer stands off to the side, his large arms crossed over his chest like he's waiting for the bomb I'm about to drop and already thinking of ways to handle it.

"Spit it out," Sawyer demands.

"Then take a seat, you're making me nervous as fuck, shithead."

Reluctantly, my remaining two brothers take a seat around the coffee table in the sitting area of our tasting room. I look at each of my four siblings, surrounded by the rich history of our family distillery, the grounds that we all grew up on, the business that runs deeply through each of our veins. The lights are low, everything dark around us except for the single overhead light where we're sitting. I take a deep breath and prepare myself. Reaching for the whiskey, I pour five glasses with a heavy hand, figuring they all might need it.

"Damn, pulling out Liam's good stuff," Kinsey says as she reaches for her glass.

"It's the family's, not Liam's," Sawyer corrects, and we all roll our eyes in unison. Swiping my glass off the table, I toss it back in one go, the whiskey burning a trail down my throat, warmth spreading through my veins.

"I'm bisexual."

"*Fuck*," Sawyer says on a rough exhale, my spine stiffening, eyes falling closed, air sucked right out of my lungs. Shit, was Finn right? "Goddamn, that's the big news? No offense, Casanova, but I thought you were about to tell us you knocked someone up or had some baby dropped off at your doorstep." My eyes snap open, my head jerking to look at my siblings.

Liam's head drops back in a loud laugh. "For real! I was not expecting this, just for the record, but for fuck's sake, I'm with Sawyer."

"Christ. The fuck?" I ask, genuinely surprised by their reactions. I guess my extracurricular activities would make them wonder when I've gambled every time I stuck my dick into a willing female, wrapped up or not.

"Soooo, no surprise baby then?" Dallas asks for clarification.

"No, brother. No babies. Just also like dick, apparently. Or one dick," I say, shaking my head. "Still not quite sure yet on the logistics."

Dallas snaps his fingers loudly, forcing our attention on him.

"Does that mean we can call you cum-guzzler instead of Casanova?"

I can't help it; I burst out laughing, a deep belly laugh that settles my nerves instantly. Leave it to Dallas to bring light to the situation. My brother's an idiot, but damn if he doesn't make us all laugh.

"Dude. That's a good one, but maybe too soon?" Liam tells him, holding back his laugh.

"Definitely don't want that nickname, dumbass."

"Well, obviously we love you no matter who you love. But it's honestly a little inconvenient for me. I was looking forward to not being outnumbered, and if you end up with a man, then I'm still going to be. I've already got too many brothers. Adding in Ivy, Blaire, and Han is obviously nice, but we're still outnumbered with you overbearing dickweeds. What the hell?" Kinsey says with a huge, teasing smile.

I laugh at my sweet sister and give her an apologetic wince. "Sorry, little sis. You'll like him, though, I promise."

"I'm just giving you shit. Maybe he'll be on my side for a change. You protective assholes need to let me breathe and live a little."

"Fuck no."

"Never."

"Nope."

"Not gonna happen."

Kinsey rolls her eyes and I feel bad for her for a moment, but it's for her own good. We know how men are, and we want to protect her from the pieces of shit out there. We never want her to feel heartbreak, fear, or pain. We can't protect her forever, but maybe we can protect her until the right man comes along and takes over.

"So, you met someone, huh?" Sawyer asks.

I scratch at my jaw nervously.

"Yeah . . ."

"Well? You gonna give us some details?"

I push Sawyer's untouched glass of whiskey in his direction. He looks at it before raising his eyebrows. "Fuck, really?"

"Drink up, big brother. You haven't thawed out enough since Ivy returned or Grace was born. Down the hatch."

Sawyer takes a long pull from his drink, setting it back down on the table.

"I'm not returning home drunk to my wife and newborn daughter. That's all you're getting from me."

"It's Griffin Nash."

Dallas whistles as Liam flops back into his seat, eyes huge. Kinsey looks back and forth between all of us, clearly confused. But it's Sawyer's reaction I'm waiting for.

"You're fucking Griffin Nash? The dickhead writer at the Northwest Explorer? The same asshole who has made your life hell for months?"

I can't help but wince. Thank fuck they don't know the raw, dirty details of how Finn ad I have manipulated and blackmailed each other and all the grit in between.

"The one and only."

"Just over that weekend? That quick?"

Fuck. These bastards weren't gonna let me off the hook easily, but I was really hoping to skip this shit.

"Uhh," I start, pausing and scratching my nails against the back of my neck. "Started a bit before that. We hooked up once, and I didn't know who he was. As soon as I did, I panicked and went into cleanup mode. I fought it as long as I could but he's a persistent fucker."

"Sounds exactly like what you need, you stubborn asshole," Liam says.

I chuckle, thinking about how stubborn and stupid I've been and how Finn has taken every punch I've thrown. He never gave up on me, always so goddamn confident in us. *Thank fuck.*

"Yeah, he is," I say with a smile. "I'm in love with him."

"Daaaamn. I never thought I'd see the day. When do we get to meet him?" Dallas asks.

"I'll set something up, but you fuckers need to chill out. He's an only child, not used to this big family shit. His family is really rough around the edges. I don't want to air their issues, but he just ended his relationship with them, and all he's got is me. The dynamic of our sibling shit is gonna be new for him and I don't want you to scare him off."

"We'll be on our best behavior. You've got nothing to worry about."

Like fuck I don't.

We spend the next few hours sitting in the old distillery just us five, talking about life—Sawyer transitioning into being a dad, his plans for getting Ivy pregnant with baby number two, Dallas' ideas for proposing to Blaire and give her the wedding of her dreams, and how Liam and Hannah are settling into wedded bliss, as if they weren't already living it before they even got married.

"I'm going to take Reid up on his offer to rent the studio apartment above Rogue," Kinsey announces, four sets of eyes narrowing in on her. It's silent for a moment, and I wait for Sawyer and Dallas to jump down her throat. But I don't want them to shatter her hopes. She's a big girl and can make smart decisions.

"I'm for it."

Sawyer's head spins in my direction so fast I almost suggest he see a chiropractor after we leave here.

"You what?"

"I think it's a good idea. She's not moving to Timbuktu. She's moving across town, into a loft apartment above, what I would argue, is one of the safer places for her to be. It's Aspen Ridge, you Neanderthal. What's going to happen to her? With Reid downstairs and me right down the street? She needs freedom, and she's not getting that at Dad and Mom's house. You do remember we've all trained her to defend herself, right? She could probably kick all our asses if she needed to." I told her I'd have her back, and I'm pulling through on that now.

Kinsey beams at me, and it makes me relax slightly, even if I'm bracing myself for Sawyer's wrath.

"Are you fucking insane?" Sawyer stands abruptly, and reflexively, so do I. He's in my face a moment later.

"I'm thinking pretty clear, brother, and I'm choosing Kinsey right now. She's got this."

"Like fuck she does. She's barely twenty-two. We're supposed to be a united front to keep her safe. After everything we've been through with Ivy and Blaire. No."

"She will be! She'll be safe!"

I see the flash of one of Sawyer's brain-rattling punches pull back a moment too late, his fist connecting with my face in a hit that I'm thankful missed my nose. The impact rings out in my head, forcing me flat onto my back on the couch. I barely register Kinsey's scream as she scoots away from me, Dallas and Liam shooting to their feet.

"Are you insane, Sawyer?" Kinsey yells at him. "What is wrong with you?"

"I want to keep you safe, Kins! I'd never forgive myself if something happened to you. Almost losing Ivy twice nearly killed me. It nearly broke Dallas after what happened to Blaire . . . she's still recovering! You were there watching it! Next to her while she suffered! We wouldn't survive it if it were you."

"And I love you for it, Sawyer. I love you all so much. But you're suffocating me. Do you know how hard it is to make friends? Real girlfriends? My entire life so many of them only wanted to be my friend because they had crushes on you four dumbasses. And guys won't come near me. How many twenty-two-year-old virgins do you idiots know? Even at college, I wasn't given freedom. Do you have any idea how lonely it's been? I love you all so much, but if you don't let me breathe, I'm going to leave Aspen Ridge. It will literally break me, but I can't live in your shadows anymore."

The room falls into silence as we watch our baby sister break down and cry. The realization of our behavior hovering over all of us, and how in our efforts to protect her, we've made her life that much harder.

All four of us are moving before she registers it, Sawyer scooping into her side, Liam on the other, with Dallas and I at her feet. Together, we hug our little sister, who's definitely not so little anymore, and needs to live her life for herself. After everything Finn has been through, I know now how important it is to just give support. We can't protect her out of fear of the unknown.

"She's moving out of Mom and Dad's and into Reid's loft. And we're all going to back off, I say as I stand up and look down at them all.

"Since when does Casanova make decisions?" Dallas asks.

"Since I'm watching our baby sister cry, and I know what it feels like to not be comfortable with your situation and have no idea how to fix it."

Kinsey bats the tears off her cheeks before walking up to me and wrapping her arms around my waist. I return the hug and glare at each one of my idiot brothers. Liam is the first to move. Wrapping Kinsey's other side in a hug.

"I support you. You're right. I'm sorry, Kins. I love you."

Dallas is next, joining in on what is turning into a huge-ass family hug that I didn't realize I needed as much as she probably does.

"I've got you, little sis. I'm sorry for being such an overbearing ass. Blaire calls me out on it, too."

Kins chuckles against my shirt. "Yeah, but she likes it. I don't."

"That's true," Dallas agrees.

With a huff, Sawyer joins in, wrapping his tree limb arms around all of us.

"We'll get through whatever happens. It's hard to be sorry when I'm just trying to protect you, but I understand you need to live, and I'll work on being more supportive. I just love you so much. And I really will kill anyone who hurts you."

"Oh, gladly. With a smile," Dallas adds.

Liam nods his head in agreement. "Facts."

"Yep," I agree, because it's true.

"I love you too," she laughs. "But let this be your lesson so that you aren't this way with Grace, Sawyer. She'll run hard and fast, and I know you don't want that."

"We good?" Sawyer asks, and we all agree.

I may have spent the last twenty-five years not really knowing my place, but I know at the end of the day, my family and I are a team and that we've got each other's backs no matter what. While we'll all be able to cash in when we need each other, it's time we all focus on our own families that we're creating, and mine is at home waiting for me. A place I can't wait to move him into.

The drive back into town passes in a blur. For the first time in my life, I'm hopeful about what's to come. I'm eager to get it started and fight for what I want. And that's life with Finn.

As I enter my house, he's not exactly how I pictured—in my bed naked with his glasses on—he's pacing in the small living room, hair disheveled, barefoot, wearing a pair of plaid PJ pants that hang low on his hips, and a plain white T-shirt. He freezes as he sees me, the blood draining from his face as he looks me over. I took a brief glance at my face in the sun visor when I hopped in my car, but I know the swelling has gotten worse as the minutes go by, especially because I can barely see out of it, my eye practically swollen shut.

"Holy shit, are you okay?"

"Looks way worse than it is, I promise."

"For fuck's sake, Carter, it went that bad? You said I didn't have anything to worry about! Go sit your ass down, let me get some ice!"

"It's fine! I'm fine."

"You're not fucking fine! Look at your eye! It's already bruising! What the hell happened?"

I have to laugh at Finn's over-the-top reaction. He's going to have one hell of a time acclimating to how physical my brothers and I are if he's going to fit in. Maybe I should take him to Dom's with me, get him some lessons. Probably a smart idea.

A tub of Tillamook ice cream gets tossed into my lap with a hand towel, and I look at him with my good eye, confused.

"That's all you have that's frozen, so put it against your damn face and talk. It went that bad? Shit, I should have been there with you. Which one had the issue? I'm so damn sorry, Carter."

"It didn't go bad. Will you calm the hell down and let me talk?"

"I'm sorry, you're right. Coming home with an eye that's swollen shut should give me the warm fuzzies; it clearly went great. I'm going to head to bed now," Finn deadpans.

"They don't care that I'm bi or in a relationship with a man. They were actually relieved when I said I was bisexual because every single one of those fuckers thought I was about to drop a bomb that I knocked some random chick up."

"For real? So you got in a fight with what? A door?"

I laugh under my breath, which causes me to wince. "No, this definitely came from one of Sawyer's haymakers."

"What the fuck, Carter, it's not funny."

"Listen, everything went great. They're happy for me, and they can't wait to meet you. We all started talking and Kinsey said she wanted to move out of our parents' house, something I told her I would back her up on if she decided to. So, I followed through on my word to her and Sawyer didn't like it."

"So, he hit you?"

"There was a scuffle," I lie so I don't sound like a pussy. Then again, he should probably know that when Sawyer wants to swing on you, your ass is going down hard. "But this is normal, I promise. If Sawyer doesn't come at you with his fists at some point, he doesn't love you."

"Man, I thought my family was fucked."

"Ha! Just wait. Hope you know what you signed up for, baby. Should probably get you some boxing lessons."

"I'll take whatever they have to offer if it means I get to keep you."

"Yeah?"

"Yeah. Now, go strip and lie down in bed. I wanna play doctor and patient."

My ass moves fast, my cock already hardening. Everything's going to be okay.

carter

MY SIBLINGS WERE THE EASY PART, AND EVEN THOUGH I feel a massive weight lifted now that my siblings know, I still have one last hurdle to get over. Especially now that I know our parents knew each other—at least in some aspect—in college.

I take the stairs two at a time, knocking quickly on my parents' front door before walking in. They've always had an open-door policy, even for our friends growing up, and if one of my mom's kids knocked and waited for her to come, she would "make them wait until they leave." She's been the best mom, and I know that coming out to them isn't going to be cause for concern. The kicker will be with who I'm in love with if they remember who Finn's dad is, like he remembers them.

"Dad? Mom? Your favorite son is here!"

"Dallas, is that you?" my mom's voice rings out from where she's working on a puzzle with my dad at the kitchen table.

"Funny. You know we all think he's your favorite, right? I should text them all and let them know you just admitted your preference, but I don't want it to go to Dallas' head."

"Oh stop it, right now! I don't have favorites. You walked right into that one by calling yourself it."

"Sure, sure, Mom, sure."

"Have a seat, my boy. Any update on your worries? Sawyer said all has been quiet."

"Kinda wanted to talk to you about that. We don't have to worry about anything. I was overly paranoid, but I had my reasons."

"That's great! But that's not Carter-visit worthy, so what else is going on?"

My dad sits back in his chair, crosses his arms, and raises a brow, waiting for my news.

"I'm bisexual."

My dad just kind of looks at me, but my mom stands up out of her chair and grabs my face, forcing me to look at her.

"I love you, my boy. I'm proud of you for telling us, and it makes me so happy that you know you can come to us about anything."

"Thanks, Mom."

"Your mom is right. I love you and I'm proud of you. No matter who you love, man or woman, as long as you're capable of feeling the emotion and giving it in return. It's life-changing."

"Thanks, Dad. On that same note, I met someone. He's the reason I even realized that I was bisexual in the first place."

"Oh, honey! I never thought I would see the day! When do we get to meet him?" my mom gushes.

"Well, before you get too excited. It's more complicated than that. The writer at the Northwest Explorer I was telling you about who I was freaking out over? That's who I'm in love with. I was grasping onto everything that could give me an out because I didn't want to accept that I had fallen in love with someone. He would never do anything to hurt me or anyone else."

"What's his name, son?" my dad asks, his tone a little more firm. My blood starts to go cold as my cheeks heat, but I shake my hands out, willing myself to stay calm.

"The man I fell in love with is Finn Nash. His dad is Griffin Nash."

If my mom's reaction is any indication of how this revelation would be received, my panic is warranted. She gasps softly, covering her mouth with her hand before looking at my dad.

"Well, isn't that a turn of events, huh?" my dad says with a laugh. I go from panic to confusion in about one point two seconds.

"Finn and I know there's something up. Will you please explain it to me? I love our family so much, but I also love Finn, and I want to spend the rest of my life with him. We need to understand what's going on. Look, his dad controlled every aspect of Finn's life and held what he loved most over his head to get him to fall in line. He forbade him from speaking with us, which is why he was being sketchy about meeting me for the interview. When I say his dad lost his mind when he found out we were together, I'm not exaggerating. You two clearly know their last name. Please, explain it to me."

"We know who Griffin Nash is, son. We aren't denying that. But maybe this is a conversation to be had when Finn is here also. We'll explain everything."

I settle further into my chair and take a deep breath. I don't want to wait any longer to understand this, but I can handle it, and Finn will want to hear it with me.

"Thank you. It's important to me that you all accept him. He no longer has a relationship with his family, he gave up his job at the magazine—I'm all he has, and I want to share my family with him. I hope that you both can be open to that someday."

"We're looking forward to meeting him, honey."

Finn is waiting for me when I get back from my parents' house and it feels so good. I never thought I would want to share my space with another person. In fact, I purposefully put boundaries in place to keep it from ever happening. But having Finn here at the end of my day is fucking bliss. We still need to take the time to pack up the majority of his things from his mini-mansion, but all of the things that matter are already here. We've easily made space for him in my—our—bedroom, and sharing space just feels natural. We're fully aware of the speed at which we've taken this, but when a love like this comes along, you grab it and hold on to it for dear life.

"Hey, baby! I'm home!"

I find Finn sitting in front of his laptop, bare feet resting on the coffee table in front of him, wearing nothing but a pair of navy blue boxer briefs. His glasses have fallen down the bridge of his nose, his hair is tousled, and he looks so fucking sexy my mouth waters at the sight. His runner's legs are muscular in all the right places, his toned abs and chest looking so good I'm practically salivating.

"I want to ask you how it went with your parents, but the look you're giving me right now is making me want to ask you to get on your knees instead."

"Oh, baby, you don't have to ask. Take that cock out for me," I tell him as I pull my shirt over my head and push my pants down.

"You want it, Hayes? Come and get it."

Quicker than I'm expecting him to, Finn drops his laptop on the couch and jumps up, taking off toward the other end of the house. I respond quickly, running after him. He jukes my first attempt at grabbing him, quickly moving to the side as he hits the threshold of our bedroom.

With the bed in front of him, I tackle him, launching both of us tumbling onto the mattress. We bounce twice as I grab at the waistband of his briefs, yanking them down his legs.

"You gonna be a good boy for me, baby?"

"Are you gonna be a good boy for *me*, lover?"

I toss the briefs behind me, looking down at my man spread out on our bed. His thick, uncut cock rests heavy against his pelvis and just as he moves his hand up to reach for it, I bat him away. "Mine," I growl, making him laugh.

"C'mere, I want you in my mouth."

"Nu-uh, I want to suck yours until you blow for me."

He arches his eyebrow at me, giving me that devilish smirk that I love so much, when it registers exactly what he wants. Flipping around, I scoot up to him on my side, Finn lying on his, as I feed my cock into his waiting mouth. Grabbing his length, I pump him twice before sticking my tongue into the hood around his dick and swirling it around. His moans vibrate through my shaft, turning me on further. Matching his rhythm, I suck him fully into my mouth, loving the way his dick feels against my tongue. His hips buck forward, pressing him to the back of my throat, forcing me to gag around his length.

His tongue is doing crazy things to my cock at this angle and it's making my head spin. Why the hell haven't we done this until now? Every new experience Finn gives me blows my ever-loving mind, always leaving me boneless and out of breath.

Wanting to make him blow first, I double down, gripping his hip and forcing him to the back of my throat. When I pull back, I hollow out my cheeks and suck him hard. His moans are gurgled around me as his thighs start to shake. I continue to suck him hard, rolling my finger in the built-up saliva and his base before slipping it around to his hole. I swirl my finger around the spot for a moment before slowly pressing in as Finn pops off of me.

"Oh fuuuuuuck," he yells as I breach the tight rim of his ass.

"You like that, baby? You like it when I play with your ass with your cock in my mouth?" I rasp as I heave air into my lungs.

I dip my head back down, sucking his dick like I need to survive while fingering his ass. I know I've found his sweet spot when he's no longer able to focus on blowing me, and that is more than okay with me.

"Fuck me, fuck me, Carter, please." His sweet whines go straight to my throbbing cock, and I wouldn't deny him anything he begs for. I release his dick from my mouth, letting it smack hard against his abdomen.

"You want my cock in your ass, baby? Tell me exactly what you want."

"Fuck my ass, Hayes. Fuck me hard."

I stay where I am for a few more moments, working his hole open so that I can slide in without hurting him. Finn languidly laps at my dick, kissing and licking up my length, nuzzling his face into my pelvis. It's so fucking erotic and I almost can't take anymore.

Once he's good and open for me, I sit up, spinning around and positioning myself between his legs. Finn spreads open for me and I grab his legs, hooking his knees over my forearms and opening his ass up wide for me.

"You ready, baby?"

"Fuck me."

I use his body to position him where I need him, lining up my hard cock and pressing in slowly just as he's pushing out. I slip right in, and my mind turns to fucking mush.

"Your ass is sucking me, so fucking greedy to be fucked, baby."

"Gah, yes!"

I thrust slowly in until we're flush against each other. I pause, giving him a moment to adjust, but he thrashes his head side to side, begging me to move. Wanting to give him exactly what we both want, I pull out and slam back in. Finn grapples to reach his thighs, grabbing them and pulling them further back for me as I fuck him hard.

"You like it when I fuck you into the mattress? My pretty boy likes taking my cock, huh? So fucking good for me, Finn, so. Fucking. Good."

"Ohgunuhgod!"

"Touch yourself, baby. Come with me," I urge him, knowing I'm about to blow. His ass feels so tight, so damn good. Too good.

He releases one of his legs, grabbing his leaking cock and jerking it hard and fast. I watch with rapt attention as we bring each other to orgasm. My cock swells in his perfect ass, my hips stuttering just as the first spurt of cum releases from his cock.

"That's it, baby. Look at you coming for me."

He moans out unintelligible words as I fill his ass with my

spend. Wave after wave is released from me, and just when I think I've never come harder, I surprise myself.

I meet his face, lust-drunk and drowsy, looking so good freshly fucked, and I'm so goddamn grateful that everything has led me right here with him.

I slowly start to withdraw from his body, watching as my dick drags my cum out with it. Once I'm out, I push up his legs toward his chest.

"Hold 'em."

I watch in awe as my cum spills from his used-up hole. Just a slow trickle of pearly white cum that claims him as mine. I don't know what comes over me or why I do it, but I don't fight the need.

Swiping through the mess, I gather up my cum on my fingers, stuffing it slowly back into his ass, watching my fingers disappear. It's one of the hottest things I've ever seen, and I may have unlocked a new kink.

"Oh fuck, babe, Jesus."

"Hold it in, baby. I want it to stay there."

"Oh, fuck me."

"Don't tempt me, this looks so fucking hot right now."

"Get up here and hold me."

I do as he says, resting his legs back down and climbing up to pull his chest flush with mine. His arms immediately wrap around my torso, holding me just as close.

"I love you," I tell him for the millionth time. I have a feeling he didn't hear it much growing up, and I intend to change the course of the rest of his life. He's going to hear it so damn much that everything before me is a faded, deluded memory of a past life.

"I love you. I take it it went well with your parents?"

"It did. They're excited to meet you. But when I told them who you were, they admitted to knowing your dad. They said they'd sit down with us and tell us the whole story.

"Even though I don't care what his reasoning was behind his

actions, they were still shit and nothing they say will make it justifiable in my eyes."

"Same, baby, same."

———

Sundays are spent at my parents' house, unless you're dying. And since I'm not on my deathbed, I'm on my mom's shit list for skipping so many of them lately. But I figure the best way to have them all meet Finn is to do it all at once.

"You seriously gonna give me the lowdown again on your family? Pretty sure I've got it down. Sawyer's the oldest, married to Ivy, they just had a newborn—Grace—Dallas is his twin, he's with Blaire—the only redhead—Liam's married to Hannah, and they have Charlotte, and then your sister, Kinsey. Parents are Craig and Amy Hayes.

"Yeah, you think you do, but just wait. You've got their names down, sure. They're a rough bunch. Protective isn't a strong enough word."

"People love me. I'm not worried."

I snort a laugh and look at him, raising my eyebrows.

"Okay, maybe not everyone. You like me now."

"You wore me down."

"Thank fuck for that, or you wouldn't know how much you liked my dick."

I slap Finn's chest, his quick reflexes grabbing my hand and pulling it to his mouth. I look at him quickly, trying to keep my eyes on the winding roads ahead of me. His lips connect with the back of my hand, my lips curving upward into a smirk. He trails up my skin, just a ghost of a touch before reaching my fingers. He licks up my pointer finger before pulling it into his mouth, swirling his warm, wet tongue around it, sucking it up and down slowly like he does my cock.

"Mmm."

"You like that? Bet it would be better if my mouth was wrapped around your dick."

I pull my hand away, quickly shifting gears to slow us down, my heart racing as I picture him bent over the console with my dick buried down his throat while I drive.

"I know it would, but you're not going to meet my family with my cum on your tongue."

That gets a laugh from him, a sound I love to hear. He behaves the rest of the way to my parents' house, much to his dismay. My parents live on a gorgeous piece of land in the same house they raised us kids in. Aspen Ridge is surrounded by a forest of Sitka spruce trees, but somehow my parents found one of the only properties without them right up on the ass of the house. Sitting in the middle of a gorgeous wild lupine field is our family home, with its long gravel driveway, flowers in full bloom, the purples, pinks, and blues showing off as the rare Washington sun shines down on them.

I pull my car into the full driveway, everyone having beaten us to arrive, nerves filling my stomach, but not on the verge of panic. Turning to look at Finn, his dark hair mussed slightly from running his nervous hands through it, blue eyes piercing my own, his faltering confidence only noticeable to me behind the rim of his glasses. God, I love those glasses.

"Not too late. We can leave here right now and keep you hidden forever."

"Get out of the car, Hayes. I want to meet them."

"You're gonna eat your words, Nash. Let's go feed you to the wolves."

Shoulder to shoulder, Finn and I walk to the back of my parents' house, where the noise is loud and traveling in the wind. I give him a quick shoulder bump as we reach the large patio, readying him.

"Hey! We made it! Sorry we're late!" I announce. My mom is sitting between my dad and Blaire, a tiny baby Grace cradled in her arms as my dad looks up at us. Finn follows me up the stairs of the deck, my siblings and our friend Reid standing together in a circle. Wonder how they got the big beast here. He's invited every week, and every week he's a no-show.

"Hey, fuckers," I say to the small crowd as they part for us. "Play nice. This is Finn, my . . . boyfriend." Fuck. I've never introduced my family to a girlfriend, mostly because I've never had one, and now I'm introducing them to my boyfriend. What is life?

"Hey, you must be Sawyer," Finn says as he reaches his hand out to greet Reid, who's standing with Ivy sandwiched between him and my brother. Fucking shit. Off to a great start.

Sawyer growls and Finn pulls his hand back, looking in his direction as Reid makes a choking sound. "The fuck did you just say?" Sawyer grinds out the words through gritted teeth.

"Down boy, innocent mistake," Ivy tells him, trying to talk him back.

"The fuck it is," he snaps.

Putting my hand flat to Finn's chest, I move him a step backward so that I can get between him and my shithead brother if I need to. Not that Finn can't handle himself, but I've been fighting this twat face since I was a kid and know what to expect. Plus, he wouldn't kill me. Jury is still out on everyone who isn't blood or family by marriage.

"That's Reid. He's best friends with both of them. That growly bastard is Sawyer."

"Damn, my bad, man. Sawyer, it's nice to meet you. Ivy, you as well." It doesn't go unnoticed that Finn doesn't make eye contact with Ivy; even if he is into men, better to not poke the bear any further. Smart man.

"Think I better make the introductions so you don't get torn to shreds before we get a chance to eat. This is my brother, Dallas; his girlfriend Blaire is sitting in the shade with my parents. This is Liam and his wife, Hannah, their little girl is Charlie, who's around here somewhere."

"Hey, it's nice to finally meet you all. I've heard a lot about you."

Dallas snorts, and I shoot him a glare.

"What? We're just hearing about him, but you've been talking us up?"

"Dal, don't fuckin' start shit. I can keep things private."

"Yeah, dumbass, kinda like you kept Blaire a secret until you brought down the barrel house," Sawyer snaps.

Ahh, fuck, here we goddamn go. The group collectively takes a large step back, Ivy and Hannah rolling their eyes and joining my parents and Blaire on the couch. Finn looks around confused as fuck, so I grab his arm, pulling him to give my brothers space. He leans into me, whispering in my ear, "Am I missing something?"

"These two have a bad habit of getting physical over the dumbest shit, just give it a moment."

"I don't want to hear her name out of your goddamn mouth, shithead!"

"It's not like you haven't walked in on me and Ivy, dumbass! God forbid you utilize knocking like a normal fucking human!"

"Ever heard of a lock? Oh, whoops! CEO shithead doesn't need to lock his door because he's special and everyone should respect his space!"

"At least we use my office and not the spare barrel house, you dumbass Neanderthal!"

"The fuck did you just call me?"

Dallas steps into Sawyer's space and gives him a shove, Sawyer unmoving, the fucking beast.

Tilting my head into Finn's, I whisper, "Aaand 3-2-1."

Dallas' arm clocks back swinging a quick jab toward Sawyer's cheek. Sawyer dodges, landing a hard punch to Dallas' stomach.

"Holy shit, you weren't kidding. They take it seriously," Finn says next to me. He's standing there watching my idiot brothers fight each other on the deck of our parents' house with his arms crossed, bemused.

"Definitely wasn't lying."

I roll my eyes and rush forward, grabbing Sawyer's arms and hauling him back. Liam does the same to Dallas, shoving them apart.

"Nice first impression, idiots. Thanks."

"Hey, I didn't mind it, just remind me not to piss you two off," Finn says, making Dallas smirk at him.

"I like him. Keep him," Dallas insists.

Sawyer grumbles. "Jury's still out."

I walk back over to Finn, reading his unaffected facial expression.

"He'll come around. You kinda bombed it with him. There was an issue when Ivy came back involving Reid, and you probably just reopened a sore spot. Don't worry about it. Let's go meet everyone else."

We walk side by side up to my parents, and I don't know why, but I'm suddenly nervous.

"Dad, Mom, this is Finn Nash. Finn, my parents, Craig and Amy."

It's eerily quiet for a moment, my usually outspoken, welcoming mother waiting to see how my father will react. Even though we spoke already so that they weren't caught by surprise, I'm nervous. I hold my breath, Finn appearing otherwise stoic, but the slight tick of his jaw tells me that he's just as nervous about this meeting.

My dad starts to speak, and even with his stutter, his voice is strong and sure.

"So, you're Griffin's son?"

"Yes, sir, unfortunately. It's nice to meet you." Finn sticks his hand out, unwavering, and waits for my dad to shake it. I still haven't taken a breath, the anticipation a steady pulse between my ears, my brain foggy.

Finally, *finally*, my dad extends his shaky hand and clasps Finn's, and my body immediately settles. This can work. This is going to be okay.

"Welcome to the family, Finn," my sweet mom says as she stands and greets him with a welcoming, affectionate hug. We finish with greetings, doing the rounds and introducing him to everyone. He meets the headstrong women of our family next, and they're just as welcoming as my mom.

"Nice to meet you, Finn, Hayes brood. Good seeing you all!" Reid announces.

"You're not sticking around?" I ask.

"Sorry, got somewhere to be. Just needed to drop something off to Sawyer."

Reid heads out, which is normal. The man has been invited to every Sunday dinner for the last decade and he's declined every single one. We all sit together for a bit and enjoy small talk when I realize I haven't seen my favorite family member.

"Li! Where's my dog?"

Finn's eyes get big, mouthing "you don't have a dog," making me laugh.

"He's not your damn dog, Casanova. He's Charlie's!"

"You didn't leave him at home, did you? He doesn't like to be left alone!"

"For fuck's sake, he's running around with Charlie. Go find him yourself."

Finn follows me like my shadow as I jog down the back steps of the porch and into the large yard, easily spotting Charlotte in the distance, running circles in the flowers with a small dog chasing her.

"Yo! Pipsqueak! Your favorite uncle is here!" I yell with my hands cupped around my mouth.

"Screw you, Casanova, you aren't her favorite!" Sawyer yells from behind me, making me laugh.

"Dude, your family is batshit crazy."

"I tried to warn you, but like always, you don't damn well listen."

"Yeah, but it's awesome. I like them."

"Let's survive dinner and then you can reevaluate."

"Uncle Carter!" Charlie squeals as she gets closer, running as fast as she can until she launches herself into my arms. I swing her around, nearly knocking her feet into Finn's face as her little laugh echoes around us.

"You're here! Dad said you were bringing a boyfriend, and I learned all about types of families already, and I know that two boys can get married! Are you going to get married like Dad and Mom did? Then I'd have anoooooother uncle. I'd have five aunts and five uncles! Ms. Katie taught me that five plus five equals TEN! I have the most in the whole class!"

"Oh yeah? That's a lot of aunts and uncles. Are you sure you're counting correctly?"

"Yep!" she says, popping her 'p.' "Auntie Lo, Auntie Hailey, Auntie Ivy, Auntie Blaire, Auntie Kinsey theeeeen, Uncle Sawyer, Uncle Dallas, yooooou, Uncle Graham, and now him," she says, pointing to Finn. "That's TEN!"

"I guess you're right, that is a lot of aunts and uncles. You're so lucky you have all of us. Are you ready to meet my boyfriend, pipsqueak?"

"Yep!"

"Finn, this is Liam and Hannah's daughter, Charlotte, but everyone calls her Charlie."

"I was named after a bear," she deadpans, and I laugh.

"Were you now?" Finn asks, sitting down on his haunches after I set her down on the ground so he's eye level with her. Finn's face lights up while they talk, Charlie telling him all about starting kindergarten in the fall and how Ms. Katie is going to be her teacher again. My heart pangs in my chest, a sharp, steady stab that makes my throat tighten.

Fuck. How could we not talk about this kind of stuff? *Because you've been trying to digest the fact that you have feelings for someone for the first time in your life, plus all the other drama.* If Finn wants children someday, this could end before it even gets started. I don't have any interest in being a father. It's so far from my radar, it isn't even a tiny blip.

Finn stands, Charlie running off with her dog, Billy, hot on her tail. He must read the unease and rising panic on my face because he steps into my space, putting his hands on either side of my face.

"Hey, where'd you go?"

"Do you want kids?"

"Carter, don't spiral. One day at a time."

"Do you?"

"Honestly? I don't. Not after the childhood I had. I want to travel and write. If you want them though—"

I kiss him. Not giving one single shit that we're standing in the middle of a lupine field a hundred feet from my family. I kiss him because he's the one person on earth who was made just for me. Maybe fate and soulmates really are real.

Loud whistles hoot behind us and I release Finn's mouth, both of us laughing. I take a deep breath, calming down. This really is going to work. We're going to be okay.

finn

CARTER'S FAMILY IS EVERYTHING A BIG FAMILY SHOULD be, and it's hard not to hold out hope that I can be one of them someday. Amy's eyes are focused solely on us, a serene smile on her face as she watches the exchange between us, and I feel my face heat. Carter takes my hand, leading me back up to his family.

"I've never seen you so comfortable in your own skin, my boy, so happy and at ease. I'm so happy for you."

Carter beams at his mom like he needed to hear those words as much as I did.

"We should probably tell you both what happened." Everyone is off doing their own thing, so Carter and I take a seat in two of the patio chairs next to his parents.

"I was in a relationship with your father, Finn. For a little over a year in college. Carter, your dad was my best friend—always had been. But he was in a relationship with Samantha Harkin, and that was a whole thing. But even though we always felt something for each other, the time was just never right for us. Finn, it's not a secret that your father comes from money, and with that money comes a certain level of expectation that his father put on him, and I'm assuming that has trickled down to you."

"It has."

"Well, your dad was destined for big things in the city, and I was destined for a small life here in Aspen Ridge. I wanted a husband who put me at the center of his world, a big family with tons of kids and chaos, and to live in a tiny town where everyone knows everyone. Your dad wanted a trophy wife to throw money at in his penthouse in the city. Our life aspirations didn't align. I cared about him, Finn, deeply at the time because I saw a side of him that clearly no longer exists. He was kind, and I know he loved me. When I realized that we would never work long-term, that he would never leave the life he had planned out in front of him, I broke up with him. Only to have the stars align and immediately start a relationship with Craig. I got pregnant with the twins not long after that. Your dad was irate. He accused Craig of taking me from him and spent months trying to get me to reconsider. He was adamant that I was stolen from him, as if I was a piece of property that could be controlled. He stalked me, stalked us, and in order to protect me and my unborn babies, I was forced to get a restraining order against him, which I'm sure did not go well for him with his family's status. It's been over thirty years. And based on your age, I'm assuming you came not long after my twin boys did."

"I found out recently that I was a surprise baby and was not wanted by my dad. It sounded like my mom willingly got herself pregnant with a Nash's baby to secure her position in life."

"I'm sorry, sweetie. And I'm sorry that something that should have been put to rest thirty years ago caused you and Carter so much harm."

"I don't know what to say. I had no idea you were such a heartbreaker, Mom," Carter says, trying to make light of the situation.

"It's probably anticlimactic to you both, I'm sure you were expecting a huge scandal."

"No, just really wanted to know the reason he hated you all so badly, that he wanted me to stay away, but that tracks. My dad holds deep grudges. He's a very angry man, and that's the only version of him I know. I don't have a single tender memory," I confess.

Carter reaches over and squeezes my hand lovingly and confidently, grounding me.

"I'm going to help you make them; we're going to be just fine," he promises.

"You've decided to no longer have a relationship with him?" Carter's dad, Craig, asks.

"Correct. Since the moment I was born, I was expected to be a mini version of him, expected to comply, never ask questions. I fell in love with writing, with being a travel writer, especially, and he knew it. He knew I had found something that he could hold over my head to keep me in line, and up until I met Carter, it worked. Your son gave me the strength to live my life how I want to, to break the cycle my dad was trying to continue. It's funny, though. You left him because you wanted a quiet, peaceful life surrounded by family in a small town, and that's all I want, too. It's all I've wanted for as long as I can remember. That and writing."

"I'm proud of you. Of both you boys," Amy tells us. "I'm sad that your dad's life is full of hatred. I hope he can find peace someday." I nod my head in agreement.

The rest of the evening goes by in a wild blur. Carter wasn't kidding when he said that his family is pure chaos. It's loud and obnoxious, but it's amazing. Each one of them is so full of life and so happy, and I desperately want to be accepted into the fold.

"Hey, you gotta few to chat?" Sawyer says to me, towering over me from where I'm sitting on a patio chair.

"Yeah, man. Lead the way."

Carter visibly stiffens next to me, his hands clenching into fists as if he's ready to brawl his older brother on my behalf right now. I nod to him, letting him know that I'm okay, and follow Sawyer into the house.

"This where you kill me?" I ask with a smile, trying to ease some of the tension.

"Nah. I'd do it where everyone could watch to serve as a warning." Something in me tells me that he's not joking, and I have to actively work hard not to bristle.

"Noted."

"You love my brother?"

"Without a doubt in my mind."

"Good. We won't have problems then. I've never seen him so . . . comfortable. Or happy. He's always the fun one, but this is different. I see the difference now and feel like an asshole for not reading the signs. I've always wondered but wasn't sure. Now I am. He wasn't fully happy before, because it's clear he is now."

"I'm glad you can see that, but don't beat yourself up. The walls he had up were thick. It took a lot to break through him."

"I fucked him up, huh?"

"He loves you more than anything, and seeing you hurt? He didn't ever want to see it again or feel it for himself. But look at where it brought him. He's okay."

"You'll take care of him?"

"We'll take care of each other."

"Alright."

Sawyer shocks the shit out of me by shaking my hand and pulling me in for a hug.

"We good?"

"Yeah, we're good."

Later that night, Carter and I are heading to meet Trey for drinks. It's been a lot of introductions all at once, but we're playing catch-up after keeping our relationship a secret for so long.

"You worried he's not gonna like you?"

"Nope."

"You worried you're not gonna like him?"

"Nope. I'm excited. Everything you've told me about him makes me respect him as much as I respect my own brothers. I'm eager to meet the only person who's had your back all these years."

Trey is eager as shit; he's been at me wondering when he can meet him and I've been putting it off. I'm glad the time has finally come. I pull up to The Whispering Well, and Carter and I step out of my SUV. I reach for his hand on instinct, and he squeezes it back in return.

We walk into the bar, and the hostess leads us to Trey, who's already sitting at a table on the bottom floor this time. His face brightens in a huge smile as he stands to greet us. I pull him into a quick hug and whisper, "Be nice."

He pulls back and mocks being offended.

"So you're the man who took my boy from me?" Trey says by way of greeting Carter.

"How about we share him? You get every other weekend?"

"I'm down for that. I'm Trey."

"Carter. I've heard a lot about you."

"Same. You guys want a beer? They've got the best drinks, and the whiskey is damn good," Trey says with a smirk.

"They better be serving Aspen Ridge if you're saying that shit."

I take a deep breath of relief. Everything is fitting together seamlessly now that we've closed the gorge that separated us. I should have known. Everything else has been as easy as breathing when it comes to Carter. It was all the other shit that was difficult.

"So, you knew this guy as a teenager? What was that like?"

"Back in his still-trying-to-convince-himself-he's-straight era is what I like to refer to it as."

"Nice, dickhead!" I say, smacking him on the back of his head.

"It's true! Want me to tell him about what it was like to watch you make out with a chick who you were not into?"

Carter laughs, throwing his head back and making me smile. I fucking love that sound.

The three of us talk, and Carter and Trey each have two rounds of drinks when, suddenly, he stiffens across from me. With a gentle nod of his head, Trey signals for me to brace myself as one of two people I loathe is approaching our table. The first one is in Seattle, I know without a doubt his ass isn't walking into The Whispering Well at eleven at night to talk to me. So that only leaves one other option.

Nick.

Despite Trey's warning, I feel absolutely nothing. I may have felt discomfort and annoyance the last time I saw him, but I'm so confident with where I'm at in life and in my relationship that I feel absolutely nothing at all. But he runs in the same group that Trey does, so I guess it'd be rude if his group didn't pop over to say hi.

The group of three of them reach our table, and two of Trey's friends fist-bump him. When they turn to face me, they give me a nod. Trey's the first one to speak up.

"You guys already know Finn. This is his boyfriend, Carter."

Carter must clock Nick's reaction because his fingers twitch against my thigh where his hand is resting. Moving his hand to the back of my neck in a possessive display that sends shockwaves of lust down my spine, he pulls me closer, pressing a delicate kiss on my neck and whispering, "I love you," into my ear, making me shiver. I can feel Carter's eyes focused only on me, as if I'm the only person in the room. It's a heady feeling and one I bask in.

"Hey, guys," I say as I nod, not giving Nick any attention. I don't care what he thinks or feels. I hope he's found happiness like I have.

They walk off as Trey's eyes get big.

"Fucking awkward. Why does Nick have to make shit so weird?"

"So that's the asshole who cheated on you?" Carter asks for clarification.

"Yeah, babe, it is."

"What a fucking tool. You definitely leveled up."

Laughs burst from both Trey and I. "I definitely did."

"So, what now?" Trey asks.

"Now, we both find jobs," I reply. "I'm building my travel blog, but it's going to be a little bit before I'm making a livable wage from it. I'll be living off my trust until then."

"I don't know what the hell I'm gonna do, but something will come together."

"Why don't you come work at the distillery? Finn said you were his assistant, right? If you like admin work, it's no different. Our intern, Marcus, is done with school and moving back home to Virginia."

"Really?"

"Yeah, why not? As long as you can take some shit, my brothers are crazy."

"He's not exaggerating. They're all batshit crazy."

Trey laughs, but he's in for a rude awakening.

"Yeah, man, I'd like that. Who doesn't want to work at a distillery?"

We spend the next few hours talking and hanging out until I have to physically drag Carter out of the bar because he's having so much fun. He's a little tipsy, and it's the first time I've seen him like this.

The moment we're in my SUV, Carter's hands are on me, pawing my chest, rubbing his palm over my rapidly hardening cock through my jeans. His mouth connects with my neck, licking a line from the base to my ear, sending chills over my body.

"Pull over. It can't wait. I need you now." His voice is thick with lust, turning me on further. I reach for the waistband of his pants, unbuttoning them and slipping my hand inside, easily finding his waiting, hard dick, wanting to give him some relief.

"Fuck. Already hard for me, lover?"

"Ugnh," is all he can reply. I fucking love how responsive he is when I touch him.

I navigate off of the road, the car bouncing as I drive us through a small field and come to a stop right outside the tree line, thanking fuck that it's pitch black and we're in the middle of nowhere. I'm pretty confident I've got us sitting in a place where we won't get arrested for indecent exposure.

I've barely cut the engine before Carter has his seatbelt unbuckled, pushing it off of his body and crawling on top of me.

"Fuck, lover. That desperate for me, huh? Tell me what you need."

He moans against my mouth as he settles on my lap, pressing his hard dick into my stomach, rubbing my length between his legs.

"You looked so hot in there. Fuck, do you have any idea how sexy you are, Finn? All night, I couldn't keep my eyes off of you. Couldn't believe that of all the men and women in that place, you were mine. *Mine.*"

His words hit me hard, and I grip the sides of his face with my palms, yanking his mouth into mine. Our tongues tangle, the taste of my favorite whiskey exploding on my tongue.

"Fuck me, baby," he begs, and fuck if I don't want to do just that.

"Right here?"

"Yeah, fill me. I need you."

"Fuck, lover. You want my dick inside that ass?"

"Yes," he practically whines, dry humping me like a goddamn teenager. I nuzzle my head into the crook of his neck, sucking and lapping at the skin there while my hands dip under his shirt, connecting with smooth skin and strong abs. I groan against his neck, wanting to give him what we both so desperately crave.

"Lube?"

"Wallet."

Carter lifts off of me while I shimmy out of my shorts, and then we're both trying to rip his off of him in the most unsexy, uncoordinated rush. The horn blares, and we both freeze before laughing.

"Get these fucking things off or I'll rip a hole in them," I demand before pushing him back into the passenger seat where he pulls them down his legs. He's on me again before he's even tossed them into the backseat. My hard cock rests between his legs, pressing right against his taint, my thick head nudging his balls. My hands find their home on either side of his face, tilting his head forward as much as the position allows so that I can claim his mouth.

After I coat my fingers with lube, I slip between us, pressing firmly against his hole, swirling around the area, teasing him before sliding a finger firmly inside. Carter groans loudly against my mouth, his body shivering against me.

"Fuck, your ass is so tight. So fucking sexy. I can't prep you the way I should, Carter. This angle, there's not enough room, babe. I don't want to hurt you."

"I'm fine, I'll tell you if it's too much. I want you so fucking bad. Don't make me wait, baby. I want it. Fuck me."

I quickly clock how many drinks he had and over how many hours, looking at his eyes.

"You're with me? You didn't drink too much?"

"I can hold my alcohol, baby, and I'm fine, I just want this big dick inside me and I don't want to wait."

"As you wish, lover."

I stretch him the best I can with two fingers for a moment before slipping free. I use my clean hand to help lift him so that I can coat my dick in a heavy layer of lube. I use way more than is probably needed, but I don't want to hurt him, knowing he's not nearly ready. But he's frantic and impatient, and his need for me is overriding all logical thought.

I line up my dick with his hole, and the moment I nudge inside, Carter takes over, slamming himself down on me, taking my entire length in one swift, hard drop.

"Fuuuuuuuuck! Carter! Fuck . . . Fuck, baby!"

Our moans fill the cabin of the SUV as he rides me hard, my dick rubbing against his prostate, based on how his body trembles above mine.

"Oh fuck. Jesus Christ!" he yells, and I still him with my hands on his hips.

"Fuck, am I hurting you?"

"Fuck no, it just feels so fucking good. I never want it to end."

"You're so goddamn perfect, Carter. Look at you taking my cock. Riding me so fucking good. Making me feel so good. You're so fucking tight, you know that? Fuck. Fuck."

"Not gonna last, baby?"

"Not with how tight this is and with you riding me so hard."

I grab his dick then, my hand still coated in lube, his dick jerking hard between us.

"You're going to come with me, lover. Now make me fill that ass with cum. I want it leaking until we get home."

I jerk him harder, running my thumb over his crown on every pass as he lifts and crashes down on my thick length. My legs are shaking from pleasure and the strain of being squished into the passenger seat with Carter on top of me. It's all too much. Too damn good.

"You're making me come. Fuck, come with me, I can't . . . oh, fuuuuck." He moans unintelligible words and grunts as I stroke him brutally through his orgasm. Carter falls forward, his head resting on my shoulder as I continue to slam into him from below. He grips my biceps hard as he accepts everything I'm giving him, and then I'm coming, filling his ass up with my load, jerking inside him and feeling like I'm going to float away from the magnitude of pleasure.

After a moment, the post-orgasm haze clears and my muscles start to ache with Carter's big-ass body crushing me into the front seat.

"Fuck, Carter. I love fucking you, but if you don't get off me right now, I'm gonna throw you. My leg is cramping so fucking bad," I say through a smothered laugh.

"I think my shin is stuck between the seat and the door. Shit, hold on," he replies, laughing at the absurdity of the mess we put ourselves in. He slides off my dick, the audible wet smack of it hitting my abdomen making us both laugh harder. We get unstuck, his naked ass flopping into the passenger seat with a thud.

"Fuck, we're too damn large to be fucking in the front seat of a car," I tell him, laughing some more as I pull up my pants, wiping my sticky hand against the fabric. "There's no way to clean up in here, you jackass."

Carter just laughs as he fights with his clothes. "You weren't complaining while you were balls deep inside me."

"'Cause you turn my brain to mush with your sexual prowess."

He barks out a laugh again, which makes me chuckle in return. "My sexual prowess?"

"Yeah, plus, I can't say no to you, lover. From the moment I saw you, I was yours."

"Yeah, you are. But I'm yours, too."

I lean over the center console and drop a hard kiss to his forehead. Wanting to get us home to shower, I reverse out of the field, praying like hell we don't get stuck. Calling a tow right now would really suck.

We're both exhausted by the time we fall into bed after showers, but it feels so damn good to have someone to lay next to and experience life with. Especially after we both had resigned ourselves to spending it alone. I pull Carter in tight, his head resting on my chest, his hand splayed out over my heart, his leg thrown over my hip. My fingers trail up and down his spine as I hold him close.

"I love you, Carter."

"I love you, too, Finn."

After a few quiet moments, Carter's breathing evens out, and just as I start to doze off, his voice fills my ears.

"The hard shit is all over," he whispers. "Now we get to live."

carter

Finn and I haven't left the house for almost a week. We've spent the entire time wrapped up with each other, arguing over which movie marathon we'll start next and exploring each other without any pressure from the outside world. We turned our phones off and focused on just the two of us. After everything Finn has been through, after the turmoil of our rocky start, we just wanted a moment to breathe. What was supposed to be a few days turned into five. I'm not complaining. For the first time in my life, I've found a place that makes me feel at home. Finn stripped me to my barest form, and with him, I'm completely myself.

"Have you had enough of me yet? Ready to face the world?" he asks, his breath warm against my lips as he lies next to me, our heart rates coming down from the mind-blowing sex we just had. Before I can answer, his tongue darts out, licking across the seam of my lips, begging me to open for him. It's a slow, erotic swipe that instantly fans that ember burning within me. Instead of giving him what he wants, I lean in, nipping at his bottom lip and pulling it until it pops free. The growl that works its way up his throat goes straight to my cock, even though I just came. It's never enough with him. I always want more. More. More.

My hands caress the clammy, bare skin of his rounded shoulder, down his strong arm, my fingers tracing over the bulging veins of his forearm. "Mmm. I'll never get enough of you, Finn. But I am ready. I was thinking I would take you out to a bar. When I wasn't at Temptations, I would hang out there. It's a good spot, but everyone knows everyone here; we're gonna run into people. People I've probably slept with."

Finn cringes ever so slightly but then settles as my hand cups his sharp jaw, forcing him to meet my eyes. My thumb smooths across the soft skin under his stormy blue eyes before I speak. He's so beautiful that it nearly causes me pain to look at him. I can't believe he's mine.

"You are it for me, Finn. I will tell you that as many times as you need to hear it."

"What if you crave a female? It's normal, and it's all you've had until me."

"Because it's not about what's between your legs, Finn. It's about who you are. Your company, the connection and chemistry we have, the comfort and safety you bring me. Jesus Christ, the peace? Finn, that's what matters. You could be a green alien with two cocks and a tail, and I would still be in love with you. It's who you are here." I place my hand against his chest, his heart beating rapidly beneath my hand. "It's how I feel when I'm with you. It's that I love *you*. You're the first person I've ever been with that I had to force myself to walk away from."

And fuck if that isn't the truth. Never in my twenty-five years of life did I think I would end up with a man or be bisexual. But even more than that? I never thought I would be open to love. Sex with Finn has always made sense, and I fought the love he was giving me and pulling out of me in equal measure as hard as I could. But I've never been able to fight Finn and win. For that, I'm so fucking thankful. He's my person in every single way.

Finn laughs and it's the best damn sound I've ever heard.

"A green alien would be pretty cool, though," he says.

"Honestly, I'm only slightly disappointed that you aren't," I reply with humor. "You ready?"

"Yeah, take me out, lover. I don't remember the last time I saw sunshine."

"Hate to break it to ya, baby, you live in Aspen Ridge now, and that shit doesn't come out often. Hope you like overcast, moody skies."

"Looks like I'm just gonna have to 'cause you're here. I wouldn't be anywhere else."

"You'll love it."

"I already do."

Finn smacks my ass hard as I crawl out of the bed, growling as I turn around to face him.

"What was that for?" I snap.

"I'm still pissed at you for branding that fine ass, Hayes."

A laugh bubbles up from deep within me. "Yeah, well, take it up with my asshole brothers, Nash."

While Finn goes to shower and pull himself together, I power on my phone to text the group chat our plans and see if any of them are free.

> Me: Finn and I are getting drinks at The Night Owl

> Me: Come join us fuckers

Sawyer: Not gonna happen shit for brains, can't exactly bring Grace into a bar now can I?

> Me:

Dallas: Blaire and I are already heading out tonight. Glad to know you'll be in AR though *wink emoji*

Liam: Do I even want to know wtf that means?

> Me: Nope

Dallas: Not a chance in hell

Liam: Charlie is already in bed so Han and I
are stayin' in to watch Scream

Kinsey: I'll come. Bringing Olivia

Me: You and Lo still not talking?

Kinsey: After the shit she pulled with Han and
Hailey? Hard no.

Sawyer: Good. Stay away from shit friends
Kins

Kinsey: Yes, of course, brother almighty. Next
time I'll be sure to ask my keepers to vet my
friends first

Dallas: Only your boyfriends

Sawyer: No boyfriends

Liam: None

Me: For fuck's sake, Kins- meet us there.

Tossing my phone to the bed, I grab the bottle of lube from the floor and jog to the bathroom to find Finn standing under the spray. Pulling open the glass door, I step in to join him. My fingers glide over his wet hips, pulling him back flush against me.

"Fuck, I love you like this," I growl into his shoulder, his skin pebbling with goosebumps from my touch. My hands move down to spread his ass, my hard dick finding its home between them.

"Mmm. We're in here to get clean. We're going out, remember?"

"Perfect place to get messy again, in my opinion."

"You're insatiable, lover."

"For you I am, baby," I tell him between kissing across his

strong shoulder blades. "Let me fuck you. Want you leaking my cum while we're out."

His head drops back onto my shoulder, and I take full advantage of his exposed neck, licking up the column and back down again.

"Oh, fuck, when you talk like that," Finn whispers.

"You turn to putty in my hands."

Finn just moans as I slip a finger into his hole, pumping him firmly.

"You gonna let me fuck you out of your mind now?"

"When have I ever said no to you, Carter?"

"That's my good boy, baby."

I make good on my promise, pumping him so full of my cum there's no chance he won't be leaking it all night.

The Night Owl is hopping as Finn and I walk in. I've imagined this moment more times than I can count. Shelby, the owner, nods to me as I take the only seat available at the far end of the bar, Finn next to me, saying he'd prefer to stand. We order two whiskeys—Aspen Ridge—and as Finn picks up the glass and brings the cold liquid to his lips, I take a moment to study the side of his face. It takes a lot of courage to do what he's doing. Moving to a small town where everyone knows everyone, a place where his boyfriend has quite the reputation for getting around with the female population, and trusting that I'm going to stand by him and own what's between us. As if I would let him down.

My fingers twitch against Finn's hip as Maya DiAngelo walks up to us with wide eyes. Finn's spine straightens as if he's bracing for it, but I give him a squeeze in reminder that I'm here with him. That I chose him—the only person I've ever chosen. Maya and I hooked up a few times, and she was one of the few who thought she could nail me down.

"Carter. This is quite a surprise," she says as she arches a brow, looking at Finn. He's wearing a pair of denim jeans that hug his ass and thighs perfectly, and a navy blue button-up shirt with the sleeves rolled up to his elbows. He looks so goddamn good, I'm sure she's jealous I nailed him down and not the other way around. She'd be crazy not to.

"Is it?" I ask, pulling Finn between my spread legs as I turn in her direction, my thumb rubbing against his hip through his soft shirt.

"I mean, if I really think about it, it makes total sense. Of course it would take a man to settle your wild ass down."

I laugh lightheartedly because she's not completely wrong. "Nah, just needed him."

"Well? Are you going to introduce me?"

"Maya, this is my boyfriend, Finn. Finn, Maya." I give the introductions with confidence and pride, and it doesn't go unnoticed by either of them, both grinning at me with huge smiles. My face flushes from the unwanted attention, and I grip Finn harder.

"Happiness looks good on you, Carter. It was nice to meet you, Finn."

Finn nods his head before spinning in my arms, his hands hooking around my neck as I look up at him.

"See? That wasn't so bad, was it?" I ask, trying to make light of the situation.

"I love you," is all he says in return before leaning down and pressing a soft, chaste kiss against the side of my turned-up lips. The contact immediately lights that fire, and I quickly wrap my fingers around the back of his neck, forcing the kiss deeper, longer, the rest of the world fading away as it always does.

A loud smack rips us apart, Finn's lips red from the force of my kiss. I look at the asshole to find my sister looking at us like we've lost our minds.

"I'm sure lots of people are enjoying the show, but you're my brother, so cut it out! Get a room if you need to! I did not come over here to watch my brother suck face with his boyfriend. K?"

"Damn, calm yourself down, pipsqueak. What's gotten into you?"

"Just ready for my freedom! I love you all, Carter, but I feel like I'm suffocating some days, and I just want to experience life without you Neanderthals hovering over me like a pack of rabid wolves."

"Hey," I say, putting my hands in the air defensively. "I didn't give you any shit about the friends or boyfriend then, I'm trying, Kins."

"I guess." She shrugs.

"It'll be better once you move into your own apartment. Next week, right?"

"Yeah, Reid said he wanted to do a little work on something in there and then it was all mine."

"I've got a ton of furniture I was going to donate if you want to look at any of it for your place," Finn offers, and Kinsey beams at him.

"I would love that! Thank you."

"It'll work out, Kins. We've got you. We're in your corner," I vow to her.

"I hope so. 'Cause I'm ready to start living for me, and you four are going to need to let me."

A sharp pang hits my heart, but I nod through it. She's right. We can't keep protecting her from everything, and we have to let her live her life how she wants to and hope that we've all prepared her enough. She's got this, and we'll love her, wherever her path leads her.

We spend the next few hours sipping on drinks and chatting with my sister, whose best friend couldn't make it, before walking up Main Street and back to our house.

Our house.

I thread my fingers through Finn's and yank him close to me so that our shoulders bump.

"What was that for?"

"I've imagined this so many times this summer. Wondered what it would feel like to walk up this street with you by my side."

"Yeah? How's it compare to the real thing?"

"This is a million times better than my dreams, baby."

"Good, 'cause you've got me forever."

"Forever."

Finn matches my pace step for step as we jog through the trail on the coast of Emberleigh. It's been almost a year to the day since Finn and I met at Temptations, wrecking everything I thought I wanted for myself and out of life. He's the best thing that's ever happened to me, and as cliché as it is, I can't imagine my life without him.

The last year has been the best of my life. My family loves him, and we all joke that Finn's taken my mom's favorite son position from Dallas. He lives for Sunday dinners over there, and no matter how hard I try to convince him to skip some weeks with me, he will drag me there against my will—even if I am only protesting because I like to rile him up.

Finn has worked tirelessly to build his travel blog, and just like I knew it would, it took off. His first article? Aspen Ridge and the Aspen Ridge Distillery. It boosted business, especially the event side. It was exactly what my family was hoping for, and we're so grateful to Finn. People know his name, and his writing speaks for itself. It proved to him that it was never about the Northwest Explorer or his dad, or hell, even the Nash name; it was about him. He writes with passion and love, and it bleeds through in his words. Watching him shine has been one of the highlights of my life and I feel like one lucky sonofabitch that I get to be by his side as he continues to grow.

After Finn planned his first weekend-long trip to Alaska last fall, I knew I couldn't be away from him. Lucky for me, most of my job can be handled remotely, and while it's taken some growing pains on my family's part to let me breathe a little, traveling with Finn while he does what he loves, watching him shine when he meets new people, and being able to continue to work with my family for the distillery has been the perfect situation for us. I didn't realize how much I wanted to get out and explore until our Maine trip, and I've loved everything about all the places we've seen so far. We're building our life together and it's goddamn perfect with him by my side.

We came back to Emberleigh on my request, to revisit the place where I fell in love with him. We rented a tiny little studio on the beach, and it's perfect for the weekend.

Jogging over the same path we did last year, when I was still so lost and confused but couldn't fight the pull to him, is so surreal. It feels like a lifetime ago that he blackmailed me into going to Maine with him and I let myself imagine just for a moment what it would be like to occupy my small house just the two of us, to walk through downtown Aspen Ridge together holding hands, to run every morning together, to build a life that we both want. Now, we're living it. Finn opened my eyes to an entirely new world, and I've waited long enough to ask him to start the next chapter with me. Because I can't wait any longer.

"You up for some surfing today?" he asks me, breaking me from my thoughts. Sweat glistens on his perfect body, the sun hitting him just right. He's gotten more muscular this year, having taken up weightlifting with my brother Liam, and while he's always looked good to me, I'm enjoying his current physique. He looks over at me as we run side by side, and his face reflects so much damn love that I nearly melt on the spot. Fuck it.

"Baby, I can't wait any longer, I'm sorry. I had such an incredible night planned, but you know me, once I make a decision, I'm all in."

Finn comes to a halt, looking at me with quizzical concern. It's not until I drop to my knee, in the center of downtown, with people walking around and going about their lives, that his eyes go wide.

"Finn, I thought I never wanted to give another person the power to wreck me, until you came along. You broke down all my walls and showed me how perfect love can be when you hand over that trust. You've stolen my heart, and there's no way I'll ever get it back. I trust you with it. I love you with every fiber of my being. My life stops and ends with you. I will choose you again and again, in this life and the next. You're my person in all things, and I can't wait another minute without asking you to be my husband. Please, marry me, baby."

Finn drops to his knees in front of me, grabbing my face between his palms and slowly, methodically, kissing me. And with every brush of his lips, every lash of his tongue, I know his answer.

"Yes."

epilogue

REID

Unknown: Time to pay up

also by jenn plummer

Aspen Ridge Series

Unravel Me

Crave Me

Love Me

Complete Me

Aspen Ridge Holiday Novellas

Ready or Not

Sweet Girl

Daddy Issues

Standalones

Nothing to Fear

acknowledgments

I hope you enjoyed reading Carter and Finn's story as much as I did writing it. When I started the Hayes family character development in January of 2024, everyone came very clear to me, except Carter. He was elusive, quiet, unsure, and I didn't really know where he fit within the family dynamic. When I met with my editor in May to work on Unravel Me, I told her that I think Carter will end up with a man, that I was fairly certain that our Aspen Ridge playboy is bisexual but he doesn't know it yet. I left that conversation feeling like I finally had clarity with Carter. That he was speaking to me and yelling "yes! This is my path!"

In December 2024 when I finally sat down to start writing his story, I was obviously apprehensive, because being a bisexual man is not my lived experience. But throughout the writing process, I stayed true to the story that Carter wanted me to tell. As I typed the words The End to my most elusive character to date, I'm emotional and I feel a sense of wholeness. I gave Carter the story he was meant for and I am truly proud of it.

Michael,

Night after night you've come home from work over the last four months to find me still working. You've taken off your uniform top, and built me a website, created an online store, packaged orders for my readers, handfed me while I wrote, and held me while I got overwhelmed or just needed to be close to you. You've spent your weekends doing laundry while I worked tirelessly, you've picked up all the balls I've dropped and you just continue to kiss me and tell me to keep going. Being your wife is the highlight of my life. Thank you for taking care of me when I fail to take care of myself, for loving me and pushing me every day to keep going. I love you, Daddy.

My editor, Katie,

This one wouldn't have been possible without you. Thank you for all of your guidance, your help, your encouragement. This one truly wouldn't be possible without you pushing me and being there for me to lean on. I can't believe this is book seven. I love our relationship, both personally and professionally and I'm thankful to have you in my life. Thank you for being my guiding light and for turning my books to gold. They wouldn't be the same without you. I love you.

Meighan,

Thank you isn't even enough. You completely took care of everything so I could focus on writing this book (and Daddy Issues!) Your daily tasks were endless and you worked so hard to support me while I got through this one, but I really want to thank you for encouraging me. For telling me to keep going, for pushing me to write and to focus, for letting me crumble and vent and cry and then reminding me of why I'm doing this and to get it together and keep going. Thank you for loving me. I love you.

My Betas, Tiffanie, Em, Clair, Laura, & Britt,

I am so thankful for the time, care, attention, and support you've given me and this book. I am so thankful to each of you for all of the feedback, the conversations, the hype, and the questions that got me thinking! Thank you for helping shape our boy's story!

Heather & Michael,

Thank you for being such an incredible role model of what a supportive, loving parent looks. You've always fostered a loving, open environment in your home, and you've been a safe place for your own children, and so many surrogate children, myself included. Thank you for allowing me to be apart of your family.

To every bookstagrammer, reviewer, and blogger,
    Thank you for reading. Every post, review, and tag means the world to me. Thank you for your support!

To every reader,
    You are making my dreams come true. Thank you for reading!

about the author

Author, wife, mother, lover of reading, overcast skies, chilly weather, and hockey.

A romantic at heart, Jenn has always been a lover of books and is constantly dreaming up heart-wrenching stories that will have you reaching for tissues and make you blush.

When Jenn's not writing, she can be found reading a spicy romance novel, watching scary movies, and enjoying her quiet life in New England, living out her real-life romance story.

Follow along for updates on new releases and book news.

www.jennplummer.com
Instagram @authorjennplummer
Goodreads @jennplummer
Amazon @jennplummer
Threads @authorjennplummer